W9-CCB-574

**Praise for the Fatal Series
by *New York Times* bestselling author
Marie Force**

"This novel is *The O.C.* does D.C., and you just can't get enough."
— *RT Book Reviews* on *Fatal Affair* (4½ stars)

"The romance, the mystery, the ongoing story lines… everything about these books has me sitting on the edge of my seat and begging for more."
— *TheBookPushers.com*

"The fast-paced 12th installment in Force's Fatal Series is a testament to her talent for blending romance with politics and suspense with sex."
— *Publishers Weekly* on *Fatal Chaos*

"I highly recommend this series to anyone who loves crime thrillers, mysteries, and certainly romance."
— *Bewitched Bookworms*

"The suspense is thick, the passion between Nick and Sam just keeps getting hotter and hotter."
— *Guilty Pleasures Book Reviews* on *Fatal Deception*

"The perfect mesh of mystery and romance."
— *Night Owl Reviews* on *Fatal Scandal* (5 stars)

The Fatal Series
by *New York Times* bestselling author
Marie Force

Suggested reading order

**And look for the next sizzling book
in the Fatal Series**

Fatal Accusation

MARIE FORCE

FORCE

Fatal
RECKONING

HQN™

If you purchased this book without a cover you should be aware that this book is stolen property. It was reported as "unsold and destroyed" to the publisher, and neither the author nor the publisher has received any payment for this "stripped book."

ISBN-13: 978-1-335-01765-9

Fatal Reckoning

Copyright © 2019 by HTJB, Inc.

Recycling programs for this product may not exist in your area.

All rights reserved. Except for use in any review, the reproduction or utilization of this work in whole or in part in any form by any electronic, mechanical or other means, now known or hereafter invented, including xerography, photocopying and recording, or in any information storage or retrieval system, is forbidden without the written permission of the publisher, HQN Books, 22 Adelaide St. West, 40th Floor, Toronto, Ontario M5H 4E3, Canada.

This is a work of fiction. Names, characters, places and incidents are either the product of the author's imagination or are used fictitiously, and any resemblance to actual persons, living or dead, business establishments, events or locales is entirely coincidental.

This edition published by arrangement with Harlequin Books S.A.

For questions and comments about the quality of this book, please contact us at CustomerService@Harlequin.com.

® and TM are trademarks of Harlequin Enterprises Limited or its corporate affiliates. Trademarks indicated with ® are registered in the United States Patent and Trademark Office, the Canadian Intellectual Property Office and in other countries.

www.HQNBooks.com

Printed in U.S.A.

For the Chairman of the Board,
George B. Sullivan
Forever in my heart

Fatal
RECKONING

CHAPTER ONE

As she had every morning for seven days, Sam reached across the bed, looking for Nick, finding his side of the bed cold and unoccupied. He would be home from his trip to Europe later that day. Thank God. In his absence, she'd been forced to make do with rushed FaceTime conversations on their son Scotty's phone, texts and the press coverage of the trip that had included an audience with Queen Elizabeth. Sam had been sorry to miss the chance to meet a woman she idolized, but she'd remained at home to care for their son, Scotty, as well as Alden and Aubrey, the five-year-old twins who'd recently become part of their family after their parents were murdered. At this early hour, Scotty and the twins were still sleeping, but the younger kids would be up soon.

She'd put the time away from work to good use, getting "the littles," as Nick had nicknamed the twins, back on a schedule that included a return to their kindergarten class. Dr. Trulo, the Metro Police Department psychiatrist, had helped her find a qualified therapist who would work with the children together and individually to help them cope with their terrible loss. And she'd fielded phone calls from their mother's family members, who were suddenly concerned about the children's well-being now that the men responsible for their parents' murders had been brought to justice.

Sam couldn't stand hypocrites and had gritted her teeth each time a member of a family that had initially expressed no concern whatsoever for the children called to check on them. Fortunately, the twins' parents had made their older brother, Elijah, their legal guardian, and he'd asked Sam and Nick to serve as the children's custodial guardians while he finished college at Princeton. What would happen after he graduated, Sam didn't know and couldn't think about. Not now when the children needed everything she and Nick and their devoted assistant, Shelby, had to give them to get their lives back on track, or as close to it as they could get without their beloved parents.

One step at a time, she told herself, just as she often did while working a homicide investigation. The activity with the littles had been good for her as she served a seven-day suspension for taking in the children of her murder victims, something she'd do again in a hot second. Was it a conflict of interest? Absolutely, but she hadn't thought about that when she saw two babies in need of something she could give them. It had only taken a few days after she brought them home for everyone associated with their household to fall in love with the twins.

She moved from her pillow to Nick's, which bore faint remnants of his distinctive cologne, the scent of home. If her time-zone calculations were correct, he would be on Air Force Two by now, about to begin the seven-hour flight home from France. Her phone rang, and she wondered if it was him, telling her he'd be home soon. Greedy for anything from him that she could get after a week apart, she grabbed the phone and flipped it open without checking the caller ID.

"Sam!" The urgency she heard in her stepmother's voice had Sam sitting up in bed.

"Morning. What's going—"

"Sam, it's your dad. Something's wrong."

"I'm coming." Sam was out of bed and running before she gave a thought to the fact that she was wearing pajama bottoms, Nick's favorite ratty Harvard T-shirt and no bra. She bolted from the bedroom, past the shocked Secret Service agent in the hallway and down the stairs as she held the phone to her ear and tried to beat back a tidal wave of panic. The agent working the front door opened it for her, thankfully without asking any questions. As she didn't have Secret Service protection, Sam could come and go as she pleased, and the agents had gotten used to her mad dashes.

Barefoot and oblivious to the cold October air, she sprinted down the ramp Nick had installed so her dad could visit their home and covered the short distance between her home and her father's in seconds, cruising up the ramp to his front door and bursting into the house.

"Back here."

Following Celia's voice, Sam went from the living room through the kitchen to her father's bedroom in what used to be the dining room. With one quick glance, she noticed his color was all wrong, and his lips were blue. In that moment, none of her training or years of emergency experience was available to her. In that moment, she wasn't a decorated police officer. She was only a daughter staring at the lifeless face of the first man she'd ever loved.

"Sam! What should we do?"

Celia's frantic tone and her fearful expression

nudged Sam into action. With shaking hands, she called 911 and requested help.

The operator asked for specifics.

"Sixty-four-year-old unresponsive quadriplegic." She recited the Ninth Street address. "Tell the Secret Service that Lieutenant Holland said to let them in."

"Of course, Lieutenant." The operator perked up when she realized who she was talking to. "Do you know the victim?"

"Yes." Sam tried to swallow around the huge knot of fear wedged in her throat. "He's my father." *My touchstone. My hero. My best friend forever.* "Please hurry."

"EMS is on the way. Has your father had any recent health issues?"

"Nothing other than the paralysis." He'd been doing better in the last year after surgery to remove the bullet that had remained lodged in his neck for three years. He'd regained some sensation in his extremities, but he seemed to become frailer with every month spent immobile. Sam walked around the hospital bed to comfort Celia, who was stroking Skip's face and hair and begging him to open his eyes, to talk to her.

"Please don't do this," Celia pleaded with her husband between sobs. "Not yet. Don't leave me."

Debra Nixon, the lead agent on Scotty's detail, appeared in the doorway, probably after having been told of Sam's sprint. "What can I do?" She assessed the situation with sharp eyes.

Sam held the phone to the side. "Tell the agents at the checkpoint to let in EMS."

"Done. What else?"

"Ask the agents at the house to keep an eye on the kids? Don't let Scotty come over here." Dear God, Scotty... He adored his gramps. All at once, Sam couldn't breathe as the potential magnitude of what was happening registered, leaving her staggered, her legs nearly buckling under her. Somehow she remained standing, but only because Celia needed her to keep it together. Inside, she crumbled.

"EMS has arrived," the operator said. "I'll pray for your family, Lieutenant."

"Thank you." Sam slapped the phone closed.

Debra went to let in the paramedics, who brought equipment and badly needed competence. They immediately took over, tending to Skip as Sam and Celia stood with their arms wrapped around each other. Watching one of her worst fears play out, Sam wondered if she might be dreaming this. It had to be a dream because the possibility that this could be real was too frightening and heartbreaking to entertain.

The lead paramedic looked to Sam and Celia. "Has he had any recent health issues?"

"Nothing other than the paralysis and a persistent urinary tract infection." Celia dabbed at her tears with a tissue. "He's been on antibiotics for that."

"Has he ever been unresponsive like this?"

"No." Celia shook her head. "Never."

Sam knew she should call her sisters but couldn't bring herself to move or do anything other than hope and pray.

The paramedic listening to her father's heart shook his head, and the other one sprang into action, setting up a portable defibrillator. Seeing the paddles and understanding what they were doing snapped Sam out of the dreamlike trance she'd slipped into as the surreal scene unfolded around her.

"No." Sam said the word before the thought had fully registered. *"No."*

"*Sam!* What're you doing?"

Sam stared at the face of the man who meant the world to her. "It's not what he would want." She knew it without a shadow of a doubt. In some ways, the most difficult decision she'd ever made was also the simplest.

"Please, Sam." Celia sobbed helplessly. *"Please."*

Sam met the intense gaze of the lead paramedic. "He has a DNR."

Hearing that, the paramedics stepped back.

Sobbing, Celia pulled free of Sam's embrace to lean over her husband, kissing and caressing the half of his face that had retained full sensation after the shooting and the stroke that'd followed. Long after his injury, Sam and her sisters learned that, for quite some time before the shooting, he'd been dating Celia, who became his devoted nurse and, later, his wife.

The lead paramedic cleared his throat. "Lieutenant, would you like us to transport him?"

A lifetime of holidays, celebrations, parties and other events in this house ran through her mind in a flash. Skip Holland had lived there for most of his adult life. It seemed only fitting that his life should also end in the home he'd loved. If he was in pain, he probably couldn't feel it. She took comfort in that.

"No, thank you." Sam's heart hurt, her hands trembled and her mouth had gone dry from fear. How would she ever go on without him?

The paramedics stepped out of the room.

Sam wanted to beg them to stay. She couldn't handle this. She couldn't bear it. *Tracy. Angela.* She had to call them. Her hands were shaking so badly she could barely make the call to her eldest sister.

"Are you losing your mind without your man?" Tracy's teasing tone barely registered with Sam.

"Trace."

"What? Sam? What's wrong?"

"It's Dad. You need to come. Tell Ang too. Hurry."

"*What?* What's wrong?"

"He's… Just come. As fast as you can."

"Sam."

"Call Angela and get over here. Now."

"We're coming."

Sam moved around to the other side of the bed and gazed down at her dad's face. Tears threatened, but she fought them off, determined to stay strong for Celia, who was hysterical.

They'd been on borrowed time for almost four years now, during which Skip's once-robust world had been reduced to three rooms. He'd been trapped in a kind of hell she wouldn't wish on her worst enemy. All that time, she'd known that at some point his body would surrender the fight.

Knowing it could happen at any time didn't make the reality easier, though.

Her sisters lived close by, so it didn't take them long to get there, rushing into the room and bringing the scents of cold and wood smoke with them. They took one look at Skip and broke down into heartbroken sobs when they realized what was happening. Sam didn't acknowledge them or do anything other than stare at the face of the man who'd occupied the very center of her life.

Tracy's husband, Mike, stood behind Sam and her sisters. "What can we do?"

"Nothing." Sam gazed down at her dad. "We have to let him go because he wouldn't want heroic measures." Later, she'd probably wonder where the composure had come from. All she knew for certain was that her dad had demonstrated amazing grace since his devastating injury, and it was up to them now to let him go with the same grace in which he'd lived his remarkable life.

Angela went around the bed to try to comfort Celia, who was inconsolable.

Tracy wrapped her arms around Sam. Only with her sister's warmth pressed up against her did Sam realize how cold she was.

As she wondered if he could still hear them, Sam thought about what she should say to him while she still could. But there was no need for last-minute platitudes. Nothing had been left unsaid between her and her father. He would leave this world knowing exactly where he stood with her and the rest of his family. Skip Holland had been loved and respected and adored by his wife and daughters, and had returned those sentiments tenfold.

They were all there, the four people he loved the most, when Skip took his last breath at 8:37.

Sam noted the time, because she knew it would matter. For a long time after his chest stopped moving, she continued to stare down at him. Through the fog of disbelief, she understood what had happened, and in one tiny remote part of her, she felt relieved *for him*. She'd never been a particularly religious person. However, the thought of Skip walking tall and proud, freed from the difficulties of his egregious injury, into the kingdom of heaven, brought badly needed comfort.

But when she thought about Celia, herself and her sisters, Skip's beloved grandchildren, devoted sons-in-law, colleagues and friends—the many people who had loved him—she ached for everyone who would be left to go on without him. And in the corner of her soul that belonged to her family in blue, she seethed with rage, directed at the nameless, faceless criminal who'd taken Skip from them far too soon.

ON THE WAY home at last, Nick thought, watching the Paris skyline get smaller as Air Force Two climbed to altitude. He had a million things to do, emails that had given birth to more emails while he'd been away, briefing documents to review before he returned to the White House on Monday and a press corps on board hungry for interviews.

But all he could think about was eight more hours until he could see Samantha. That felt like an eternity after missing her terribly for an endless week apart.

They were absurd. He knew it. She knew it. They didn't care who knew it. What had started as a crazy wildfire of attraction the night they met had been denied for six long years until they were reunited at a crime scene, of all places. Sometimes Nick thought they were still making up for lost time almost two years after finding each other again.

That was the best explanation he had for the absolutely ridiculous love they had for each other, the kind of love that made a life worth living. He was eager to get home to spend time with Scotty and the littles, who had recently joined their family. But he was absolutely *desperate* to see his wife, to hold her, kiss her, make love to her, breathe her in and stare at her gorgeous face. He could do that for hours and never get tired of the view. Her face was his favorite view in the world.

A knock on the door that separated his cabin from the rest of the plane drew Nick out of his thoughts. "Come in."

His lead Secret Service agent, John Brantley, Jr., stepped into the room, his expression serious and professional as always. Brant rarely cracked a grin or removed the all-business facade that made him such an effective agent.

"What's up?"

"We received a call from Agent Nixon."

As Debra Nixon was his son's lead agent, Nick's first thought was for Scotty. "What?" He fought back a burst of panic.

"Your father-in-law."

"What about him?"

"I'm sorry to have to tell you that he passed away a short time ago. Mrs. Cappuano, her sisters and stepmother were with Deputy Chief Holland when he passed."

Sam. Oh no, no, *no*. "I need to speak to my wife."

"We're attempting to reach her now. She's not answering her phone."

"Call one of the other agents and have them find her."

"Yes, sir."

Nick's entire body felt cold with shock and despair as he imagined Sam dealing with such an awful loss, and while he was hours away from her. He'd never felt more useless or despondent as he thought about what she must be going through.

Brant returned a short time later, speaking on a secure satellite phone. "Hold on just a moment. Here he is." He handed the phone to Nick.

"Sam?"

"I'm here." Her dull, flat tone told him so much but nowhere near enough.

"Babe… I'm so, so sorry."

"Thank you. I know you loved him too."

"I did. So much. I would give anything to be there with you right now."

"I wish you were here too."

"What happened?"

"Celia called when she couldn't wake him. The paramedics came, but I told them he wouldn't want to be resuscitated."

Oh God, she *had been the one to make that call?* Nick closed his eyes, put his head back against the seat and released a deep breath, thinking about what it must've cost her to make that decision on her father's behalf. "What can I do for you?"

"It helps to hear your voice. I have to go tell Scotty, and the kids will be getting up."

"Samantha…"

"I'll see you when you get here, okay?"

"I love you so much, and I'm just heartbroken for you and Ang and Trace and Celia."

"Thanks. I love you too. I can't wait to see you."

"Me too, babe."

The line went dead, and he handed the phone back to Brant.

Visibly shaken, Brant took the phone from Nick. "I'm very sorry for your loss. Is Mrs. Cappuano…"

"She sounds bad. Flat."

"She's in shock."

Nick leaned forward, elbows on knees, head in hands. *Skip is dead.* Tears filled his eyes and spilled down his face, his thoughts full of Sam, Scotty and the rest of their family. This would be a devastating loss for all of them. And it was a devastating loss for him. Skip had been a friend and father figure to him since the day Nick met him. Even paralyzed from the neck down, Skip had managed to completely intimidate Nick with the formidable blue-eyed stare that had put him on notice. *Take care of my baby girl, or you'll deal with me.* Few things had ever mattered more to Nick than keeping the promises he'd made to Skip Holland that first day.

Brant's voice interrupted his thoughts. "I'm going to ask Mr. O'Connor to step in, if that's all right."

Nick nodded and used the sleeve of his shirt to mop up his tears.

Terry came into the cabin, shock etched into his expression. "I just heard the news. I'm so sorry, Nick."

Nick insisted his chief of staff call him by name when they were alone. "Thanks."

"Were you able to talk to Sam?"

"Briefly."

"I won't ask how she is." Terry took a seat. "Did you hear what happened?"

"He was unresponsive this morning. They chose not to resuscitate him. He had a DNR."

"What can I do for you?"

"Get me home to her as fast as you can. I don't care what has to happen."

"I'll arrange for Marine Two to meet us at Andrews. We can land on the south lawn of the White House and have you home within minutes."

"Thank you." That would be quicker than being conveyed to the city via motorcade, but it was still going to take far too long.

CHAPTER TWO

As soon as she could put two thoughts together and identify her most pressing need, Sam called Shelby Faircloth, their devoted assistant and friend.

"Morning." In the background, Sam could hear Shelby's son Noah's baby chatter. "Noah says hi too."

"Shelby."

"Sam? What's wrong?"

For the first time, Sam had to say the words out loud, each of them like a sharp knife to her heart. "My father died."

Shelby's gasp came through the phone. "Sam... Oh God. I'm so sorry."

"I know it's Sunday and you have a life, but the kids—"

"I'm coming. I'll be there in fifteen minutes. You tell me what you need, and I'll do it. Whatever it is. I'll do it."

"I haven't had a chance to tell Scotty, but he'll be asleep for a while yet. The littles will be up, though. The agents are there." She didn't have to tell Shelby that childcare wasn't the Secret Service's job.

"I'm on my way. Don't worry about anything other than your family. I'm on it."

"Thank you." Overwhelmed by Shelby's support, Sam closed the flip phone without the usual satisfying slap. Then she reopened it and placed a call to her captain.

"Well, if it isn't my favorite lieutenant. I really hope you had a good week off, because I'm ready to have you back. Doing your job on top of mine is an even bigger royal pain in my ass than you are."

"Cap."

"What's up?"

Jake Malone had been one of Skip Holland's best friends. "My dad…"

"Sam?"

"He's gone."

His anguished cry took her breath away. "*What? What happened?*"

"He died in his sleep."

"Oh my God. I'm so sorry. I don't even know what to say."

"Will you notify Uncle Joe and the others?" Sam couldn't recall the last time she'd called her chief by the name she'd used for him as a child. "I just can't…"

"Yes, of course. I'll take care of it. What else can I do?"

"Nothing for now."

"There'll be an inspector's funeral with full honors."

"Yes." The term, adopted from the New York Police Department, was used to describe a funeral to honor an officer killed in the line of duty.

"I don't have to tell you this, but Skip Holland was the finest man I ever knew."

Sam closed her eyes against the rush of emotion. "That means a lot to me, and it will to my family too. Your friendship meant the world to him and us."

"He meant the world to us. Call me if I can do anything. I mean it."

"I know, and I will. I guess I'll be out for a while longer."

"Take whatever time you need."

"Will you notify my squad? Make sure everyone keeps it off-line until we're ready to release the news."

"I'll take care of everything. Don't worry about a thing."

"Thanks again." Sam ended the call and went into the living room, where her sisters were comforting Celia. She sat across from them. "Captain Malone is notifying the department."

Celia wiped the tears from her face. "You should go home to your family, Sam."

Sam realized her stepmother was pissed. "I'm sorry if you didn't agree with me in there, but you know it's better for him."

"How can you say that?" Celia's voice caught on a sob. "He wanted to be *here* with us!"

"Not like that." Sam hoped that the nurse in Celia would eventually see that Sam was right. For now, Celia was thinking like a heartbroken wife and not as a medical professional.

"This hurts like hell for all of us." Tracy's face was swollen from crying. "But Sam is right. He couldn't go on that way indefinitely."

"Earlier, I had this vision of him standing up from the chair and walking through the gates of heaven, whole and strong and full of the power he used to have." Sam forced a smile. "I liked that vision."

Angela sniffled. "I like that too."

The front door opened and Angela's husband, Spencer, came rushing in, fresh from the gym.

Angela stood and flew into his outstretched arms, both of them sobbing.

Mike came out of the kitchen, where he'd been on the phone and sat with Tracy, his arm around her.

Sam wanted Nick more than she ever had before, but he wouldn't be home for hours yet. In the meantime, her stomach ached at the thought of her beloved stepmother being angry with her. That only made a horrible situation worse.

"We need to make a statement." Sam hoped the others would agree with her. Under normal circumstances, seeking out the press was the last thing she ever wanted to do, but in this case, they needed to take control of the story. "Before it gets taken out of our hands." She didn't need to tell her family that this would be a huge story, not only because of who Skip had been to the department and the city but because of his son-in-law, the vice president.

"What do you suggest?" Tracy asked.

"I'd like to call Darren Tabor from the *Star*. He's a friend. He'll do right by us and Dad."

Tracy looked to Celia. "Would that be all right, Celia?"

Celia nodded but still didn't look at Sam. "Whatever you all think is right is fine with me."

"There'll be a police funeral with full honors," Sam said.

Celia looked up at her with fierce determination in her gaze. "As there should be."

"I'll call Darren." Sam had developed a rapport with the reporter and could trust him to properly handle the important news of her father's passing. She got up, grabbed a fleece jacket of Celia's and went outside to the front porch, appreciating the blast of cold fresh air. Finding the number for the *Washington Star*'s Darren Tabor in her contacts, she put through the call.

"Don't you ever take a day off?" His voice was gravelly with sleep.

"I need a favor."

"Will this favor result in you owing me one?"

"Yeah. Maybe a couple."

"Everything okay?"

"Nope." She nearly laughed so she wouldn't cry. "My dad passed away this morning, and we need to release a statement. I thought you might be able to help me with that."

"Are you at home?" Darren sounded wide-awake now.

"I'm at his house, three doors down from mine. It's the other one on the street with a ramp. Tell the Secret Service I said to let you in. They'll call me to confirm."

"I'll be there in twenty minutes—and you won't owe me any favors for this one."

"Thank you."

"I'm really sorry, Sam. I know how close you were to him."

"Yeah, thanks. It's a tough one, but I'm finding comfort in knowing he's free from the difficult reality of his life over the last four years."

"That's a good way to look at it. I'm on my way."

Sam closed the phone and stood for a long time on the front porch, memories of growing up on Ninth Street filling her heart and mind. Right in the middle of all those memories was the larger-than-life man who'd raised her with high expectations. He'd made her want to be a cop. He'd made her into the cop she was today. He'd made her into the human being she was today. Before Nick, Skip had been the most important person in her life. Everything she'd ever done had been with the goal of making him proud.

That doesn't have to change, she told herself in the first hour without him.

She glanced down the street and saw Shelby rushing up the ramp to their house, a flash of pink with blond hair. Fifteen minutes later, at the Secret Service checkpoint, she watched Darren jump from a cab, and took the call from one of the agents.

"We have a Darren Tabor for you, Mrs. Cappuano."

"Please send him in."

"Right away, ma'am. And may I express my condolences for your loss?"

"Thank you." From her father's front porch, she waved to Darren so he'd know where to go. As he came up the ramp, Sam realized they didn't need the ramp anymore. Not here or at her house. The thought hit her like a punch, rendering her temporarily breathless.

Darren came to a stop a foot from her. "Am I allowed to hug you?"

She forced herself to breathe, to keep pressing forward, to do what needed to be done. "I suppose I could tolerate that for a second or two."

He gave her an awkward hug and patted her on the back. "I'm really sorry, Sam."

She swallowed the lump in her throat and nodded. "That's enough."

Darren stepped back and took an assessing look at her, his brown eyes sharp and warm at the same time. His light brown hair was a mess, as if he hadn't taken the time to brush it before running out the door. "How're you holding up?"

"I'm surprisingly okay, for now anyway. It hasn't really sunk in yet."

"Had he been ill?"

"Nothing more than the obvious complications of life as a quad. But in the last few months, he'd gotten very frail. Four years in his condition is actually a long time."

"Do you mind if I take notes?"

"Not at all." She gestured for him to have a seat and lowered herself into a chair across from him, only realizing when she was seated that her legs were trembling. It never came naturally for her to unload on a reporter, but Darren had earned her trust and respect over the years, and she was counting on him to do right by her dad. Not to mention his death was an opportunity to remind the public that his shooting remained unsolved.

"How old was he?"

"Sixty-four. Make sure you refer to him by his title, deputy chief, and that he was egregiously injured in the line of duty three months prior to retirement." She recited the date of the shooting, which was a date that had divided her life into "before" and "after."

"And the case remains open, correct?"

"Yes, and I firmly believe someone out there knows what happened to my father. I would hope that anyone with information pertaining to his shooting on G Street would come forward to ensure that justice is done on behalf of a decorated police officer who devoted his entire adult life to ensuring the safety of our city and its citizens." She gave him the number for the Metro PD tip line. "This is now a homicide investigation, and no piece of information is too small. If you know something, report it."

"Talk to me about what he meant to you personally."

Sam huffed out an ironic laugh. "What did he mean to me... Well, he was the best father anyone could ever hope to have. And he was an outstanding police officer, respected by everyone who ever worked with or for him. He was a frequent contributor to cases investigated by my squad. He recently consulted on the Beauclair case, offering wisdom and insight. His mind was as sharp as ever, and he frequently homed in on things the rest of us had missed. In many ways, he was my best friend."

"Was Skip his real name?"

"It was Charles, but he never went by that."

Darren took detailed notes. "Talk to me about the family members who should be listed."

Sam recited the names of her stepmother, sisters, brothers-in-law, son, nieces and nephews, as well as a devoted cadre of friends, many of them fellow MPD officers. "He would also want his former wife, Brenda Ross, to be mentioned." Despite the acrimonious end to their marriage, Skip never forgot that Brenda had given him three beautiful daughters and afforded her the respect she deserved as the mother of his children.

"I'd like to use the quote you gave me on the phone about taking comfort from him being free. Would that be all right?"

Sam nodded. Perhaps the thought would bring comfort to others who'd loved him.

"Here's what I'm thinking. Tell me if you approve.

"Retired Metro Police Deputy Chief Charles 'Skip' Holland, 64, passed away in his sleep on Sunday, nearly four years after being shot in a traffic altercation on G Street. The incident occurred three months before he was due to retire after thirty-two years on the force. Holland, who was left a quadriplegic in the shooting, had contended with a number of health challenges in recent years, but continued to actively consult on cases led by his daughter, Metro PD Homicide Lieutenant Sam Holland. Lieutenant Holland is the wife of Vice

President Nick Cappuano, who was out of the country at the time of his father-in-law's passing. The vice president is due home Sunday evening from a weeklong diplomatic trip to Europe.

"'We're taking comfort in the thought of him being set free from the difficult reality of his life over the last four years,' Lieutenant Holland said shortly after her father's death.

"Deputy Chief Holland is also survived by Celia, his beloved wife and devoted caretaker, as well as daughters Tracy Hogan and her husband, Mike, and Angela Radcliffe and her husband, Spencer, as well as six grandchildren: Brooke, Abby and Ethan Hogan, Jack and Ella Radcliffe, and Scott Cappuano. He leaves his former wife, Brenda Ross, his brothers and sisters in blue in the Metro Police Department and many faithful friends. Deputy Chief Holland will be given a police funeral with full honors on a date to be named shortly.

"Lieutenant Holland noted that her father's case is now considered a homicide investigation and anyone with information about the shooting should contact the MPD tip line."

He recited the number and finished with "'No piece of information is too small,' Holland said."

Darren glanced at her. "How is that?"

His unusually gentle tone had Sam taking a deep breath, determined not to break down in front of the reporter, who was often a thorn in her side. Today, he'd been a friend. "It's good. Add something about how, in lieu of flowers, the family requests donations be made to the Metro PD Memorial and Museum Fund and give them the link. It's on our website."

"Will do. Green light to release?"

Sam glanced at her own home, where her son still slept, oblivious to yet another huge loss in his young life. Her next order of business would be to go home and tell him the news. She dreaded that.

"Sam?"

This would make the unimaginable official. "Green light to release."

CHAPTER THREE

WITH THE STATEMENT seen to, Sam placed a call to Detective Cameron Green, who answered on the second ring.

"Lieutenant, I just heard from Captain Malone. I am so very, very sorry. Your dad was a great man, and I enjoyed getting to know him over the last couple of months."

"Thank you. I was wondering if you could make a call to the family business on our behalf." Cameron's family owned the Greenlawn Funeral Homes, which were highly regarded in the region.

"Consider it done."

"It'll be a big deal, so you might want to warn them."

"Understood. Don't worry about a thing. I'll have someone at your father's home within the hour to take care of everything."

"I appreciate it."

"If there's anything else I can do, anything at all, please let me know."

"There is one thing…"

"Name it."

Sam debated whether it was the right thing, but in the end, she decided it wasn't up to her to decide. "If you could track down Cruz in Italy and let him know, I'd appreciate it. Please emphasize I do *not* want him to come home, but I did want him to know." Her partner,

Freddie Cruz, was on his honeymoon, but he'd been close to her father.

"I'll call him myself. What about Sergeant Gonzales?" Gonzo had recently checked into rehab to contend with an addiction to pain meds and PTSD from the shooting death of his partner, Detective A. J. Arnold, earlier in the year.

"Can one of you check with his fiancée, Christina, to see how we should handle that?"

"Will do."

"Thanks, Cameron. If you need help, call on the others in the squad."

"We're on it. Don't worry about a thing. I wish there was something I could say to you. I only knew him a short time, but I feel richer for having had him in my life."

"That helps."

"Call me if you need anything else."

"I will."

Sam closed the phone and ducked her head inside to let the others know that Darren had been given the statement, that someone from Greenlawn would be there shortly and she was going home to speak to Scotty. "I'll be back."

She was halfway down the ramp to the sidewalk when her sister Tracy called for her to hang on. Sam turned to face her sister.

"You don't have to do all this yourself, you know." Tracy smoothed Sam's hair, tending to her the way she had for Sam's entire life. Though Skip Holland had loved all his daughters fiercely, that he shared a special, deep bond with Sam, his youngest, was no secret to anyone.

"Yeah, I kinda do, so if you guys wouldn't mind indulging me…"

"I don't mind, and Ang won't either, but you have to let us help you. *We* need that."

"Fair enough. How pissed is Celia?"

"She's shocked and grief-stricken. She won't hold it against you."

"As awful as it was, it was the right thing to do."

"I agree, and he would too. I don't know how he withstood it for as long as he did."

"I need to go home and tell Scotty before he wakes up and sees it on his phone."

"I called Brooke, and I have to pick up Abby and Ethan from a sleepover at Mike's brother's house. I'm dreading having to tell them."

"Same. Poor Scotty has already had enough loss in his life." After his mother and grandfather died when he was very young, Scotty had ended up in foster care before landing in a state home in Virginia, where Nick had met him on a campaign stop.

"He'll be okay with all of us around to support him."

Sam hugged her sister. "I'll be back shortly. Make sure someone is with Celia, and we should call her sisters. And Mom."

"I'll take care of that."

Sam nodded and left to go home. As she covered the short distance between her father's home and her own, her phone rang incessantly. She let it ring. She couldn't do another thing until she talked to Scotty.

Nate, the agent working the door, opened it for her. "My sincere condolences, Mrs. Cappuano. Your father was a wonderful man."

"Thank you so much. I agree." Sam went into the kitchen, where Shelby was making breakfast for

Alden and Aubrey. The sight of their adorable little faces brought tears to Sam's eyes. She kissed them both as Shelby looked on with concern. "How'd you guys sleep?" Sam caressed their soft blond hair.

"Okay." Aubrey gave Sam a knowing look. After what she'd endured, she knew disaster when she saw it. "Can we go to the park later?"

"Maybe. Let's see what happens, okay?" Sam didn't want to add to their grief by sharing hers with them. Not yet anyway. "I need to run upstairs and shower."

"Do what you need to, Sam." Shelby's big blue eyes were tearful and full of compassion. Sam expected nothing less from her. "We're all set here."

She gave Shelby a quick hug before leaving the kitchen to trudge upstairs, where Debra stood watch outside Scotty's door. Giving the agent a grim smile and receiving an empathetic look in return, Sam went into her son's room and shut the door behind her, taking a second to gather the fortitude she would need for this.

It killed her that what she was about to tell him would devastate her son, but he was too old to be treated like a baby. If she had her way, nothing would ever hurt him again, as unrealistic as that was. She went to his bed and sat on the edge of the mattress, reaching out to run her fingers through the silky dark hair that was so much like his father's. Though they didn't share DNA, father and son had several physical similarities that gave them the look of family. "Hey, bud." She gave him a gentle nudge.

He groaned. "Go away. It's Sunday. No school."

"I need to talk to you."

His eyes opened, immediately on alert. "Don't tell me something happened to Dad."

"No, not Dad." Her throat closed, and she had to look away from his sweet, earnest face or risk losing it.

"What, then? Just say it. You're freaking me out."

"Gramps."

"No." He shook his head. *"No."*

"I'm so sorry to have to tell you this. But the good news is he went peacefully in his sleep, and he's free now."

Tears rolled down Scotty's handsome face as his chin quivered.

Sam held out her arms to him. "Come here."

He sat up and fell into her outstretched arms, sobbing his heart out. "I'm not ready for this."

"I know, sweetheart. None of us are."

"You really believe he's free?"

"I do." Sam spoke the truth even as she ached on the inside. "You didn't know him before he was shot. He was so big and brawny and brave. At his funeral, there'll be lots of photos of him in uniform, and you'll see what I mean." She pulled back from him, wiped the tears from his face and smoothed the hair that stood on end after sleeping. "His great big life was so greatly reduced after he was shot, and it was hard for us to see him like that. I can't begin to imagine what it was like for him to be so trapped physically while being completely aware mentally."

"That had to suck so bad."

"It did, and that's why I believe that he's in a better place now, a place where paralysis doesn't exist, and people are made whole again." She kissed his forehead and continued to run her fingers through his hair, which she didn't get to do often enough these days for her liking. "I hope it makes it easier to bear to think of him as free."

"It does."

"He was so proud of you and loved you so much. You amused him endlessly and made his last few years so much richer. He would say, 'That kid is just too much. I love him to pieces.'"

"I loved him too."

"He knew that. He would tell me your visits were the highlight of his days. You were very faithful to him, and we all appreciated that."

"I loved talking to him. That's why I was always over there. I liked having a grandpa again."

"I know, and I'm so sorry you have to lose someone else you love. You've already had way too much loss in your life."

"Yeah, but I was lucky too, because I got to have them for a short time, and they loved me."

"Yes, they did, and that's a good way to look at it. Are you okay?"

"I will be."

"Do you promise you'll talk to me about anything you're feeling?"

"If you do the same. This is way harder for you than it is for me."

"I promise, and it's hard for all of us."

"How's Celia?"

"She's hurting, as you can imagine."

"I'll go see her."

"I'm sure she'd love that."

"Does Dad know?"

She nodded. "The Secret Service got word to him on Air Force Two, and he called me."

"He must be freaking out that he's not here when we need him."

"He is, but he'll be home soon."

"I'm really glad he's coming home."

"So am I." *That*, Sam thought, *is the understatement of my lifetime.*

CHAPTER FOUR

THUS FAR, ITALY had been about three things for the new Mr. and Mrs. Cruz—great food, great wine and *great* sex.

Late afternoon in Rome, and the newlyweds hadn't made it out of bed yet. *Thank goodness for room service*, Freddie thought, *the best invention since coffee.*

He ran his hand over Elin's soft, silky skin, feeling more relaxed than he could ever recall being. No work, no murders to solve, no demands on his time or hers, no nothing but him and her and endless hours to fully wallow in the magic of marriage.

"We should've done this a long time ago," he said, breaking a long, contented silence after yet another round of lovemaking. He couldn't get enough of her and was beginning to realize that a lifetime wouldn't be long enough to spend with her.

"Done what?"

"Gotten married and stayed in bed for days at a time."

"What we should've done is stayed in a hotel in DC since we've barely seen a thing since we've been here."

"We've got another week to sightsee."

"You think we'll do it?"

"Oh, we'll do it." His dirty tone made his wife laugh. *His wife.* He'd never been more thrilled by anything than he was to have the extraordinary Elin Cruz as his *wife*. "We'll do it and do it and *do it*."

"We've already done that. I want to see the Colosseum and the Vatican."

"Tomorrow. We'll get up early and put in a full day. I promise."

"Tomorrow." Her hand slid down to encircle his cock. "Or the next day. Whenever."

Her touch made him instantly hard, something that still amused him almost two years after meeting her. Hell, all she had to do was *look* at him with heat in those dazzling blue eyes of hers, and he was a goner. Having two full weeks to focus exclusively on her and them made this the best time in his entire life.

"I love being married."

Elin laughed. "You love having nonstop sex. You're still making up for your first twenty-nine sex-free years."

"It's going to take decades to work off all that pent-up desire."

"Dear God. What've I gotten myself into?"

"Too late to turn back now, Mrs. Cruz. You're stuck with me and my out-of-control libido."

"Somehow I'll make do."

He kissed her, lingering on the sweet taste of her lips, which were swollen from hours of kissing and other delightful things. This might go down as the best day of his life, even better than their wedding day, which had been magnificent. "PS the nonstop sex is awesome, but I love being married because I get to have nonstop sex—and everything else—with *you*."

"I love being married too. Best thing I ever did."

"You really think so?" Sometimes it still amazed

him that a goddess like her had chosen a regular guy like him.

"Freddie... How can you ask me that? You know how much I love you."

"That makes me the luckiest guy ever."

"We're both lucky."

He kissed her more intently as she stroked him until he was hard and aching for her all over again.

"Freddie."

"Hmm?"

"I think your phone is ringing."

"Ignore it."

"Babe..." She pulled back from him. "The only way anyone would call us while we're here is if something was wrong."

Not wanting to think about anything being wrong when everything felt so *right*, he said, "Whatever it is will keep." He went back to kissing her, focused exclusively on her, groaning against her lips when the phone rang again. Dropping his head to her chest, he took a deep breath and got up to retrieve his phone and see who the hell had the nerve to intrude on his honeymoon. Cameron Green. What the hell?

"Hey." He tried not to sound annoyed or freaked out but felt both those things. "What's up?"

"I'm so sorry to bother you, but I thought you'd want to know that Skip Holland passed away this morning."

At first, Freddie wasn't sure he'd heard his colleague correctly. And then, as the words registered, Freddie dropped into a chair, his legs going weak beneath him.

"I'm really sorry to do this to you, bro, but the LT said you'd want to know. She also said, quite emphatically, to tell you *not* to come home. She said to tell you she's fine, and she wants you to enjoy the rest of your trip. She was very clear on that."

One thing Freddie knew for certain—there was no way on God's green earth that his best friend and partner was "fine" after losing her beloved father.

"What happened?"

"He died in his sleep."

Imagining the shock and dismay of Sam, her sisters and stepmother, all of them like family to him, made Freddie hurt for them.

Tuned in to disaster unfolding across the room, Elin sat up in bed. "What is it?"

He put a hand over the phone. "Skip Holland passed away."

"Oh no. Oh, Freddie."

"I'm really sorry to drop this on you," Cameron continued, "but Sam said you'd want to know."

"Yeah, of course. Thanks for calling, Cam. Do me a favor and keep me posted?"

"Absolutely. Will do. I'll be in touch."

"Thanks again."

"Sorry to be the bearer of bad news."

"It's okay. Sam was right. I definitely want to know. Take care."

"You too."

Freddie ended the call and sat perfectly still for a long time, trying to decide what to do next.

"Call her, Freddie."

"She's probably overwhelmed with calls and people."

"She'd want to hear from you."

"I'll try her." Someone had told them about a free app to make calls while they were overseas, but he hadn't expected to need it. He opened the app, dialed Sam's number and waited for it to go through. It rang and rang before her voice mail picked up. Closing his eyes, he tried to find the right words. "Hey, it's me. I just heard the news. Call me if you get a second. I'm so sorry, and I'm thinking of you all, and I'm thinking of Skip... I, um, I don't even know what to say, Sam. Elin and I love you guys."

Sighing, he ended the call and put his phone on a table. It occurred to him that Nick would be on his way home from the Europe trip today and wouldn't have been there when disaster struck. That only made Freddie feel worse for Sam—and Nick, who'd be beside himself.

Elin got up, put on one of the silk robes she'd received as a shower gift and came to him. "What can I do?"

Freddie brought her onto his lap and wrapped his arms around her. "This helps." Outside their hotel, the sound of cars going by, horns and sirens blaring, could be heard in the heart of Rome. But his mind was thousands of miles away, in DC with the ball-busting older sister he'd never had. She had to be absolutely reeling.

Elin kissed his neck. "We should go home."

"Sam told Cameron to tell me *not* to come. She doesn't want that."

"She doesn't want to interrupt our trip, but what do *you* want?"

They'd waited such a long time for this trip, had scrimped and saved to be able to afford it and were thoroughly enjoying it. He absolutely hated the idea of cutting short their time in Italy, but more than that, he hated the idea of Sam going through hell without him there to prop her up in any way that he could. And he'd truly loved and admired Skip Holland, who would be given a funeral to befit a hero. In the end, there was no decision to make.

"I need to be there."

"I agree. I'll call the airline and get us on the first possible flight home."

"I'm so sorry about this, babe."

She kissed his forehead. "Don't be sorry. We can come back for our anniversary."

"Maybe by our tenth we'll be able to afford it again."

"It'll be something to look forward to. And you know what the good news is?"

"There's good news?" He felt terribly sad over the loss of a great man and a tiny bit selfish at the same time.

"Uh-huh. The honeymoon doesn't have to end just because we're going home."

"That's very good news indeed."

"I'm so sorry you lost your friend and that Sam lost her dad."

He hugged her tightly, grateful for her strength and support. "Thank you."

"Let me up, and I'll see about getting us home."

As A LIFELONG devout Catholic, Joe Farnsworth never missed Sunday mass with his wife, Marti, who sang in the choir. He used the quiet hour of contemplation to reflect on the past week and to pray for the four thousand men and women who served under him in the Metropolitan Police Department. They had no idea he prayed for them, their safety and their families, who also sacrificed so much. They didn't need to know that in addition to the obvious requests for their safety, he also asked the good Lord to keep his officers honest in all their dealings and to serve their city and its citizens with honor and distinction.

His prayers weren't always answered, but he offered them anyway. In the last year, his department had suffered the tragic loss of Detective Arnold, a young officer who'd shown tremendous promise, and had seen several in their ranks cross lines that could never be uncrossed. He mourned for the losses of life and grieved over those who'd disappointed them all by stepping out of bounds. And mostly he prayed for the patience and fortitude to lead his department through turbulent times for law enforcement officers.

After mass, he waited in the back for Marti to join him for the walk home. She'd put a roast in the oven for their midday meal before they left. He enjoyed their routines and appreciated the weekends that passed without a crisis that brought him back to work.

As his lovely wife made her way toward him, surrounded by friends from the choir, he said a little prayer of thanks for her. Thirty-five years after they said "I do," he was still crazy about her. She smiled brightly at the sight of him and damned if his heart didn't give a little jolt of appreciation for the way she still looked at him.

Marti slipped her arm through his. "See you all at rehearsal on Tuesday."

Cathy, another woman from the choir, gave him a good once-over, as she always did. It annoyed the hell out of Marti but only amused him. He had eyes only for the woman he'd had the good fortune to marry. There would never be anyone else for him. "Ladies." Joe nodded to the others. "Have a good week."

"Bye, Joe." Cathy's suggestive, breathy voice did nothing for him.

They said their goodbyes and began the five-block walk home, still arm in arm, as the brisk autumn air swirled around them, scattering fallen leaves on the sidewalk.

"If I stab her eyes out, will you have to arrest me?" Marti's question, asked when they were two blocks from the church, made Joe laugh—hard.

"No one is above the law, my dear, not even the police chief's wife."

"I should have some advantages after all the nonsense I have to put up with as the police chief's wife. Late-night phone calls and messed-up dinners and vacations, as well as interruptions to *private* activities."

As chief of police, he never ignored a phone call. Ever. And that had led to some rather unfortunate interruptions in his married life. Luckily, his wife mostly rolled with the demands of his job. But some things, she said, should never be interrupted. He agreed and looked forward to the day, hopefully a few short years from now, when he would retire and give her all his time. In the meantime, he took the calls. "Your sacrifices have been significant, my love, but you still can't stab her eyes out. If you were, however, to accidentally stick your foot out when she was walking by... Well, those things happen to the best of us."

She snorted out an inelegant laugh. "That's a very good idea. She's in *church*, for heaven's sake, and lusting after someone else's husband. What is *wrong* with her?"

"She is only human after all, and your husband is a rather handsome sort of guy."

"My husband is a stud, and she can eat her heart out. He's all mine."

"And he wouldn't have it any other way." Putting his

arm around her, he kissed her temple. "You know you have absolutely nothing to worry about."

"Of course I do, but it still annoys me when she looks at you like you're an all-you-can-eat buffet and she's starving."

Joe laughed so hard he had tears in his eyes, recovering himself to notice someone waiting for them on their front porch. Immediately on guard, he reached for the concealed weapon he wore at all times on his hip.

"What?" Marti asked after he released her somewhat abruptly.

"Visitor on the porch."

She took a closer look. "Oh, for heaven's sake, Joe. That's Jake!"

Her vision was better than his, but now that she mentioned it, he could see the distinctive build of his close friend and colleague Jake Malone. At six feet four inches, Jake was a rather imposing sort of guy, and he should've recognized him more easily. Might be time for an eye exam. He tucked the weapon into the waistband of his pants.

Jake came down the stairs to meet them.

"You need to stay out of the shadows, my friend." Marti raised her cheek to accept Jake's kiss. "Blind-as-a-bat here nearly took a shot at you."

"That's not true." Joe shook the hand of his friend and detective captain. "I never came close to shooting. What brings you by?" When he took a closer look at Jake and noticed distress, Joe's stomach dropped in anticipation of bad news. "What is it?"

"Skip Holland passed away this morning."

"Ah, no." Marti sagged against him.

Shock hit Joe like a punch to the gut. He put his arm around Marti as much to comfort her as to be comforted. Images from decades of friendship cycled through his mind, one right after the other, beginning with his and Skip's first days at the academy. And then he thought of the young, brash lieutenant who headed up his Homicide division, the woman who was like a niece to him, who'd called him Uncle Joe until she joined the force and he became her deputy chief and, later, her chief. "Sam…"

"Is holding up okay."

"We need to go to them." Marti took charge in his moment of shock. "Give me a minute to gather up the dinner I made. We'll take it to them."

She always made extra so they got a couple of days without having to cook. Why was he thinking of such things at a time like this? Skip was dead. He repeated the words to himself, hoping that would make them easier to process.

Marti gave his arm a squeeze and went up the stairs, moving quickly because she knew he'd want to see Celia and the family.

"You okay?" Jake asked when the two men stood alone on the sidewalk.

"I don't know." Jake Malone was one of three people in the world Joe Farnsworth completely trusted. The other two were Marti and Skip. Now one of them was gone. "You?"

"Even though we knew this could happen at any time in the last four years, I'm still completely stunned."

"Me too." He glanced up at Jake. "You're sure Sam is okay?"

"I only talked to her for a minute, but she sounded better than I would've expected."

Hands on hips, Joe tried to wrap his head around this

latest development. "We'll need the biggest damned police funeral this city has ever seen."

"Absolutely. I've already put the word out to notify all the other departments once we have a plan."

"We'll get tens of thousands for this one." Not just because of who Skip had been, but because of who his daughter and son-in-law were to the city and the country.

"No doubt about it. And we've upgraded the charges in his case from attempted murder of a police officer to murder. That was the first thing I did when I heard the news. I've also arranged for an honor escort from Ninth Street to the funeral home."

Joe nodded in agreement. "Thank you for taking care of that."

"Sam included mention of the tip line in the announcement that went public fifteen minutes ago. Let's hope we get some new leads. It would give me great pleasure to lock up the son of a bitch who did this to him."

"You and me both."

They exchanged a fierce look that told Joe they were on the same page, as they usually were. Getting justice for Skip Holland would now become their top priority.

CHAPTER FIVE

BY LATE AFTERNOON, Skip's house was overrun with family, friends, fellow police officers and neighbors who'd come to offer comfort and consolation to the grieving family. They'd brought food and booze and baked goods and love—lots and lots of love. While Sam appreciated the outpouring of support, the only love she wanted was from Nick, who was still several hours from home.

The clock seemed to move in reverse during that long, difficult day. She'd received a voice mail message from her partner, Freddie, that had touched her deeply. It pained her to think of him receiving this news when he was so far from home and supposed to be enjoying his new wife and their honeymoon.

Timing, as they said, was everything. She'd texted him to thank him for the concern and told him to carry on with his trip and that she was okay.

The undertakers had removed Skip's body from the house several hours ago. Sam had stood with her family on the sidewalk to watch the Metro PD escort Skip to the funeral home with lights and sirens befitting a fallen hero. She had kept a distance from the proceedings to avoid the throng of reporters that had gathered outside the Secret Service checkpoint.

A member of the department would remain with Skip until his burial. Before she'd had a family of her own to care for, Sam would've wanted to be that officer. Now her responsibilities to her son took precedence. She had to believe Skip would want her to stay close to Scotty while other members of the department stood watch over him.

Around three, she went outside to speak to Debra. "What time is Air Force Two due to arrive at Andrews?"

"Shortly after five. Marine Two will be standing by to bring the vice president into the city. He should be here by six at the very latest."

"Will you please pass along my thanks to whoever took care of all that?"

"I believe it was Mr. O'Connor, but I'll make sure he's told."

"No need. I'll tell him myself when I get the chance. Excuse me." Sam went down the ramp to greet her father-in-law, Leo Cappuano, and stepmother-in-law, Stacy, with hugs.

"We came as soon as we heard the news." Leo had the same brown hair, hazel eyes and olive-toned skin as Nick, the son he'd fathered while still in high school. The two had struggled over the years to form a relationship but were closer now than they'd ever been.

"I'm sorry I didn't call you myself."

"Don't be," Stacy said. "We can't begin to know what you must be going through."

"I feel like I keep saying this, but I'm comforted to know he's free. I keep thinking he's running around in heaven and dancing like a fool the way he used to."

"I love that." Stacy swiped subtly at tears. "We admired him so much and always enjoyed the time we spent with him."

"That means a lot. Thank you."

"What can we do for you?" Leo asked.

"Snap your fingers and get your son home right now?" Sam said with a small grin.

"If I could, I'd do it in a second for you. He's due home tonight, right?"

Sam nodded. "I'm told he'll be here by six."

"If you don't mind, we'll stick around until he gets here."

"That'll be great. Scotty will be happy to see you."

Sam escorted them inside. Scotty was seated on the sofa next to Celia, where he'd stayed for most of the day. In between greeting guests and visiting with friends, Celia had leaned against the boy who'd become her grandson over the last few years. Brooke, Abby, Ethan, Jack and Ella were there too, but it was Scotty who never left Celia's side, making his mother very proud during that endless afternoon of people and condolences.

Marti Farnsworth slipped an arm around Sam's waist. "Have you eaten anything, Sam?"

She shook her head. Food had been the last thing on her mind that day. She wasn't sure she could eat.

"Come with me." Marti led Sam into the kitchen. Conversation among extended family and friends died off when they walked in. "Would you all mind giving us a minute?"

Sam appreciated the way Marti took charge.

The others filed out of the room, leaving Sam and Marti alone until Uncle Joe walked in.

Marti fixed them each a plate from the wide assortment of food and put it on the table in front of them. Then she discreetly left them alone, letting the kitchen door swing closed behind her.

When they were alone, Sam glanced at him. "Your wife is the best."

"I've known that for more than thirty-five years."

Sam picked at the food, forcing herself to chew and swallow a few bites so she wouldn't do something embarrassing like pass out.

Joe pushed his own food around with the same lack of interest Sam felt. "This is a tough one, for all of us, but mostly for you."

Sam shook her head. "He didn't belong just to me."

"Didn't he?" Joe offered a small smile. "You had him so firmly wrapped around that powerful little finger of yours, the same little finger that has me and Jake and many others firmly wrapped." He wiped his face with a paper napkin and smiled warmly at her. "I remember the day you were born. He never said so, but we all knew Skip wanted a boy."

Sam had always known she'd been her father's last great chance for the son he'd craved. In many ways, she'd spent her entire life trying to fill that void for him.

"You know what he said to me that day when I went to visit you in the hospital?"

Sam shook her head. They'd never talked about this before.

"He said he took one look at you and realized it didn't matter if you were a boy or a girl. All he cared about was that you were healthy."

"That sounds like him."

"He also said he had a sneaking suspicion that this one, this little one, was going to turn out to be the best friend he'd ever have. It was as if he took one look at you and knew what you'd mean to him."

Sam dabbed at the tears that flooded her eyes, refusing to give in to them out of fear that she'd never stop once she started. "Thank you for telling me that."

"It's nothing you didn't already know." He covered

her hand with his much bigger one. "No question this'll leave a huge void for you, but you are *not* alone, and he'll never be truly gone, Sam. Anytime you need him, he'll be right there to tell you what to do. He's so deep in your DNA there's no getting him out."

Sam nodded in agreement. That was certainly true. It had always been true.

"If there's anything I can do, anything at all, you tell your uncle Joe what it is—now and in the future. You hear me?"

She turned to him and accepted the tight hug he gave her, one of the few she'd gotten from him in years as they worked to maintain the fine line between family and superior officer on the job. Today, they were family.

"You'll speak at the funeral, right?"

"Absolutely."

"Thank you for everything, particularly your devoted friendship to him these last few years."

"I enjoyed every minute I ever spent in his presence. He was the cop we all wanted to be, and so are you. He was so incredibly proud of you."

"Even when I'm insubordinate?" she asked, needing a moment of levity.

Joe laughed. "Especially then. He'd never say so, but he secretly admired your renegade spirit. Remember that day you came into this house during the O'Connor investigation, prepared to do battle with us because you knew we were going to try to take you off the case after your car blew up?"

"I remember. The old-boy network was trying to flex their muscles."

"While he watched you, *I* watched *him*. He all but beamed with pride watching you mouth off to your chief, who also happened to be one of his best friends.

He loved the way you do the job, even if it gives me and others heartburn at times. Skip freaking loved it. Don't you ever think otherwise."

Hearing that made her smile for the first time in hours. "He always seemed to lean more toward your side than mine."

"I think he was afraid you'd completely go rogue if he let you see his approval."

Sam laughed. "Instead of only partially rogue?"

"Exactly. He was always on your side, Sam. And he always will be."

"I appreciate you more than you could ever know, and I'm well aware that I present a constant challenge to you and the fine line we walk between personal and professional."

He leaned in, his voice low. "You continue to do you, and I'll continue to tally up the successes we achieve together. And if you ever quote me on that, I'll deny it with fire and fury as I demote you so fast your head will spin."

Sam pretended to lock her lips and throw away the key and then leaned her head on his sturdy shoulder, grateful for his words and his support. "Love you, Uncle Joe."

He kissed the top of her head. "Love you too, sweetheart."

THE LAST LEG of Nick's trip home, the chopper ride from Andrews to the White House and the motorcade from the White House to Ninth Street, seemed almost as long as the seven-hour flight that preceded it. As the motorcade finally approached the Ninth Street checkpoint, Nick felt like he was coming out of his skin while he waited for Brant to open the door. The second the door opened, Nick bolted.

Would there be hell to pay with Brant later? Ask him if he cared. The only thing he cared about was getting to his wife after an endless week and hours of heartbreak on her behalf. He ran past his own house to her father's and up the ramp in three strides, bursting into the living room and taking everyone by surprise.

Celia's face crumpled at the sight of him.

His son jumped up from the sofa and ran into his outstretched arms.

Scotty sobbed as he clung to his father, who held him close. "I'm here, buddy. I'm sorry it took so long. But I'm here now." He scanned the crowded room for the one-in-a-million face of his wife but didn't see her.

Marti Farnsworth squeezed his arm. "She's in the kitchen with Joe."

Nick kissed the top of Scotty's head. "I need to see Mom."

Scotty nodded. "Yes, you do."

Nick brushed the tears from his son's face, his heart breaking for him. "Are you all right?"

"I'm trying to be."

"I'll be right back, okay?"

"Okay." Scotty released him and went back to Celia, who received him with outstretched arms.

As Nick moved toward the kitchen, people got out of his way to let him through, which kept him from knocking them over in his haste to get to her. He pushed through the door to the kitchen, where Sam leaned on the shoulder of her beloved chief and uncle, Joe. When Nick walked in, she gasped and lit up with pure pleasure at the sight of him. No one had ever looked at him the way she did.

"I'll give you two a minute." Joe released Sam, stood and shook Nick's hand on the way out of the room.

Sam stood and launched herself into his arms.

Gathering her into his embrace, Nick could finally breathe again because he was back where he belonged, with the only woman he'd ever truly loved wrapped around him, bringing the distinctive fragrance of jasmine and vanilla that he would recognize anywhere in the world as the scent of love.

"Thank God you're home."

"I'm so sorry it took so long and that I wasn't here when you needed me."

"You're here now. That's what matters."

Over her shoulder, his gaze landed on the empty hospital bed and wheelchair in the dining room, his eyes filling with tears. He would dearly miss Skip and his steady presence in their lives, his words of wisdom and the way he looked out for Sam as best he could, even after his devastating injury. The loss would leave a huge hole in all their lives that could never be filled, but no hole would be bigger than the one left for Sam.

"Your dad and Stacy are here."

He'd been so intent on getting to her, he hadn't noticed anyone else besides Scotty. "Nice of them to come."

"Everyone has been so incredibly nice."

"Everyone loved him."

"You should go see them."

"I will." He buried his face into her hair. "But first I need some more of this."

She held on tighter to him. "So do I."

THEY SPENT HOURS greeting friends, members of Sam's squad and others from work, including her father's good friend Deputy Chief Conklin, as well as Dr. Lindsey

McNamara, FBI Agent Avery Hill, Dr. Trulo, Detective Erica Lucas, Lieutenant Archelotta and all three of the identical Miller triplets, who served as Assistant U.S. Attorneys for the District of Columbia. The people kept coming all afternoon and into the evening.

Around eight, Sam helped her sisters divide the food that had been brought among their four households. They were cleaning up the kitchen when Scotty escorted their mother, Brenda, into the room.

"I was in Richmond for the weekend and just heard the news." Tears filled Brenda's eyes as she hugged each of her daughters. "I'm so sorry."

Sam returned her mother's embrace, thinking that this was the first time she'd seen her mother in this kitchen in more than twenty years, which was bizarre to say the least. "Thanks for coming."

"I was hoping Celia wouldn't mind if I came to see you girls."

"She doesn't mind," Tracy said.

"How is she?" Brenda asked.

"Not great," Angela said. "Which is understandable. She's devoted her life to his care for almost four years. What would we have done without her?"

"He wouldn't have lasted this long without her," Sam said bluntly, sagging against the counter, losing her steam now that the house had begun to empty and the gritty reality began to set in.

"True," Tracy said.

"I think it's time to get the kids home and into bed," Angela said.

"Are you sending Scotty to school tomorrow?" Tracy asked Sam.

"Only if he feels up to it. I'll let him decide." She

hugged her mother again. "Thanks for coming by. We appreciate it."

"Please let me know if I can do anything for any of you in the next few days. I'm here for whatever you need."

Sam appreciated the kind offer. "What I need right now is some time with the kids, some time with my husband and some sleep. I'll check in with you guys in the morning."

She hugged her sisters and went into the living room, where Scotty was still seated with Celia and her two sisters. Mike, Spencer and Nick were still there, along with Brant and Debra, who were there because of Nick and Scotty.

Nick stood when she came into the room. "Ready to head home, babe?"

Sam nodded and then turned to her stepmother. "I'll be over in the morning for the meeting with the department rep at ten, okay?"

Celia nodded. "Thank you."

"Celia—"

"Go get some rest, Sam. We're all going to need it."

Celia's anger cut Sam to the quick. But now was not the time or the place to address it. There would be time for that after they laid her father to rest.

"Let's go home, Scotty."

He hugged and kissed Celia. "I'll be over tomorrow."

"Thank you for being the sweetest boy I know. You really helped me today."

"Love you," Scotty said.

Celia teared up as she hugged him. "Love you too. Your gramps was super proud of you."

Scotty swiped subtly at tears as he got up to join his parents for the short walk home.

Sam put her arm around him. "You made me very proud today. Thank you for being so good to Celia." They walked slowly as Brant and Debra kept a respectful distance behind them.

"I love her."

"I know you do, buddy."

"She'll still be, like, my grandma even though Gramps died, right?"

"Of course she will."

"Is she mad with you about something?" Scotty asked.

"Yeah, she is," Sam said with a sigh.

"Why?"

"When everything happened earlier, I was the one who told the paramedics that Gramps had a DNR and wouldn't want extraordinary measures."

"What's a DNR and what do you mean by extraordinary measures?"

"DNR stands for *do not resuscitate*, and it's a form people sign when they don't want medical personnel to go all out to save their lives."

"Why would he sign something like that?"

"Because, pal," Nick said, "if his body shut down on him, he wanted to be allowed to pass away peacefully and not be brought back to life."

"Gramps didn't want to die," Sam said, "but he also didn't want heroic measures if his body decided it was time."

"You have to think about the way he'd been forced to live for the last four years," Nick added. "He made it look easy, but it was a very, very difficult thing to contend with on a daily basis. As much as we'll miss him, I'd like to hope he's in a better place tonight where there's no such thing as paralysis."

"That would be nice." As they went up the ramp to their home, Scotty glanced at his mother. "Will Celia forgive you?"

"I sure hope so. I really think it was the best decision for Gramps, or I never would've done it."

"She'll realize that, babe." Nick squeezed her shoulder. "When she's had time to process it."

In the living room, Shelby was curled up on the sofa with Noah asleep in her arms and Avery stretched out on the sofa, his head on her leg as they watched a movie.

"So sorry to keep you guys so late," Sam said.

Avery sat up and straightened his hair. "How're you holding up?"

"I'm okay. How're our littles?"

"They're tucked into bed and their backpacks are ready for the morning," Shelby said. "I'll be here to get them off to school."

"Do I have to go to school?" Scotty asked his parents.

"That's totally up to you," Sam said. "You can decide in the morning if you feel up to it."

Under normal circumstances, the chance to take an unscheduled day off from school would've been met by jubilation. Tonight, Scotty said, "I'll think about it."

Sam hugged him. "If you need us during the night, you know where we are."

When Sam released him, Shelby stepped up to hug him after handing Noah to Avery. "Hope you're hanging in there, pal."

"Thanks, Shelby." Scotty hugged Nick. "I'll see you guys in the morning."

After he trudged upstairs, Shelby reached for Noah's

blanket. "We'll get out of your hair. I'll see you in the morning?"

Sam hugged her. "Thank you so much for today."

"No need to thank me. I'm glad there was something I could do."

Sam and Nick waited for Shelby and Avery to depart with Noah before they headed upstairs to bed, looking in on Aubrey and Alden, who were sound asleep in the big bed they were sharing for now. They preferred to be together, which was fine.

Debra was on duty outside Scotty's room.

"Isn't it time to go home?" Sam asked.

Debra shrugged. "I offered to give a few more hours."

"That's very good of you."

"I hope you're able to get some rest."

"I'm going to try," Sam said. "Good night."

"Night."

Nick ushered her into the bedroom and closed the door. "We're not the only ones who love that boy of ours."

"Debra was amazing today. If there's anything you can do for her…"

"I'll pass it along." He put his arms around her and held her close. "I wish there was something I could say or do that would ease your grief, sweetheart."

"Having you here really helps."

"I'll always be sorry I wasn't here earlier when you needed me."

"It's okay. I was very well supported, and I'm very glad to have you home."

"Me too. Let's go to bed."

Sam went into the bathroom to brush her teeth and then dropped her clothes in a pile on the floor to be dealt with tomorrow. She slid naked into bed and held out her arms to him when he joined her a minute later. After a week of craving the feel of his skin against hers, she sighed with relief.

Nick held her tight against him. "There you are. I missed you so much."

"I missed you just as much." She ran her fingers through his thick dark hair. "It's a little bit ridiculous that we can't spend a week apart without losing it."

"Tell me what you need, babe." He caressed her back in small, soothing circles. "I'm so worried about you."

"I'm…surprisingly all right and strangely relieved for him."

"I can understand why."

"You didn't know him before. He was just so vibrant and full of life."

"Like his daughter?"

"Yeah, I guess."

He tipped her chin up and kissed her gently. "Whatever you need, I'm right here. Terry cleared my schedule for the week, so I can be with you and the kids and the rest of the family."

"More kisses would be good."

"You're in luck. I have an endless supply with your name on them."

Her joy at being reunited with her beloved husband helped her contend with the grief that had marked this surreal day. And while her heart ached over the loss she'd sustained, it soared with love for Nick. Soaring highs, crushing lows—the story of her life. And Nick… He was the highest of highs. Kissing him, touching him, being loved by him, somehow made everything better than it would've been otherwise.

Kissing her with a week's worth of desire, he

smoothly rolled her under him before easing back from the kiss to gaze down at her with concern, love and desire.

She reached for him, raising her hips in invitation. "I'm okay."

He kept his hazel eyes open as he joined his body with hers. "Samantha... I can't bear to be away from you."

She curled her arms around his neck and her legs around his hips, feeling complete for the first time in a week. "I feel the same way. No more traveling."

He dropped his forehead to rest against hers. "I told Terry if they want me to travel, you have to go with me, or I'm not going."

"Can you do that?"

"They're not going to fire me." He kissed her lips and then her neck as he moved in her, filling her heart, soul and body the way only he could. "This was one of the longest days of my life, knowing you were suffering and I couldn't get to you."

"I felt almost worse for you than I did for myself. I knew you'd be losing it because you weren't here."

"I *was* losing it, and I hate that I wasn't here when you needed me." He picked up the pace, and they clung to each other, chasing the release that occurred in a moment of near-holy perfection, his body straining against hers as they came together, the tension inside her subsiding in the aftermath and leaving bone-deep exhaustion in its place.

She had wondered if she'd be able to sleep tonight, but safe in the arms of her love, she found the peace and comfort she needed to close her eyes and let it all go until the morning.

CHAPTER SIX

SCOTTY CHOSE TO go to school because, he said, that was what his gramps would want him to do. "He was always telling me that there was nothing more important than a good education," Scotty said over his usual bowl of cereal. "I'm going to try to take school more seriously for him. You think that would make him happy?"

Holding a cup of coffee as she leaned against the counter, Sam smiled and nodded. "That would make him very happy. He wanted to see you reach your full potential."

"He was always saying the sky was the limit for me."

"He really believed that."

"Are you sure you don't need me here today?"

"I always need you here, but I'll be okay until you get home. You're going to miss school for the funeral, so it's a good idea to go today so you don't get too far behind."

He polished off the cereal, downed a glass of OJ and then stood to put the dishes in the sink. "How old do I have to be before I can have coffee?"

Sam handed him her mug, enjoying the surprise that lit up his expressive face.

He took a sip. "It's kinda bitter."

"It's an acquired taste. Have some more."

He took a second bigger taste. "Not bad."

"Go brush your teeth."

As he dashed out of the kitchen, he passed Nick, who was coming in. "Mom let me have coffee."

Nick raised a brow in Sam's direction. "Did she, now?"

"He had two sips. No biggie."

"Don't get him addicted to a morning boost or he'll be a bear like you are until you get your fix."

"A bear?"

"A gorgeous, sexy, delightful bear." He kissed her forehead and then her lips. "But a bear nonetheless."

"Only you can insult and compliment me all in the same breath."

"It's my special gift." Resting his hands on her hips, he gazed down at her. "How'd you sleep?"

"Surprisingly well thanks to you and your special bedtime remedy."

"It fixes a world of hurts."

She put her mug on the counter and wrapped her arms around him. "Yes, it certainly does."

"What do you need today?"

"You, right here with me."

"Nowhere else I'd rather be every day, but especially today."

"We're meeting with the department rep at ten and then the funeral home. We probably ought to have Brant and Debra at the meeting with the rep so they know what we'll be doing and when."

"I'll let them know. Anything else you want or need, you just tell me."

Scotty returned to the kitchen, backpack on his shoulder, and came to a stop when he saw them wrapped up in each other. "There's a child in the room."

Nick smiled at Sam as he released her. "Nothing to see here."

"I suppose some kissing is to be expected in light of her loss, but let's keep it respectable. Alden and Aubrey are too young to be exposed to such goings-on."

"Go to school." Sam tried not to crack up. That would only encourage him.

He grabbed the lunch Shelby had made for him the night before and tucked it into his backpack. "Later, peeps."

"Have a good day, and if it turns into a rough day, call us," Nick said.

"I will. You take care of her." Scotty nodded to his mother.

"I'm on it. Don't worry."

Scotty was almost to the door when he turned back. "Hey, Mom? Do you think I could maybe say something about Gramps at the funeral?"

"I think that would be awesome."

"Okay. I'll work on it." He was out the door like a shot, talking to the agents who would accompany him to school.

"I can't believe he didn't take the chance to stay home," Nick said.

"He said Gramps would want him to go, and you'll be glad to hear that he's going to start taking school more seriously, also because Gramps would want that."

Feigning shock, Nick rested his hand on his heart. "Don't mess with me about this. It's too important."

Sam laughed. "It's true. He said it."

"I need a minute to process this development."

"Don't start calling Harvard quite yet. We still have to get him through high school math."

"True." He checked his watch. "Let's go rouse our littles so they're ready when Shelby gets here."

Bringing a second cup of coffee with her, Sam went

ahead of him up the stairs to the bedroom Aubrey and Alden were sharing.

Sam sat on the bed next to Aubrey. "Good morning."

The little girl looked up at her with big eyes. "Is Mommy here?" Then she seemed to remember what'd happened.

Every time they asked for their late parents, Sam's heart broke all over again for them.

"Sorry." Aubrey hugged her stuffed bear a little tighter. "I forgot."

"It's okay, sweetheart. That's apt to happen for a while."

"I heard somebody say that your daddy died too."

"He did."

"Are you sad?"

"I am."

Aubrey sat up and held out her chubby little arms to Sam, who leaned into her embrace, closing her eyes against the rush of emotion.

Nick cleared his throat and turned his focus on Alden, who was watching them with the wise, knowing way that made him seem older than his years. He had witnessed the horror at his home the night his parents were killed. The therapist had told Sam it was hard to tell what he would remember later, but it was possible the memories of the awful night that had changed his life forever would never fade completely.

Sam and Nick worked together to get the children washed and dressed for school.

As they trooped down the stairs to see to breakfast, the front door opened and the Secret Service admitted Freddie and Elin. At first, Sam was so shocked to see them that she didn't immediately react. "*What* are you doing here?" She greeted her partner and his wife with hugs.

Freddie held Sam for a long moment. "You know what we're doing here."

"You didn't have to come home."

"Yes, we did." He released her but kept his hands on her shoulders. "What can we do?"

"Since you defied my orders and came home when I told you not to, will you be part of the honor guard with the rest of the squad?"

"Of course I will. What else?"

"I don't know yet. Can I get back to you?"

"We're here for whatever you need."

"We're so sorry, Sam." Elin's eyes were bright with unshed tears. "For the rest of my life, I'll never forget him getting us pole-dancing lessons as a bachelor party gift."

Sam laughed at the memory. "Trust me, neither will I."

"He was the best," Freddie said.

"Yes, he was. I'm sorry that your honeymoon was interrupted. He would've hated to be the cause of that."

"We wouldn't have been able to enjoy it," Freddie said. "There's talk of a candlelight vigil at HQ tonight."

"Is there?" Sam asked, touched by the gesture.

Freddie nodded. "People remember what happened to him, Sam. They've never forgotten."

"That's good to know. Hopefully, we'll get some new leads to follow."

"I hear the tip line has been doing robust business. We'll dig into that as soon as we give him the send-off he deserves."

"Yes, we will." Her father's death had relit the fire inside her that burned for justice on his behalf. In the four years since he'd been shot, she'd investigated countless leads that had led nowhere. Skip had somewhat calmly accepted his fate, but Sam had seethed with outrage. While her father contended with his new reality, the person who'd put him in a wheelchair remained free. The sheer unfairness of that was almost more than she could bear at times.

"There's a massive scrum of reporters at the gate," Freddie said. "Just so you're aware."

"Ugh," Sam said. "What do they want from us? We gave them a statement."

"You know that's never enough where you guys are concerned."

Shelby came bustling in with Noah strapped to her chest. "Sorry we're running late. Someone was cranky this morning."

"Avery?" Sam asked.

Alden and Aubrey went dashing over to see Noah, who, along with Scotty, had become their favorite part of living there.

Shelby laughed. "Nope, not Avery. This little man didn't want to cooperate with his mama. It might've been the first time, but I suspect it won't be the last." She corralled the children into the kitchen. "Let's get some grub into those bellies so we can head to school."

"We're going home to sleep for a bit," Freddie said, "but we'll be back later to check on you."

Sam hugged him again. "Thank you for this. It shall be remembered forever."

"Skip will be too."

Because she didn't trust herself to speak, she nodded and saw them out. "I can't believe they came home."

"I can," Nick said. "He'd never let you go through this without him. You'd do the same for him."

"Yeah, I guess I would. I'm going to run up and take a shower while I can."

"Take your time. I'll help Shelby."

"Maybe you should take the kids to school this morning so Shelby doesn't have to deal with the reporters by herself."

"Good call." He gave her a quick kiss. "I'm on it."

While he went to alert Brant that he'd be taking the kids to school, Sam dashed upstairs to prepare for another long, emotional day.

THE OUTPOURING WAS nothing short of astonishing. Food, flowers, cards, people... Five minutes at her dad's house and Sam could see they were overrun and in need of the kind of assistance only one person could provide. Sam placed a call to her White House chief of staff, Lilia Van Nostrand.

"Sam." In recent weeks, Lilia had finally conceded to calling Sam by her given name whenever possible. "I was just going to try to call you. I can't begin to tell you how sorry I am for your loss. Harry and I were away for the weekend, and I barely glanced at my phone."

"That, in and of itself, is one hell of a coup by my good friend Harry."

"He is very distracting."

"I can hear you blushing over the phone."

"You can't *hear* someone blush."

"In this case, I can."

"I'm trying to be serious and express my heartfelt condolences."

"Thank you."

"Are you doing all right?"

"I'm muddling through. It's a shock, but in many ways, it's also a relief. Seeing him so diminished every day for the last four years was far more painful than I realized until it was over."

"That's a very interesting perspective. What can I do for you?"

"We're being slammed with kindness. I could use someone to manage it all for us."

"Say no more. I'll be there within the half hour."

"There's a meeting with the department rep at ten to go over what's going to happen. Can you attend that too?"

"I am at your disposal and honored to help in any way that I can."

Sam breathed an audible sigh of relief. In Lilia's hands, this wouldn't turn into the total shit show that it would be without Lilia and her mad organizational skills. They needed all the help they could get to record the tsunami of gifts and condolences, so they could be properly acknowledged later.

"Lilia is coming to help." Sam joined Celia, Tracy and Angela, who were seated around the kitchen table making checklists and going over the details for the next few days. "And Freddie and Elin cut their trip short. They came by this morning. He said the department is holding a candlelight vigil tonight at HQ."

"Oh, Freddie," Celia said, dabbing at tears.

"I can't believe they came home," Ang said. "That's so amazing."

"Do you think Gonzo will come too, Sam?" Tracy asked.

"I'm not sure if he can."

AT THAT VERY MOMENT, Sergeant Tommy Gonzales was locked in a standoff with his counselor and the director of the Baltimore-area rehab center. They'd called him into the office after his morning group session to share the news of Skip's passing, the shock of which was still reverberating through Gonzo's heart. Imagining what Sam and her family must be going through made him feel sick. Then they'd told him it was in his best interest to stay in treatment, where he'd been making good progress.

Like fuck it was in his best interest.

"There's no way I can miss this funeral. No. *Way*. He is not only my boss's father, but he was also a good friend to me. I never would've survived the immediate aftermath of losing Arnold without Skip Holland. You can't keep me here against my will."

Standing with his arms crossed, his counselor, Josh, seemed tense. "No, we can't. But we can advise you to send your condolences and stay put. This is a very important juncture in your treatment. You're a week sober and fully detoxed. One slipup puts you right back at day one. If you stay here, that won't happen. If you leave, you're risking the hard work you've already put in."

"I'm going to a funeral, not on a bender."

"Research indicates that most people who leave rehab after the first week don't come back."

"I'm not most people. I've got my entire life and career on the line here. I'm not going to fuck it up."

A knock on the door annoyed the director. *"What?"*

The receptionist stuck her head in. "I'm sorry to interrupt, but Sergeant Gonzales has a guest who's insisting on seeing him."

The director scowled. "He's not allowed to have guests—"

Gonzo didn't stick around to see how that sentence was going to end. He turned and headed for the door, brushing past the receptionist in his haste. In the outer office, Christina waited for him with Alex in her arms. His son let out a happy cry at the sight of his father and strained against his mother's hold as he reached for Gonzo.

The sight of their faces sparked a tidal wave of emotion in him. Since he'd detoxed, his every emotion hovered at the surface, threatening to spill over at any second. He'd bawled his head off in group therapy two days ago, recounting the night he'd lost his partner, and he was about to lose it again now in the presence of the two people he loved the most.

"We came to bring you home." Christina handed Alex over to him. "I figured you'd be losing your mind here after you heard about Skip."

"You figured correctly." Gonzo breathed in the scent of baby shampoo coming from his son's hair. "They just told me the news. How's Sam?"

"I haven't seen her yet, but Freddie cut his trip short and saw her earlier. He said she seems to be holding up okay. Can you come home?"

"They're saying no, but they can't keep me here against my will. I'm going."

"I'll take you under one condition."

"What condition?"

"That you come back right after the funeral and that you're with me every second you're not here. I guess that's two conditions."

He met her determined blue-eyed gaze without blinking. "I can live with both of those conditions."

Josh came out of the director's office. "Tommy..."

Keeping his greedy gaze on her gorgeous face, Gonzo found his center. "I'm leaving, Josh. I'll be back after the funeral, and I'll be with Christina the entire time I'm gone."

"I won't let him out of my sight," Christina said.

"I can only tell you that I don't recommend you do this." Josh seemed resigned now.

"I hear you and I appreciate your concern, but I'm going. Let me grab a few things from my room. I'll be right back." When he handed Alex back to Christina, the child let out a squawk of protest. Gonzo kissed his soft cheek. "I'll be right back, buddy."

He moved quickly to return to his room. In the hallway, he passed a guy named Tony, who he'd come to know over the last week.

"Hey, Sarge. What's your rush?"

"Going home for a funeral. I'll be back at the end of the week."

"Whoa. What'd Josh have to say about that?"

"He's not happy." Gonzo spoke over his shoulder, not wanting to slow down for any reason. He feared that maybe they *could* keep him there and were plotting to make that happen while he was dicking around. "But I have to go."

"Sorry for your loss."

"Thanks." He felt odd accepting condolences on behalf of Skip and his family, but as part of the thin blue line, he was family to Skip. The law enforcement community was a brother-and-sisterhood formed by tight bonds that became even tighter when one of their own was taken from them in a criminal act. Skip had lived for almost four years after being shot, but his death would be ruled a homicide.

As he threw clothes and personal items into a bag, Gonzo hoped the classification on Skip's case had already been upgraded. He'd be surprised if that hadn't been the first order of business for the department after learning of his death. Upon zipping the bag and hoisting it to his shoulder, he stopped just short of the doorway to realize with sudden clarity that he was thinking like his old self again for the first time in months.

His mind was clear and focused, his determination reminiscent of the way he'd been before disaster struck, and his resolve to get back on track firm. Glancing at the room he'd called home for the last week, he had to acknowledge that the treatment was working.

He would be back.

But first, he would see to his family in blue, especially his beloved friend and lieutenant.

CHAPTER SEVEN

JOE FARNSWORTH ACCOMPANIED the department's liaison, Officer Charles, to the ten o'clock meeting to discuss Skip's funeral. Though Celia, Tracy and Angela were surprised to see the chief, Sam was not. She knew he'd want to personally oversee every detail of the send-off for one of his oldest and dearest friends. His involvement would ensure that Skip was afforded every honor he was due.

Joe hugged and kissed each of them before taking a seat at the table and placing his hand over Celia's. "How're you holding up?"

"I'm lost. I don't know what to do with myself without Skip to care for."

"It'll take some time to figure out what's next. In the meantime, you let us know what we can do to help. Anything you need, you let Officer Charles here know, and it'll be taken care of."

"Thank you, Joe. Everyone has been so incredibly kind."

"Skip meant a lot to our department. He won't be forgotten."

Leaning against the counter, Sam crossed her arms and looked down at the brown plaid linoleum floor that was original to the house.

Nick slid his arm around her waist, offering silent but steady support.

Officer Charles, a young African American woman with kind eyes and a slim, athletic build, outlined the various plans the department had made. "Tonight, there will be a candlelight vigil at nineteen hundred at the MPD headquarters building in honor of Deputy Chief Holland and the sacrifice he made on behalf of the city. At zero eight hundred tomorrow, Deputy Chief Holland will be escorted from the funeral home to City Hall, where he will lie in state for twenty-four hours. His viewing will be open to the public from zero nine hundred until eighteen hundred. After that, the family will greet personal friends and family until twenty-one hundred hours. The department will provide around-the-clock escort and security."

Brant spoke up from his post by the door. "The Secret Service will need more detailed information about the proceedings."

"I took the liberty of preparing an in-depth report for your needs." Officer Charles handed the report to Brant. "Please let me know if I missed anything."

"Thank you." Brant seemed impressed by her thoroughness.

Sam was too. "Well done, Officer. Thank you for anticipating that request."

"Anticipating all your needs is my job."

Lilia slid past Brant and into the crowded kitchen. "And mine."

"This is Lilia Van Nostrand, my chief of staff at the White House." Sam felt slightly mortified to be introducing her White House staff to her MPD colleagues. Worlds colliding always made her uncomfortable. "She is the most ruthlessly organized human being in the universe, so put her to good use."

Officer Charles shook hands with Lilia. "Happy to have the assistance."

The two of them could probably overtake the government if they put their minds to it, Sam thought.

"Wednesday morning at zero eight hundred, Deputy Chief Holland will be escorted from City Hall to Saint Mark's Episcopal Church at Third and A Street Southeast for the funeral service." Officer Charles handed a printout to everyone in attendance. "This is the route the motorcade will take and Patrol will oversee traffic and crowd control."

"Crowd control?" Celia asked.

"In light of the outpouring we've received at headquarters," Joe said, "we believe the crowds will be massive. We're expecting upward of ten thousand officers to attend from departments all over the country."

"Wow." Tracy blinked back tears. "That's amazing."

"At the conclusion of the service, a police escort will take him to his final resting place at the Prospect Hill Cemetery," Officer Charles said. "An invitation-only reception for close friends, family and MPD colleagues will be hosted by the DC Police Union in the ballroom of the Hay-Adams, which has donated the space to us."

Sam glanced at Nick, who offered a small smile. The last time they were in the ballroom of the Hay-Adams had been on their wedding day.

"We'll need a guest list for the reception as soon as possible," Officer Charles concluded.

"We'll need to vet that list," Brant said.

"I'll get it to you as soon as I have it." Officer Charles looked to Celia. "With your permission, the plans will be made public in a press release that's already been prepared."

"You've done a wonderful job organizing everything." Celia seemed overwhelmed by the magnitude.

"That's my job, ma'am, and I'm happy to help. If there's anything you'd like to change, you need only to let me know."

"I wouldn't change a thing." Celia glanced at Sam. "Does it meet with your approval?"

"Absolutely." Sam was relieved to be consulted by her stepmother. "Go ahead and issue the release."

Officer Charles made a note on one of the many pages on the table. "The funeral service itself will be planned by the family."

"The pastor is coming to meet with us at two," Tracy said.

"President and Mrs. Nelson would like to attend the service," Lilia said, "but only if Vice President and Mrs. Cappuano would welcome their presence and only if they can do so without causing any sort of disruption."

The crimes of the Nelsons' son still hung heavily over the relationship between the first and second couples. Sam glanced at Nick to gauge his reaction.

"Completely up to you," he said.

"I have no objection if no one else does," Sam said, deferring to Celia.

"Your dad would be astounded and honored to have the president and first lady at his funeral," Celia said.

"I'll let them know," Lilia said.

"If I can assist in any way," Officer Charles said, handing business cards to each of them, "I am at your service. And again, please accept my deepest condolences on the loss of an extraordinary man."

Celia sniffled and dabbed at raw, red eyes with a tissue. "Thank you so much for everything."

"It is the very least we can do in light of his ultimate

sacrifice." She glanced at the chief, who nodded. "I'll be on my way, but please call if you need anything."

When she stood, Sam stepped forward to shake her hand. "Thank you for a job very well done, Officer."

She shook Sam's hand and then Nick's. "It's an honor, Lieutenant, Mr. Vice President."

When she had departed, Celia said, "She's an impressive young woman."

"Indeed, she is," Joe said. "I have very high hopes for her career in the department."

Gonzo came rushing into the kitchen and walked right up to Sam to hug her. "I'm so, so sorry. I got here as fast as I could after I heard the news. Are you okay?"

"I'm okay." She smiled at her friend and colleague, who looked more like himself than he had since before his partner's tragic murder. "Did you bust out?"

"Just about."

"Means a lot that you're here."

"I couldn't imagine not being here."

At the table, Joe put an arm around Celia. "Is there anything else we can do for you?"

"I can't think of anything. Skip would be so very pleased with the show of support from the department."

"He was one of us. He will *always* be one of us."

"That meant everything to him."

"We'll give him a send-off fit for a king," Joe said, his voice gruff and filled with emotion. "And we'll remember him always."

OVER THE NEXT two days, Sam, Nick, Scotty and the rest of the family went through the steps of public mourning, including the candlelight vigil attended by thousands outside HQ and the hours of greeting strangers and friends alike who came to pay their respects to

Skip at City Hall. The outpouring of sympathy, respect and adoration for Skip and his family was so great as to be completely overwhelming.

Sam's heart swelled with emotion at the pageantry of the MPD motorcycles that led each procession with sirens blaring and blue lights flashing. In dress uniforms of every shade of blue, thousands of law enforcement officers and honor guards from across the country—led by Chief Farnsworth and her colleagues from the MPD—marched through the city, accompanying Skip to his funeral. Along the route, the streets were lined with citizens ten-deep waving flags and applauding as the hearse went by.

Again because of Scotty and her desire to remain close to him throughout the proceedings, Sam rode with her family in the Secret Service vehicle that followed the hearse rather than marching with her MPD colleagues. In a gesture of goodwill and generosity to the family of a fellow law enforcement officer, the Secret Service provided a motorcade for the entire extended family.

Sam took it all in with a sense of pride and a surreal feeling of loss that had only begun to permeate the numbness. But it was the bagpipes outside church that broke her composure with their distinctive wail of mourning. That sound… It brought back a lifetime of memories: police events, parades and sadder times, such as Arnold's funeral. The wound of his loss was still raw as she fought to contend with this latest blow. Aware that the eyes of the city, the country and the world were on her, Sam battled her way through the emotions, determined to do her grieving in private.

Her squad—Cruz, Gonzales, McBride, Green, Dominguez and Carlucci—each of them in full dress uniform, white gloves and badges shrouded by black bands of mourning, served as personal escorts to the Holland family. Sam was also in uniform in honor of her father. The last time she'd worn her uniform had been for Arnold's funeral.

On this day, she suspended all her usual rules against public displays of affection while in uniform and was thankful for the arm Nick kept firmly around her shoulders as they walked into the church. Celia was escorted by Scotty. Tracy, Mike, Angela, Spencer and their families followed with Sam and Nick bringing up the rear of the family procession. As each guest came into the church, they received a printed program from Tracy's children Abby and Ethan. On the cover of the program was one of Sam's favorite photos of Skip smiling in his deputy chief's uniform. He'd been so damned proud of that last promotion.

Halfway up the long aisle, Celia stopped to embrace Sam's mother, Brenda.

Sam watched as the two women who'd loved Skip Holland exchanged a few words and dabbed at tears before Celia continued to the front of the church. As she went by her mother, Sam reached out a hand to her.

Brenda squeezed Sam's hand. "Love you."

The church was completely packed, with overflow crowds outside, who would listen to the service on speakers. At the request of the family, the service would not be televised, even though the MPD and White House had received numerous requests from the media wanting to broadcast it.

After the family was seated in the front rows, Sam's squad rolled Skip's casket down the center aisle, followed by Chief Farnsworth, Deputy Chief Conklin,

Captain Malone and a cadre of retired officers who had served with Skip, each of them in dress uniform.

The Reverend Canon William Swain, a childhood friend of Skip's, presided over the service along with an archbishop and another clergy member. Her father hadn't been particularly religious, but he'd maintained a close friendship with Reverend Swain, who'd been a frequent visitor during the last few difficult years.

The reverend began with a prayer of thanksgiving for Skip's life and his service to the city he loved. "Skip Holland was of the District, for the District. Having lived in the Capitol Hill neighborhood his entire life, from Brent Elementary School to the highest ranks of the Metropolitan Police Department, this city was his home. And we will lay him to rest today in the neighborhood where he lived a life of honor, service, family, faith and community."

Sam's eldest niece, Brooke, gave the first reading, Freddie did the second reading, Ethan and Jack presented the Offertory gifts and Joe Farnsworth gave the first of three eulogies.

"Part of me still can't believe this has really happened." Joe propped his arms on the lectern as if he needed the support of the wooden structure. "Even as he lived on borrowed time for four long years, Skip rose above the daily challenges to continue providing love, friendship, wisdom, humor, grace and guidance to those of us who'd relied on him for those things long before his injury.

"Only a giant like Skip could've continued to be such a huge presence in our lives with only half his face and one finger to work with. In the last few days, I've found myself wanting to turn to him for advice about how to handle the loss of my closest friend, my brother in arms, my moral center and my true north. Since I can't do that, I've taken comfort in asking myself 'What would Skip do?' By answering that question, I have found my way through the difficult hours and days since we lost him. As we go forward without his daily presence in our lives, we should regularly ask ourselves what Skip would do. If we follow his example, we'll do the right thing, the honorable thing, the noble thing."

When Scotty sniffled, Nick raised his arm and put it around his son.

"I will remember his humor, the eyebrow that conveyed so much with only the subtlest of lifts, the parties… The *epic* parties. No one could throw a party like Skip Holland. I'll never forget the time Patrol responded to a report of a wild party on Ninth Street only to realize their deputy chief was the host and their chief was a guest." Laughter rippled through the church. "I'll remember the dancing…"

Those who'd known him before his injury lost it laughing. Skip had been a *horrible* dancer, and everyone knew it except him.

"The enthusiasm with which he did everything was a hallmark of his remarkable life and distinguished career. Celia, Tracy, Mike, Angela, Spencer, Sam, Nick, Brooke, Abby, Ethan, Jack, Ella and Scotty… You were his heart and his soul. His love for you was the most important thing in his life, his pride in his family boundless. I was never with him that he didn't tell me something about one of you that made him glow with happiness. I honestly believe he survived an injury that should've killed him because he wasn't ready to say goodbye to all of you. He wanted to be here to marry his love, Celia, and to meet Nick, Scotty and Ella. His work here wasn't finished yet, but it is now, and he can go to his final reward knowing his three beloved girls and precious grandchildren will be well cared for by sons-in-law he deeply loved and respected. Marti and I hope you will take comfort, each of you, in knowing you were well and truly loved by the greatest man I've ever known."

As he came down from the altar, Joe stopped to hug and kiss Celia, Tracy, Angela and Sam.

"And now," Reverend Swain said, "we'll hear from Skip's grandson, Scott Cappuano."

Wearing the blue blazer, light blue dress shirt, khaki pants and red-and-blue-striped tie that Scotty referred to as his "work clothes," he made his way to the altar and placed a piece of paper on the lectern before adjusting the microphone to his height. He looked so grown-up and composed that Sam's heart swelled to overflowing with love for him.

Nick gave her hand a squeeze.

She held on tight to him, hoping she could get through this without losing it. They'd asked the other grandchildren if any of them wanted to speak, but they'd demurred, agreeing to allow Scotty to speak for all of them.

"I was five years old when my first grandpa died. I don't remember much about him, except for the smell of cigars and that he loved baseball. I've only had my grandpa Skip in my life for a little over a year, but I'm really thankful that I'm older now and will remember every minute I ever spent with him. When I first came to live with my mom and dad, my grandpa Skip made me feel like I was his real grandson, which always meant a lot to me.

"He wanted to hear anything I had to tell him, and

we had long conversations about politics and why none of Washington's sports teams could seem to win a championship until the Caps finally did it this year. I talked to him about kids at school, and if he were here right now, he could tell you the names of the bullies, because he remembered the details. 'Boyo,' he would say, 'the devil is in the details, especially when it comes to police work.'

"He said I should always take the high road and never stoop to the level of the bullies. He had no patience for mean people or powerful people who did what they wanted because they could. Whenever I was annoyed by the constant presence of Secret Service agents, he would remind me that they feed their families by providing safety and security for mine, and that I was to respect them and do what they tell me even if I didn't like it. Their only job, he would say, was to keep me safe.

"I know that my cousins Brooke, Abby, Ethan, Jack and Ella would agree that we were lucky to have Skip as our gramps. I loved him, and I'll miss him for the rest of my life. Oh, and, Celia, I'll still be over to visit every day after school, so keep buying those cookies I like."

Nick handed Sam a tissue that she used to dry her suddenly damp eyes as she watched Scotty hug and kiss Celia on his way back to them.

"Sam?" Reverend Swain said.

Sam and Nick stood to hug Scotty when he returned to their pew and then walked hand in hand to the altar. She had asked Nick to come with her in case she couldn't get through her eulogy. He would finish for her if it came to that.

As she took a moment to gather her thoughts, she looked out at a sea of faces, realizing everyone she loved was there along with countless friends and acquaintances. President and Mrs. Nelson were seated next to Graham, Laine and Terry O'Connor, Lindsey McNamara and Byron Tomlinson. Sam saw her friend Roberto Castro and his girlfriend, Angel. They had also attended the candlelight vigil. Her gaze took in Shelby, Avery, Elin, Christina, Harry, Lilia, Archie, Marti, Leo, Stacy, Will Tyrone, Erica Lucas, A. J. Arnold's parents, Jeannie McBride's husband, Michael Wilkinson, and Dr. Trulo. Nick's friends Derek Kavanaugh and Andy Simone and his wife were there along with Freddie's parents, Darren Tabor and Scotty's former guardian, Mrs. Littlefield.

Sam noted the teary-eyed gaze of Alice Coyne Fitzgerald, widow of Skip's first partner, Steven Coyne, who had been killed decades ago in an unsolved drive-by shooting. Skip's faithful devotion to Alice after Steven's death had caused strain in Skip's marriage to Sam's mother.

"On behalf of the Holland family, I want to thank you for being here and for the tremendous outpouring of love and support over the last few days. To my brothers and sisters in the Metropolitan Police Department, I thank you for your presence here today, as well as the unwavering respect you afforded my father in the years since his devastating injury. It meant the world to him to feel as if he still belonged among the ranks of the department he served so faithfully for thirty-two of the best years of his life—and those are his words, not mine. He loved everything about being a cop, the job he was born to do, and he did it with honor and love for this city and its citizens.

"He was a fiercely proud Washingtonian who took lifelong delight in seeing the monuments lit up at night and the cherry blossoms blooming in the spring. He loved the parades, the protests, the politics, the madness and the energy of his hometown, referring to anyone born on the 'wrong' side of the 14th Street Bridge as a carpetbagger.

"You've already heard from Reverend Swain, Chief Farnsworth and my son, Scotty, about my father's well-calibrated moral compass, so I won't belabor that point except to say that my sisters and I are the people we are today in large part because of Skip and that strong inner compass that guided him throughout his life. Whenever the job gets to be too much for me, as it often does, I would turn to my dad to talk me through the latest challenge with words of wisdom and experience that only someone who has done the job would have. He liked to say that we will never know what we prevented simply by getting up and going to work every day. He would remind me, like no one else ever could, of why we do this job and why it matters so much. And whenever my ego got the best of me, he knew just how to keep me humble with a well-placed but loving barb that would bring me right back to reality." As the others laughed, Sam took a moment to breathe. "At times, it hasn't been easy being Skip Holland's daughter in the Metropolitan Police Department. The high standard he set for himself and the people who worked with and for him is one that I aim to emulate every day I spend on the job.

"I have no idea how…" Her voice broke, and she gave herself a minute to find her composure, determined to get through this without making a spectacle of herself.

Nick's hand on her back reminded her he was, like always, there if she needed him.

She cleared her throat and took a deep breath. "I have no idea how I'll do the job without him on my team, but I'm confident that his deep, distinctive voice will always be with me, showing me the way. He would say, 'You've got this, baby girl. You've got this.'

"My dad loved the Old Irish Blessing and quoted it often. It is now my wish for him. 'May the road rise up to meet you. May the wind be always at your back. May the sun shine warm upon your face; the rains fall soft upon your fields, and until we meet again, may God hold you in the palm of His hand.'

"Until we meet again, Dad, I will carry you with me everywhere I go, for you are as much a part of me as the nose on my face, the hair on my head, the smile on my lips and the fire in my belly to get justice for those who need it most.

"On behalf of myself and my sisters, I extend my heartfelt love and appreciation to my stepmother, Celia Holland, without whom none of us would've survived the last four years. Celia, your tender, loving care of Dad before, during and after his injury gave him years he wouldn't have had otherwise. Your love gave him a reason to get up each day and keep persevering through the best and worst of times. We will never have the words to properly thank you for all you did for him and for us. We are so lucky to have you in our family, where you shall remain forever a Holland."

Celia acknowledged her words with a tearful smile, full of the love she normally directed Sam's way.

Sam fixed her gaze on the honey-colored wood coffin. "To you, Dad, I say rest in peace and dance like a fool in the arms of your heavenly Father." She saluted him. "Deputy Chief Holland, thank you for your dedicated service to the Metropolitan Police Department, the District of Columbia and its citizens. We've got the watch from here, sir."

She held the salute for a full thirty seconds, during which she vowed to devote every ounce of energy, heart and soul she had to finding the person who'd put him in that box.

CHAPTER EIGHT

THE MPD AND Secret Service did a masterful job of getting the family and their closest friends into the cemetery with a minimal amount of fuss. Skip was officially laid to rest in a spot he had chosen himself. When the time came, Celia would be buried alongside him. Sam appreciated that his final resting spot was only a short distance from Ninth Street. She took comfort in knowing he would continue to be close by as he had been all her life.

At the conclusion of the service, Reverend Swain hugged each of them and told Celia he'd be by to see her in the next few days.

Sam hugged each member of her squad and thanked them for being Skip's honor guard.

"It was an honor, Lieutenant," Detective Jeannie Mc-Bride said tearfully. "Thank you for asking us."

The others walked away to give the family a few final minutes with Skip.

Flanked by her sisters, Celia stepped forward to place a red rose on his casket. Then she stepped back so his daughters, sons-in-law and grandchildren could place their flowers. Watching her nephew Jack, in his father's arms, place that rose on his grandfather's casket was almost more than Sam could bear. She had to look away.

She'd had a lifelong aversion to cemeteries, and now

was no different. After she, Scotty and Nick had placed their flowers, she took Nick's hand and let him lead her back to the car, relieved to get the hell out of there even if it was painful to leave her father behind.

The motorcade left the cemetery and conveyed them to the Hay-Adams.

"I remember this place." Scotty smiled at them when the iconic hotel came into view.

Nick's eyes twinkled as he glanced at Sam. "We had a little party here once."

She appreciated their attempt to bring some levity to a difficult day. "You were brilliant today, Scotty. Your words about Gramps meant so much to all of us."

"Thanks, Mom. I hope he would've liked it."

"He would've loved it. I have no doubt."

"Yours was really good too," Scotty said.

"I'm glad you thought so."

"It's crazy how many police officers came from all over for him."

"More than ten thousand."

"Wow. That's amazing."

"Anytime an officer is killed in the line of duty, the rest of the thin blue line shows up in force."

"What does that mean?" Scotty asked. "Thin blue line?"

"Law enforcement is known as the symbolic thin blue line that stands between order and chaos in our society."

He appeared to give that concept serious thought. "You said Grandpa Skip was killed in the line of duty, but he was retired."

"He was definitely killed in the line of duty. It just took four years for him to die from his injuries."

"I see. Are you going after the person who shot him?"

"You know it. With the case elevated to homicide status, that puts it under my purview. We'll be taking a fresh look starting tomorrow."

"Don't you think you should take a few days before you go back to work, babe?"

"No."

Nick raised a brow. "Just no?"

"Just no."

"Ruh-roh," Scotty said.

"I've heard from Freddie and Malone that the tip line has received some new information. No time like the present to seize the day while his death is still fresh in the minds of people who know what happened to him."

"We'll talk about it later," Nick said.

"Nothing to talk about. I'm going back to work tomorrow."

They pulled up to the Hay-Adams a minute later, ending the conversation for now. Sam had full confidence that she and Nick would go-around about it again later, but she was not relenting. She fairly burned with the need for justice on her father's behalf, like she had at the beginning, when it first happened. Then, she'd been driven almost to madness tracking down every lead and clue that had led nowhere.

A busy life and the unrelenting pace of murder in the city had pushed her father's case to the back burner, where it had remained on simmer. Now it was time to turn up the heat again and bring it to a boil once and for all.

The Secret Service asked them to wait until they could clear the lobby to bring them in, so they sat in the car and watched one familiar face after another go by.

"It's weird that this is our party and we're the only ones who can't go in," Scotty said.

"You should've seen how it was in Europe," Nick said. "I had to wait everywhere we went. Once for an hour until they were satisfied."

"We haven't had a chance to even talk about the trip," Sam said.

"Eh, it was fine. The highlights were meeting the queen and the pope. Otherwise, it was meetings, dinners, photos, glad-handing. A lot of it was boring because my two favorite people weren't there with me."

"Maybe we can do something this summer when I'm on vacation," Scotty said.

"I'll let them know we'd be up for that if Mom can get the time off."

"I'll get the time off." She'd been encouraged to see Gonzo looking and sounding more like his old self than he had in months after one week in rehab. Maybe by the summer, he'd be ready to be left in charge for a few weeks so she could get away with the guys.

"We have to go back to the beach again too," Scotty said.

"That's a given," Sam said.

"Best vacation ever," Nick said.

"One of the best." She winked to remind him of Bora-Bora and the times they'd had there for their honeymoon and first anniversary.

"One of the best."

They were escorted into the hotel a short time later. As they walked through the lobby, everything seemed to stop and all eyes turned to them.

"Goldfish," Nick muttered, referring to his frequent comment that being vice president was like being a goldfish in a glass bowl. Everyone was always looking at him and them when his family was with him. Always the politician, he gave a little wave to the people who stared at them but didn't stop moving so they wouldn't be encouraged to approach.

Today wasn't for the public. Today was for the family and friends gathered in the rooftop ballroom who awaited their arrival. For the first time in days, Sam was ravenously hungry and sat with her sisters to eat delicious roast beef, chicken, potatoes and steamed vegetables.

"I feel like I could eat the entire buffet," Sam said.

"Me too," Tracy said. "I haven't eaten more than a few bites in days, but now I want everything in sight."

In contrast, Angela pushed the food around on her plate with a decided lack of enthusiasm.

"You okay, Ang?" Sam asked.

"I feel kind of sick inside."

"Heartsick or physically sick?" Tracy asked.

"Some of both, maybe." She glanced up at them with watery eyes. "I was going to tell you guys, but then everything with Dad happened."

"Tell us what?" Sam asked, stricken with fear of another looming disaster.

"I think I might be pregnant again." Angela winced as she said the words, which made Sam feel awful.

"Ang… Don't do that. It's fine. I swear. I have Scotty and the twins now and baby Noah underfoot every day. I'm okay, and I'm thrilled for you and Spence."

"I'm glad you are." Angela dabbed at her eyes. "This one was definitely not planned."

"But it's still a blessing," Tracy said. "And we're all in bad need of some good news right now."

"It breaks my heart that this baby will never get to know Dad," Angela said.

"He or she will know him through us," Sam said.

"Won't be the same," Angela said.

"Nothing will be," Tracy said bluntly, "but we have to keep doing what we've always done and make him proud of us by taking care of each other."

Nick approached their table. "Sam, Graham and Laine were hoping for a chance to say hello."

"Duty calls." Sam leaned in to kiss Angela's cheek as she got up.

Nick escorted her across the crowded room to where Graham and Laine were seated with Leo, Stacy, Terry and Lindsey. "Everything okay?"

"Angela is pregnant and sad that Dad won't get to meet the new baby."

"Well, that's some big news." He took a careful look at her, as if to gauge her reaction to yet another baby in their midst while she continued to be unable to conceive.

"I'm fine."

They had a nice visit with Graham and Laine, who'd been like adopted parents to Nick over the years. And Sam finally got a chance to thank Terry for his efforts to get Nick home as quickly as possible the other day.

"I wish it could've been faster."

"We appreciated the effort."

After the O'Connors left, Freddie came over to talk to her. "How're you doing?"

"I'm okay." Sam felt like she'd said those words a thousand times over the last few days. She kept looking around for Skip and his wheelchair, thinking there was something she should be doing for him. Knowing he was finally at peace helped, even as she burned with the need to get back to work and start pulling every thread she could find in pursuit of justice on his behalf.

Freddie eyed her with concern. "It was a beautiful tribute."

"That it was. I'm going back to work tomorrow with one goal in mind."

"I'll be there to help."

"You're on vacation until Monday."

He returned her fierce stare with an equally fierce look. "I'll be there to help."

Realizing there was no point in arguing with him, she nodded.

"Everyone's going to O'Leary's after this to raise a glass to Skip. Can you come?"

"Yeah, I'll be there." She wouldn't miss it. O'Leary's had been Skip's favorite haunt. Sam had frequently met him there for an after-work drink, including the night when she met Nick for the first time. "Spent a lot of time with my old man in that watering hole."

"I know you did, and I also know, at some point, the reality of this is going to set in and it's probably not going to be pretty. I'll be right there for you when that happens."

"There's never going to be a time when I'm not pretty," she said with a teasing grin.

"Either way, I'll be there."

Regardless of who might be watching, Sam rested her head on his shoulder. "Means everything to me that you were here for this."

"I wouldn't have missed it for anything."

MUCH LATER, SURROUNDED by her brothers and sisters in blue, as well as her husband, Sam raised a shot of whiskey in tribute to her father and downed the liquor in one gulp that burned all the way through her.

"To Skip!"

That shot was followed by another and another, until Sam caught a comfortable buzz that took the edge off her raw emotions.

Then Archie busted out a heartfelt, soaring rendition of "Danny Boy," surprising and delighting his colleagues with a beautiful voice that brought tears to Sam's eyes that she didn't try to contain. She didn't have to in this crowd where she was surrounded by friends who'd loved her father almost as much as she had.

Nick stood behind her with his hands on her shoulders as Gonzo and Cruz flanked her.

Gonzo drank only water.

Sam was well and truly plastered by the time Nick and Freddie helped her into the Secret Service vehicle that waited at the curb to take them home. She pretended she couldn't hear Nick and Freddie talking about her.

"It's probably good for her to blow off some steam," Freddie said.

"Agreed," Nick replied. "But she'll regret it in the morning."

"She said she's going to work."

"I want her to take another day."

That's not going to happen. Sam tried not to puke in the pristine Secret Service SUV. Comfortable numbness was much preferred to the ache that came with profound loss.

Nick said good-night to Freddie and got in next to her, gathering her into his embrace.

She'd tried to tell him he didn't have to come to

O'Leary's, that it was a cop thing and he could go home if he wanted to, but he'd insisted on sticking with her. Scotty had gone home with Celia and would spend the night there.

"I'm glad you came with me." Her words were slurred, but she didn't care.

"So am I."

"Wanna know why I'm glad you came with me?"

"Can't wait to hear this."

"You come with designated drivers."

"Is that all I'm good for?"

"That's one of many things you're good for." She rested her hand on his leg and started to slide it upward when he stopped her. "Don't be a stick-in-the-mud."

He laughed. "Will you remember any of this tomorrow?"

"I've never forgotten a second that I spent with you." She pushed his hand away and continued her quest to get at what she wanted.

"Samantha."

"Yes?"

"Can you hold that thought until we get home?"

"As long as I'm allowed to indulge that thought when we get home."

"You can indulge all you want when we're behind closed doors."

"Okay." She leaned her head against his shoulder, closed her eyes and sighed, the stress and strain of the last few days leaving her in a whoosh of air. "Nick…"

"I'm right here."

"My dad…"

"I know, honey."

"What am I supposed to do now?"

He held her tighter, his lips skimming her forehead.

"You're supposed to keep doing what you do and keep making him proud just by being your perfect self."

Tears burned her eyes, so she closed them. Just for a minute.

HER QUESTION BROKE Nick's heart. What would she do without Skip? He couldn't begin to know, but he hoped she would take comfort in being reminded of how proud her father had been of her. Her body went lax against his, and he was relieved that she had fallen asleep.

When they arrived at Ninth Street, Nick lifted Sam into his arms and carried her up the ramp, into the house and straight upstairs, where he helped her out of her uniform and tucked her into bed. He was kind of glad she'd let loose with her colleagues and had gotten a little drunk after the week she'd had.

He went to look in on Aubrey and Alden sleeping peacefully after spending the evening with Shelby and Avery, who were asleep with Noah in the guest room. Thank God for good friends at times like these.

Keyed up after the long, emotional day, Nick changed into sweats and a T-shirt and went downstairs to have a drink. He'd abstained during the day so Sam could let loose. But now he needed to take the edge off.

Bourbon, he decided, having been weaned on it at Graham O'Connor's table while at Harvard with Graham's son John. He poured a healthy shot and took it to the sofa, pulled out his phone and checked his messages for the first time all day. Work stuff could wait for the morning, he decided, not wanting to fuel his insomnia with stress. He read a text from Freddie.

I'm worried about Sam. Has she cried yet?

Not that I've seen, Nick replied. I think she was holding it together in public.

She says she's going back to work tomorrow. Is she ready for that?

I suppose we need to let her decide that.

Yeah, I guess. I'll be there to keep an eye on her.

That'll help. It meant so much to her that you came home to be with her.

I wouldn't have missed it. What a day this was.

I know. It was amazing. He would've loved it.

Yes, very much so. Try to get some sleep.

You too.

Nick already knew that she hadn't cried yet. He'd checked with her sisters as well as Scotty. Now Freddie had echoed his concerns.

Brant came out of the room the Secret Service used as an office, the bag he carried to and from work on his shoulder. "Mr. Vice President. I almost didn't see you there in the dark."

"Heading out?"

"Yes, sir. I'll see you in the morning?"

"Hey, Brant?"

"Sir?"

"Thank you for all you do. The last few days couldn't

have been easy for you or the others, but you made it easy on us. It's very much appreciated."

"Thank you, sir. Everyone on our team was fond of Deputy Chief Holland. We were honored to serve you and your family this week." He paused, seeming to consider his next words. "But if you ever run away from your detail again, I won't be responsible for my actions. Understood?"

Nick laughed. "Sorry about that."

"I understand why you did it, and I might've done the same thing myself under the circumstances. However..."

"Say no more. I got it."

"Is Mrs. Cappuano doing all right?"

"She's better now that she has a belly full of whiskey. Not sure how she'll feel in the morning, though."

"It's a tough loss for her. It was obvious to everyone how close they were."

Nick stood to shake the agent's hand. "Thanks again for everything."

Brant shook his hand. "It's an honor to work with and for you. Tomorrow, we need to talk about the plan for the Armstrong children. I've been in touch with headquarters about providing them with security. You should be aware that the GOP minority leader has inquired about whether taxpayer dollars should be used to protect children you voluntarily brought into your family while in office."

"I'm not surprised. I expected some backlash."

"But since you and Mrs. Cappuano will be their legal, custodial guardians, they're entitled to protection, and we recommend they have it."

"Agreed."

"If it meets with your approval, I'll work with headquarters to coordinate their protection."

"It does. Thank you."

"Very good. I'll see you in the morning, then."

"You should take a day off one of these days."

"And do what?"

"Get a life?"

Brant laughed—as hard as Nick had ever seen the always-serious agent laugh. "That'll be the day. My life is protecting your life."

"That doesn't count as a life of your own. We need to see about getting you a girlfriend."

"*Good night*, sir."

Nick wished he could see if Brant was blushing. He wouldn't be surprised. "Good night, Brant." He finished his drink and went upstairs to join Sam in bed, even if he didn't feel tired. He rarely did without some form of medication that made him groggy the next day.

Sliding into bed next to his beloved, he snuggled up to her and took comfort from her nearness, her scent, her heat, the silk of her hair and the softness of her skin.

Freddie would keep an eye on her at work. He would keep an eye on her at home. Together, they would get her through this. Whatever she needed, whatever it took. He would be there for her—always.

CHAPTER NINE

AFTER SAM AND Nick left O'Leary's, Gonzo pointed to the door, letting Christina know he was ready to go too. Tomorrow morning, she would return him to the rehab in Baltimore. His parents had taken Alex for the day and night so they could tend to their friends. That gave him a night alone with Christina that he wasn't about to waste.

He'd been thankful throughout the days of mourning that no one had asked him where he'd been for the last week or when he'd be back to work. He had been prepared to tell them he was dealing with some fallout from Arnold's death, which was true, but it wasn't the entire story, and he wasn't comfortable blaming his late partner for the mess he'd made of his life all on his own.

The temptation to self-medicate his way through the relentless grief that followed Arnold's death hadn't gone away. Gonzo struggled through each unmedicated day full of raw emotions and painful memories. His counselor at rehab had told him there was no shortcut he could take to speed up the process of coping with tragedy. He had to experience each emotion, no matter how painful, and that muting those emotions would only extend the ordeal.

Intellectually, he agreed with the theory. Emotionally, he was drained, even more so after the funeral for Skip Holland, a man he'd loved and respected.

As they stepped into the chilly autumn evening, Gonzo put his arm around Christina, hoping the gesture would be welcome. She'd been present but distant since picking him up two days ago, most of her focus on their son while she kept her word about spending every minute with Gonzo so he wouldn't fuck up again.

That was what it had come to—the cop being policed by his own fiancée. Not that he didn't deserve the scrutiny, because he did.

She didn't shake him off as they walked to the car, and he took that as a small victory.

He held the passenger door for her. "One hell of a day."

"It was an amazing show of respect. I'll never forget it."

As he went to close the door, he caught the uncertain, wary look she directed his way, as if she wasn't sure whether she could trust this version of him.

It would take time and persistence on his part to get things back on track with her, but he was determined to try. They drove home in tension-filled silence and trudged up the stairs to their apartment. After they hung their coats on a tree in the foyer, he turned to her. "Did you hear from my mom?"

She nodded. "Alex had a good day and was asleep by eight. He's asking for you. Your mom told him he'll see you tomorrow. They're going to bring him home early so he can see you before we leave."

"The poor kid isn't going to understand why I have to go again."

"We'll get through it." She sounded exhausted.

"Hey, Chris…"

She was on her way to the bedroom but stopped and turned to face him.

"I'm really sorry for what I've put you and Alex through. I'm trying to do better."

"I can see that, Tommy. I really can. I'm proud of you."

He shook his head. "You shouldn't be. Not yet anyway. But hopefully, someday…"

She came to him and rested her hands on his chest, her right hand next to the gold badge he wore so proudly, even after everything he'd experienced on the job. The good still outweighed the bad, even if the bad had gotten the upper hand lately. "I'm always proud of you, of the difficult job you do so well, of the way you care so much about the people you work with that the loss of one of them nearly killed you too. As hard as it's been to watch you go through that, knowing you love so deeply makes me feel very lucky to be loved by you."

He put his arms around her and held her tightly, breathing in the familiar scent of her hair and skin. "I love you so much. I'd be lost without you and Alex."

"We can't wait to have you home again, but we want you whole and healthy. I pray for you to find some peace, Tommy."

"I want that too. More than just about anything."

"Come to bed with me." She took his hand and led him into the bedroom.

When he would've begun to remove his uniform, she stopped him. "Let me."

He dropped his hands to his sides and let her tend to him, watching as she worked with determination to unbutton, unhook and undress him. She stripped him down to his boxers, laying each piece of his uniform over the back of a chair. "My turn."

She turned to give him her back and he unzipped the black dress that was demure, respectful and sexy. The dress dropped to the floor. He rested his hands on her shoulders and kissed the top of her head. "Thank you for standing by me through all of this, babe."

Turning to face him, she gazed up at him with the big eyes that had captivated him since the night they met, almost two years ago now. "I love you. There's nowhere else I want to be than smack in the middle of your life—and Alex's."

"Despite how it may have seemed recently, there's nowhere else I want to be than in that life too."

She raised her hands to his face and brought him down for a kiss that quickly spiraled into desperation.

He couldn't recall the last time he'd kissed her this way or made love to her or even wanted to. He'd been so numb for so long. Desire came roaring back to life in a tidal wave of want and need. "Chris…" Overwhelmed by the emotion, he wrapped his arms around her and held on tight. "I'm so sorry for everything." His eyes burned with tears that he struggled to contain.

"It's okay, Tommy." Her soft voice soothed him as she caressed his back. "We're going to be okay." She gave a gentle tug to guide him into bed with her where she welcomed him into her loving embrace. The silk of her skin brushing against his triggered a craving for more of her.

"Do we need a condom?" Before Arnold was killed, they'd been trying for a baby. It shamed him to realize he had no idea if she had gone back on birth control.

"If we don't want to chance pregnancy we do. If we don't care, we don't."

"Do you still want to have another baby?"

She gazed up at him with her heart in her eyes. "I want everything with you."

"I want everything with you too." He kissed her. "After I get home, let's get married."

Combing her fingers through his hair, she said, "You don't think we ought to wait until things settle down a bit?"

"Things are never going to settle down. I want to be married. I want you to officially adopt Alex. I want us to be a family."

"We already are a family."

"Then let's make it official. Planning a wedding will keep you busy and out of trouble while I'm gone."

Smiling, she said, "You don't think taking care of a two-year-old will keep me busy enough?"

"Marry me, Christina." Kissing her again, he poured his heart and soul into showing her how much he loved her. He could only hope that, over time, he could make up for being absent from their life for so long. "I promise I'll never again take you or what we have for granted."

"Yes, you will. And I will too."

He entered her slowly, giving her time to accommodate him. "I won't take you for granted. I mean it when I tell you I want to be better for you and Alex."

She ran her hands down his back to cup his ass and gave a gentle tug to bring him deeper into her body.

"Love you so much." He touched his lips to hers. "You'll never know how much. I want you to be my wife. I want my ring on your finger and you right here with me, where you belong forever."

Tears leaked from her eyes.

"What's wrong?" *Please don't say no. Please don't.* He wasn't sure he could handle that on top of everything else.

"For once in a very long while, nothing is wrong."

"Then why are you crying?"

"Because I'm happy. I've missed my Tommy so much."

He couldn't contain his own tears as he made love to her. His tears mixed with hers as he experienced genuine joy for the first time since his partner's murder. The feeling gave him hope, something that had been in short supply over the last nine months. He tried to last, but it had been so long that his control was sorely lacking.

And when she cried out in pleasure, he let himself go with her, clinging to her, his life raft in the storm. He was wise enough, after what he'd been through, to know the storm was far from over, but he had a new reason to believe that they might emerge on the other side stronger for the struggle.

"You never answered my question." His comment followed a long period of contented silence. "Are you going to marry me?"

"Yes, Tommy. I'm going to marry you."

He had five more weeks of rehab to get through before they could get on with their lives, but she'd given him something to look forward to, something that would sustain him as he worked to put his life— and hers—back together.

THE DRUMS OF hell beating in her brain woke Sam the next morning. She was afraid to so much as breathe out of fear of her head exploding. Since breathing was necessary, she took a tentative breath and winced.

"It was such a good idea at the time," Nick muttered from his post, facedown next to her. "Right?"

"Mmm." She winced again. Her mouth tasted like dog shit, and her eyes were gritty. And she needed to get Scotty up, see to the twins and get her ass to work.

"Take one more day, Samantha. No one expects you to show up today."

She was sorely tempted, but then she thought about the wooden box and her determination to find the person who had put her father in that box. If he could bear what he'd been through for four agonizing years, surely she could get through a day at work hungover. "I'm never drinking again."

"Could I have that in writing?"

Sam grunted in reply because that was less painful than forming words. She dragged herself out of bed and made a beeline for the bathroom to brush her teeth before taking a shower. As she stood under the pounding hot water, she began to feel slightly human again.

Nick stepped in behind her and wrapped his arms around her waist, his lips landing on her shoulder. "Take another day, babe."

"I really can't. I was out all last week on suspension, and we've got shit to do. I need to get back to normal." Nothing in her life had been "normal" since the day she'd arrived at the scene of Alden and Aubrey's nightmare. Between taking them in, seeing to their needs, solving their parents' murders, agreeing to be their long-term guardians, Nick's trip and her father's death, Sam hadn't had one normal minute in ten days.

She craved normal, and she needed to dig into her father's case with fresh leads and a new resolve to finally get the answers that had eluded her for so long.

He held her tight against him. "I'm worried about you."

"I'm okay."

"You haven't cried yet."

"Yes, I have."

"No, you haven't."

"So what? Do you think that means I'm not sad enough about my father's death? Because let me assure you—"

He turned her to face him and rested his index finger over her lips. "That's not at all what I think. I know better than just about anyone how very sad you are."

"I choose to expend my sadness and anger productively rather than rolling into a ball and sobbing."

He gave her a good long look. "Fair enough."

"I need to do this my way, even if it's not what you or other people would do. And I need you to let me."

"Whatever you need, babe. That's what I want you to have."

"Then let me go to work, and don't spend all day worrying about me."

"I can do the first part. The second thing might be harder. Will you call me if you need me?"

"Who else would I call?"

He gathered her into his embrace, their bodies responding to each other the way they always did when her skin came into contact with his.

Because she couldn't resist him, she rubbed against him suggestively.

"I thought you were hungover and cranky."

"I am." She curled her hand around his hard cock and stroked, drawing a deep groan from him.

"Babe…"

"Hmm?"

"We don't have to."

"I know, but I want to." No one could take her mind off her grief and stress the way he could. And even with her head pounding and her stomach feeling iffy, she wanted him.

"Scotty…"

"Celia will get him up."

He kissed her neck and fondled her breasts. "You sure you feel like it?"

"I definitely feel like it, but there's a very real possibility my head could actually explode."

"We'll go nice and easy." His words and lips rendered her powerless to resist him, not that she ever wanted to do that. "I'll give you my magic elixir for hangovers."

"Even after brushing my teeth, it's possible my breath stinks like sewer gas."

The low rumble of his laughter echoed off the shower walls. "Thanks for the warning."

"I'm serious. It's a toxic waste dump in there."

"I'll steer clear." He pressed her against the shower wall and lifted her effortlessly, which she found ridiculously sexy. "Hold on to me. I'm right here whenever you need me."

"That makes everything that's wrong better."

"I would do anything to spare you this pain."

"I know you would."

He slid into her and dropped his head to her shoulder, holding her tight against him as he throbbed inside her.

Nothing in the world could top the high she got from making love with him. Sam buried her fingers in his hair and held on tight to her love. She was thankful for him every day, but never more so than at times like this when he seemed to know what she needed before she did. And as he moved slowly and carefully so as not to jar her tortured head, she was able to let it all go and be carried away by him.

They came together, gasping and clinging to each other, and when she floated down from the high, she realized her head didn't hurt as badly as it had before, which made her laugh.

He scowled playfully at her. "Are you mocking my technique?"

"Hardly. I'm celebrating your hangover elixir."

"Did it work?"

She tipped her head to the left and then the right, waiting for the pain that didn't come. "I think it did."

"Then my work here is nearly finished." He withdrew from her and got busy washing her while she leaned back against the wall and let him tend to her, knowing he needed that as much as she did. Watching the play of his muscles, the fall of his hair over his forehead, the morning scruff on his jaw, she was tempted to take one more day off to spend with him.

But then she thought of that goddamned wooden box that contained the ruined body of her father, and her resolve returned with a fiery thirst for vengeance. She straightened out of the slouch she'd fallen into under his tender ministrations and kissed his cheek. "Thank you."

"I wish there was more I could do."

"People say it will take time."

"We'll get through it, no matter how long it takes."

Knowing he would be by her side through it all made the unbearable slightly more bearable.

"Let's go get our littles up and spend some time with them before I have to go."

NINETY MINUTES LATER, she walked into HQ for the first time in ten days, entering through the morgue entrance to avoid the media scrum planted outside the main doors. Lilia had reported receiving hundreds of requests for interviews from reporters wanting to know how she was handling her father's death. How did they think she was handling it? She'd asked Lilia to release a statement that said Second Lady Samantha Holland Cappuano and her family deeply appreciated the outpouring of condolences and sympathy since the death of her father and that she would have no further public statement about her loss.

You'd think that politely worded request would take them off the scent of a story, but alas, the bloodhounds were still salivating.

Between Nick's shower elixir, six hundred milligrams of Motrin and two cups of coffee, she was feeling slightly more coherent than she had upon awaking. However, she still felt "off," the same way she had after her father's shooting, when she'd waded through every minute of the unfolding nightmare with an unrelenting ache in her heart. In some ways, that had been worse than this. As sad as she was to know she'd never see him again, the weeks after he'd been shot, when they'd been forced to confront the new reality of his devastating injury, had been among the darkest days of her life.

Sam went into her office, flipped on the lights and sat behind her desk, searching for the mojo she usually brought to the job and hoping it would find her as the day progressed. Firing up her desktop computer, she began the arduous task of sifting through ten days' worth of emails. She'd been so busy last week with Alden and Aubrey that she'd barely looked at it and couldn't find the wherewithal to bother now with emails about mandatory training or time-sheet updates or anything other than what she was there to do.

She was about to get up to find Captain Malone

when he appeared in her doorway. "What're you doing here?" he asked.

"Last I checked, I work here."

"You don't need to be here today, Sam."

"Yes, I do. I want to see what's come into the tip line since Sunday."

He eyed her warily. "We've assigned people to that."

"You're assigning *my* people, not just any people."

"Sam…"

She held up a hand to stop him. "Don't. Please don't. You told me the other day to tell you what I need. I need this. I need to do something to make this right for him. Please don't put up obstacles that don't need to be there."

They held each other's gaze for a tense moment before he blinked and looked away. "I'll get you a report."

She pointed to the items he'd brought with him. "What's all that?"

He placed two huge stacks of cards on her desk. "Condolences the department has received since your dad passed. We thought you'd like to see them."

"Thank you."

"We're inundated with media wanting interviews with you."

Sam shook her head. "I don't have anything more to say."

"They want to know how you are, Sam. People care. Can you give them five minutes?"

Though it was the last thing she wanted to do, she sighed in defeat. "Fine. Whatever."

"I checked out your father's files from Records and everything is in my office."

"I'll send someone over to get it."

"You're sure about this?"

"Never been surer about anything in my life."

He continued to stare at her for a long time before he nodded. "Okay. We'll do it your way, but I want to be involved as the official lead on this so there can never be any claims of conflict of interest or anything else that messes up the case."

"I can live with that."

Freddie came to the door. "Morning."

Malone seemed surprised to see him. "What're you doing here? You're off until Monday."

"I cut my vacation short. We've got things to do."

Freddie's fierceness matched Sam's. He'd loved her father and would do anything he could to support her in this next phase of the journey to find the shooter.

He glanced at her. "What can I do?"

"Bring my father's files from the captain's office to the conference room?"

"On it."

After Freddie had walked away, the captain seemed reluctant to leave. "I'm worried about you. We all are."

"I'm okay."

"That's what worries me."

"You're worried because I'm okay?"

"I'm worried because I'm well aware that losing Skip is a big fucking deal to you, and you've been all calm, cool composure when I'd expect you to be a hot mess."

Sam considered his words for a moment. "Maybe I'll be a hot mess at some point in the future, but for right now, I'm trying to stay focused on justice for my dad and our family. That's getting me through, as well as the thought of him being free from the difficulties of the last four years."

Malone sagged against the door frame. "I give you

credit. You're handling this a lot better than I am. I'm just so fucking *enraged*."

"As am I, Captain, despite how it might appear. We need to ride that rage straight to a suspect. If we can find the person who did this, then maybe we can find some peace for ourselves at the same time."

He stood to his full, imposing height. "I'll get you the info from the tip line."

"Thank you for everything. You were a great friend to him."

"He was a great friend to me, and we're going to get this motherfucker if it's the last thing we ever do."

With a lump lodged firmly in her throat, Sam offered a small nod.

"Will you do one thing for me? Will you check in with Trulo?"

She rolled her eyes. "If I must."

"The situation with Gonzales has me realizing we need to do better when it comes to PTSD and the other mental health concerns that go along with this job."

"I'll talk to him."

"All right, then. Carry on and keep me posted."

"Will do."

She decided to get the press briefing out of the way first so she could get on with the rest of her day. Though it went against everything she believed in to willingly address the media, she'd agreed to give them five minutes, and she would keep her promise. Steeling herself and buttoning down her emotions, she walked from the pit to the lobby, where she encountered the chief conferring with Malone.

What were the odds they were talking about her? High.

Seeing her coming, Chief Farnsworth waved her

over. "The captain tells me you're going to give the media a few minutes. I'll go out with you."

"Appreciate that, sir."

"Shut it down if you need to. That's an order."

"I will. Let's get this over with."

CHAPTER TEN

SAM LED THE way through the double doors to the court-yard, where the media set up shop on a regular basis. As she approached the podium, the reporters began shouting questions at her.

How are you?

How is your family?

How did the vice president learn of your father's death?

Have you received new leads?

Why were you suspended last week?

Are the Armstrong children still living with you and the vice president?

Sam waited for them to shut the fuck up before she spoke. "On behalf of myself and my family, I'd like to thank the people of the District, the Capitol region and across the country for the outpouring of sympathy and condolences on the passing of my father. I'd also like to thank my colleagues at the Metropolitan Police Department for their support over the last few days, as well as the men and women in blue who came from all over the country to pay tribute to my father and his service. I'm not going to lie to you. This is a tough loss for all of us, but we're continuing to do what he'd expect of us, and for me that includes getting back to work. I'll take a few questions and then I've got to get to it."

"Lieutenant," a female reporter from one of the TV

stations said, "in announcing your father's death, you requested information on his unsolved shooting. Have you received new tips as a result of that request?"

"We have, and we'll be pursuing each one of them. In light of his death, his case has been elevated to a homicide, and my father will receive the same attention all homicide victims in this city receive from my team. I'll restate my earlier request that anyone with information pertaining to the shooting of Deputy Chief Holland call the department's tip line." She gave the number and then repeated it. "If you know something, now is the time to come forward to help us take a violent criminal off the streets."

"Is it a conflict of interest for you to investigate your own father's shooting?" another female reporter asked.

Sam wanted to punch her in the face. "I'm not the lead investigator on the case. Captain Malone is taking the lead, so no, it's not a conflict. We all want to see the person who shot a decorated police officer brought to justice. My father's life was cut short by decades as a result of that shooter. He or she needs to be brought to justice so no one else can be harmed."

"You've been working this case for almost four years already," Darren Tabor asked. "What'll be different this time?"

"That's a good question, and it's hard to say. Hopefully, the requests for tips will generate new leads, and it never hurts to put fresh eyes on a cold case. We've added several new detectives to the Homicide squad in the last two years, and they'll be seeing much of the information about the case for the first time. All we can do is try."

"Can you confirm that the children of Jameson and Cleo Armstrong, also known as Beauclair, are residing with you and the vice president?" one of the male broadcast reporters asked. Their expensive suits and fastidious grooming set them apart from their newspaper colleagues.

"Per the wishes of their brother, Elijah, who is their legal guardian, they are currently under our care, where they'll remain until Elijah finishes college in eighteen months."

That announcement was met with stunned silence followed by more rapid-fire questions about the children, their extended family, Sam's family and protection for the children in light of Nick's job. So many questions were fired at her in the span of two seconds that she could barely process them all.

She held up her hands to quiet them. "Thank you for the compassionate coverage of my father's life and death and for continuing to air our request for tips in his case. My family appreciates it. That's all I have to say for now. We'll provide updates as they become available." They continued to shout questions at her as Sam turned and walked quickly toward the double doors.

The chief held the left side open and followed her inside. "You handled that well. Thank you for doing it."

"Hopefully, it'll keep the tips rolling in." Sam dug her phone out of her pocket. "Since I just confirmed that the Armstrong children are living with us, I probably ought to let Nick know there could be a shitstorm coming his way."

"Probably not a bad idea," Malone said. "I've got a couple of things to do, and then I'll be over to help."

"Thanks, Cap." Sam put through the call to Nick as she walked toward the pit.

"Are you already in trouble?"

She smiled at the question. "Not yet, but I may have

caused some trouble for you by confirming our tempo-
rary guardianship of Aubrey and Alden to the media."

"And you did this willingly?"

"I was compelled by my command to feed the beast
hungry for info about how I'm handling my father's
death. They asked. I answered, because I figure we'll
have to eventually. Sorry I didn't consult with you
first."

"No worries. I'll let Terry and Trevor know. They'll
deal with it."

"All right. I just wanted to give you a warning."

"Appreciate it, babe. Are you doing all right?"

"I've got a lot to do. That helps."

"I'll let you get to it. Be careful with my wife. I love
her very much."

"She loves you too. See you later."

"Call me if you need me."

"I will." Sam closed the phone and stashed it in her
pocket, planning to put in her shift and go home to
her family as soon as she could. Her father's case had
been lingering for four years. It wouldn't be solved in
a day of new effort. Hell, it still might never be solved,
a thought that profoundly depressed her.

When her cell phone rang, she took the call from
Gonzo. "Hey, what's up?"

"Can you come outside for a minute? Morgue entrance?"

"I'm coming." Before heading for the morgue, she
ducked her head into the conference room, where Cruz,
Green and McBride were sorting through boxes containing her father's files. "I'll be back in a few. Feel
free to dive in."

"What're we looking for, Lieutenant?" Green asked.

"I have no idea. I just hope we'll recognize it when we see it."

"Got it. We're on it."

She took off for the morgue entrance and had the spectacularly bad luck of encountering Sergeant Ramsey coming down the stairs from the second floor, back from serving his latest suspension. She noted with satisfaction that he had nasty scabs on his face and hands from when he'd fallen through the window.

"Awww, so sad about your daddy." His condescending tone had become familiar to her. "Who's going to protect you now?"

Having learned her lesson after punching him once before, she resisted the urge this time and kept moving, determined not to give him the satisfaction of rattling her. But if consequences weren't a factor, she'd happily stab the son of a bitch through the heart with the rustiest steak knife she could find.

She pushed open the exit door by the morgue and stepped into the chilly autumn air.

Across the parking lot, Gonzo stood outside Christina's car, arms crossed.

Christina waved to her from the driver's seat.

"Thanks for coming out. I didn't think it was a good idea to go inside when I'm supposedly on sick leave."

"No problem." He looked good, Sam thought again, relieved by the return of the sharp-eyed gaze she remembered from before disaster struck. "Whatever they're doing for you in Baltimore seems to be working."

"So it would seem."

"You're going back?"

He nodded. "We're leaving now, but I wanted to see you before I go."

"I'm glad you came by."

"I wish I could help with what I'm sure you're working on today."

"You need to focus on yourself and your health. That's what I want you to do. We need you whole and healthy."

"I'm working on it. Are you okay?"

"I'm hanging in there. It'll help to give the case a fresh look."

"I won't keep you." He stepped forward to hug her. "Take care of yourself, Sam. Ask for help if you need it. Sometimes I wonder what might've been different if I'd done that."

She returned the hug. "I hear you. Thanks for being here for everything. Means a lot."

"I wouldn't have missed it. You know how much we all loved him."

"I do. Your friendship meant a lot to him."

"I'll see you in a few weeks."

"Let us know when you can have visitors." She smiled. "We'll get the Secret Service to drive us up."

"I'll do that." He went around to get into the car.

Sam knocked on Christina's window. "Call me if you need anything," she said after Christina lowered the window.

"You do the same."

Sam nodded and waved them off, comforted to see her sergeant and close friend seeming better. Finally. There had been times over the last nine months when she'd had cause to wonder if he'd ever get past the awful tragedy of Arnold's death. She'd wondered if he would be able to continue to do the job.

Detective Will Tyrone had left the department after his close friend Arnold's death, because he couldn't bear to do the job anymore. Gonzo had told Freddie that Will was lucky to be able to quit, something Gonzo didn't have the luxury of doing with a family to support. Now, perhaps, it was safe to hope he would get the help he needed, find a way to cope and get back on track in all areas of his life.

As she went back to the pit, she was waylaid again, this time by Dr. Trulo, the department shrink. "A word, Lieutenant?"

With him it was never *a* word. It was always *a lot* of words. Resigned to everyone wanting something from her today, she led him into her office. "I just saw Gonzo. He's heading back to rehab."

Trulo closed the door. "I thought he seemed much better when I saw him at the funeral."

"Agreed, but it's early days yet. I'm taking it as a good sign that he's willingly returning to treatment."

"It's a very good sign." He gave her an assessing look, his gaze sharp and focused as always. "How're you holding up?"

"I'm okay." Maybe if she kept saying it, people would eventually quit asking.

"Really, or are you telling me what you think I want to hear?"

"Would I do that?"

He laughed. "Never."

"I'm going to miss him like crazy, but I won't miss the wheelchair or seeing him unable to do anything but lift an eyebrow. I won't miss that at all."

"Understandable. He wasn't my father, and I found it excruciating to see him reduced to what he was left with after the shooting. I imagine you're attacking his case with fresh eyes and new leads after the call for tips."

"You imagine correctly."

"I want you to prepare yourself for the possibility of more of the same. There's a fresh wave of interest and grief that'll give you hope and resolve that could lead to more disappointment."

"I know what you're saying, and I'm prepared for the possibility that we may never close the case. But don't we have to try?"

"We absolutely have to try. And if there's anyone who can figure this out once and for all, it's you."

She released a huff of laughter. "I haven't had much luck thus far."

"My money is on you, kid."

"Thanks. Appreciate the support, and my dad did too. The department was good to him after the shooting. None of us will ever forget that."

"We loved him." The simplicity of his statement brought tears to her eyes.

"I've been thinking about something the last couple of days that I might want to talk to you about in more detail when things settle down."

"What's that?"

"It's rough at this point, but going through the paces after my dad died, I started thinking about all the people I meet on this job who're victims of violent crime. I'm a victim of violent crime. My family members are victims. I think about Nick's friend Derek Kavanaugh, who lost his wife to murder, and the people who were caught up in the drive-by shootings, like Vanessa Marchand's dad and Joe Kramer, who lost his wife. I think about my niece Brooke, who was raped the night of the Springer murders. We get justice for them, but then what? What happens to them after we close the case?"

"It's a good question."

"There're *so many* of them, Doc. It seems to me like we could be doing more to support them."

"What do you have in mind?"

"I'm not sure yet, but maybe some sort of support group or something that brings them together in a way that lets them know they're not alone. I don't know... Like I said, it's rough at this point."

"I like the idea a lot."

"Really?"

He nodded. "I think it could be a tremendous community service project for you to take on as the Homicide lieutenant and as a victim of violent crime yourself. You're uniquely positioned to lead something like this."

"Whoa." Laughing, she held up a hand to stop him. "I never said anything about leading it."

"Didn't you? It's your idea, and who better to make something like this happen than someone who not only sees the need on a daily basis but who has also been on this journey herself?"

"I don't know, Doc. I barely have time to see my husband and family as it is. Not sure I could take on something else."

"You wouldn't be doing it alone."

"Does that mean you'd be interested in working with me on something like this?"

"Absolutely. It would be my honor to help you make this happen."

"Let me give it some more thought and get back to you when things calm down."

"Sounds like a plan. Before I leave you to your work, I'll remind you that my door is always open to you. These are difficult days for you, your squad, your family. I'm here if I can be of assistance to any of you."

"That helps. Thank you."

"I hate to bring up other wounds when you're dealing with a new one, but with Stahl's trial coming soon, I'd like to set up some time to talk about how we're going to get you through that challenge."

"I appreciate the sentiment, but I don't think I need it. I'm very resolved to testifying and helping to put him away for life."

"Sam... Please don't underestimate the trauma of having to face off with the man who tried to kill you—twice."

"I'm not underestimating it. I'm simply refusing to give him any more of my time or attention than he's already gotten."

"Fair enough, but if you should change your mind, you know where to find me."

"I do, and I appreciate you. I really do."

"I'll let you get on with your day, Lieutenant, and I'll wish you well in the effort to apprehend your father's shooter. We're all hoping for a successful resolution to his case."

Sam nodded and gave him a grateful smile.

After he left, she took a minute to settle her overloaded emotions. The reminder of Stahl's upcoming trial was just another thing on her already overflowing plate. Adding the organization of a support group for the victims of violent crime to her to-do list was probably madness. She didn't have time to breathe most days. However, the recent drive-by shootings and the family members left behind had been weighing heavily on her mind.

Most of the crimes they investigated were senseless. Some, like the drive-by shootings, were more so than others. Probably because the victims were simply in the wrong place at the wrong time. That was their only "mistake." She'd never forget Trey Marchand and his unspeakable grief at the loss of his six-year-old daughter. Sam had wondered how he was holding up in the weeks since his daughter's death and had wished there was more she could do for him besides get justice for a little girl who was gone forever.

Justice helped, but that was only one part of the complicated maze of grief that followed such a tragic loss. She would give the idea more thought and test the feasibility of making it happen. No, she didn't have time for anything else, but the idea had taken root anyway, compelling her to do something with it.

She left her office and went into the conference room, where Freddie, Cameron and Jeannie were reading case files. "How's it going, people?"

"Nothing new yet," Freddie said. "I'm sifting through the tips and making some notes on the ones that might be worth pursuing. A lot of it is more condolences than actual tips."

"People are stupid," Sam said.

"Sometimes."

She took the lid off one of the boxes and began going through the contents.

"Your dad's reports put every report I've ever written to shame," Cameron said.

"He was known for having the best reports in the department. He was a great writer. Before he was shot, he used to talk about writing crime fiction in his retirement."

"He would've been awesome at it," Cameron said.

"Just another thing that was taken from him by whoever shot him."

They spent the next few hours combing through the

boxes and the files on the case thus far, and parsing through the information that had come into the tip line.

"I'd like to talk to this one." Sam referred to a man named Frank Davis, who had called the tip line to say he'd been on G Street the day of the shooting and might've seen something. "More than anything I'd like to know where the hell he's been for the last four years."

Freddie checked his watch. "We can get that in before our tour ends if you want to head over there now."

"Let's do it. I'll see the rest of you tomorrow. Thank you for your work today."

"We want to catch this person almost as much as you do, LT," Jeannie said.

"That means a lot. Thanks." To Freddie, she said, "Let's take separate cars so we can head home after."

He handed her a piece of paper with the Adams Morgan address for Davis. "See you there."

Sam went into her office to get her keys and to lock up before leaving for the day. As she approached the morgue exit, she ran into Lindsey McNamara.

"How's it going, Doc?"

"I was just coming to ask you that very question."

"I'm working the case, pulling the threads, doing what I do."

"If there's anything I can do for you, you know where to find me."

"I do. Everyone is being so supportive. Well, almost everyone."

"Do I take it you ran into your good friend Ramsey?"

"You would be correct. He's very concerned about who's going to clean up my messes for me now that my daddy is gone."

Lindsey rolled her green eyes. "Someone ought to take that mess right out of our department."

"Haven't you heard? He has *rights*."

"He's an asshole, and everyone knows it. Don't let him get to you."

"Eh, he's the least of my concerns. I'm going to talk to a guy who was on G Street the day my dad was shot."

"Where's he been the last four years?"

"My question exactly. I'll see you tomorrow."

"Sam… If you need anything, you have a lot of friends. I hope you know that."

"I do, and it helps. Tremendously. Take care, Doc." She pushed through the double doors into the waning daylight, zipping her coat as she walked to her car. The temperature had dropped about fifteen degrees since she'd been out earlier. Winter was coming and bringing with it long nights and a deep chill.

As she crossed the parking lot, she was struck by a memory from four years ago, on a similar late afternoon when she'd encountered her father returning from a meeting at City Hall as she left for the day.

"Taking a half day, baby girl?" That'd been one of his favorite jokes. Anything less than twelve hours was a half day in Skip Holland's book.

"Haha," she'd said, weary after a long eight hours on the job. She'd been a detective sergeant then, working under Stahl's command while married to Peter and generally hating her life and her job.

"How was your tour?"

"Just another day in paradise." She'd always been careful to avoid too much complaining to her father, who outranked her boss.

"I hate that you're working for that son of a bitch."

"I'm handling it."

"I wish there was something I could do to make it better."

"Don't you *dare*. Don't even think about it."

"I won't do it, but you can't tell me not to think about it."

"I am telling you. Stay out of it, Dad. I mean it."

"Are you being insubordinate to a superior officer by any chance?"

"Always." Her cheeky grin had made him laugh.

It'd been excruciating for him at times to gracefully handle the way she was treated by Stahl and others simply because her last name was Holland. And he'd absolutely despised her husband—he'd had Peter's number long before Sam had figured him out. It'd given Skip great joy in his final years to see her divorce Peter, ascend to Stahl's command and marry Nick, and it gave her pleasure to know that the changes in her life had been met with his approval.

As she drove to Adams Morgan, she thought about those last days of normal with her dad still on the job, wearing the uniform of the deputy chief. They'd met for coffee most days before work as Sam had tried to navigate the shark-infested waters that came with being the daughter of one of the department's top officers. His support and guidance had been as critical to her then as they had been later, when she assumed command of the Homicide squad and regularly relied upon his advice and counsel.

She wished she could ask him now how she was supposed to live without him.

"Don't go there." She was determined to keep her emotions out of the equation, so she could focus on the job. That was what he'd tell her to do if he were there. He'd tell her to do the job. And today, her job was getting justice for him.

CHAPTER ELEVEN

SAM FOUND THE address in Adams Morgan and saw Cruz's beat-up Mustang parked down the block. He waited for her on the sidewalk, so she double-parked and left her hazards flashing as she got out to join him.

"That one." He pointed to the building in question.

"Lead the way."

She followed him up two flights of stairs to an apartment on the third floor.

He knocked on the door. "Metro PD."

Sam rested her hand on her service weapon, wary after having recently been shot at through a closed door.

A series of locks disengaged, and the door swung open to reveal a man with wild white hair and wilder blue eyes. He took a quick assessing look at them and then gasped. "It's you! The VP's wife."

"Frank Davis?"

"That's me."

She flashed her badge while Freddie did the same. "Lieutenant Holland, Detective Cruz. May we have a minute of your time?"

"Yeah, sure. Come in."

Sam waited for Frank to lead the way before she followed him in. She tried to never turn her back on anyone on the job, which was one of many things her father had pounded into her head when she first started. *Keep your eyes on them always. Never turn your back. Be ready for anything. Expect the unexpected. Don't bring the job home with you.* Everything she knew about how to do this job had come from him.

Davis led them into a tidy kitchen that smelled of freshly brewed coffee. "Care for some?"

"I wouldn't mind a cup."

Sam scowled at her partner. She hated anything that dragged things out, especially when she was eager to go home.

Freddie smiled and shrugged as he accepted the mug from Davis.

"Cream is on the table. I don't have any sugar. Not supposed to have it cuz of my diabetes, so it's easier not to have it in the house."

"Cream is fine. Thank you."

Sam glared at Freddie before returning her attention to Davis. "You called the MPD tip line about the shooting four years ago of Deputy Chief Holland?"

Davis nodded. "He's your father, right?"

"Yes, he was."

"Sorry for your loss."

"Thank you." Sam wanted to pound her fist on the table and tell him to get on with it, but he seemed like a nice enough man, and if he had info she needed, she didn't want to piss him off. "What can you tell us?"

"Like I told the officer the day it happened, I was walking on G Street after work."

"What officer did you speak to the day it happened?" She had long ago memorized every detail of her father's case and had no recollection of a report about the shooting by anyone named Davis.

"Conklin."

What the fuck? "Tell us what you saw."

"I worked then at the Government Accountability

Office—GAO. We work for Congress, doing investigations."

"Yes, we're aware of what GAO does."

"So I left work that day and saw the cop in the unmarked car pull over another car. I kept walking past where it was happening. I was about two blocks away when I heard the gunshot. I turned around and saw the officer go down."

Sam took frantic notes, her heart racing at the implications. An eyewitness. A fucking *eyewitness* she hadn't known about *for four fucking years*? Her hands shook, and her heart raced. She could feel Freddie's gaze on her, but she didn't dare look up or venture a glance at him or do anything other than write down every word Davis was saying.

"I called 911 and ran over to see if I could help him. He was bleeding from his neck. I did what I could to stop the bleeding, but it was bad." He shook his head. "Real bad."

Sam realized she was talking to the man who'd probably saved her father's life in those first few fateful moments. *Where had this information been for four long years?*

"You didn't see the other car?" Even her voice felt shaky.

"No, it was gone by the time I ran back."

"And you told all of this to Conklin?"

"Yep. He's the deputy chief now, right?"

"Yeah, he is." She looked at Freddie, who was wide-eyed and equally shocked.

Freddie got to work on his phone, produced the web-page that featured photographs of the department's top leadership and handed the phone to her.

"Are you *sure* it was Conklin?" She handed Freddie's phone to Frank.

While she and Freddie held their collective breath, Frank took a close look at the officers. The leadership team was more or less the same as it had been then, with one notable exception. Skip Holland was no longer the deputy chief. When he was medically retired, Conklin had moved up to deputy chief and Malone had taken Conklin's place as detective captain.

"That's him there." Davis pointed to Conklin. "He's the one I talked to that day. I figured I'd hear something from the detectives looking into the case, but I never did."

Sam felt as if an earthquake had struck, tilting the ground beneath her and leaving her breathless. During the recent investigation into the drive-by shootings, they'd discovered that Conklin had kept secret the fact that a retired MPD officer and a close friend of his had been missing for more than two weeks. Sam had uncovered that detail, which had led to Conklin's suspension. And now this… "You've been very helpful."

"I wish I could tell you more. After that day, I followed the stories about Deputy Chief Holland, and I was sad to hear he'd passed away."

Sam fought back the rage and disbelief. "I believe that what you did that day saved his life. It made it possible for him to marry the woman he loved, to meet two more of his grandchildren and to see me happily married. What you did made a huge difference to his entire family, and we owe you a long-overdue thank-you."

He shrugged off her thanks. "I did what anyone would've done in that situation. It's unbelievable to me that someone could randomly shoot a guy who's out there protecting all of us. It's madness."

"Yes, it certainly is." Sam took down his phone number and left him with their business cards in case he thought of anything else.

Outside, Sam sucked in badly needed deep breaths. Freddie spoke first. "Oh my *God*. What the *hell*?"

Shock reverberated through every cell in her body. This couldn't be happening. All this time...

"What do we do?"

"I'm going straight to the chief with this."

"Sam... Let me go with you. You shouldn't be driving right now."

That was when she realized her hands were shaking violently. "Yeah. Okay."

They got into her car, with Freddie at the wheel. He did a U-turn and headed for HQ while Sam put through a call to Farnsworth's cell phone, using a number she'd had for years but had rarely used in all the years she'd worked for him.

"Sam?"

"I need to see you right now. Are you still at the office?"

"I was just getting ready to leave."

"Meet me in the morgue parking lot. Ten minutes."

"Sam—"

She closed the phone because she couldn't say another word until her uncle Joe was standing in front of her, telling her what to do with this bombshell she'd been handed. Another thing her father had told her on day one—*If you learn something your superior officers should know, no matter what it is, tell them immediately. Don't sit on it for even five minutes, or you're part of the problem.*

She'd taken that advice to heart when she'd stumbled upon the fact that Conklin hadn't told anyone that retired Captain Kenneth Wallack had gone missing two weeks before Sam talked to his wife as part of the drive-by investigation. And now this… What else did the deputy chief know about his predecessor's shooting? Her dad had counted Conklin among his closest friends. That he could've had this information for all this time… She couldn't wrap her head around it.

To his credit, Freddie didn't say another word on the ride back to HQ, through rush-hour traffic that made the trip ten minutes longer than she'd predicted. Outside the door to the morgue, the chief waited for her, leaning against his department-issued SUV.

Freddie pulled Sam's car into the spot next to the chief. "You want me to come?"

"Yeah."

She got out of the car and forced herself to move on legs that felt wooden. Her stomach ached, and she feared she might vomit in front of the chief.

"What's wrong?"

"We followed a tip-line lead to a man named Frank Davis, who lives in Adams Morgan. He was on G Street the day of the shooting, saw the cop car pull over another car, heard the gunshot, called 911, ran back and rendered aid. And even though he reported all of this to Conklin, it's the first I've heard of any of it. I've never heard the guy's name before today."

"How do you know he reported it to Conklin?" Farnsworth's shock was apparent in the set of his jaw and the rigidity of his posture.

"He said he reported it all that day to Conklin. To be certain, we showed him the top brass on the website, and he picked out Conklin." It took everything she had not to lose her shit completely. She wanted to scream and rage and punch something. "All this time… What else does he know?"

"I'd like to consult with Malone on this before we proceed. Are you okay with that?"

"Whatever you think is best."

"I'm sorry this happened, Sam. We'll get to the bottom of it."

"All this time… Has he known what happened to my father and didn't tell anyone?"

"If that's the case, I'll see him prosecuted to the fullest extent of the law."

"What should I do?" She vibrated with rage and energy and hope. In the midst of the shock, hope shone through. Would this be the break they'd been waiting for? Or would it be another dead end.

"Go home. I'll call you later."

"Chief—"

"Go home, Lieutenant. I will call you."

Sam didn't want to go home. She wanted to stay and find out why a superior officer she'd liked and respected, a man her father had considered a close friend, would've kept this information from her and other investigators for *four years.*

Freddie took her by the arm and gave a gentle tug. "Come on."

She allowed him to lead her to the car and nudge her into the passenger seat.

And then he drove her home to Ninth Street, where they were waved through the checkpoint by the agents on duty. He parked in her assigned spot in front of the house, killed the engine and glanced over at her. "We have to trust the chief to handle this properly. He always does the right thing."

"Are there, like, three or four people in the entire

department who always do the right thing, or does it just seem that way lately?"

"It's way more than three or four people. The bad ones are few compared to the good."

"*How* could he have done this to us? To my dad, who was always a good friend to him? He *lived* with us for a short time when his first marriage ended."

"Did he? I've never heard that."

"My dad dragged him out of a bar and brought him home to our house so he wouldn't do something stupid and lose his career."

Freddie's deep sigh said it all.

Desolate and grief-stricken all over again that someone she respected and trusted could've done something like this, she couldn't seem to fully process this new information. "I don't understand."

"Maybe it'll turn out that he had a good reason."

"What *possible* good reason could he have had?"

"I don't know."

Sam glanced at her house, where it seemed every light was on, whereas Celia's home was dark. "I should go in."

"Call me if you hear anything?"

"I will. Take my car home and pick me up in the morning. We'll get yours then."

"Will do. You gonna be okay?"

"What choice do I have?" She got out of the car, and though she desperately wanted to see Nick, Scotty and the kids, she walked over to Celia's, aching at the knowledge that her dad wasn't there and never would be again. How she wished she could share what she'd learned today with him. But in a way, she was glad he would never know what his friend had done—or failed to do.

She went up the ramp and rested her hand on the doorknob, prepared to walk in the way Celia had always insisted, but uncertain of her welcome, she stopped short of opening the door. Raising her hand, she knocked and waited.

Celia opened the door. "Why are you knocking? You know the rules."

"I...I wasn't sure if the rules had changed."

"They haven't." Celia turned and led the way into the kitchen, where a glass of wine sat on a table covered in cards and other piles of paper. "Drink?"

"I'd love one."

Celia poured her a glass of chardonnay.

"What're you doing?"

"Thank-you notes."

"The girls and I can help with that."

"Eh." She waved her hand. "Gives me something to do."

"Are you okay?"

"I've been better. I'm sure you have too."

"I'm sorry, Celia. I know you're angry with me about what happened and how it happened, and I honestly can't bear to think that I made this worse for you in any way."

"It was the right thing. I couldn't see it at the time, but you were right to intervene. It was what he would've wanted, even if I didn't agree."

Hearing her say that filled Sam with relief so profound it nearly permeated the shock of what she'd uncovered about Conklin.

Celia looked up at her. "It took a lot of guts for you to do the right thing for him. I'm glad one of us was thinking clearly. I certainly wasn't."

"He was your husband and you loved him. I hope I never have to confront what you did that day."

"I hope you don't either. Even knowing it was the best thing for him... It's the worst thing for me." She teared up and used her sleeve to dab at her eyes. "Just when I think I've shed all the tears I'll ever have, there're more."

Sam sat next to her and held out her arms.

Celia leaned into her. "He loved you so much."

"He loved you just as much."

"I don't know about that." Celia laughed. "He had a soft spot a mile wide for you."

"We were both lucky to be loved by him."

She patted Sam's arm. "Thank you for what you said about me at the service."

"I meant every word of it. You gave us four years we wouldn't have had without you."

"Even when it was awful—and it was awful a lot of the time—they were the best years of my life."

"I think he would say the same."

"Not sure that's true..."

"He loved every minute he spent with you. We all saw the way he looked at you."

"You're going to figure out who did this to him, right?"

"Our entire team is devoted to new leads, and we're very determined." Sam hesitated to say more, but she had to prepare her stepmother for the possibility that they could still be unsuccessful, even after the bomb-shell they'd uncovered that day. She couldn't say any-thing about that until they knew more, but she wished she could share it with Celia. "Four years is a long time. The case is cold. But we're going to do every-thing we can."

"That's all I can ask. It won't bring him back, but the thought of someone out there enjoying his or her life while he's dead and buried…"

"I know. Believe me. I get it."

Celia sat up and wiped her face. "Sorry to be such a waterworks."

"Don't apologize."

"It's good of you to come by and see me. Scotty was here earlier. That boy is such a gem."

"I know. He adores you. You won't be getting rid of any of us."

"That's fine with me. I'm not sure what I'd do without you."

Sam finished her wine and leaned in to kiss Celia's cheek. "You want to come over for dinner? I have no idea what we're having, but I'm sure Shelby left something."

"She was over earlier with Noah and the twins. They brought me enchiladas, so I assume that's what you're having too."

"Yum." Sam's stomach growled. "She's the best."

"Yes, she is. We're surrounded by good people and lots of love that will get us through this."

Sam nodded. "I'll check on you tomorrow."

"I'll be here."

As she got up from the table, Sam had to force herself not to look in the dining room for someone who wasn't there anymore or listen for the whir of the wheelchair. As she walked out the door, she realized it wasn't her dad's house anymore. It was Celia's house now. A while ago, he'd talked to Sam and her sisters to let them know he was taking steps to ensure Celia was cared for in the event of his death. Sam was glad that he'd seen to those details, because Celia deserved to be well cared for after having given so much to Skip and the rest of them.

Sam went up the ramp to her house, one of the ramps they no longer needed. They'd become such a regular part of her daily routine that she barely noticed them, but she couldn't imagine the street without them anymore.

Nate, the agent working the door, nodded to her. "Evening, Mrs. Cappuano."

"Hi, Nate."

She stepped into bedlam, Scotty on the floor with Alden as Aubrey danced around them.

Nick watched over them, beer in hand and a smile on his face.

It occurred to Sam that her husband finally had the family he'd always wanted, which made her happy on a day that had left her numb with shock. Even in the midst of despair and sorrow, joy crept in to remind her that life went on even when you didn't think it possibly could.

Aubrey let out a happy shriek when she saw Sam and ran over to her.

Sam scooped up the little girl, who smelled of peanut butter, and kissed her soft cheek. "What's going on here? I left you in charge of the boys."

Aubrey giggled. "Scotty tickled Alden and then that happened."

Alden had Scotty pinned. "Admit defeat."

"Never!" Scotty toppled Alden, which restarted the wrestling and the screaming laughter from the little boy.

His laughter was one of the best things Sam had ever heard, especially after the days of silence that had followed the deaths of his parents.

Aubrey squiggled in her arms. "I need to help Alden."

"Don't hurt my Scotty."

Aubrey dashed over and landed on top of them, drawing a loud *ooph* from Scotty.

Sam glanced at Nick, who slid an arm around her and kissed the top of her head. "Should we be allowing this?"

"They're working off the last of their energy. They'll sleep well." He looked down at her. "How'd it go today?"

"I'll tell you after we get the kids in bed."

"Uh-oh."

"Yeah. I heard there're enchiladas?"

"You heard correctly, and they're amazing."

"You got this? I need to eat."

"I got it. Go ahead." He gave her another kiss and released her. "Five minutes to bath time."

"Haha." Scotty playfully headlocked Alden. "You gotta take a bath."

"You have to take a shower," Nick said to Scotty.

Alden laughed and stuck his tongue out at Scotty.

Amused by their sibling-like banter, Sam went into the kitchen to eat while Nick supervised baths. She finished eating the delicious enchiladas and went upstairs in time to snuggle up to Alden while Nick read them a story about hungry bears breaking out of a zoo and running free in a neighborhood. The story and the voices Nick used to read it made both children laugh.

While she was physically present with her family, her mind was still on the situation with Conklin as she wondered if she would hear from the chief tonight.

CHAPTER TWELVE

THE FIRST THING Joe Farnsworth did when he parted with Holland and Cruz was call Jake Malone. "Where are you?"

"Almost home. What's up?"

"I need to see you right away."

"Everything okay?"

"I don't think so."

"Ah, fuck. What now? You want me to come back to HQ?"

"Meet me at my place in twenty?"

"I'll be there."

As he drove home, Joe took a call from Marti. "Hi, honey."

"Hi there. I'm leaving for a meeting at church, but I left dinner in the oven for you. It's on low, but if you leave it there too long it won't be any good."

"I'm on my way."

"All right. I'll be home by eight."

"See you then. Love you."

"Love you too."

He told himself that no matter what kind of shit show was about to blow up around him and his department, he would still have her, and she made everything bearable. When he arrived at home, he saw Malone waiting for him on the porch, illuminated by the glow of the light Marti had left on for him.

Joe got out of his SUV and went up to the porch.

Malone eyed him warily. "What fresh hell is upon us now?"

"Holland and Cruz followed up on a lead called into the tip line from a guy named Frank Davis. Ring any bells?"

"Nope. Should it?"

"Apparently, he was on G Street at the time of Skip's shooting and gave a detailed statement to Conklin the same day."

Malone tipped his head as if he hadn't heard the words correctly. "He gave a statement to Conklin."

"That's what he told Holland and Cruz. To be sure, they showed him the page of department leadership from the website, and he identified Conklin as the officer who'd taken his statement. Apparently, Davis rendered aid to Skip after the shooting and perhaps saved his life by putting pressure on the wound until the paramedics arrived."

"Are you fucking kidding me right now?"

"You have no idea how much I wish I was." Joe sighed. He should've retired years ago. Then this latest nightmare wouldn't be his problem.

"Did Davis see the shooter or the car?"

"No. He only remembers seeing the cop car pull over another car, but he had moved past them when he heard the shot."

"Jesus."

"First Wallack and now this. What else is there?"

"I don't even want to know." Crossing his arms, Jake looked at Joe. "What're we going to do about this?"

Joe expected nothing less of the colleague and friend who always had his back. "We need to go talk to him."

Joe needed someone there to witness whatever transpired, and he trusted Jake to help him navigate this situation.

Jake checked his watch. "He's probably home by now."

"Let me go turn off the oven and then we can go." Dinner would have to wait.

Twenty minutes later, they crossed the 14th Street Bridge in bumper-to-bumper late-day traffic on the way to Conklin's home in Alexandria. Normally they'd be talking sports or politics, but today they coexisted in tense silence. It took forty-five minutes to make the five-mile trip.

"What's our plan?" Jake asked when they pulled into a guest spot in the condo complex.

"Let's ask him to come out and talk, so we can't be overheard." Conklin was remarried, but none of them knew his second wife that well. She didn't often socialize with them.

"I'll do that," Jake said.

While Joe stood next to the car, Jake went up the stairs to the front door and rang the bell. A minute later, the inside door swung open. Conklin seemed surprised to see Jake. He pushed opened the storm door.

"Can we talk?" Jake gestured to where Joe waited. "Out here?"

Conklin glanced at Joe and then at Jake. "Uh, yeah. Sure. Let me grab a coat."

Jake came down the stairs and joined Joe at the car.

Conklin joined them a minute later. "What's going on?"

Joe took the lead. "We've been following up on some info that came into the tip line after Skip died. Does the name Frank Davis mean anything to you?"

Conklin thought about that for a second. "No. Should it?"

"He claims he was on G Street the day Skip was shot, rendered aid to him in the aftermath of the shooting and gave a statement to you that we have no record of."

"He said he talked to *me*?"

"He named you and picked you out of photos of the department's top leadership."

"I never talked to anyone on G Street that day. I wasn't even there. I went to the hospital after I got the call about the shooting."

"You're sure about that?"

"I'm positive. I was at HQ when the officer-down call came in, and I went straight to the GW ER." His stance took a defensive edge. "You really thought I'd keep something like this to myself for four years? Just because I didn't tell you about Wallack? Skip was my *friend*. He saved my life and my career once upon a time."

The story of Conklin's downward spiral after the end of his first marriage was well-known by Joe and Jake.

"Who brought this to you?"

"Holland and Cruz."

"Of course it was her." Conklin's laugh had a bitter edge to it. "Why'd I even ask?"

"Don't blame her," Joe said sharply. "What was she supposed to do with this and the Wallack info?"

"No worries." Conklin scoffed. "I certainly know whose side you both are on. Everyone knows."

"I'm on the side of the department and the honest men and women who serve this city," Joe said, infuriated. "Are you? I didn't take your badge on the Wallack thing, but if I find out that what you told us about Davis isn't true, you're done—and I'll see you prosecuted. So think about it tonight. Think long and hard about that day and make sure you're remembering correctly. You know where to find me in the morning." To Jake, he said, "Let's go."

They drove by Conklin, still standing where they'd left him, as they exited his development.

The drive back to the city was no less tense than the first half of the trip had been.

"You believe him?" Jake asked after a long silence.

"I don't know what to believe."

"We could ask him to take a polygraph."

"And what if it gets out that we're polygraphing our deputy chief?" Joe cringed at the thought of that PR nightmare.

"So, it's basically the word of a guy we've known and worked with for decades against this Davis dude, who swears he talked to Conklin that day?"

"If the thing with Wallack hadn't happened, I'd take Conklin's word for it. But after that… I just don't know what to say."

Jake looked over at Joe. "Why don't we dig into Davis a little deeper and get a sense of how credible he is?"

"We can take a high-level look but nothing too in-depth. I don't want to rip the guy's life apart after he was good enough to call the tip line."

"One question I have is where's he been the last four years? He gave the report to Conklin, and that was the end of it for him?"

"He probably thought we'd do the right thing with the info and what more could he do?"

"I dunno. If I witnessed something like what he did,

every time Sam mentioned the case was still open, I'd
be calling to see if I could do anything more to help."

A knot of dread tightened in Joe's gut. "Maybe he
did."

"What do you mean?"

"Get Davis's phone number and then *personally*
take a look at the records of every call Conklin has received in the office since the day Skip was shot. Find
out whether Davis ever called him after that day. Ask
Archelotta for the records for all the top leadership so
he won't know who we're focused on. Tell him to call
me for approval."

"I'll take care of it first thing, and I'll ask Holland
and Cruz to take a high-level look at Davis."

"Maybe Davis remembered incorrectly."

"What if he didn't? Will you really bring charges
against Conklin?"

"You bet your ass I will."

SAM HELPED NICK tuck Aubrey and Alden into bed and
then went in to check on Scotty. "Everything ready for
tomorrow, bud?"

"Define *everything*."

She rolled her eyes at his predictable comment. "Is
most of the homework done anyway?"

"Define *most*."

"Scotty!"

He laughed. "Chill, Mom. It's all good. Dad has already gone through my planner and my backpack to
make sure I did everything."

Hearing him call her Mom never got old. "Thank
God for Dad."

"He really is essential to the entire program."

"You know it. Celia said you were there this afternoon. She really appreciated your visit."

"I love going there after school. It's weird that Gramps isn't there, though. I keep waiting for him to come rolling in."

"I know. I was just there and felt the same way. I can't bear to look in the dining room."

"Will we take down the ramps?"

"Eventually, I suppose. I don't think we need to do that right away."

"It'll be so different out there without them, like it's different without him."

Sam nodded.

Scotty sat up, reached for her and gave her a hug that brought tears to her eyes.

She held him for as long as she could before he began to squiggle to get free. "Thanks. I needed that."

"No problem."

She leaned in to kiss his forehead. "Love you."

"Love you too."

"Lights out." She waited until he'd shut off the light before she left the room and closed the door, recalling when her father used to do the same with her. Every night, she turned the light back on, and every night, he came busting in to catch her, scaring the crap out of her. Then they would laugh. The joke never got old.

Her whole life, they'd had the ability to crack each other up. She could meet his gaze across a crowded room and know exactly what he was thinking and vice versa. They understood each other on a cellular level. It had been no surprise to anyone who knew them that she'd followed him into the MPD. She hadn't seriously considered any other profession.

Until Nick, she'd never had that kind of connection

with anyone but her father. That feeling of being so deeply understood would be the thing she would miss the most about her dad. Thank God she had Nick to fill some of the void.

He was in bed, wearing sexy reading glasses and flipping through a binder full of briefing documents, or what he referred to as his nightly trip through hell. As vice president, he was privy to things most people would never know about, and for that, he said, they should be thankful. No wonder his insomnia had been worse than ever since he became vice president.

Her cell phone rang and she took the call from the chief. "Hey. Did you talk to him?"

"Yeah. He says he was never on G Street that day. He says he went right from HQ to GW after he got the call about your dad being shot."

"So that's it? He's going to deny it, and that's the end of it?"

"Did you get a phone number from Davis by any chance?"

"Yeah, hang on." Sam retrieved her notebook and gave him Davis's number. "Are you going to call Davis?"

"I'm going to investigate further. That's all I can say right now."

"You can't tell me anything else?"

"I can only ask you to be patient and trust me."

"Patient," she said with a laugh. "*Four years*, Chief, and the guy who replaced my dad as deputy chief has possibly been sitting on a bombshell all that time? You'll have to pardon me if my patience is sorely lacking."

"I understand, and I feel the same way. I have to do this by the book."

"I hear you."

"If there's anything to it, you'll be among the first to know. That's the best I can do."

"Okay."

"Try to get some sleep. If nothing else, we know more today than we knew yesterday."

Oddly enough, that didn't bring comfort. She thought of all the meetings and encounters she'd had with Conklin in the last four years, the visits he'd made to her father and the friendship he'd shown them both. Had it all been an act? Had he been hiding critical information about the shooting while pretending to be a friend and ally?

"Sam?"

"Yeah, I'll talk to you tomorrow." She closed the phone and put it on the bedside charger.

"What the hell was that?"

In as few words as possible, she told Nick about the conversation with Davis and what it had yielded. He was the only person who was ever privy to information about her cases that no one else could know. She trusted him implicitly.

Nick stared at her, his face blank with shock.

"Farnsworth confronted Conklin about it, and he says he was nowhere near G Street that day."

"Can you prove otherwise? Is there security film or something you could check to see if he's lying?"

"It's on my list for tomorrow to check with Archie to see what we have."

Nick's sour expression made her laugh when she didn't think that was possible. He'd recently found out about the brief fling she'd had with Archie after her first marriage ended. "Knock it off."

"Don't wanna." He held out his hand to her. "Come here."

"Give me one minute to change." She went into the bathroom to brush her teeth and change into pajama pants and a tank before snuggling up to him in bed.

He wrapped his arms around her. "This thing with Conklin has to be a gut punch."

Safe in his embrace, she finally exhaled after the shock delivered by Mr. Davis. "It is."

"Any chance the guy is mistaken about who he talked to that day?"

"He picked him out of the photos of the department's top leadership. I don't think he's mistaken."

"What can I do?"

"This helps. This always helps."

"I wish it was more. I hate to see you suffering."

"If the suffering leads to a break in my dad's case, it'll be worth it." Sam gave herself permission to relax—for now—so she could hopefully get some sleep. There was nothing more she could do tonight to pursue the lead she'd been handed by Davis. And besides, the chief had put her on notice that she would not be the one investigating it anyway. "Scotty mentioned the ramps. He asked if we're going to take them down now that Dad is gone."

"What do you want to do?"

"I can't imagine our house or his without them. I can barely remember what Ninth Street looked like before there were ramps."

"There's no need to decide anything about that right away."

"Remember the day you had the ramp installed and I thought someone had blown up our front door?"

His low chuckle echoed through his chest. "My Samantha is always a cop first and foremost."

"I'm trained to think the worst." She moved so her chin was on his chest and she could see his handsome face. "In case I forget to mention it every day for the rest of our lives, that was one of the nicest things anyone has ever done for me."

He curled her hair around his fingers. "I wanted your dad to be able to visit us."

"You say that as if it's no big deal, when it was a huge deal to him and to me."

"Anything for you—and him."

"He loved you. I hope you know that."

His warm hazel eyes filled. "I loved him too."

"Remember when you were afraid he was going to have you killed for being in my bedroom?"

"I remember everything, and I'm quite certain that even in his paralyzed state, he could've arranged it."

Sam laughed. "Oh, he definitely could have, but he knew you were different from everyone else the first time he saw us together."

"After your ex-husband tried to blow us up?"

She rolled her eyes. "Ahh, yes, those were some good times, huh?"

"The best times of my entire life."

"You need to get out more."

"I don't need anything other than what and *who* I have right here in this bed and this house." Smiling, he gave her a gentle tug to bring her fully on top of him, putting her lips into kissing range. Anytime he looked at her that way or kissed her so sweetly, her insides still fluttered. "I think about our first days together all the time. In the midst of the madness of John's murder, there you were, the woman I'd dreamed about for six long years."

"Did you really dream about me?"

"I thought about you constantly. My only regret in this life is that I didn't go after you when you didn't return my calls."

"My only regret is that I didn't hunt you down when you didn't call me like you said you would."

"I called you the second I got back from the trip to Europe. I called you from the airport."

"You did? You've never told me that."

"If you had answered the phone, I would've come straight to you."

Sam groaned at hearing that. "It's a good thing Peter is dead, or I might be tempted to do it myself." Her ex-husband had been her platonic roommate at the time Sam first met Nick. Since Peter had been interested in her himself, he'd failed to give her the critical messages from Nick. "What do you think would've happened if he'd given me those messages?"

"We'd be married for almost eight years rather than almost two."

Sam dropped her head to his chest. "I can't even think about it or I'll go mad." Raising her head, she met his loving gaze. "Thank God we found each other again, because I wouldn't be able to survive this life without you. You can't ever leave me."

"*Leave you?* Where would I go when I can't breathe without you? I almost lost my mind having to live without you for a week, even when I talked to you every day."

"There are other ways you can leave me." She couldn't think about the people who hated him and what he stood for as vice president. If she did, she'd lose what was left of her sanity.

"I don't want you to worry about me. I'm very well protected."

"And yet still I worry."

"Let's talk about a worst-case scenario, then."

She recoiled. "Do we have to?"

"We never have before, and every day I have to send you out there to hunt down criminals who would think nothing of taking you away from me. As much as you might worry about me, let's face it, it's much harder being me in this marriage."

"I know."

"So let's talk worst-case. Maybe if we do, it won't have the power to frighten us the way it does now."

"There are about twenty million other things I'd rather talk about. Such as…" She shifted her pelvis to press against his cock, which sprang to life under her.

"Quit it. I'm serious."

"So am I." She kissed his neck and took a gentle bite under his jaw.

He buried his fingers in her hair and compelled her to look at him. "Tell me what you would do if the worst thing happened. I really want to know."

"Whereas I can't bear to even think about it."

"Humor me."

Sighing, she realized he wasn't going to let this go. "After my six-month stay in a padded room, I'd probably take up drinking for a living. I'd do whatever it took to dull the worst pain I could ever imagine feeling. Just thinking about it is unbearable."

"For me too."

"What would you do?"

"I'd make sure that you were honored for your service the way your father was, for one thing."

"You're so much better at this than I am. I'm in a padded room while you're seeing to my legacy."

The sound of his laughter went a long way toward relieving some her tension and reminded her that despite the what-if game, he was very much alive. Thank God for that.

"I'd be out of my mind with grief," he said. "Don't ever think otherwise."

"Would you remarry?"

"Would you?"

"I asked first. Answer the question."

"I probably wouldn't. How would I ever top this?"

"What if someone came along who made you happy again?" She seethed with jealousy at the thought of him with anyone but her.

"What would you want me to do?"

Sam flashed a big goofy grin. "Stab her with a rusty steak knife?"

"Why did I know you were going to say that?" His fingers sifted through her hair in a soothing rhythm.

"If I'm truly gone and you find someone who makes you happy, I *suppose* it would be okay with me if you married her, but you can't be as happy with her as you were with me. That's my line in the sand."

His gorgeous hazel eyes danced with amusement. "I suppose that's fair enough. Now, tell me what you would do."

"I would never remarry."

"Even if you found someone who made you happy again?"

"Even then."

"Why?"

"Because I'd want to be Samantha Cappuano for the rest of my life."

"Aw, babe, that's very sweet of you."

"So maybe I would live in sin, but I wouldn't get married again."

With his hands on her face, he kissed her. "No matter what happens, I'd want you to do whatever it took to be happy. I don't care what that entails. Just be happy, Samantha."

"I could never, ever, *ever* be truly happy again without you."

"Yes, you could."

"No, I really couldn't, so please don't let anything happen to you."

"I'm not going anywhere without you, but in light of what we do for a living and the crazy-ass world we live in, I think it's important that we have this conversation."

"Maybe so, but I hope you're not expecting me to sleep tonight as I contemplate the horror of life without you."

"Sounds like I need to make sure you're completely exhausted by your very much alive husband so you'll get the sleep you need." He rolled her under him and kissed her more intently.

She responded to him the way she always did, body and soul, but as he removed her pajamas and made love to her, the morbid conversation and the feelings of dread stayed with her long after they reached a highly satisfying conclusion. Sam fell into restless sleep plagued by worst-case scenarios.

CHAPTER THIRTEEN

As PLANNED, FREDDIE picked her up at six thirty the next morning, and they stopped to pick up his car where they'd left it the day before in Adams Morgan. Sam was grouchy and out of sorts after a rough night of disturbing dreams—or rather, nightmares. Because if any of them ever came to fruition, they would be her worst nightmare come true. She understood why Nick had wanted to talk about what they would do if the worst possible thing happened, but the dreadful topic had left a pit in her gut that she rubbed anxiously as she settled into her office and fired up her computer.

Somehow she was managing to survive losing her dad. Despite what she'd said to Nick last night, she'd never survive losing *him*. Life as she knew it would be over without him. She'd give up everything but Scotty. Aubrey and Alden would have to go somewhere where they could be properly loved, because she wouldn't have it in her.

"Stop." She said the word out loud, hoping her spinning mind would hear and take heed.

Dr. Trulo came into her office. "What are we stopping?"

"My disturbing thoughts."

"Why are you having disturbing thoughts? Other than the obvious, of course."

She waved him all the way in and gestured for him

to close the door. "Last night, Nick wanted to talk about what we'd do if the worst thing happened to either of us."

"Oh." Trulo took a seat in her visitor's chair. "I take it that left you feeling anxious."

"That's one word for how it left me feeling."

"It's a tough topic, but one that should be addressed in a marriage, especially one as high profile as yours."

"I suppose."

"It's unthinkable, right?"

"Completely."

"Last week, it was unthinkable that you could lose your father, and here we are. Somehow life goes on."

"Not if Nick dies, it doesn't."

"Yes, it will. Whether you want it to or not."

Sam put her hands over her ears and shook her head.

Trulo chuckled. "If there's a cost to having great love in our lives, it's the fear of losing it."

"Leave it to you to sum it up in one sentence."

"Why, thank you. That's my job. Nick is showing you how much he loves you by making sure you'd be okay if the worst thing should happen. I'm sure that's his only concern."

"It is. And vice versa, as long as he's not *too* happy with my replacement."

Trulo laughed hard at that. "Which I'm sure you mentioned."

"Duh."

"I know it's hard when you've allowed yourself to entertain a worst-case scenario, but you should put it out of your mind. You had the conversation. Now you need to convince yourself that it was just a conversation. It hasn't actually happened, and there's no reason to believe it will."

"Working on that." She offered a wan smile. "This helps, thanks. I assume you didn't come down to talk about my doomsday prophecy."

"I didn't, but I'm always glad to help you. I hope you know that."

"I do, and I appreciate it."

"I came to talk about your support group idea. I can't stop thinking about it since you brought it up."

"It's been on my mind a lot too."

"In my experience, whenever I get something in my head that won't get out, that means it's an idea I need to pursue."

"I agree. Is it something we need to run up the flag-pole before we go any further?"

"Probably, but I expect it'd be well received. But I was thinking…and tell me if this is way out of line…"

Intrigued, Sam said, "I'm listening."

"What if we did it in conjunction with both your roles—as the lieutenant of the Homicide division *and* as second lady?"

She mulled that over. "I wouldn't want to do something like this for the attention it would bring to me."

"Understood, but I think it could help to shine the light on the fallout of violent crime, the people who're left behind. It could also help to promote your efforts as second lady to support law enforcement. I don't want to pressure you to do something you aren't comfortable with. Think about it and let me know. In the meantime, I'll run the idea up the flagpole, giving you full credit, of course."

She waved that off. "I don't care about the credit."

"You deserve the credit for a brilliant idea. I can see this becoming a national effort to better support the victims we encounter on the job—and to better support the law enforcement officers, like Sergeant Gonzales and Detective McBride—who suffer in the aftermath of things they experienced on the job."

Sam nodded. "Our culture encourages officers to keep their suffering to themselves or run the risk of encountering trouble on the job. That's another thing I'd like to address through this group."

"That stigma is something I spend a lot of time on a daily basis to overcome with the officers I work with. Anything we can do to bring attention to the very real traumas police officers face on the job would be beneficial."

"I'll talk to my team at the White House—and yes, it's still weird to say that sentence."

Trulo laughed. "I can't imagine that sentence ever gets routine."

"It won't for me. That's for sure. But I'll get some opinions and let you know."

"Let's keep in touch about this—and the trial."

At the reminder of Stahl's upcoming trial, Sam sagged into her chair. "Don't remind me."

"You could ask Faith to request a continuance. The judge would take into consideration your recent loss."

"I want to get it over with, so I never have to think about him again. The sooner the better."

"Come see me if you need to before you testify."

"I will. Thanks." Not that long ago, she would've dodged him, made excuses, gone out of her way to avoid anything that smacked of headshrinking. However, having seen the benefit of therapy after Stahl attacked her, she was thankful to know Trulo was available if she needed help in weathering this next storm.

"Speaking of Stahl." Sam checked her watch. "I have an appointment with Faith Miller in three minutes."

Trulo stood. "I'll let you get ready for that. I'll be in touch." He smiled and winked on his way out the door.

Sam shook her head in amusement. The doctor who'd once represented a formidable obstacle to returning to duty had become a trusted friend and colleague since he helped her find a way through the nightmare of being kidnapped, attacked and certain she was going to die at the hands of her former lieutenant. Stahl hated her for being Skip's daughter, for being good at her job, for being well regarded by her fellow officers, and who knows what other reasons had twisted his mind to the point that he could wrap her in razor wire and threaten to set her on fire.

She shuddered thinking about that day and the absolute certainty that she would never see Nick, Scotty or her beloved family again.

A knock on the door had her looking up at Faith, who, like her identical triplet sisters, had soft brown hair, green eyes and a curvy figure. As always, she wore a sharp suit with her signature stiletto heels.

"Come in."

Faith stepped into the office and closed the door.

Sam wanted to know what her team was doing in the conference room and what was happening with Conklin, but she had to endure this meeting before she could get back to what she should be doing.

"How're you doing?"

"Just great." Sam poured on the sarcasm. "I've been looking forward to this meeting for days."

Faith laughed. "I'm sure. Sorry that we have to do it, but you know the drill by now."

"All too well."

Having their story straight and her testimony rock-solid would be critical to ensuring Stahl never saw the light of day again. She would do anything she could to make sure of that.

It took ninety minutes to go through the testimony step by step.

Sam recited the facts of the two times Stahl had attacked her from memories she would never forget. In some ways, testifying had never been simpler. She'd lived every second of it, done everything she could to survive and went through the details one after the other in response to Faith's strategic questions.

"I think we're ready," Faith finally declared.

Sam's stomach hurt, and a headache had settled over her left eye. Talking about shit she'd much sooner forget never came naturally, but it was a necessary evil in situations like this. Underline the word *evil*.

"You're going to be great. The key thing, as you know, is to not let his presence in the courtroom get to you. After you identify him, don't look at him again."

"I won't, don't worry. He's the last thing I ever want to look at." Her plan was to look directly at Nick, who'd vowed to be in the front row when she testified, as much as she wished he wouldn't come. He'd never let her go through that without him, but it pained her to think of him hearing those details again. That day had been worse for him, in many ways, than it had been for her.

Faith put her legal pads and pens in her tote bag and stood to leave. "I wanted to say that I thought the services for your dad were amazing, and your eulogy was so…" She shook her head, grimacing when tears filled her eyes. "I'm sorry. I don't mean to make it about me, but losing him has been hard for a lot of us. I hope you know that."

"I do and I appreciate the affection directed his way and mine."

"We loved him, Sam. Everyone loved him. He was so nice to my sisters and me when we started at the USA's office. We were young and green and learning the ropes, and he was endlessly patient with us, answering questions and generally helping us in any way he could."

Sam had never heard that before but certainly wasn't surprised. "That sounds like him."

"I remember the last time I saw him before the shooting. I had a meeting with the chief and when I came out your dad was in the lobby talking to Helen. He was making her laugh, and I just remember thinking what a great guy he was. He had that messenger bag he used to carry…"

"We called it the man purse."

"Yes!" Faith laughed. "Everyone teased him about it, but he wore it like part of his uniform across his chest. He cracked a joke about running late for happy hour at O'Leary's that made us laugh. The next time I saw him, months later, he was in that chair and…" She released a deep breath. "I loved him. I just wanted you to know that."

Sam got up, came around the desk and hugged Faith. "Thank you so much for telling me that."

"I hope you know how much we all wish there was something we could do to make this easier for you."

"I do know, and it's very much appreciated. We've been amazed and overwhelmed by the outpouring of love and support."

"He deserves every bit of respect and admiration we can give him."

"I agree."

Faith took a deep breath, recovered her composure and offered a small smile. "I'll see you in court, if not before."

"I'll be there."

Faith left and Sam gave herself a minute to regroup to prepare to join her team in the conference room. Faith's memories of Skip had touched her deeply. In the years since his injury, it had been difficult at times to remember how he'd been before the shooting. But she could picture the scene Faith had described—Skip making everyone laugh as he took off for an end-of-shift drink with whoever showed up to join him at O'Leary's. On many a day, Sam had been one of the officers bellied up to the bar with him, constantly reminding him not to call her baby girl in front of their colleagues.

He would laugh and remind her that she'd always be his baby girl and anyone who had a problem with that could kiss his ass. If he hadn't fully comprehended how difficult it could be for her in a department in which her father was the number two officer, well, he'd had far more positive qualities than negative. His greatest "sin" in her mind had been wanting to make things easier for her, which was one thing they had argued about. She hadn't wanted any special treatment—ever. But he didn't know any other way to treat her but specially. It had been their one major bone of contention in a lifetime as soul mates.

Her throat tightened as a swell of emotion blindsided her. *Not here. Not in the office. Not now.* Remembering him as the tall, strong, robust, muscular man he'd once been made her burn to find the person who'd taken that and so many other things from him and the rest of them. Faith's mention of the man purse reminded her of days she hadn't thought about in a very long time.

She'd been too busy coping with the new normal that had followed his injury to think of the little things that had made up their routine before the shooting.

Determined to soldier through, to stay focused on the case and the new leads that were continuing to pour in, she gathered up her notes and the personal files she'd kept since the shooting and started for the conference room, stopping short halfway there.

The man purse.

Where was the man purse? Feeling as if her body had been plugged into an electrical outlet, she forced herself to move, to go into the conference room, where the others were reading and talking as Cruz added info to one of the big dry-erase boards they used to detail their cases. Murder boards, they called them. There was now a murder board for her father, complete with photos of Skip before and after the shooting.

They stopped what they were doing when she came in. "Where's my father's…"

Freddie pointed to a box on the floor.

Sam knelt next to it and took the lid off to begin going through the family photos, awards, citations and other items that were taken from his office after he was medically retired. The bag wasn't in there, but why would it be? It had been with him at the time of the shooting. So where was it now?

She stood so quickly she experienced a head rush. "I'll be back."

"Where're you going?"

"I need to go home." She headed for the door, aware they were watching her the way they would a lunatic.

"Sam!" Freddie followed her. "What's going on?"

"I—I'll be back." Had she ever seen the man purse again after that day? She couldn't recall, and the not knowing would make her crazy until she found it. Maybe it was nothing, but until she knew for sure, she had to find it. In her office, she grabbed her keys and ran for the morgue exit, aware of Freddie giving chase.

They pushed through the double doors into the chilly autumn breeze. "What's wrong?"

She'd forgotten her jacket but wouldn't be going back for it. As she jumped into the driver's side of her black BMW, Freddie got in the passenger seat, barely closing the door before she peeled out of the parking lot and pointed the car toward Capitol Hill.

"Tell me. You're freaking me out."

"My dad carried a messenger bag to and from work."

"Okay…"

"Faith said something about it earlier, and I told her we used to call it the man purse."

"That's funny."

"He took a lot of ribbing about that bag."

"So what's that got to do with where we're going?"

"I can't say for certain that I've seen that bag since the shooting."

He gasped. "Whoa."

"Yeah. May be nothing. May be something." She tightened her grip on the wheel, frustrated and furious with herself for not thinking of it sooner.

"Don't, Sam."

"Don't what?"

"Don't be thinking that you should've thought of the bag before now."

"Well, I *fucking* should have! He had it with him every goddamned day!"

"I've asked you not to use the Lord's name in vain."

"Has there ever been a better time for a good *goddamn*?"

"Sam!"

"Well, has there? What if all this time…"

"Stop. Don't go there until you know. There's no point in speculating."

She drove faster than she should have, dodging in and out of traffic, refusing to let anything as ridiculous as traffic keep her from getting to Ninth Street as quickly as she could. Swerving to avoid a car, she nearly took out a woman pushing a stroller in a crosswalk.

"Sam…" Freddie grasped the handle above the passenger window. "Slow down, will you? The last thing we need is more paperwork if you kill someone."

She eased off the accelerator. Slightly. Ten minutes later, they pulled up to the Secret Service checkpoint and were waved through. Outside her dad's house, she jumped from the car and was halfway up the ramp before she heard Freddie's door—and hers—close behind her.

"That's okay. I'll get the doors."

Under normal circumstances, she might've complimented his sarcasm, having taught him everything he knew about the fine art. Today, however, she couldn't spare the time. She burst into the house, scaring the hell out of Celia, who was on the sofa, a pile of cards and papers stacked next to her.

"Sam." Celia rested her hand over her heart. "What is wrong?"

"The man purse."

"The what?"

"The bag Dad carried to work with him. Where is it?"

"I'm not sure what bag you mean."

Sam told herself to calm the fuck down, to be patient, not to snap when she wanted to scream. "The old beat-up leather messenger bag he carried to and from work."

"I've never seen that. Before the shooting, I only saw him after work, not coming and going." Her heart-shaped face lit up with a pale pink blush at the reminder of how they'd dated in secret before Skip was injured. Afterward, she'd volunteered to be his lead caregiver, and later, Sam had learned they'd been dating for quite some time.

Hearing that Celia didn't know where the bag was left Sam feeling deflated after the punch of adrenaline that had brought her rushing home.

"There's some stuff in the attic—"

Sam was halfway up the stairs before Celia finished saying the word *attic*.

Freddie followed. "I'll just go with her."

In the upstairs hallway, she reached for the cord hanging from the ceiling and yanked down the stairs to the attic, charging up the stairs into murky darkness. *Where the fuck is the light?*

Freddie used the flashlight on his phone to illuminate the light.

Sam pulled the string to turn it on and took a look around at stacks of boxes, a steamer trunk and milk crates full of crap that she and her sisters had brought home from college and never touched again. In the far right-hand corner, a stack of boxes drew her attention because they were the same boxes that were used at the MPD to house evidence and files. The sight of them made her feel light-headed.

She bent at the waist, propped her hands on her knees and stared at the two boxes as if they were filled with dynamite. "Those boxes have been sitting here, *in his house*, right under our noses, and I had no idea.

I had no idea." For a brief moment, she feared she was going to be sick.

"It might be nothing, Sam. More of the same."

"Or it might be everything."

"Let's find out." He stepped around her, picked up the stack and carried them down the stairs.

After closing the attic door, Sam followed on legs that felt rubbery and weird, as if someone had kicked them out from under her. *Four years. Four fucking years.* She wanted to punch something or someone.

"Did you find the bag?" Celia asked when they came downstairs with the boxes.

"Not sure yet. Take them into the kitchen." *It was the shock*, she thought, the shock that had followed the shooting and the stroke her father had shortly afterward, that had knocked her off her game. For months, she'd been in a fog of grief, sorrow, fear and rage, helping to care for Skip and trying to hold on to her own job, while her marriage to Peter crumbled and her battles with Stahl intensified. He'd had absolutely no empathy whatsoever for what she and her family were going through after her dad was shot. The enmity between them had escalated significantly during that time.

Those days, weeks and months were a blur, the most stressful period of her life, a time she'd much rather forget than relive. But when she allowed herself to wallow in the memories of that dreadful time, she was able to see how things that would normally be important had slipped off her radar. The delivery of items from the office would barely warrant a notice when keeping him alive and comfortable had consumed their days and nights.

Had those boxes been there all that time, containing the answers they'd needed so badly? Sam was almost afraid to find out.

CHAPTER FOURTEEN

IN THE KITCHEN, Freddie took the cover off the first box and pulled out a stack of files that he placed on the table.

Sam stared at the files. "Why did some of it end up here and the rest is still at HQ?"

"Who knows? Maybe this was more personal stuff?" He took the first file and opened it, sifted through the pages. "These are all his performance evals."

There were files with awards, citations, letters from citizens Skip had helped or befriended that Sam would pore over when she had time, letters from children he met at school visits and pictures they'd drawn of him in his uniform. Something about those pictures got to her as she recalled his joy in interacting with kids and teaching them to respect law enforcement officers. That had been one of his favorite things to do as deputy chief.

They went through every piece of paper in both boxes but didn't find anything new that could help with the case.

The adrenaline drained out of her, leaving Sam exhausted and frustrated.

Celia came into the kitchen. "Anything?"

Sam shook her head. "Where else would that bag be? Any idea?"

"You can go up and check his closet in the bedroom.

Everything is still where he left it, except for the clothes he wore afterward."

Afterward. Life divided between before and after the shooting.

"Let's go check the closet." Sam trudged back up the stairs.

Freddie followed her into her father's bedroom.

Celia had chosen to use one of the other empty bedrooms, so Skip's room was virtually untouched, right down to the framed family photos on the dresser, the red-and-blue-striped comforter he'd bought after Sam's mother moved out and the queen-size bed that had belonged to Skip's mother, Sam's beloved grandma Ella. Angela's daughter had been named for her.

Freddie's hand on her shoulder reminded her of what they'd come in there to do.

She went to the closet, opened the door and was greeted by the faint scent of the Polo cologne her father had worn his entire adult life. The familiar scent nearly brought her to her knees. She gripped the doorknob as she took a quick visual inventory of the closet—dress shirts, polo shirts, dress pants, jeans, uniforms, shoes and a stack of sweaters on the shelf. The man purse was not among the items in the closet.

"Is there anything behind the clothes?"

Sam divided the hanging clothes and looked behind them. "Nope."

Another dead end. Backing away from the closet, she sat on the edge of the bed to collect her thoughts. "When I was a kid, I used to come running in here first thing every morning to wake him up. It didn't matter how early it was, he always got up with me, shushing me so I wouldn't wake everyone else. He would carry me downstairs and make me pancakes. We'd watch the news together while he drank coffee and I had chocolate milk. He'd ask me questions about things we saw on the news and tell me it was important to be aware of what was going on in the world."

Arms crossed, Freddie leaned against the dresser and listened.

"I followed him around like an annoying puppy, but he never acted annoyed."

"He adored you."

She ran a hand over the familiar striped comforter. "Used to drive me crazy when I was first on the job and he'd light up at the sight of me, no matter who else was around. The guys would tease me about being a daddy's girl, and I couldn't even deny it."

"We're going to figure this out, Sam."

She glanced at him. "*When?* When are we going to figure it out?"

"We've already got three things we didn't have before—the statement from Davis, the info about Conklin and the reminder of the messenger bag."

"Which could be anywhere at this point."

"We should check the evidence locker at HQ."

She shook her head. "We've already done that. It wasn't with the stuff from the shooting."

"We weren't looking for the bag then. This time we would be."

He was right. It was worth a shot. "Yeah, I guess so." She opened her phone and called her sister Tracy, who answered on the second ring.

"What's up?"

"I need a favor."

"Sure thing."

"Do you remember the messenger bag Dad used to carry to work?"

"The man purse?"

Sam smiled. "Yeah."

"What about it?"

"One of my colleagues mentioned it earlier today, and I realized I'd forgotten about it—and that no one has seen it since the shooting. So we're looking for it."

"Have you checked the house?"

"Freddie and I just went through the stuff that was sent home from HQ after he retired and his old bedroom and closet, but it's not here."

"What can I do?"

"A more thorough search of the house? I don't want to ask Celia to do it."

"I'm on it, and I'll get Ang to help."

"Thanks, Trace. You're the best."

"We'll do anything we can to help figure out who shot him."

"This is a big help. Thanks."

"I'll keep you posted."

Sam closed the phone, took a deep breath and pushed herself up from the bed, taking a last look at the familiar room that reminded her so profoundly of her dad and the way life had been before the shooting.

Freddie stopped her with a hand to her arm. "Give yourself a minute if you need it."

"I'm okay." She said what he needed to hear, but she wondered if she'd ever truly be okay in a world that no longer included her beloved father.

JOE WAITED UNTIL two o'clock before he went to find Jake in his office, surrounded by four stacks of paper. "How's it going?"

"Slow."

"Want some help?"

"Wouldn't say no to that." Jake gestured to the piles. "These are all the calls to Conklin's extension, one stack for each of the last four years. I'm almost through the first year. Three more to go."

"Give me a year and the number we're looking for."

Jake handed over the pages and a sticky note with Davis's number written on it.

"Just like the old days, huh?"

"You mean back when we were useful?"

Joe laughed, which he wouldn't have thought possible. He'd been up all night, overtaken by the stress of Conklin's possible involvement in Skip's shooting and what he might have to do about it if it turned out to be true. The very idea that Conklin could've kept something like this from them intentionally was so overwhelming and revolting. And if it was true, what else was there? What other secrets had his deputy chief been keeping?

They worked in silence, scrolling through page after page of numbers. It would've been easier to have Archie do a computer search for the number, but Joe was afraid to tip his hand about what they were looking for. So they did it by hand, the old-fashioned way.

Joe broke the long silence. "Remember when we used to be all about the paper?"

"I remember. I like computer searches better."

"Me too, but that's not an option this time." He glanced at Jake. "Did Archie have anything to say about the request?"

"Nope. After he confirmed it with you, he printed it out and handed it over."

The lieutenant who led their IT department was one of the best officers Joe had ever worked with— thorough, competent, discreet and meticulous. "We probably could've told him what we were looking for and let him do it."

"Probably."

While they respected and admired Archie, they didn't trust anyone with a situation this potentially explosive for the department. They went back to scanning the pages.

Another twenty minutes passed before Jake gasped and sat up straighter. "Pay dirt. He called Conklin's extension on the first anniversary of the shooting." He shuffled through another stack of papers. "And the second anniversary. You've got the third year—check the date of the shooting."

Joe sifted to the back of the pile to check the December dates, scanning for the date of the shooting, his heart sinking when he saw the number they were looking for. "And the third anniversary." Joe glanced at Jake. "He called every year, looking for an update on the case." He handed the page over to Jake, who ran a highlighter over the line in question and put it with the other two pages.

Jake blew out a deep breath and sagged into his chair. "What do we do?"

For a full minute, Joe's mind went blank. He couldn't formulate a single thought that made sense.

"Joe?"

"I'd like to consult with Tom Forrester." Bringing in the U.S. Attorney would make this a big deal, and he didn't do that lightly, but what choice did he have?

"Jesus."

Joe stood, handed the stack of paper to his friend. "Keep digging and see if he called any other time. Check the half-year dates and let me know."

"I will. Joe…"

"I know. Believe me, I know." Joe left Jake's office and returned to his own, walking past Helen, who said something that he acknowledged with a raised hand. She'd worked for him long enough to know when not to disturb him. Closing the door, he leaned back against it, reeling from the discoveries that pointed to his deputy and longtime friend having withheld evidence in a case that had struck so close to home.

They'd all come up together—Holland, Farnsworth, Conklin and Malone. The possibility that one of them could betray the others, as well as the department and city they served, was unfathomable. He wanted to go back to yesterday, before he'd known about it. As he lowered himself into his desk chair, the weight of command sat heavier on his shoulders than it ever had before.

Only one choice existed in this situation. He had to report it or he'd be as guilty as Conklin. As he reached for the extension on his desk, a wave of nausea hit him. This call would lead to an epic scandal that would engulf him and his department. As he battled through the nausea, he thought for a second that he might actually vomit.

He put down the phone, opened a bottle of water from the bagged lunch Marti made for him each day and chugged most of it. As he thought of Skip and the horrific ordeal that had followed the shooting, he focused on breathing through the nausea. Every detail of the day Skip was shot remained vivid in Joe's memory. From the first call of "Officer down" to endless hours in the hospital waiting to see if Skip would survive the first twenty-four hours, the first forty-eight hours, the first seventy-two hours, every minute an epic battle. Then he'd had a stroke that had left him further diminished.

Through it all, Skip's resilience and will to live had astounded them all. Joe remembered weeping with

Marti over what'd happened to their dear friend, the
fear of what could happen to any of them who wore
the uniform and the heartbreak of it all. And now this.
Confirming that Conklin had known something he
hadn't shared with the rest of them broke Joe's heart
all over again.

Sometimes doing the right thing hurt. This was one
of those times.

He picked up the phone, requested an outside line
and put through the call to Forrester's office. "This is
Chief Farnsworth with the MPD. I need to see U.S. Attorney Forrester ASAP."

ON THE WAY back to HQ from Ninth Street, Sam took
a call from Dispatch.

"Holland."

"Lieutenant, we have a report of one DOA on
12th Street. Witnesses state that the victim was hit by
a stray bullet."

"Detective Cruz and I will respond." Sam fumed at
another delay. Four years of delays, distractions and
dead ends. What was one more on top of hundreds of
others? She directed the car toward 12th and noted the
flashing lights from the Patrol cars that had already
arrived on the scene.

The closest she could get was a block from the activity, so she double-parked and put on the hazards
before getting out of the car. She flashed her badge to
the crowd gathered on the sidewalk. "Let us through."
Sam wanted to ask the gawkers if they'd want someone staring at their dead body on a sidewalk if this had
happened to them.

A few of them seemed to recognize her, and a ripple of
gasps went through the crowd. When one of the women

would've stopped her to say something, Sam's fierce scowl had her thinking better of it. They pushed through the crowd to where a young man in a bloodied shirt and tie lay on the sidewalk. Upon a quick look, Sam could tell he'd been extremely handsome, and the ring on his left hand indicated he was married. The senselessness of it struck her hard, as it always did, knowing someone's world would be shattered by the loss of this young man.

"What do we know?" Sam glanced up at the male Patrol officer, whom she did not know.

Reading from a notebook, the officer recited the facts. "Patrick Connolly, aged thirty-one, an agent with the DEA, according to a badge found in his pocket." He offered the man's home address, which he had found on his driver's license.

"Sam." A familiar male voice had her turning to face Darren Tabor, who stared down at the body with a stricken look on his face. "I work with his wife. They... they just got married a few months ago."

She nodded to Freddie, silently asking him to see to Darren.

"Come on, Darren." Freddie led him away from the body.

"Let's get these people out of here," Sam said to the Patrol officer. "And have you called the ME?"

"Yes, ma'am. She's on her way."

Sam took off her jacket and placed it over the dead man's face. "If I see pictures of this man anywhere online, I'll hunt you down and throw your asses in jail." She said that loud enough for everyone around her to hear. "He's someone's husband and son. Show some respect and back off."

The crowd backed away, leaving Sam alone with the dead man until Lindsey showed up a few minutes later.

"Young and newly married," Sam told her.

"Ah, damn. What happened?"

"Caught a stray bullet."

"What the hell are people doing firing a gun in a crowded area in the middle of the day?"

"If I had the answer to that question, we'd probably be out of business." Sam looked around at the staggering array of places a bullet could've come from. "It'll be a hell of a job figuring out where the bullet originated." They would analyze the angle of entry and work backward from there.

"Crime Scene is on the way, Lieutenant," the Patrol officer said.

"Let's not move him until they get here," Sam said to Lindsey.

"Right." Lindsey raised the jacket to view his face, her eyes softening with emotion. "His poor wife."

Sam took a deep breath and released it slowly. "I've got to go find her."

"I don't envy you that."

"Someone's got to do it." Sam tried to be cavalier about what would be a dreadful task, but her heart ached at the thought of destroying the life of a woman who'd thought she had things figured out. In one second, everything changed. "I'll see you back at the house."

She went to find Freddie and Darren, who were standing off to the side of the fray. A nearby shop owner had given Darren a bottle of cold water. Sam had never seen the young reporter look so pale or freaked out. Like her, he saw a lot of crazy shit in the course of a day, and this had clearly rattled him.

"Can you take me to the wife?"

Darren nodded. "Yeah."

To Freddie, she said, "Start a canvass. Talk to everyone who was on the street and find out everything you can about where the bullet came from. Get the others here to help you."

"Will do."

"Let's go, Darren." She led him to her car.

Darren got into the passenger seat. "I…I'm not sure I can do this. She's the nicest person, and she was so happy with him. I went to the wedding."

"What's her name?"

"It's Veronica, but we call her Roni."

"What does she do at the *Star*?"

"She's our obituary writer." He blew out a deep breath. "How could this have happened?"

"I ask myself that question every day as I encounter one tragic death after another."

"I don't know how you do it."

"Someone's gotta do it. May as well be me."

They were silent on the ride to the K Street office of the *Washington Star*. Darren directed her to a guest parking lot and flashed his ID to building security. "She's with me." The officer waved her through after Sam showed him her badge. They took the elevator to the third floor.

Sam had never seen the *Star* newsroom before and took a quick look around at a beehive of activity as she followed Darren down a long corridor of offices behind glass walls that afforded zero privacy to the people inside. That was probably strategic, so their employer could keep an eye on them. People stopped what they were doing to gawk at her as she went by.

God, she hated that goldfish feeling and yearned for the days when she'd been able to move freely around the city without attracting attention everywhere she went. She was so proud of her vice president husband, but his higher profile had led to hers being raised as well, and that made things more difficult for her on the job. Not that she'd ever tell him that. He worried enough about her as it was.

Darren stopped outside an office and used his chin to tell Sam this was the one.

A dark-haired woman faced away from the door, earbuds in as she worked on a laptop.

Darren opened the door. "Hey, Roni." He spoke loudly enough to be heard over the music.

She turned, tugged out one of the earbuds and smiled. "Hey. What's up?"

Sam stepped into view and watched as the woman immediately recognized her.

"Oh my God! You're here! In our office!" She got up and came around the desk, hand outstretched to shake Sam's. "Darren speaks so highly of you. How'd he get you to come in? He says you play hard to get with him."

Sam wanted to die over what she had to do to this poor, sweet woman. "Could we talk for a second?"

CHAPTER FIFTEEN

RONI GLANCED AT DARREN, her brows furrowing. Perhaps something she saw in his stricken expression alerted her to impending doom. She took a step back and shook her head. "No. Please…"

"Roni…"

She began to cry and put her hands over her ears.

Darren closed the office door behind them.

"I'm so sorry to have to tell you that Patrick was shot and killed a short time ago." Sam said the words quickly, the way she'd learned to do at times like this, so as not to drag out the process.

She would never forget the sound of Roni's heart-broken scream. It pierced her heart and left her bleeding inside for a woman she'd never met, for a couple whose life together had ended in the most tragic way possible.

Darren rushed forward to catch Roni when she would've collapsed and held her as she cried hysterically.

"Not my Patrick. He's got a desk job! He said this would never happen. He promised me…"

"He was hit by a stray bullet while walking on 12th Street," Sam said. "We don't believe he was targeted, but we don't know that for sure yet."

"What am I supposed to do?" She shook with sobs. "I don't know what to do, Darren."

"Is there a family member we could call for you?" Sam asked her.

"Her sister is local." Darren helped Roni into her desk chair, where only a few minutes ago she'd sat doing her job, unaware that life as she knew it was over. "I'll call Rebecca for you, Roni. Would that be okay?"

She nodded and handed him her phone. "She's on my favorites."

Standing next to Darren, Sam saw that Patrick's name was at the top of Roni's list of favorites. That small detail broke Sam's heart all over again.

He placed the call to her sister and told her the news. The sister screamed so loudly that Darren held the phone away from his ear. Outside the office, Sam noticed a crowd had formed, probably tuning in to the disaster unfolding for one of their colleagues.

"I want to see him." Roni turned her shattered gaze toward Sam. "Can I see him?"

"I'll arrange for that." She sent a text to Lindsey asking to be notified when the victim had been moved to the morgue and that the wife wanted to see him.

Thirty minutes, Lindsey replied.

"Have the sister meet us at HQ," Sam said to Darren, who conveyed the information to Roni's sister. "I can take you to see Patrick now."

Roni shook her head. "He can't be dead. He just can't be."

"I'm so, so sorry." Sometimes Sam tried to imagine what it would be like to receive this kind of news about her own husband, but even after the conversation they'd had last night, she couldn't bear to let her mind go there. She just couldn't. She had no idea how people survived this sort of thing, how they managed to go on, to put shattered lives back together again. People like Roni were the ones she never forgot, the ones she wanted to help with the new support group. "Darren, go tell your colleagues what's happened and ask for some space so we can get her out of here."

He ducked outside to share the news.

Sam watched as shock rippled through the crowd, which began to disperse after Darren asked them to move along.

Roni had her arms wrapped around her body as she rocked back and forth, clearly in deep shock. After Sam took her to see Patrick, they would have to determine if Roni was in need of medical attention.

"Are you able to walk?"

"I…I think so."

God bless her. Sam would have to be carted out on a stretcher.

Darren helped Roni into her coat and put an arm around her to escort her to the elevator, walking her past stunned coworkers. The formerly buzzing newsroom had gone completely silent.

Sam grabbed the woman's purse, phone and keys from the credenza next to her desk and followed them, keeping her head down to avoid eye contact with curious bystanders.

The three of them rode the elevator to the lobby. Darren guided Roni to Sam's car and settled her in the passenger seat before belting her in.

It had been, Sam realized, a full hour since she'd given a thought to her father's death or the effort to find his killer. Murder had a way of making a day go sideways. The victim of the moment—and their family— took precedence over everything, even her own family at times.

As they drove to HQ, Roni continued to weep softly,

her sniffles the only sound in the car. Traffic made the trip longer than it should've been, and by the time they pulled up to the morgue entrance, the ME truck was parked outside, indicating Lindsey had returned with Patrick's body.

Sam met Darren's gaze in the rearview mirror and saw tears in his eyes.

"Do you want to wait for your sister to arrive?" Sam asked.

Roni shook her head. "I want to see Patrick."

They helped her inside and stepped into the cold, antiseptic-smelling morgue, where Lindsey waited for them with the body on a table, covered by a sheet.

"Roni, this is Dr. Lindsey McNamara, the medical examiner. Lindsey, this is Roni Connolly."

"I'm so very sorry for your loss." Lindsey's green eyes brimmed with the compassion that made her so damned good at her dreadful job.

Roni stared at the body on the table as she trembled uncontrollably.

Lindsey lifted the sheet.

Roni screamed, her knees buckled, and only Darren's arms around her kept her from collapsing. "Patrick! Oh God... *No. Patrick.*" She sobbed uncontrollably and launched herself at the body, lying on top of him.

Sam's heart broke for her.

Darren wiped away tears.

Lindsey came around the table to comfort Roni.

"Patrick." Roni's moans echoed through the room.

Sam's phone rang, and she ignored it. Only when it rang a second time did she excuse herself to take the call from Freddie. Stepping through the automatic doors, she said, "What's up?"

"We got the guys." He sounded breathless, as if

he'd been running. "They were fighting over a woman across the street, one of them pulled a gun on the other. The second one lunged, and the gun discharged with the bullet that killed Patrick Connolly."

"Do we know them?" Drained by yet another killing that would ruin multiple lives, sometimes Sam feared becoming numb to it all, of getting to the point where she had no reaction whatsoever to yet another life ended prematurely.

"The one with the gun has a lengthy sheet."

"Somehow, I knew you were going to say that." She closed her eyes and leaned against the cinder block wall, the sound of Roni's wails audible through the glass doors.

A Patrol officer approached with a woman who was almost as hysterical as Roni. The sister, Sam thought. "I gotta go," Sam said to Freddie. "I'll see you back here."

"We're on our way in."

Sam closed the phone. "Rebecca?"

The woman nodded.

"I'm Lieutenant Holland."

"I know who you are."

"Would you like me to take you in to see your sister?"

"Is he... Is Patrick..."

"His body is here, yes."

She covered her mouth as tears flooded her eyes and spilled down her cheeks. "How could this have happened? My God. He was *thirty-one* and such a *good* man."

"I'm so sorry for your loss."

"What is she supposed to do now? They were so in love. They just got married." She looked up at Sam. "I don't know what to say to her."

"Just be there for her. That's what she needs right now."

Nodding, she wiped her tears and tried to pull herself together. When she seemed as ready as she would be, Sam escorted her into the morgue, where she stopped short at the sight of Roni lying over Patrick's body. Afraid that Rebecca would faint, Sam stayed close to her, just in case.

Darren stood next to Roni, rubbing her back, trying to offer whatever comfort he could while Lindsey hung back to give Roni the space she needed.

"Roni," Sam said. "Rebecca is here."

Roni stood upright and launched herself at her sister, the two of them sobbing hysterically.

Sam tipped her head at Darren, and he came with her to the hallway. "We got the guy with the gun."

"Already?"

Sam filled him in on what Freddie had told her. "Sometimes it's easy." Rarely, but it did happen.

"You gotta be kidding me. So a good and decent man is dead because two idiots were fighting over a woman?"

"That's the gist."

"How does Roni begin to make sense of this?"

"It'll never make sense to her."

Darren sighed and leaned back against the wall. That he wasn't jumping on the exclusive she'd just handed him said a lot about how deeply the day's events had affected him. "You and me, we see a lot of crazy shit on our jobs."

"We do."

"This…"

"I know." Patrick Connolly's murder was right up there with the drive-by shootings, orchestrated by a worthless piece of shit with an ax to grind against the city that had fired him from a low-level job.

"I suppose I should get back to the office to write about this." He made no move to leave. "Their wedding… One of the best I've been to. They were truly happy. That was obvious to everyone who knew them."

"I'm really sorry this happened to your friends."

"So am I. Will you email me the report?"

"As soon as I have it."

Together, they went back into the morgue to let Roni know that they'd gotten the guy who'd fired the gun. The news barely seemed to register with her. What did it matter? Her beloved husband was still dead. Darren hugged Roni, told her he would check on her later and then left to go write the story of his friend's murder.

Sam waited until the sisters departed before she trudged to the pit, which was deserted because her team had been called out to work on the Connolly case. She went into the conference room, where papers and files were spread out on the table. The murder board had been updated, and she took a closer look to see if there was anything she didn't already know.

There wasn't.

Another day, more delays and distractions, not that she would qualify Patrick Connolly's murder as a distraction, but it had taken her team off her father's case yet again.

"Hey," Captain Malone said as he stepped into the conference room and closed the door. "What happened on 12th?"

Sam filled him in on the details she knew thus far.

He shook his head in disbelief. "Just when I think I've heard everything."

"By all accounts, a really good guy. Newly married."

Malone grimaced. "Taken out by a scumbag who probably should've been locked up years ago."

"Probably." Sam glanced at the murder board and then at the captain. "Anything new?"

"We found proof that your guy Davis called Conklin every year on the anniversary of the shooting."

Sam grasped one of the chairs for support. "I don't understand this."

"Neither do we. The chief has an appointment with Tom Forrester tomorrow morning."

"I feel sick."

"I know that feeling."

Sam sat because she wasn't sure she could remain standing. "He was my dad's friend. Was it all a big lie?"

"I don't know, but we're going to find out."

She thought of the evidence locker that needed to be searched for her dad's messenger bag. "Faith said something that reminded me of the leather messenger bag that he carried back and forth to work every day. I hadn't thought of that bag in years, since before the shooting. I can't find it at the house. I was going to search the evidence locker for it."

"Want some help?"

"You remember the bag?"

"The man purse?" He smiled. "Of course I do."

"Why didn't I ever think to ask what'd become of it before now?"

"Sam, come on… Give yourself a break. Don't you remember what those first weeks were like?"

"Not really. It's kind of a blur." She remembered fear and heartache and stress over the problems she'd encountered with Peter and Stahl at that time, neither of whom had had an ounce of empathy after the trauma of her father's shooting. When Peter accused her of spending too much time with her recently paralyzed father, that was when she'd moved out of the home she'd shared with him and back into her childhood home to help care for her father. She'd stayed there until right before she married Nick.

"I remember every chilling, horrifying, agonizing detail, and the last thing on any of our minds was what had become of the man purse." Malone opened the door. "Let's go take a look."

Sam got up to follow him, but they were waylaid by the arrival of FBI Special Agent in Charge Avery Hill, who was visibly rattled.

"Is it true? Pat Connolly was killed?"

"Yes," Sam said. "By a stray bullet fired by a career criminal arguing with another man over a woman across the street."

Hill exhaled and bent at the waist, hands on his knees. "Oh my God."

"You knew him?"

Without looking up, Hill nodded. "He interned with me out of grad school. I helped him get the job at the DEA. He was *brilliant*. One of the best up-and-coming federal agents I ever worked with. He was going to do big things."

Lieutenant Archelotta came into the pit, looking pale and shocked. "Pat Connolly was murdered?"

"You knew him too?" Sam asked.

"Yeah. He was in IT at the DEA. We worked together several times, and I knew him also through an IT association for LEOs." He used the acronym for law enforcement officers. "He was…"

"Brilliant," Avery said again.

"Indeed," Archie said. "I can't believe it. And he just got married."

"His wife was here," Sam said. "It was dreadful."

Archie groaned. "Ugh."

They were still standing there when Freddie, Cameron and Jeannie came into the pit, looking tired and spent.

"The shooter is in Booking," Freddie said.

"Thanks for a great job, all of you," Sam said.

"We had some good help from people who saw it go down," Cameron said.

"We'll need to make a statement to the press," Malone said to Sam. "Can you do that and then I'll meet you in the locker?"

"Yeah, okay." She conferred with Freddie, wrote down the pertinent info and scanned the rap sheet that Jeannie printed out, detailing the lengthy criminal record of the man charged with shooting Connolly. "What the hell was this guy still doing on the streets?"

"That's a very good question." Cameron sounded frustrated. "And now an innocent guy is dead. It's so fucking *wrong*."

Sam had never heard the überprofessional Green drop an f-bomb. "Yes, it is, but at least we got swift justice for his family."

"Cold comfort," Freddie said.

"Let's call it a day here and pick up my dad's case in the morning." Sam had a feeling she wouldn't get much out of them at this point in the day. "Thanks for your good work on behalf of Agent Connolly." While they prepared to leave, she headed for the lobby to make a statement to the press. When they saw her coming, they snapped to attention. Before they could begin shouting questions at her, Sam stepped up to the podium.

"At just after two thirty eastern time today, thirty-one-year-old Drug Enforcement Administration Agent

Patrick Connolly was killed instantly by a bullet discharged from a weapon fired during an altercation between two men. Agent Connolly, who was on the sidewalk across the street, was shot in the chest. James Zander, who is well-known to the MPD and has a lengthy record, was arrested a short time later by Homicide detectives who credit eyewitnesses for assisting in the speedy resolution of this case. Mr. Zander will be charged with one count of felony murder, and I expect that additional gun charges will be filed by the U.S. Attorney. Agent Connolly was newly married and leaves his wife, Veronica. He was described by colleagues as brilliant in the area of information technology as it pertains to criminal investigations. That's all I have at this time."

She ignored their shouted questions as she turned to go back inside to meet Malone in the evidence locker, where he was already working.

"This is everything from that December." He gestured to a shelf in the vast storage area where he'd removed several boxes and plastic tubs from the shelf. "How'd the statement go?"

"Fine."

"Another tough one, huh?"

"They're all tough, but some are worse than others, such as the well-respected and newly married DEA agent who was in the wrong place at the wrong time."

"You want to pick this up tomorrow?"

"No, I'd like to get it done."

They spent two hours going through every piece of evidence collected during the month of her father's shooting, as well as the items from the month after, but there was no sign of the bag. "Where would it be?" Sam wanted to punch something.

"Tomorrow, you should interview the first responders who were on the scene. One of them might remember seeing it."

"We'll start there. Thanks for the help in here."

They put the room back to rights before heading out. When she was in the car, Sam placed a call to Nick, who answered on the second ring.

"Hey, babe."

The sound of his voice filled her with relief. "Are you still at work?"

"Yep. You?"

"Just leaving. Are you heading home anytime soon?"

"Not quite yet." He sounded tired and stressed.

"You mind if I stop by?"

"Is that a rhetorical question?"

Sam smiled. He was so damned sweet. "I don't want to interrupt world domination or anything."

"Please come and interrupt me. I just got out of a budget meeting that made my head hurt and gave me heartburn. No end in sight for this continuing resolution that's running the government at the moment."

"I don't know what that means, and I don't want to know, but I'm sorry about the headache and the heartburn. I'm on my way."

"I'll be here."

CHAPTER SIXTEEN

SAM LEFT HQ and directed the car through rush-hour traffic as she made her way to Pennsylvania Avenue to go to her husband's office at the White House. And yes, that sentence still made her want to giggle madly nearly a year after he'd accepted the president's invitation to be his new vice president. They'd had no idea then the many changes his new role would bring to their lives, primarily the security that surrounded Nick and Scotty at all times.

That had been quite an adjustment, to say the least, not to mention that it took thirty minutes for Nick to leave the house. He hated that, and so did she. They both missed the ability to be spontaneous, to come and go as they pleased, to operate in the anonymity people took for granted until they lost it forever.

At the White House gate, she was waved through. After all, she was the second lady—another thought that still made her laugh. She was probably the worst second lady in history, but she was also considered a trendsetter for continuing in her job, without Secret Service protection, while her husband was in office.

Coming here was almost routine at this point. Underline the word *almost*. It would always be surreal to swing by the White House to see her husband during his workday. She even had her own parking space. Hilarious. Inside the West Wing, she made her way to

Nick's office, nodding at people who recognized her and said, "Hello, Mrs. Cappuano," as she went by. Here, she was Mrs. Cappuano, and that was fine with her when not that long ago she would've chafed at being Mrs. Anything. She'd never changed her name after she married Peter, a topic that had caused conflict between them, but then again, everything had caused conflict between them.

She'd happily changed her legal name when she married Nick, probably because she knew this marriage was forever whereas the first time around had been a mess from the get-go. Marrying Peter when she'd been pining for Nick had been among the biggest mistakes of her life. And then when she'd learned that the reason she'd never seen Nick again was because Peter hadn't given her his messages…

God, she couldn't think about that without her blood boiling, even after all the time she'd been back together with Nick. She'd never forgive Peter for what he'd denied her and Nick with his lies and deceit. He was gone now, a victim of murder at the hands of someone who'd been trying to discredit her and Nick, and while she was sad for the way his life had ended, she remained bitter about the hell he'd put her—and Nick—through.

Outside Nick's office, one of the admins—Sam could never remember all their names—smiled and told her to go on in. "He's expecting you."

Three little words that made her heart flutter with anticipation, knowing he was on the other side of the door and that he'd taken the time to tell his staff she was coming. She opened the door and stepped inside.

He was behind the big desk that had belonged to another vice president—she forgot which one—and looked up at her, smiling.

God, that smile, that face, those eyes... She loved him unreasonably.

He got up and came around the desk, holding out his arms to her.

She went to him, let him wrap her up in his warm, loving embrace and immediately felt better.

"This is a nice surprise." He kissed the top of her head. "To what do I owe the pleasure of a visit?"

"I needed this." She held on tighter, and so did he.

"I'm always happy to provide this."

They stood that way, wrapped up in each other, for a long time before he guided her to the sofa and brought her down on his lap. "What's wrong? Besides the obvious, of course."

"Tough homicide today. A newly married, highly respected DEA agent cut down by a stray bullet fired during an argument across the street."

"Ah, God. That's awful."

"It was awful. The poor wife. She works with Darren, so he took me to her." Sam shook her head. Recalling Roni's awful shock and grief was unbearable. "It was bad."

"I'm so sorry you had to deal with that so soon after your own shocking loss."

"It's not about me."

"They're all about you, Sam. You take them all personally, which makes you damned good at your job."

"I guess. It's just so fucking sad. I kept thinking that she had her whole life figured out, and then it's just gone in the blink of an eye." She glanced at him. "Even though we played worst-case scenario last night, I don't know how I would ever deal with that if it happened to me."

"It won't."

"Please don't make promises you can't keep."

"I never do. Kiss me."

She knew he was trying to change the subject, to take her mind off the pervasive sadness, but she never said no to kissing him. Her lips connected with his, which was all it took to make her want much more than she was going to get while they were in his office. He leaned his forehead against hers, stroking his fingers through her hair and generally making everything that was wrong in her world right again just by caring so much.

"I'm sorry you're hurting, babe."

"Lots of people are hurting."

"I'm sorry *you* are hurting."

"I've been talking to Dr. Trulo about maybe doing something for people like the woman today, something to support them more than we do now."

"Like what?"

"A support group, maybe, for the victims that're left behind when someone is murdered."

"That'd be amazing."

"He suggested I do it as both the Homicide squad commander and as second lady. He thought it might become a national movement if I lend my lofty title to it. What would you think of that?"

"I think that's a fantastic idea on his part—and yours."

"It's in the earliest stages, but this thing today brought home again how badly it's needed. I took her to see her husband at the morgue, and in most cases, I wouldn't see her again until the case goes to trial. The thought of being able to do something more for her and so many others is very appealing to me."

"I love it. You'd help a lot of people even more than you already do with something like this."

"Perhaps I'd also help myself at the same time."

"No doubt." He guided her head to his shoulder. "I know you have to be missing him something fierce."

"I am but working on his case again is helping. We're actually making a little headway."

"Wouldn't it be something…"

"Yes, it would."

"What's the latest with Conklin?"

"Farnsworth and Malone are investigating that personally and were able to prove that Davis called Conklin every year on the anniversary of my father's shooting."

"Oh my God."

"Farnsworth is taking it right to Tom Forrester."

"Holy crap."

"What I don't get is why he would keep that from the rest of us. I can't stop asking *why*."

"It's possible the answer to that question might be the break you've been waiting for."

"Maybe, but at what cost? You know? What was Conklin involved with that was more important than getting justice for my dad?"

"If anyone can figure out the answer to that question, you can."

"It's going to come down to money, power or sex. If you're looking for motive in most crimes, it usually involves one of those three things. Part of me doesn't want to know."

"I can understand that."

"I should go so you can get back to work and finish up."

"I can take work home with me. I've had enough of this place today."

"Is everything okay?"

"The budget crap is draining."

"And? What else?"

His deep sigh put her on immediate alert. "There're apparently some major rumblings from the other side of the aisle about us taking in two kids who'll require Secret Service protection at taxpayer expense."

"*Seriously?* What if we'd had twins of our own when you were in office?"

"From what I hear, that would be viewed differently than volunteering to take in other people's children."

"That's such bullshit. We have the right to expand our family if we choose to."

"And that's exactly what I told Terry to pass along to those who have objections."

"How big of a deal is this going to be?"

"We've had reporters from CNN, NBC, the *Washington Post* and the *New York Times* call for statements today."

Sam experienced a sinking feeling at realizing it would be a very big deal with those outlets nosing around. "What did you tell them?"

"The same thing you just said—that we have the right to expand our family at any time, even when I'm in office, and that we also have the right to have our family protected from people who'd do us harm simply because of the office I hold. Terry thinks it's going to be a bit of a *thing*."

"I'm sorry."

"For what? You haven't done anything."

"I brought home two kids without a thought as to what it could mean for all of us."

"And I'd certainly hope if you had it to do over again, you'd do exactly the same thing despite any heartburn it might cause us. As I've said repeatedly—our heartburn is nothing compared to their heartache."

"I love you so much, Nick. All the time, but the way you've gone to bat for two kids who aren't yours makes me love you even more than I already did."

"Same goes, babe. I love the way you saw them and had to help. I'll never regret stepping up for them."

"Even if there's a massive shitstorm?"

"Even then. *Especially* then." He kissed her again. "Let's get the hell out of here and go home to our family."

HOURS LATER, AFTER spending quality time with the kids, which included lasagna for dinner and a competitive game of Candy Land that Scotty had won, baths, bedtime stories and a few tears from two little ones, who were still missing their beloved parents, Sam curled up to Nick in bed, exhausted and drained.

He caressed her arm as she breathed in the familiar scent of him, the scent of home. "I used to dream about having what we do now," he said. "A family to call my own. There's nothing else quite like it."

"No, there really isn't. I just worry about what'll happen when Elijah finishes school."

"You want my prediction?"

Sam eyed him with surprise. "You have one?"

"Babe, you know me. I'm always thinking ten steps ahead, and my guess is by the time he graduates, the kids will be so settled with us, he wouldn't dream of disrupting them. And besides, he's going to be a twenty-two-year-old recent college grad. What's he going to do with two seven-year-olds?"

"Don't forget that recent college grad will have billions at his disposal. He could pay for whatever help he needs."

"Granted, but he won't want to disrupt them—again. They're not going anywhere, Samantha. If we want them, and I think we both agree that we do, they'll be with us until they leave home."

"I'm afraid to hope for that, only to be disappointed when he comes to collect them. What if he does want them when he graduates? Maybe we should talk to him about that at some point."

He sighed. "Probably."

"So how big of a shitstorm are we looking at over the Secret Service issue?"

"Trevor just texted that he had thirty inquiries about it today alone," Nick said, referring to his communications director.

"Damn it."

"Don't worry about. We'll handle it, and it'll blow over like everything always does."

"I thought the outpouring of sympathy for the loss of my dad would last a little longer than it did."

"I'm sorry if something to do with my job is cutting short the mourning for him. You know I'd never want that."

"It's okay."

"I'm sorry you're sad tonight."

"For people I don't even know."

"It's a very sad thing."

"Yeah, for sure." As she wallowed in the loving embrace of her beloved husband, Sam thought of Roni and ached for her.

THE NEXT MORNING, Joe Farnsworth arrived ten minutes early for his eight o'clock appointment with Tom

Forrester. The admin offered him coffee, which Joe gratefully accepted. He'd had another sleepless night as his mind raced with the potential implications of what he'd come to discuss with Forrester.

If he allowed himself to delve too deeply into the why or how of Conklin's actions, he would lose his mind. That his closest aid and longtime friend could've kept something like this out of the official reporting of Skip's shooting and then continued to hide it for four years… The job of chief often overwhelmed him, but few things had ever hit him as hard as this had.

Forrester came rolling in with several aides in tow. "Hey, Joe," he said in a thick New York accent. "Come on in."

Joe followed Forrester and the others into the office.

"Have a seat." Tall and confident, Forrester had silver hair and sharp blue eyes. He was among the more competent U.S. Attorneys Joe had worked with in his long career. "What can I do for you, Chief?"

Joe eyed the young, hungry aides who were probably recent law school graduates on their way up the ladder. "I need to speak to you in private."

Forrester cast a glance at the others, and they got up to leave the room.

"What's going on?"

"I'm not entirely sure." Joe told the USA about what they'd uncovered during a new look at Skip's case.

Seeming shocked, Forrester sat back in his chair. "This guy Davis, he's credible?"

"By all accounts, a stand-up sort of guy. He's called Conklin every year on the anniversary of the shooting." Joe laid the highlighted pages on the desk, showing the calls to Conklin's line.

"What would Conklin stand to gain by keeping this quiet?"

"I have no idea. I've spent two sleepless nights wondering that myself."

"Do you think he knows who shot Skip?"

"I don't know that either. He claims he was nowhere near the scene of the shooting that day. Davis says otherwise."

"Have you spoken to everyone who was on the scene of the shooting? Every first responder?"

"Not yet."

"Let's do that. Let's find someone else who can put Conklin at the scene."

"We'll get on that today." Joe paused before asking the question that filled him with dread. "What do you see happening here?"

"If he had this information for four years and didn't share it with anyone, at the very least we'll charge him with impeding an investigation."

"Could I ask a favor?"

"You can ask."

"May I request that you handle this personally for now?"

"I'll handle it personally for as long as I can. If there's another witness able to put him at the scene, I'm going to want the investigation turned over to the FBI to keep it clean for you and your department. Agreed?"

As much as it rankled to turn anything over to the FBI, Joe knew he had no choice in this case. "Agreed. I'll put some people on it today and get back to you."

"Keep Lieutenant Holland far away from this, Joe. If this turns out to be something, the last thing we'll need is a massive conflict of interest."

"Understood. Captain Jake Malone will handle it personally."

"Great. I'll wait to hear from you."

Joe stood and reached across the desk to shake Forrester's hand. "Appreciate your time on this."

"For what it's worth, I'm sorry you're dealing with this on top of the loss of a close friend."

"It's been a hell of a week."

"My condolences. Skip was one of the good guys."

"Indeed he was. We'll miss him, and we're determined to finally get justice for him, no matter where it may lead."

"Understood. Keep me posted."

"Will do."

Joe left the USA's office and decided to make another stop on his way back to HQ. He'd thought about this during the night and had concluded that this was a conversation he needed to have, even if it was a risk. Retired Captain Kenneth Wallack had come up through the ranks with him, Skip, Conklin and Malone. They'd attended the academy together and had known each other for decades.

Recently, Wallack, a decorated sharpshooter, had been kidnapped by his former stepson and forced at gunpoint to kill innocent people in the drive-by shootings. The stepson had threatened to rape and kill Wallack's new wife, and Wallack had done what he had to in order to protect her.

Joe hadn't spoken to Wallack personally since then, but others had seen him. By all accounts, Wallack was a broken man in the aftermath of killing six innocent people, including a young girl. Wallack was another close friend of Conklin's and for two weeks after Wallack's wife reported him missing to Conklin, the deputy chief had sat on the info while he investigated personally. His excuse then had been that he feared Wallack, a recovering alcoholic, had fallen off the wagon, and he'd held the info in an effort to protect a decorated officer.

Joe had called bullshit on that and had suspended Conklin for a week. In the nearly four years Conklin had been his top deputy, that had been the only time he'd ever questioned his judgment or his integrity. Had he been a fool to trust Conklin for all these years? He liked to think he was a good judge of character, and until the Wallack incident, Conklin had never put off any vibes that he couldn't be trusted. Granted, Joe didn't trust Conklin on the same level he'd trusted Skip and Jake, but he had put considerable faith in Conklin as the department's second in command.

Joe had come up through the ranks with his eye always on the top job, and he loved being chief. Most of the time. The men and women of the Metro PD did a difficult, often dangerous job that most people weren't equipped to do. Being part of the brother-and-sisterhood that made up the thin blue line had been the second greatest honor of Joe's life, second only to being Marti's husband. The possibility that his number two officer and longtime friend could be crooked or corrupt made Joe sick—physically and emotionally.

Wallack lived with his wife, Leslie, on Montana Avenue. Joe found a parking space a block away and walked the short distance to the clapboard townhouse. He went up the stairs and rang the bell.

Looking tired and frazzled, Leslie answered the door. Upon quick glance, he deduced she was in her late fifties or early sixties, with graying blond hair and dark circles under hazel eyes. Joe had met her a couple of times at retiree events but didn't know her well. He only knew that after a difficult first marriage, Wallack was happy with her. Leslie's expression conveyed surprise to find the chief on her doorstep.

She opened the storm door.

"Sorry to drop by unannounced. I wondered if Kenny might be up for a visit."

"I'm sure he'd love to see you, but..." When she looked up at him, tears made her eyes shiny. "He's so ashamed. I worry all the time that he's not going to be able to live with it."

Joe stepped into the house. "He's been seeing Dr. Trulo?"

"Almost daily. He's been so good to both of us. So many people have been. I just don't know if it'll be enough for Kenny. He's tortured by nightmares, and he cries a lot."

"I'm not here to make anything worse."

"I understand, and he'll be glad to see you. He always speaks so highly of you and Conky and the others." She tipped her head toward the back of the townhouse. "Come on back." Leslie led him to the back of the deep townhouse, where a sunny screen porch looked out over a small, well-kept yard. "Kenny, Joe Farnsworth is here to see you."

Wallack, who was seated in a recliner with a blanket over his lap, stood and turned to them.

Joe bit back a gasp at the sight of Wallack's ravaged face. He barely recognized the man he'd known for over thirty years. Forcing himself to rally and hide the shock, Joe extended his hand to Kenny. "Good to see you."

Kenny shook his hand. "You too. Have a seat." He gestured to the other recliner.

"Can I get you anything, Joe?" Leslie asked.

"No, thank you."

"I'll leave you two to catch up."

Kenny eyed him warily. "This is a nice surprise."

"I'm sorry I haven't been by before now."

"I don't blame you for staying away. I can't imagine the trouble I've caused for you and the others."

"You haven't caused us trouble, Kenny. You were kidnapped and forced at gunpoint to do what you did. No one blames you."

"Well, they fucking oughta." Wallack blinked back tears.

"No one blames you. They blame Curtis." Wallack's former stepson had been the mastermind of the shooting spree. "This was his doing, not yours."

Wallack shrugged. "So I try to tell myself."

"You were protecting your wife."

"She's the only one who's ever truly had my back, you know? How could I let that monster do what he said he'd do to her? And he would've done it. I have no doubt about that. I've known that son of a bitch for a lot of years. I know what he's capable of."

"I get it. We all get it."

"You think Vanessa Marchand's daddy gets it?" The six-year-old had been gunned down while leaving a playground near her home.

"Mr. Marchand knows who was behind his daughter's killing, and he blames Curtis." Joe cleared his throat, determined to stick to the agenda for this visit. "Could I ask you something?"

"Sure."

"Conky." He nearly choked on Conklin's familiar nickname but was determined to keep things light with Wallack.

"What about him?"

"You know Leslie reported your disappearance to him and he sat on it for two weeks, right?"

"Yeah, I heard that. He said he was worried I was on a bender and wanted to find me himself. I don't blame him for keeping it on the down low. He was looking out for me. He knows better than anyone how bad it got when I was drinking. Without him as my sponsor and protector, I would've lost my job and my pension back in the day."

"I need to ask you something, and I need to ask you cop to cop, not as Conklin's friend. I also need you to keep the fact that we had this conversation between us. Can you do that?"

"Whatever I can do for you is the least of what I owe you all."

"It's extremely important that you not share what I'm about to tell you with Conklin. I need your word as a man and as a cop."

"You have it."

Joe hoped he was doing the right thing by confiding in one of Conklin's closest friends, but he was counting on Wallack's need for redemption to guide his actions. "We have reason to believe that Conklin knows more about what happened to Skip Holland than he's disclosed thus far."

Wallack's expression registered genuine shock.

Joe told him about the witness who'd given Conklin a statement the day of the shooting and then checked in with him every year on the anniversary. "He didn't tell any of us about this guy Davis or the annual calls."

"Wh-why would he do that?"

"That's what I'd like to know. I wondered if you might have any insight as one of his close friends."

"I can't begin to imagine what he was thinking."

"Did he ever talk to you about Skip's shooting?"

"Only about the horror of it. We all talked about that after it happened. He was no less affected than everyone else who knew Skip or considered him a friend. Of course, he was the top captain in line to take Skip's place as deputy chief when he was medically retired. I don't remember him mentioning anything about that, but it was a long time ago."

"Sometimes it feels like yesterday. Other times, I have trouble remembering him before the shooting."

"I'm really sorry for the loss. I know you two were tight."

"We were like brothers."

"I can't believe Conky would do anything intentional to impede an investigation that affected his close friend."

"Neither can I, and yet, the evidence suggests he did just that."

"Have you talked to him?"

Joe nodded. "He says he wasn't at the scene that day and has never met Davis. We'll be talking to the people who were there to see if they recall seeing him."

"And if they do?"

Joe let his grimace speak for itself. "If you think of anything that might be relevant, call me. Even if you think it's something small or trivial. Call me."

"I will. Of course I will. But I don't think he'd be capable..."

"We'd all like to think that of our friends and colleagues, but we've both seen enough to know better."

"True."

"Again, this conversation is confidential."

"I promise it won't go any further."

"I appreciate your discretion."

Wallack responded with a harsh laugh. "I appreciate yours. What I did… I put a stain on the department that I'll be ashamed of for the rest of my life."

"No one else sees it that way."

Wallack raised a brow. "No one?"

"No one who matters."

CHAPTER SEVENTEEN

AFTER HAVING BREAKFAST with the kids, Sam headed out for work. The story about the Secret Service providing protection to Aubrey and Alden was the lead in the *Star* and the *Post*, but Nick had told her not to worry about it. His office would handle it. Because she had more than enough of her own stuff to worry about, she planned to push it out of her mind and let him deal with it.

She'd woken to a text from Lilia, her chief of staff at the White House, who was dating their close friend, Dr. Harry Flynn. I know you have so much going on and it might be too soon after losing your dad. However, Harry and I would like to invite you and the vice president to a dinner party at my home on Saturday night. It will be a small group of close friends, including Andy and Elsa Simone, Derek Kavanaugh, Terry O'Connor and Lindsey McNamara. If it's too soon to socialize, we totally understand, but we wanted to invite you anyway.

Sam had responded, Thank you for the kind invite. Right at this moment, we'd love to join you, but I reserve the right to renege later if I'm not feeling up to it. Is that okay? Let me know what time and what to bring. It would be good for Nick to have some time with his friends, which he had so little of now that he was vice president and everything had to be planned so far in advance.

Absolutely fine and just yourselves. Seven o'clock. Would it be okay to invite Shelby and Avery? She's become a friend since I met you. Lilia had also provided her address in the Adams Morgan neighborhood.

Of course, Sam had replied, looking forward to an evening with friends and to trying to get things back to normal, whatever that was now.

Excellent. I'll take care of coordinating with the vice president's detail.

Thank you. A casual night out with friends was anything but when you were the vice president. Sam was thankful to Lilia for handling that detail for them. Sam texted Nick to fill him in on the plans for Saturday night.

That sounds like fun, he replied. A date with my best girl and some time with my best friends. Sign me up.

Already did! Sam replied, including heart and kiss emoji.

Thanks to rush-hour traffic, she had plenty of time to think about her next move in her father's case. Celia, Tracy and Angela had promised to keep looking for the messenger bag at the house, and Sam tried to think about where else it might be at HQ. Lost and found, maybe? How long would they keep things that went unclaimed? Was it someone's job to discard unclaimed items after a certain amount of time had passed? If so, how did she apply for that job? She'd vastly prefer it to hers lately.

Between the drive-by shootings, the home invasion that had left Alden and Aubrey's parents dead, her father's death and the shooting of Agent Connolly, she'd had about enough of death. Most of the time, she rolled from one case to another without letting the details overwhelm her. But these last few cases had been rougher than usual. Toss her father's death in on top of everything else, and a lot became too much.

Lost and found.

Her brain jumped around from one thing to another and landed back where it started. After being shot, her dad had been transported to the George Washington University Hospital. How long would they keep something in their lost and found? Had the bag still been slung across his chest when he was shot? Probably not, but it was worth checking. Turning the car toward 23rd Street, she flipped open her phone and put through a call to Freddie, all while zigzagging through traffic. At times like this, it was a good thing she was a cop who didn't have to worry about traffic violations while on the job. Otherwise, she'd probably be in jail.

"Morning." His morning perkiness usually got on her nerves, but today she was glad one of them was feeling perky.

"I'm heading to GW to check their lost and found for the messenger bag."

"Oh, good thought. Want me to meet you?"

"That'd be good. Let Malone know where we are and hit me up when you get there."

"Will do. I'm on my way."

When she arrived at the hospital, she parked in the emergency department lot and ran inside, hoping to find Dr. Anderson. They'd had far too many encounters that involved him coming at her with needles, but he'd been useful to her in the past and she hoped he would be again. At the desk, she asked for him while ignoring the people in the waiting room whispering about her.

She wished she could whirl around and tell them to

mind their own goddamned business, but she couldn't do that to Nick, who would have to explain why his wife had been a bitch to his adoring public.

The nurse working the desk placed a call to request that Anderson come out to the desk.

Ten long minutes later, he came through the swinging double doors, seeming surprised to see her. Youthful and blond, he had warm brown eyes that lit up with amusement at the sight of the people in the waiting room gawking at her. "To what do I owe the pleasure of a nonbloody visit?"

He was funny. She'd give him that, even if his humor was often at her expense. "I need a favor."

"Come on back."

Sam followed him to a small office tucked between patient cubicles. "Is this where the magic happens?"

"Nah, this is where I hide when I need to take ten."

"I know that feeling."

"Did you catch the Connolly case yesterday?"

"Yeah," she said with a sigh. "I had the special joy of notifying his wife of three months."

Anderson winced. "So fucking tragic."

"Incredibly."

"What's this favor you need?"

"I'm looking for something that's been missing for four years, and I only recently realized it."

"Okay…"

"I know it's a long shot, but my dad was brought here after he was shot. He had a messenger bag that he carried back and forth to work. A colleague recalls seeing him wearing it across his chest before the shooting. It's possible it was still there when he was shot and would've been on him when he was brought here."

"Anything he came in with would've stayed with him when he was admitted."

"Is it possible that in the effort to save his life, he could've been separated from it?"

"I suppose it's possible it was still with him if the EMTs didn't cut it off to gain access."

"If it was still with him, where would it have ended up?"

Before he could reply, Freddie appeared at the door. "Morning."

"Morning. Dr. Anderson and I were discussing where missing items land in this place."

"We have a central lost and found in the main office off the lobby," Anderson said. "It's run by volunteers."

Sam cringed at the word *volunteers*.

Anderson chuckled. "Don't make that face. They're remarkably organized and are the backbone of this place."

"If you say so."

"I say so." He consulted a directory, picked up the phone and made a call. "This is Dr. Anderson in Emergency. I have Lieutenant Holland from the Metro PD here." He paused, glanced at Sam and said, "Yes, the vice president's wife."

Sam groaned.

Anderson smiled. "She's looking for something from four years ago that possibly came in with a patient and might've ended up with you guys. Is it okay to send her over to take a look?" After listening for a second that seemed like much longer, he said, "Okay, will do." He hung up the phone. "She said you're more than welcome to look, but they don't tend to keep things that long, unless they seem valuable."

Sam's heart sank. Her dad's beat-up leather messenger bag certainly wouldn't pass the valuable test. But they would look anyway. "Thanks for your help, Doc."

"My pleasure." Using a printed map of the hospital, he showed her where to find the lost and found office. "Would you like me to punch your frequent-flyer card?"

In light of her many visits to the ER, he'd recently given her a card as a joke. "That's okay."

"Hey," Anderson said when they were halfway out the door. "I'm very sorry about your dad."

"Thank you."

"Are you holding up okay?"

"Working the cold case helps."

"I'll hope and pray you get the answers you're looking for."

"I appreciate that." She followed the directions he'd given her to the main lobby, realizing that at some point the good doctor had become a friend despite the needles. One could never have too many friends, or so her dad had always said. He'd had so many friends, people from all walks of life who'd come to pay their respects during the public viewing. She wasn't nearly as likable as he'd been, but she had her share of friends and appreciated every one of them, especially at times like these.

As she and Freddie navigated the maze of corridors and hallways, Sam kept her head down to avoid eye contact with curious people they encountered. She heard the whispers and the buzzing, felt the eyes on her and the fingers pointed in her direction, but ignored it all to stay focused on why she was here.

The woman whom Anderson had spoken to was waiting for them when they arrived in the lobby. She waved them over to a doorway, located behind the information desk. "Hi there, I'm Ann, and it's a pleasure to meet you."

Sam shook her hand. "You too. This is my partner, Detective Cruz."

"I'm sorry for your recent loss."

"Thank you. Do you mind if we take a look?"

"Feel free." Ann stepped aside to let them enter the small room. Shelves lined the walls with items contained in plastic bins.

"Is there any particular place that older items would be kept?" Sam asked.

"Not really. We've tried to institute organization, but with volunteers in and out, things get mixed-up."

"Okay, then we'll check it all," Sam said, resigned to being there awhile.

Freddie gestured toward the left side. "I'll start over here."

Sam headed for the far right and pulled the first bin off the top shelf. Inside were stuffed animals, clothing, shoes. They worked quietly and methodically, going through each bin and checking every item, meeting in the middle after more than an hour. They pulled the last two bins off the shelf and sifted through the items inside, but there was no leather messenger bag.

Freddie lifted the last two bins back onto the shelf. "What now?"

Putting aside her disappointment at not finding the bag here, she took a second to gather her thoughts. "I want to talk to every first responder who was on G Street that day."

"We've talked to them before."

"Yes, but we've never asked if they remember a messenger bag. This time we'll ask them that."

"Sounds like a plan."

Sam knew the list of people by heart. "Let's hit the fire department on the way back to HQ."

They arrived at the engine company that had responded to the call thirty minutes later, and walked in through the open doors, past the trucks to the common area in the back. The firefighters and paramedics were seated around a large table, binders open before them as an instructor led them through a class that came to a stop when Sam and Freddie walked in.

"Lieutenant." The firefighter leading the workshop wore a white shirt and captain's bars. Sam had seen him around but couldn't recall his name. "To what do we owe the honor?"

"Sorry to interrupt. We're taking a fresh look at my dad's shooting, and I was wondering if we might have a word with anyone who was on the scene that day."

"I was there," one of the men said.

Sam recognized him as David Branson, a paramedic, and nodded to acknowledge him.

"Me too," a female firefighter said.

Carmen Garcia, Sam recalled.

"Could we have a word in the hallway perhaps?" Sam asked.

The captain gestured for them to go ahead.

When the four of them were in the hallway, Sam shook hands with Garcia and Branson. "Good to see you again."

"Likewise," Garcia said. "We were sorry to hear of your dad's passing."

"Thank you."

"What can we do for you?"

"My dad carried a leather messenger bag that I had forgotten about until someone shared a memory with me and I realized we haven't seen that bag since the shooting. I know it's a long shot, but we're trying to figure out what became of it."

Branson rubbed at the stubble on his jaw as he thought about it. "I'm trying to sift through the details of that day."

"I know it was a long time ago."

"Some calls stand out more than others. That one has stayed with me."

Sam already knew that the shooting of a dedicated police officer had been traumatic for everyone who'd responded. Deaths and serious injuries of officers on the job served as a reminder to all public safety personnel of the ever-present danger they tried not to think too much about as they went through their days.

"I don't remember a bag," Garcia said.

"I can't say I do either," Branson said.

"What shift does Viera work these days?" Sam asked of one of the other paramedics who'd been there.

"Third," Garcia said. "He's probably sleeping now, but I can text him and ask him to get in touch with you."

"That would be great." Sam handed her a business card. "My cell number is on there."

"We'll get word to him," Branson said. "If there's anything else we can do, don't hesitate to ask."

"I will, thanks. It goes without saying that if you think of anything else, I'd appreciate a call." She hesitated, briefly debating whether she should ask, and in the end, the need to know trumped everything else. "One other thing I was wondering. Do either of you remember who was in charge at the scene?" Since there was no mention of Conklin being there in any of the reports, she was hoping someone besides Davis would recall seeing him and could put him at the scene.

They both thought about that for a moment.

"I can't say I recall that," Garcia said.

"I can't either," Branson said. "There were so many people there that day at various times."

"I understand," Sam said. "Four years is a long time."

"Wish we could do more," Garcia said. "We're all very sorry for your loss. DC Fire and EMS held Deputy Chief Holland in the highest regard."

"Thank you and we appreciated the outpouring of support during the funeral." Hundreds of firefighters and EMS personnel had attended the services in uniform.

"It was the least we could do," Branson said.

Sam shook hands with both of them. "Thanks again for your help."

"We hope you're able to get some answers," Garcia said.

"Me too. Take care." Sam and Freddie walked back to the car to return to HQ.

"Try not to get discouraged," Freddie said. "The more seeds we sow, the more likely they are to bear fruit."

"That's very profound, young Freddie. And it sounds like something I might've said in the past, which means it's copyrighted."

He grunted out a laugh. "While you are often profound in your own unique way, that was my own original material. You have permission to use it, though."

"That's very generous of you."

"By the way, I know we have many other things going on at the moment, and the timing is awful, as usual, but you do need to make a decision about who you want for Will's spot on the squad. We've been working shorthanded for a long time now, and with Gonzo out for who knows how long, we need that position filled."

"I know, I know. I think Malone is letting me get through Stahl's trial before he applies pressure, but your point is well taken. I'll look at the applicants today and decide something."

"I gave you my recommendations weeks ago."

"Refresh my memory."

"Beckett and O'Brien have both passed the detective's exam. I listed them as the top prospects because I know you actually like them both."

"And I don't actually like anyone."

"Exactly. So that's a plus for both of them. I chose O'Brien over Beckett, only because he's been around longer, paid his dues and he's damned reliable. Of course it's your call, but that's what I would do."

"Then that's what I will do."

He turned to look at her. "Just like that?"

"Why not? You did the legwork, we know he's qualified and, like you said, he's got the chops. I'll run it by Malone, and we'll go from there."

"Wow, that was easy."

"In the grand scheme of things, that doesn't rate as one of the more difficult things I have to deal with today. Did you hear about the press making a thing of us taking in the twins?"

"I did hear that, and it's total BS. Just because Nick is in office doesn't mean you can't add to your family. What if you'd had twins the old-fashioned way?" He stopped himself. "Ugh, sorry. I know that's a sore subject."

"It's true, though. What if I did have twins naturally? Would they object to the Secret Service providing protection for them?"

"Probably not. The uproar is about you voluntarily

taking them in, which makes them eligible for protection."

"Which, as you say, is BS. The uproar is also over the fact that their father left them billions, and that has people's noses out of joint."

"True."

"Elijah would make the money available to pay for protection if we asked him to, but I'm not going there. Nick and I agree it's the principle of it. We have the right to expand our family any way we wish to while he's in office. The public will have to pardon us if we didn't consider the cost of protection when we saw two little kids in need of a loving home."

"You should say that—just like that."

"I'm not saying anything. Nick's office can handle it. He's the one who has to answer to the taxpayers, not me. But that doesn't mean I don't think it's another totally ridiculous manufactured scandal."

"It's because he doesn't give the Republicans much to pick at, and with the next presidential election right around the corner, they're going to be looking to discredit him any way they can as the heir apparent to the job."

Though she'd heard that before, Sam's stomach hurt at the thought of Nick being heir apparent to the presidency.

CHAPTER EIGHTEEN

"THIS IS TURNING into a big deal." Terry broke the bad news to Nick shortly after he arrived at the White House. "It was the lead story on all the morning news shows."

"Must be a slow news day." Nick sipped from the travel mug of coffee he'd brought for the ride to work. If there was a benefit to having Secret Service protection, the motorcade that got him where he needed to be without being hampered by the notorious DC traffic congestion was at the top of the list.

"It is a slow day."

"Just my luck. What do you think we should do?"

Terry withdrew a piece of paper from his portfolio. "I think you should issue a statement from yourself and Sam. I took the liberty of drafting something." He extended the paper to Nick.

"Read it to me."

"'Sam and I have made a commitment to Alden, Aubrey and Elijah Armstrong, and we fully intend to honor that commitment. We love the children and are delighted to add them to our family for as long as we are lucky enough to be needed by them. We have always planned to add to our family eventually, and the addition of Alden and Aubrey is a welcome blessing to both of us as well as to Scotty, who is delighted to have younger siblings to love. Frankly, I'm not interested in seeing two children who recently suffered the tremendous loss of their parents, their home and the only life they've ever known used as political pawns. They are now a part of our family, where they will remain for the foreseeable future. As such, they will be afforded Secret Service protection to ensure that no harm will come to them while they reside with us. Sam and I appreciate the amazing support we have received since we brought Alden and Aubrey into our home, as well as the outpouring of love and sympathy for the recent loss of Sam's father, MPD Deputy Chief Skip Holland. After this briefing, we won't have anything more to say on the subject of Alden and Aubrey, and we ask you to allow the children to continue to grieve their losses in private.'"

"That's really great." Terry's heartfelt words had filled Nick with profound emotion. "Do you want to go ahead and issue it?"

"I think this one would be better coming directly from you."

"Let me run it by Sam, and then we can ask Trevor to schedule me for the daily briefing."

"Sounds like a plan." Terry placed the page containing the statement on Nick's desk. "I'll leave you to discuss it with her."

"Good work, Terry. Thanks again."

"Of course. Let me know when to give the word to Trevor." Terry left Nick's office, closing the door behind him.

Nick read through the statement again and then placed a call to Sam.

"Hey." She sounded rushed and busy as she always did at work.

"You got a second?"

"For you? Always. How's the shitstorm?"

"Pretty shitty. Terry drafted a statement he thinks I should make to the media. I wanted to run it by you first."

"I'm listening."

He read the statement to her, again feeling the tightening in his chest when he thought of the two little ones who'd captured their hearts and feeling a father's need to protect them from anything that might hurt them when they'd already suffered enough.

"I love that and thank you for including the part about my dad. Anyone who would badger the kids or us after hearing that is truly heartless."

"I'm sure there'll still be more grumbling and badgering, but hopefully the statement will take care of the worst of it."

"Well, you have my approval. Would it help if I was there when you read the statement?"

"As much as I love any excuse to see you during the day, I know you're busy. I'll take care of it for both of us."

"Okay. Let me know how it goes."

"I will."

"I know I've said it before, but it bears repeating. Thank you for stepping up for our littles the way you have. And I'm sorry if I've caused you trouble at work."

"You haven't caused me trouble and neither have they. I don't give a rat's ass what anyone says. Stepping up for them is one of the best things we've ever done, and I'd do it again in a hot second, even knowing it was going to cause a shitstorm."

"And that's why I love you so much. One of many reasons."

"Love you too. I'll text you after."

"Good luck."

"Thanks." After he ended the call, Nick let Terry know they had the green light from Sam. Then he reviewed the statement a couple more times until he knew it more or less by heart. Terry would have it put on the teleprompter, but Nick didn't like to rely on that. Once he had a handle on the statement, he turned his attention to his email and the day's briefing materials.

Terry knocked on the door an hour later. "They're ready for you in the press room."

Nick brought his copy of the statement with him when he went with Terry to the briefing room, which fell silent when he walked in. The president's press secretary was there, as was Trevor.

Nick stepped up to the podium. "I asked for a minute of your time to make a statement about the ongoing story many of you are running about the children my wife and I recently took in."

As he read the statement, he made eye contact with reporters from the outlets who'd gleefully reported the news about the taxpayers having to foot the bill for the Cappuanos' new wards. Two of them looked away after his gaze landed on them.

After he was finished reading the statement, he said, "I'll take a couple of questions."

A reporter from the *New York Times* raised her hand and Nick called on her. "Do you think it's fair that the taxpayers have to pay the cost of protecting two children that you voluntarily brought into your home?"

"I would answer your question with a question—is

it fair to judge us for how we choose to add to our family? As you know, my wife has suffered from infertility, and after we adopted Scotty, we hoped to have another opportunity to expand our family. As you also know, Sam encountered Alden and Aubrey at the worst moment of their young lives and stepped up for them in such an amazing way. She had my full support—and Scotty's—in bringing them to our home when they needed somewhere to be. We could've applied to adopt and been given the opportunity to adopt twins, and the result would've been the same—two more children in our home and our family who require protection due to the nature of my job. To us, it doesn't matter how they came to be there. What matters is that we love them and we're committed to providing them with a home for as long as they need one."

Another reporter raised his hand. "The children have aunts, uncles and grandparents on their mother's side of the family. Why are they not residing with family members?"

"Their brother, Elijah, is their primary legal guardian. He makes the decisions on their behalf, and he chose to keep them with us when he saw how well they were adjusting to our home and our family. We've surrounded them with love and support and have agreed to help Elijah for as long as we're needed." Nick wasn't about to throw their mother's family under the bus by saying they were initially unwilling to take the children and in fact hadn't even asked about them after learning their parents had been killed.

But, oh, how he wanted to say that.

"Do you understand the concern people have about

taxpayers footing the bill to protect children that do have other family members who could care for them?"

"I absolutely understand the concern, but I hope you can understand that because the children will be part of my family for some time to come, they need to be protected from those who would harm them simply because of what I do for a living. Keeping them safe and protected is one of our primary roles as their guardians." He paused, trying to decide if he should say more. Why the hell not? What did he have to lose? "One thing I've learned in my life is you never know what's right around the next corner. Did Sam and I plan to add to our family right now? No, but when the twins came into our lives, it felt meant to be from the beginning, and we couldn't be more pleased to have the honor of taking care of them at this difficult time in their lives. Alden, Aubrey and their brother, Elijah, have become family to us. It's that simple. That's all for now. If you have other questions, please contact Trevor and he'll see that I get them. Thanks for your time."

They were still shouting questions at him when Nick exited through the door that Terry held for him.

"I think that went well."

Nick wasn't so sure. "I guess we'll find out." His phone rang, and he took the call from Elijah. "Hey, what's up?"

"I saw you on TV just now. I had no idea you were taking that kind of flack about the kids. I feel really bad."

"Don't worry about it. I'm not and neither is Sam. It'll die down in a day or two. These things always do."

"I just hate to cause you any heartburn when you are doing such a huge thing for me and the kids."

"Let me tell you something, Eli. They could run me out of office, and that would be fine with me if it meant we got to keep Aubrey and Alden with us. We love them very much. They're part of our family now, as are you."

"I honestly can't tell you how much it means to me to know they are well cared for and loved when I can't be there. I'll never be able to thank you and Sam for all you've done."

"They've given us as much as we've given them. Don't worry about anything. It's all good. I promise."

"Thank you again."

Nick ducked into his office, nodded to Terry and closed the door. "Could I ask you something else?"

"Sure."

"Sam and I were talking the other night about what's going to happen when you finish school."

"About the kids, you mean?"

"Yeah. We're, um, well… We're getting attached to them, and it's just that the thought of them leaving…"

"I'd never take them away from you guys after all you've done for them—and for me. My goal is to find a job in DC so I can help out, spend time with them and be part of their lives. Maybe they can spend some weekends with me or something like that."

Nick took a deep breath and closed his eyes. That was a plan he and Sam could live with. "That'd be perfect."

"I know how easy they are to love."

"They really are. Don't you have class at one?"

Eli laughed. "Yeah, I do. You sound like my dad."

"Well, get going. You don't want to be late."

"I'm walking as we talk. I'll let you go. Tell the kids I'll call them before bed."

"They'll look forward to it. Take care, Eli."

After he ended the call, Nick composed a text to Sam, giving her the gist of their conversation.

SAM AND FREDDIE watched Nick on the TV in the conference room, her stomach churning the entire time, waiting to see how the reporters would react. She breathed an audible sigh of relief when he stepped away from the podium.

"He handled that really well," Freddie said. "But that's no surprise. He's exceptionally good at this stuff."

"Yes, he is. Way better than I am."

"You said that, not me."

She laughed. "It goes without saying that he's far more diplomatic than I'll ever be."

Freddie snorted and then covered it with a cough. "Yes, he is."

She elbowed him in the ribs. "Quit laughing at me right to my face."

"How else should I laugh at you?"

"Laughing at your superior officer isn't the best career move you can make."

Her phone dinged with a text from Nick, telling her about his conversation with Eli. She read it twice, thrilled with what she was seeing as she typed her reply to him. Well, that's a big fat fucking relief.

My gorgeous wife has a way with words. I can live with that plan. Can you?

Hell, yes.

See? It's all working out the way it's meant to.

I'm so happy that we'll get to see them grow up.

Me too, babe. Back to work for both of us. See you later.

Love you.

Love you too. Xoxo

She no sooner read the text when her cell rang with a number she didn't recognize. "Holland."

"Hey, it's Kevin Viera. Branson said you were by and wanted to talk to me?"

"Yes, thanks for calling."

"No problem. I was at the gym so I just got his text. What can I do for you?"

"We're taking another look at my dad's case with fresh leads coming into the tip line."

"I was really sorry to hear he'd passed. He was a good man."

"Yes, he was. Thank you. One of my colleagues mentioned the messenger bag he used to carry back and forth to work, and I realized I'd forgotten about it in all the chaos after the shooting. I know it was a long time ago, but I wondered if you have any recollection of there being a beat-up leather bag at the scene of his shooting?"

After a long period of silence, he asked, "Was it brown leather?"

"Yeah." Sam held her breath.

"I remember it. After he was taken from the scene, I found it on the street, realized it belonged to Chief Holland and grabbed it so it wouldn't get lost."

Sam's mouth had gone dry, her hands were sweaty and her legs wobbly. She dropped into a seat at the conference room table while Freddie stood with his hands on his hips, watching over her. "What did you do with it?" Her voice was barely a whisper.

"I gave it to Conklin and asked him to get it to the family."

Like Alice falling into Wonderland, Sam felt like a trapdoor had opened beneath her, sending her hurtling through space.

"He gave it to you, right?"

"No, he didn't." She forced herself to take a deep breath and do what needed to be done. "Listen, I know you just got off an overnight shift, but I need you to come to HQ right now. Immediately. Can you do that?"

"Ah, yeah. I guess. I'll be right there."

Sam closed her phone. "Go get Farnsworth and Malone. Hurry."

"Sam—"

"Go."

He went.

Sam took a series of deep breaths as the words *holy fucking shit* ran through her mind on continuous repeat. She'd found someone who could not only put Conklin at the scene of her father's shooting, but who could attest that he'd given Conklin the messenger bag that should've been returned to Skip's family and never was.

What the actual fuck is going on?

She continued to force air into lungs that felt compressed by the weight of the information that had landed on her in the last few minutes.

Malone came rushing into the room. "What?"

"I've got a first responder who can put Conklin at the scene of my dad's shooting, and who says he gave Conklin my dad's messenger bag to return to the family after my dad was transported."

Malone stared at her, not blinking or seeming to breathe as he absorbed what she'd said.

Freddie returned with Farnsworth a minute later, and Sam told the chief the latest.

For a long, awful moment Farnsworth stood perfectly still, his sharp gray eyes giving nothing away. "Jake, take the deputy chief into custody—quietly. No cuffs, no spectacle. Make sure to read him his rights. Dot every *i* and cross every *t*."

After another long, pregnant pause, Malone cleared his throat. "Yes, sir." He turned and left the room.

Sam looked up at the chief. "What happens now?"

"I'm calling in the FBI to interview Viera."

Every part of Sam wanted to reject that plan, but she didn't say a word, sensing that anything she said would be unwelcome.

"Behind the scenes—and I mean so far behind the scenes there's no chance your fingerprints will be anywhere near this, I want your team to take a close look at Conklin's activities in the six months before your father's shooting. Look at everything—email, phone calls, reports he filed, personal. *Everything.* Bring Archie in but no one else outside your squad. Pull any footage we have from the day of the shooting and go over it again, looking for any sign of Conklin at the scene. Put Green's name on the reports. He wasn't here then and has no personal connection to Conklin. Work quickly and don't tell anyone else in this department what you're working on. Don't breathe a word about this inside or outside HQ, not even to spouses. Am I clear?"

Sam swallowed hard. "Yes, sir."

Freddie nodded. "Yes, sir."

"Get on it." Farnsworth turned and left the room.

Sam sat staring at the wall, unseeing, her mind racing as she tried to make sense of this.

"Sam."

She looked up at her partner.

"What're you thinking?"

"I don't know what to think. This is so…" She shook her head. "It's beyond my ability to comprehend."

"Mine too. If it's too much, the rest of us can see to the chief's orders. You don't have to be here. Anyone would understand."

"I'd go crazy at home waiting to hear what was happening." Sam forced herself to stand, to get her shit together, to find her legendary mojo, to do what needed to be done. If justice for her father led to one of his closest friends, then so be it. At least then they'd know. She opened the conference room door. "Everyone in here. Now."

CHAPTER NINETEEN

FBI Special Agent in Charge Avery Hill, head of the Criminal Investigations division, was in his office when his assistant told him Joe Farnsworth was on the phone.

Avery picked up the call on the first ring. "Good morning, Chief."

"I need you at HQ immediately."

To call this request from the chief of the Metro PD unusual was putting it mildly. "What's going on?"

"I'll let you know when you get here. Can you come right now?"

"I'm on my way."

The line went dead. Holy crap. Whatever was happening, it had to be huge for Farnsworth himself to call in the FBI. And it was most likely internal. What other reason would the chief have for making that call?

"I'm going to Metro PD HQ," Avery told his assistant. "I'm not sure how long I'll be. Text me if you need me." He was already through the door and in the corridor before he finished speaking. Moving quickly, he got lucky with the traffic and arrived at HQ fifteen minutes after receiving Farnsworth's call.

The chief himself was waiting for him in the lobby and gestured for Avery to follow him to his office.

Avery nodded at Helen, the chief's admin, who watched them go by with wide eyes that fed Avery's curiosity. He'd never seen Helen with wide eyes before.

"Close the door."

Avery closed the door.

"We've arrested Deputy Chief Conklin." Before Avery could absorb that bombshell, a knock sounded. "Come in."

U.S. Attorney Tom Forrester and Assistant U.S. Attorney Faith Miller entered the room.

Avery nodded to them both.

"Thank you for coming." Farnsworth seemed cool and composed when he had to be completely undone on the inside. "I was just informing Agent Hill that we've arrested Deputy Chief Conklin."

Avery gave the chief credit for holding it together, for doing the job, for taking charge of a potentially explosive situation.

Neither Forrester nor Miller seemed as stunned by this news as Avery was.

"So you were able to connect him to Skip Holland's shooting?"

What? Holy shit!

"We have a first responder coming in now who will attest to the fact that Conklin was at the scene on G Street that day. Lieutenant Kevin Viera, a paramedic, gave Conklin the messenger bag that Skip carried to and from work and asked him to return it to Skip's family. That never happened. Lieutenant Holland has been trying to track down the bag, which is what led her to Viera and the other first responders who were there. Two days ago, Conklin looked me and Captain Malone in the eyes and told us that after receiving the call about Skip's shooting, he went right to the GW ER, which we now know was not true. At this juncture, I'm turning the investigation of Deputy Chief Conklin's actions pertaining to the shooting of Deputy Chief Skip

Holland over to Agent Hill and the FBI. I have a team gathering internal information pertaining to Conklin from six months prior to the shooting and will turn that evidence over to Agent Hill the moment it is compiled."

Farnsworth glanced at Hill. "I believe we're looking at a matter of hours, maybe less, before word gets out that our deputy chief has been arrested."

Avery nodded. "Understood."

Another knock sounded at the door. Helen ducked her head in. "Lieutenant Viera is here for you, sir."

"Show him in." Farnsworth pocketed his cell phone and came around the desk. "I'll relocate for the time being so you can use this office."

Forrester shook hands with Farnsworth. "You're doing the right thing here, Joe."

Farnsworth nodded and left the room.

Avery glanced at Forrester and Miller, who seemed equally stunned by what was happening.

Viera came into the office, stopping short at the sight of an FBI agent and U.S. Attorneys. "Um, I thought I was talking to Lieutenant Holland?"

"As the case in question pertains to her father, we'll be conducting the interview." Avery extended his hand. "I'm Agent Hill, and this is U.S. Attorney Tom Forrester and Assistant U.S. Attorney Faith Miller."

Viera shook hands with them. "What the hell is going on?"

"Have a seat and we'll tell you." Hill gestured to the conference room table on the other side of Farnsworth's office.

Hill sat at the head of the table. "Take us through what happened on G Street the day Skip Holland was shot."

"We received multiple 911 calls about an officer shot

in the neck and responded within three minutes of the shooting. When we arrived, a man was providing aide to Deputy Chief Holland by keeping pressure on the wound. I believe that man's actions saved Chief Holland's life."

Avery took notes as Viera recited the info. "Did you catch his name?"

"I did, but I don't recall it off the top of my head. He was an older guy who worked at GAO."

"What happened then?"

"We took over and attempted to stabilize Chief Holland so he could be transported. That took about ten to twelve minutes. After the ambulance left with him, we were clearing the scene and I picked up a brown leather messenger bag that was lying in the street, checked inside, saw Skip Holland's name and handed it over to then-Captain Conklin to make sure it got back to Skip's family."

"And you're sure it was Conklin?"

"Positive. I'd worked with him before, so I knew him." He glanced from Avery to Forrester and back to Avery. "Are you going to tell me what this is about?"

"Deputy Chief Conklin has been arrested for lying about the events of that day."

Viera's eyes bugged. "Whoa."

"We're going to need you to make a formal statement to the facts you've given us here."

"Okay."

Avery spent the next two hours recording every detail that Viera could recall, and when they'd nailed down the statement, he asked Viera to sign it.

The paramedic scrawled his signature across the bottom of the page. "What now?"

"Go about your business and don't talk about any of this with anyone. We'll be in touch."

SAM'S TEAM, AIDED by Lieutenant Archelotta from IT, never left the conference room for the rest of their shift, sifting through years-old reports, phone records and investigatory notes after an emergency search warrant was obtained to give them access to the contents of the deputy chief's office.

Per Malone's orders, Sam had remained in her own office throughout the afternoon, told to stay away from the goings-on in the conference room. She'd watched as officers arrived at regular intervals with boxes and other items that were delivered to her detectives. Sitting on the sidelines made her crazy, but she understood why she couldn't be in there, even if she didn't like it.

She'd been reviewing reports submitted by her team, including the one about Patrick Connolly's homicide, the details making her profoundly sad once again for the wife and family the talented young agent had left behind.

At four o'clock, she turned off her computer, gathered her keys and phone and headed out, encountering Lindsey McNamara coming out of the morgue. "Step into my office."

Sam followed her through the automatic doors that led to the frigid morgue.

"What the hell is going on around here today? Everyone is buzzing about Conklin being arrested."

"I'm not allowed to know anything about it."

Lindsey gasped. "Because it involves your father's case?"

"I can neither confirm nor deny."

Lindsey's expression went flat with shock. "You've got to be kidding me."

Sam shrugged.

"Was he the shooter?"

Sam shrugged again.

"Holy *crap*. This is going to be *huge*."

Sam nodded. "I'm on my way out. Talk to you tomorrow?"

"Yeah, of course. Sam… Are you okay? You have to be reeling—in more ways than one."

"I'm okay." She'd said those words a hundred times in the last few days and would keep saying them for as long as people asked how she was. "I'll check in tomorrow."

"I'm here if I can do anything for you—anything at all."

"Appreciate it."

As she stepped out into blustery late-afternoon chill, she thought about how blessed she was to have such great friends. Their love and support had been tremendous since her dad passed away, and they'd have her back no matter what happened with Conklin and the investigation.

Sam got into her car and started to head home but then decided to make a stop on the way. She wasn't exactly sure what she was doing in front of the building where Patrick Connolly had lived with his wife, Veronica, but something had brought her there. She put the car into Park and shut off the engine. For a long time, she stared at the vestibule, wondering whether she should do this. In the end, compelled by a need she couldn't exactly explain, she got out of the car and pushed the button next to the name Connolly on the keypad.

A female voice answered, "Yes?"

"Lieutenant Sam Holland, from the Metro PD, to see Mrs. Connolly."

The sound of commotion came through the intercom before a buzz unlocked the door. Sam went inside and took the stairs to the third floor, where a gray-haired woman stood in the doorway of 3C waiting for Sam, who withdrew her badge more out of habit than necessity.

"I'm Lieutenant Holland."

"Yes, I know who you are. I'm Justine, Roni's mother. She isn't really up for guests, but when I told her you had come by, she asked me to let you in."

"I won't stay too long. I just wanted to…" What did she want exactly? The case was closed. She had no actual business here. So what was the point? "I wanted to see how she is."

"Not good." Justine's grim expression told the story. "Not good at all. Patrick, he was…" Her eyes filled and she crossed her arms, seeming to hug herself. "I'm sorry. It's just the most awful thing. They were so happy together, and now… I don't know what'll become of her. I just don't know."

"I'm so sorry for your terrible loss. I wish there was something I could say."

"There's nothing anyone can say. The sheer sense-lessness of it is the part I can't get past."

"I know." Sam took a deep breath. "I'll only stay for a minute."

"Is there something new about the case? We were told the man who shot him was arrested."

"That's correct, and no, there's nothing new. I just…" Sam had no idea what she was doing there, but something had brought her there. "I was the one who had to tell her the news yesterday, and I just… I wanted to see her. I understand if this isn't a good time."

"Give me one second?"

"Of course."

Justine left the door ajar while she went to consult with her daughter.

Sam leaned against the wall, feeling like a jerk for disturbing these people at such a difficult time. What the hell was she doing here in the middle of their nightmare? *I ought to go.* She eyed the stairwell. *It's wrong for me to be here.* In all her years as a Homicide detective, she'd never once "stopped by" to visit victims without it pertaining to an ongoing investigation.

She pushed herself off the wall, intending to leave.

Justine came to the door. "She'd like to see you."

Sam followed her into a bright, stylish apartment where Roni was on the sofa, covered with a blanket, her face red and puffy, her hair ratty around her shoulders and her eyes… Sam could barely stand to look at the eyes that held her devastation. "Hi, Roni."

"Hi."

Sam sat next to her. "I wanted to stop by to check on you." On the end table next to Roni, Sam noticed a gorgeous wedding photo of Roni and Patrick, the two of them gazing at each other and wearing huge smiles.

"I'm still here." Roni forced a small smile. "Everyone has been so amazing and supportive."

"I'm glad you're being well loved."

Absently, Roni spun her diamond engagement ring around her finger. It sat above a diamond wedding band. "I'm just not sure what to do now, you know? Patrick… We had so many plans, and now…" She shrugged helplessly and glanced at Sam. "I don't know what to do. I write obituaries for a living, but I don't know where to begin with Patrick's."

Sam's heart broke for her. "Is there someone who could help you with that?"

"Lots of people, but I want to do it myself."

"That's understandable." Sam tried to find some words of wisdom that would help Roni, but really, what could anyone say that would truly help? "I'm sure it seems impossible today, but you will find a way through this."

"I guess so. What choice do I have?"

"If there's anything at all I can do for you at any time, please call me." Sam placed her business card on the coffee table. "My cell number is on there."

"It's very nice of you to come by. You must be so busy, and you just lost your father."

"Yes, I did, and while it's not the same thing, I know what it's like to wonder how you're going to survive without someone."

Roni's eyes filled as she nodded.

"We have something in common, you and me. We're both victims of violent crime. I've been thinking about putting together a group for people like us, those who've been left shattered by the sort of thing that happened to Patrick. If it's all right with you, I'll let you know what we decide to do. It might be helpful to you."

"That would be nice. Thank you."

"If there's anything at all I can do for you, please call."

"I will. It was good of you to come by."

"Do you mind if I stop by again to check on you?"

"I wouldn't mind. It's nice of you to care."

"I'm so sorry again for your loss. From what everyone says, Patrick was a brilliant, well-respected agent."

"He was the smartest person I ever knew."

Sam, who wasn't known for being a hugger, leaned in to hug the young woman, who clung to her for a long time. "I'll be in touch," she said when they finally released each other, both of them blinking back tears.

Roni nodded and wiped the tears from her face.

Justine showed Sam out. "Thank you for coming by."

"Please let me know if there's anything I can do."

"We will."

Sam went down the stairs and out to her car, taking greedy, deep breaths of the cool air. For a long time after she got into her car, she sat there thinking about Roni and Patrick and the terrible loss of a promising young life. Then she pounded her hand on the steering wheel and screamed with frustration until her hand and throat began to hurt so badly she had no choice but to stop.

She took a few minutes to pull herself together, pushing the rage back into the back corner, where it had lived for four seemingly endless years. After opening the window, she took several more breaths, trying to settle her ragged emotions before she went home to her family. She'd become accustomed to hiding the rage, to living with it, to carrying it with her everywhere she went. But since her father died, it had been harder to hide the ever-present fury over what'd been taken from him and everyone who loved him.

Maybe that was why she'd needed to see Roni, so the other woman would know there was someone out there who understood how she felt. Or maybe she'd done it for herself, so she could be with someone who understood how *she* felt. Whatever the reason, she was glad she'd come, that she'd had the chance to express her condolences and speak to Roni about the support group that *would* be happening. It was no longer just an idea. Roni's unspeakable grief had made Sam more determined than ever to do something for people who desperately needed a place to turn when their lives were ruined by violence.

If she could help to give them even five minutes of comfort, it would be time well spent.

Fifteen minutes later, the Secret Service waved her through the Ninth Street checkpoint. She parallel parked in her spot, behind one of the black SUVs that ferried Nick and Scotty around. As she got out of the car, she glanced toward her dad's house, where a single light burned in the living room. A wave of sadness overtook her when she thought about all the years she'd have to live without her dad's steady presence in her life, without that voice calling her baby girl, without his calming influence to talk her down when the job got the better of her.

Roni's grief mingled with her own, making the path forward seem almost insurmountable.

She had no idea how long she'd been standing there when the front door to her home opened and Nick came down the ramp.

He put his arm around her. "Heard you were out here."

"Every day when I come home I have to remind myself he's not there anymore."

"I know, babe. Me too. It's still hard to believe."

She leaned her head on his shoulder.

"You want to go see Celia? I'll go with you."

"Right now, I'd like to see you and the kids."

"I was just about to feed them. You want to join us?"

"Yeah, that'd be good." She'd check on Celia later, after she had some time with Nick and the kids.

Keeping his arm around her, Nick led her up the ramp, past Brant, who stood watch over him as always, and inside to the warm comfort of home, where she could hear the three kids in the kitchen, laughing and talking. Sometimes it was hard to believe that Aubrey and Alden had only been there a couple of weeks.

Scotty and the twins were just what she needed after another difficult day.

After dinner, Scotty decided the twins needed to see *Star Wars* or their education would be incomplete. Sam agreed to the first half, but not the full movie because they needed to get to bed. She never had been a big fan of *Star Wars*, but she sat with Nick's arms around her on the sofa and tried to follow the story even as her mind wandered through the events of the day.

When her cell phone rang, she disentangled herself from Nick's embrace and went into the kitchen to take the call from Freddie.

CHAPTER TWENTY

"HEY, WHAT'S UP?"

"How're you doing?"

"I'd be better if I knew what was going on."

"Nothing much to report. We're going through the stuff from his office piece by piece. It's slow going."

"Any smoking guns?"

"Not yet, but we're still digging. Apparently, he's making a huge stink about being arrested and continuing to claim he was never on G Street that day. Archie is sifting through archival footage from then, looking for him."

"God, I hope he finds something."

"Conklin is saying you're so desperate to solve your father's case that you're grasping at straws."

"He can say whatever he wants. The evidence led directly to him."

"Exactly. Apparently, he hired Charles Bagley to represent him."

Sam groaned at that news. "Only the biggest blowhard in town."

"The way I see it, if he's got nothing to hide, why hire a prominent defense attorney?"

"A very good question."

"People here are saying this could bring down the chief."

"How so? It's not like he knew that his deputy was hiding evidence."

"The theory is he won't survive the scandal, if it turns out to be a scandal."

"I can't worry about that on top of everything else right now. I just wish there was something I could do. I'm losing it playing on the sidelines."

"Keep working the tip line. There may be other stuff there that'll be useful to us."

"True. I'll give that some time tomorrow."

"We're closer to answers than we've ever been. Keep reminding yourself of that."

"I'm afraid I'm not going to like the answers."

"I know. I can't believe where it's led so far. We'll hit it hard again tomorrow, and Dominguez and Carlucci are on it tonight."

"Thanks for the update."

"No problem. Try to get some sleep."

"I will. You too."

"See you in the morning."

Sam closed her phone and leaned against the counter, thinking about what they'd discovered so far and where it might lead. Other than the obvious desire to be promoted, what possible reason would Conklin have had for covering up leads in her father's case? He'd never struck her as someone so ambitious that he'd stoop to attempted murder to get ahead, but how well did she actually know him and what motivated him?

Not that well actually. While he'd always been a close friend of her father's, Sam didn't *know* him the way she knew Farnsworth and Malone. She would rectify that tomorrow by talking to people who'd known him longer than she had, beginning with her mother and Alice Coyne Fitzgerald, both of whom had known Conklin for decades.

Technically, she wasn't doing anything wrong by seeking deeper background for her own information. If she uncovered anything relevant to the investigation, she'd immediately turn it over to Avery so there could be no conflict of interest claims. The last thing she wanted to do, in light of recent developments, was anything that could compromise the case they were building that might finally lead to the answers they'd needed for four years. But there was no way she could stand by and do nothing.

Nick came into the kitchen. "What's up?"

"That was Freddie checking in."

"Anything new?"

"Other than Deputy Chief Conklin being arrested for lying about his whereabouts on the day of my father's shooting?"

Nick released a gasp. "Seriously?"

"Yep. We've got a paramedic who can put him on G Street and says he gave Conklin my dad's messenger bag that day to return to the family. We never received it."

"Holy shit. Samantha… You must be reeling."

"I am. All this time, we've been looking for answers that were right in our own ranks. It's hard to believe. And PS I'm not supposed to be telling even you about this."

"No worries. I'd never repeat it to anyone. Why do you have that calculating look about you?" He refilled his glass with a small amount of whiskey, which sometimes helped him sleep. Nothing worked consistently to overcome his insomnia.

"They're keeping me far away from this for obvious reasons, so I'm thinking of ways I can assist in the investigation without actually assisting in the investigation."

"Ah, and for some reason, that makes perfect sense to me."

"Because you speak me. You get it."

"Yes, I do, and I know how hard it has to be for you to take a backseat right when things are heating up."

"It's excruciating."

"But necessary. You know that, don't you?"

"Of course I do. Doesn't mean I like it, though."

"I know, babe." He slipped an arm around her shoulders and brought her head to rest on his chest.

"Freddie said people are talking about how Conklin's involvement in my dad's case could bring down the chief."

"How so?"

"He's responsible for whatever happens on his watch. The fact that his top deputy withheld this info for four years isn't going to reflect well on him."

"It's not like he knew about it. Skip was one of his closest friends. He would've been all over it if he'd known."

"In the court of public opinion, good intentions often don't matter."

"Well, that would truly suck if Joe lost his job because of this."

"I can't imagine the department without him at the helm. He's the best chief we've ever had. Most everyone thinks so. Not to mention I'd be completely screwed without him to run interference for me." Sam couldn't bear to think about that unsettling scenario.

"Try not to go there until you have to. Nothing will happen overnight."

"I can't help thinking about the fallout if Conklin was involved with my dad's shooting in some way. It'll be ugly for the department, for Uncle Joe, for me. Hell, it may even be ugly for you."

"Don't worry about me. You've got enough to think about without taking that on."

"I've already caused you enough trouble by taking in the twins. I don't want to cause you any more heartburn."

He kissed the top of her head. "I love your kind of heartburn."

Sam laughed. "You're not right."

"If loving you is wrong, I don't want to be right."

"Now you sound like a corny country song." She glanced at him. "But you made me laugh, and I needed that, so thanks."

"That's what I'm here for. Let's get these kiddos in bed and spend some time in the loft. I think we both need a getaway."

"I'm all for that."

More than an hour later, they'd overseen baths and bedtime stories for the twins and tucked Scotty in with orders to shut off his light within thirty minutes.

"I need a shower and then I'll be up."

Nick kissed her cheek. "I'll be waiting for you."

With anticipation of time alone with her sexy husband driving her, Sam rushed through the shower and applied the lavender-and-vanilla-scented lotion he loved so much. Wearing a robe, she stepped into the hallway and was relieved to find that the agent who normally stood watch outside Scotty's door was not there. Nick probably told him to take a break because Sam hated the agents knowing that they were stealing away to their private oasis upstairs. Best husband ever.

She took the stairs two at a time, reaching the top to find Nick sitting on the end of the double lounge chair waiting for her, naked as a jaybird and fully aroused. Laughing, she shed her robe and dropped to her knees between his spread legs. "Excellent presentation."

"I thought you might appreciate that. I really hoped it was you coming up the stairs."

She laughed again. "I appreciate you."

"Mmm." He leaned forward to nuzzle her neck. "I appreciate *you* and the scented lotion that turns me on. We can't ever run out of that."

"We should buy stock in the company."

"I'll do that tomorrow."

"Only you could make me laugh and forget about the madness swirling around me."

He combed his fingers through her hair. "I like to hear you laugh. It's one of my favorite things, especially when I know you don't have much to laugh about at the moment."

"I still have a lot to be thankful for, especially a husband who understands me better than anyone ever has." She leaned in to kiss his chest and breathe him in. "And who smells so good he makes me want to do wicked things to him."

"Don't let me stop you."

Smiling at his witty reply, she kissed a path down his chest to the abdomen that rippled with tight muscles. Her hair slid over the rigid length of his cock.

"Samantha…"

"Hmm?"

"Quit torturing me."

"And do what?"

He made a sound that was a cross between a groan and a grunt.

Smiling, she skimmed her lips over the steely length of his erection, drawing a hissing sound from him as he palmed the back of her head, encouraging without pressuring. Always the consummate gentleman, even in the throes of desire. Sam decided to take mercy on him, wrapping her lips around the wide head and sucking.

His fingers tangled into her hair, his hips lifting in a silent plea for more, which she gave him, lashing him with her tongue and taking him as far as she could, letting her throat close around him the way she only ever had for him. Before him, this act had been about obligation and fair play. With him, it was about trying to give him a fraction of the pleasure he gave her.

"Sam…" He gave her hair a gentle tug. "Babe… Let's do this together."

She took her sweet time releasing him from her mouth and then looked up to find him watching her with a fierce, sexy expression. Sometimes she still couldn't believe all that was for her. Then he reached for her, brought her into his embrace and fell back on the double lounge chair, bringing her with him.

He smoothed the hair back from her face. "Hi there."

"Hi yourself."

"You sure know how to drive me crazy."

"I speak Nick."

"Fluently."

She laughed and gazed at him greedily, taking in every detail of the olive-toned skin, hazel eyes, thick eyelashes and sexy lips.

"What?"

"I was just thinking that only you could make me laugh and forget the shitstorm swirling all around me."

"I wish I could make it better for you somehow."

"You are. This is helping."

"Let me see what I can do to further distract you." He rolled them so he was on top and kissed her.

Sam wrapped her arms and legs around him, losing herself to him and the magic they created together. Nothing else could compare to this, she thought as he tugged her nipple into the heat of his mouth. "Nick." She squirmed under him, trying to move things along, even knowing how he hated to be rushed.

"You aren't being impatient, are you?"

"Yes, I am."

"And what is it that my baby wants?"

"You. Only you." She pressed her pelvis against his cock. "Right now."

He surprised her when he gave her exactly what she'd asked for in one long, deep stroke that filled her so perfectly. "Like that?"

"Yes," she said, gasping. "Just like that." She held on tight to him as he moved in her.

Then he repositioned her, raising her hips and hitting a spot deep inside her.

Sam cried out and held on tighter to him as he reached down to where they were joined to coax her to an orgasm that crashed over her like huge waves hitting the beach.

He was right there with her, his fingers digging into her hip and shoulder as he let himself go, sagging into her embrace afterward.

Sam ran her fingers through his hair, which was damp with sweat. Even when sweaty, he still smelled delicious to her.

"Am I crushing you?"

"Nope. Feels good."

"Everything about this feels good."

"I just want you to know… I wouldn't be able to deal with this without you and our family to prop me up."

"We'll always be right here for you. I just wish there was more I could do to help you through it. I know what a tough loss this is for you."

"I keep thinking I dreamed it, you know? That he's not really gone, that none of it actually happened."

"The suddenness of it makes it harder to accept. Someone at work today said that's better for him but harder for those left behind."

"I guess." She yawned and her eyes suddenly felt heavy.

"Let's get you to bed." Nick pushed himself up on his arms and withdrew from her. He picked up the robe from the foot of the bed and held it for her.

Sam dragged herself off the comfortable mattress and let him wrap the robe around her. As much as she'd prefer to stay put, they needed to be able to hear the twins if they woke up in the night. It didn't happen every night, but when it did there were usually tears involved. "We need a monitor for the twins' room, so we can hear them from up here."

"I'll ask Shelby to order one tomorrow."

Sam was so tired that her legs felt rubbery beneath her as she made her way down the stairs, past Max, the Secret Service agent positioned in the hallway outside Scotty's room. He nodded to them as they went by.

"I hate that he knows we're coming from a booty call," Sam said when they were inside their room with the door closed.

"Is it still a booty call when we're married?"

"If there is booty involved, it's a booty call."

With both hands on her ass, he gave a gentle squeeze. "And I do so *love* your booty."

"There's way too much of my booty."

"No way." He continued to nuzzle her neck. "There's a perfect amount."

"You have to say that. You love me."

"I do love you, and your perfect, sexy booty."

She wrapped her arms around him and held on for the longest time, so long she nearly dozed off standing up.

"Into bed with you." Nick nudged her toward her side of the bed. He pulled down the covers, helped her out of the robe and waited for her to get settled before tucking her in.

Sam's eyes shot open. "The messenger bag."

"What?"

"My dad's bag." She sat up and the covers fell to her waist. "I need my phone. It's in the pocket of the robe."

He got it for her and handed it over.

Sam put through a call to Captain Malone, who answered on the second ring.

"What's up?"

"Sorry to call so late, but I had a thought about Conklin."

"You're not allowed to have thoughts about Conklin right now."

"Are you searching his house?"

"First thing in the morning."

"Are you looking for the messenger bag?"

"It's on the list."

"Okay." Sam sagged into the pillows, filled with relief. "Okay."

"Try to get some sleep, will you?"

"I'll try. Talk to you in the morning." Sam closed the flip phone and plugged it into the charger she kept on the bedside table.

"Can they get that done overnight?" Nick asked from his side of the bed.

"They'll have to wake up a judge, but they should be able to make a case that it's urgent. If his wife came to see him in jail, he could tell her what to get rid of, so time is of the essence."

"You really think he had something to do with your father's shooting?"

"I don't want to think that—for many, many reasons— but I can't ignore what the evidence is telling me. Archie is looking through the footage from the day of the shooting. If he can put Conklin there, that'd be huge."

"It's not enough that your guy Davis and one of the paramedics said he was there?"

"That's damning, for sure, but the video would be irrefutable."

Nick reached for her, and Sam turned toward him, sighing as he wrapped his arms around her. "Try to shut it off for a few hours so you can get some rest." His hand made soothing circles on her back.

Even as her brain continued to spin, she couldn't keep her eyes open any longer. Wrapped up in her husband's love, she was able to let it go and relax into sleep.

CHAPTER TWENTY-ONE

LATE-NIGHT PHONE CALLS were part of the job, but they still stopped Joe Farnsworth's heart every time, usually because they involved some sort of trouble. He grabbed the phone off the bedside table and started to get out of bed so he wouldn't disturb Marti.

She stopped him with a hand on his arm. "I'm awake."

"Sorry." He took the call from Jake. "What's up?"

"Sam called me to ask if anyone had thought to get a warrant for Conklin's house in regard to the missing messenger bag. With your permission, I'm going to wake up a judge to request a warrant tonight because Conklin's wife was in to see him earlier."

Jake didn't have to spell out the need for urgency, especially in light of the wife's visit. "Do it."

"I'm on it."

"The messenger bag you're looking for... The last time I saw it, he had the Kiss Me I'm Irish key chain I brought back from Ireland for him attached to it. Not sure if it was still there that last day, but I figured I'd mention it."

"That's good to know."

"Keep me posted?"

"You got it."

Joe ended the call but kept the phone in his hand, almost as if he expected it to ring again momentarily.

Marti turned over to face him. "What's going on?"

"We're going to get a warrant to search Conklin's house."

"Oh, Joe. Dear God. Has it come to that?"

Per his orders to the others, he hadn't told her, but it would only be a matter of time before the news got out. "We arrested him earlier. He says he wasn't on G Street the day of Skip's shooting. We have two witnesses who can put him there. One of them is a man who ran back to offer aid to Skip and has checked in with Conklin every year on the anniversary of the shooting. We'd never heard his name before this week. And one of the paramedics who was on the scene told Sam that he gave Skip's messenger bag to Conklin. It's never been seen again. That's what Jake's call was about. We're getting a warrant to search Conklin's home for the bag and anything else that might be relevant."

Marti's expression registered shock and horror. "You have to be kidding me with this."

"You have no idea how much I wish I was kidding."

"Why would he withhold that information for all this time? Skip was his friend."

"Your guess is as good as mine." He paused, considered and decided to tell her what'd happened recently with Wallack. It went against everything he believed in to tell tales out of work, even to her, but this one needed to be shared if only to help him wrap his head around it. "This isn't the first time he's kept something to himself that he should've shared."

"What else?"

"He knew Kenny Wallack was missing for two weeks before we found out. Sam went to his house looking for him in the middle of the night. His wife freaked out thinking he had to be dead if she was there at that hour. That's when we found out he'd been missing for two weeks. She'd reported it to Kenny's close friend Conklin, who kept it to himself."

"Why didn't he tell you?"

"He said he was afraid Wallack had fallen off the wagon again and he was trying to protect him."

"And you believed that?"

"I didn't know what to believe, but I suspended him for a week for not following proper procedures in reporting a missing person. Ever since then, he's been keeping his distance."

"I can't believe what I'm hearing. He's always been one of your closest friends and advisers."

"I know, and because of that, his downfall could spell mine too."

"How so?"

"It's well-known that we're close friends, and if my deputy chief and longtime friend is crooked in some way, that's going to rain down on me."

"That's not fair! You knew nothing about any of this."

"The argument will be made that I should've known. The buck stops with me, honey. You know how that works."

"It's all so unbelievable."

"I know. For me too. Our academy class was known for being super tight—me, Jake, Skip, Conklin, Wallack, Steve Coyne. I was closer to Jake and Skip than the others, but I always thought any of them would have my back."

"I've been thinking a lot about Steven since I saw

Alice at the funeral. The poor thing was so broken up over Skip's passing."

"She would be. Skip was so good to her after Steven was killed, even at the expense of his own marriage when he was with Brenda."

"It's strange that both Steven's shooting and Skip's are unsolved."

Her innocuous comment hit him like a fist to the gut. Was it possible the two shootings were somehow related, even coming several decades apart? The question had him reaching for the phone again.

Marti sat up in bed. "Joe? What is it?"

He put through the call to Jake, who picked up on the first ring. "What's up?"

"Marti said something." It would be no surprise to Jake that he'd shared the latest developments with his wife.

"What'd she say?"

"About Steve Coyne and Skip both being part of un-solved shootings. It made me wonder."

"If they're related somehow?"

"Exactly."

"Jesus, Joe. I can't even let my mind go there."

"I think our minds have to go there in light of re-cent events."

"You can't possibly think…"

"I don't what to think!"

Jake took a deep breath and blew it out. "Something like this… It could bring us all down if it somehow comes back to Conklin."

"Believe me, I know."

After a long pause, Jake said, "Let me think about this. I need time to process it. We'll talk in the morning?"

"See you then. Call me if anything breaks overnight."

"I will."

Joe ended the call and plugged the phone back into the charger. He reached for Marti, and she snuggled up to him, putting her arm around his waist and resting her head on his chest.

"No matter what happens, everything will be all right. We have each other, and that's all we need."

He tightened his hold on her. "I know." She was all he needed, but he wished he believed her when she said everything was going to be all right. He had a bad feeling about where this investigation was leading.

SAM'S FIRST ORDER of business in the morning was a text to her mother. Give me a call when you're up and about.

Her phone rang ten minutes later as Sam was getting dressed. "Hey."

"Morning."

"Do you have time to grab coffee this morning?"

"Absolutely. Do you want to come by my place? I've got coffee and corn muffins."

"That sounds good. I'll be there shortly."

"Looking forward to it."

They ended the call, and Sam finished dressing in jeans, a sweater and running shoes in anticipation of pounding some pavement as she followed up on leads from the tip line. It wasn't what she wanted to be doing, but it was what she was allowed to do. Keeping busy was critical, especially when all she really wanted was to take to her bed and pull the covers up over her head to keep everyone away.

Everyone except Nick, of course. There was never a time she didn't want him close by.

A soft knock sounded on the door to the room she used as a closet. She opened the door to Nick, who held a steaming mug of coffee fixed just the way she liked it.

"Step into my boudoir."

Nick came into the room, shut the door and handed over the coffee. "How is it that you can make four little words sound so sexy first thing in the morning?"

"It's my special talent."

"One of your many special talents. I've been thinking about some of your other special talents that were on full display last night." He leaned in to kiss her, sending shivers down her spine.

"I did some rather good work last night, if I do say so myself."

"*All* your work in that department is good work."

"Glad you think so. You're my best customer."

"I'd better be your *only* customer."

She smiled at him, amazed that he could make her laugh and smile and think about things other than the pervasive blanket of grief that hung over her. "Where are my children?" He'd taken the early shift, getting the kids up and dressed so she could sleep in a little.

"Having breakfast with Shelby and Noah." His gorgeous hazel eyes skirted over her face, looking for signs of trouble. "How're you doing, babe?"

Sam took a sip of the coffee and put the mug on a nearby shelf. "I'm okay. Trying to stay busy so I don't give in to the urge to take to my bed and pull the covers over my head."

"No one would blame you if you needed to do that for a few days."

"That's not my style."

"Not usually, but you've never lost your dad before."

"No, but we've also never been closer to finding out who shot him either, and I can't sit on the sidelines while that's going on."

"Understandable, as long as you promise me you'll take good care of my wife. I love her more than anything, and I know how bad she's hurting right now. If you need to walk away, do it. And if you need me—at any time—you call me, and I'll come running."

Touched by his sweet words, she caressed his freshly shaved face. "You can't come running. The Secret Service won't let you."

"Let them try to stop me if my wife needs me."

Sam rested her head on his chest and sighed as his arms came around her. "You always know just what I need."

"That's my superpower."

"As awful as it is to lose my dad, I'd be out of my mind without you to prop me up."

"I'll always be here to prop you up. No matter what."

"That makes everything better. Thank you."

"I'm so sorry you're hurting, sweetheart."

"I know, but I keep telling myself he's free, and that brings comfort. He's running around up there in heaven, dancing like a fool and throwing big parties with not a wheelchair in sight."

"That's a good way to think of him."

"It's the only way I can stand to think of him not being here anymore." She looked up at him. "How do you think Scotty is doing?"

"He's quieter than usual, but he seems okay. We've been talking a lot about Skip and things we both remember. Last night I told him about the day I met Skip and how I was sure he was going to have me killed for being in your bedroom. He loved that."

"That was pretty funny—and the best part was that even as a quadriplegic, he could've done it if he'd wanted to."

"I know! Why do you think I was so freaked out?"

"He never would've killed you after he saw how much I love you—and more important, how much you love me. That made him very happy."

"I'm glad he had peace of mind where you're concerned."

"As much as he ever had where I'm concerned."

Nick laughed. "You must've been one hell of a handful when you were younger."

"I kept him on his toes."

"I can only imagine. What's on your docket for today?"

"Breakfast with my mother and then pounding the pavement with some of the leads that have come into the tip line."

"You're not doing that alone, are you?"

"Yeah, but I'm visiting my mom and Alice Fitzgerald, so I'll be fine. What're you up to?"

"Meetings on top of meetings. Another day in paradise."

"Not sure how you stand the excitement."

His eyes glittered with anticipation. "We're doing more budget stuff today."

"You're not right in the head if you find that exciting."

"Someone's gotta do it, and the president has asked me to take the lead in dealing with Congress to get the budget hammered out so we can be done with this continuing resolution and have an actual budget in place."

"Did I just pass out from boredom? I think I blacked out for a second there."

He gave her a gentle spank and a quick kiss. "Don't make fun of your policy-wonk husband. It's not nice."

"That was me being nice."

Leaving her with a smile, he headed for the door. "Call me if you need me today. I mean it, Samantha. I will come running."

"I know. Thank you."

"Be careful with my cop today. I love her so much."

"Be careful with my VP today. I love him so much."

Winking, he went out the door, leaving her feeling settled and loved and well supported. She finished the coffee he'd brought her and headed downstairs to see her kids before she left for the day.

FORTY MINUTES LATER, Sam approached her mother's townhouse in Arlington. The house had a white brick facade with black shutters and a black door, as well as pumpkins on each of the three cement stairs that led to the front door, where Brenda waited to let her in. Sam tipped her face to receive the kiss her mother placed on her cheek.

"This is a nice surprise." Brenda had her shoulder-length brown hair up in a bun and her brown eyes were warm with welcome for her youngest daughter.

Sam wondered if this was as weird for her mother as it was for her, seeing each other and acting normal, like there'd never been twenty years of silence between them.

"Sorry it's been a while since I stopped by." In fact, Sam hadn't been there once since she and her sisters helped her mother move in earlier in the year.

"Like your father, I suspect it takes an act of Congress to get you to cross the Potomac."

Sam sent her a sheepish grin. "That's kinda true."

Brenda laughed. "That's okay. I know how busy you are. I'll take what I can get. Come on back." She led the way to the kitchen, which was painted a dark taupe that somehow made the room seem brighter than it would've been with a lighter color of paint.

"I like that color."

"Do you?" Brenda glanced at the wall. "I'm not a hundred percent sold on it."

"It works in here."

"I'm glad you think so. I needed a second opinion. I just did it a couple of weeks ago and was hoping it would grow on me." She poured coffee for Sam and put it on the high-top table along with a small porcelain creamer. "You don't take sugar, right?"

Touched that her mother remembered that kind of detail from so long ago, Sam shook her head. "No, I don't."

Brenda toasted two corn muffins, buttered them and put them on plates that she delivered to the table.

Sam broke off a piece of the muffin and popped it into her mouth. "Thanks for feeding me."

"My pleasure. I've been thinking about you nonstop. I know how hard it must be for you since losing your dad. He loved you all fiercely, but you…"

"I know." Sam's throat closed as her eyes filled. To keep from losing her composure, she focused on the coffee and picked at her muffin. "It seems impossible to imagine going on without him."

"I'm sure it does. I remember when my father died. I wondered if I'd survive it. At the time, my mother said something that's stayed with me ever since. She said it's the circle of life, and it's important to remember that life is a fatal illness. Ain't none of us getting out of here alive."

"That's true, but it sure does suck when someone has to leave us."

"It really does. No way around that, especially when it's your soul mate."

"One of them anyway."

"He was so damned proud of you, Nick and Scotty. The day I stopped to see him and Celia, he glowed when he talked about all of you. He absolutely loved how happy you are with Nick, and Scotty was the apple of his eye."

"I'm glad he got to meet Nick and Scotty and the twins."

"How're they doing? I think about those poor babies all the time too."

"They're adjusting remarkably well. They still have their difficult moments, but we're trying to get them back on a regular schedule, and Shelby has just been a godsend. They adore her, but then again, we all do."

"She's amazing. You're lucky to have her."

"And we know it. Nick and I say all the time that she's the glue that holds the whole operation together. We'd be lost without her."

"What will happen with the twins when their brother graduates from college, or maybe I shouldn't ask?"

"It's okay to ask. Nick talked to him about that yesterday, and he agreed that we'll figure something out that'll keep them in our lives."

"I hope you're not setting yourself up for more heartbreak, Sam."

"I hope not either but offering to help them didn't feel like a decision. It just felt necessary."

"I can understand that. They sure are cute." Brenda had met them at the reception that had followed Skip's funeral, when Shelby brought them to the Hay-Adams.

"Yes, they are, and they're very sweet too. We love them very much."

"I can see why." Brenda stirred sweetener into her coffee and then glanced at Sam. "As much as I love catching up and any excuse to see you, something tells me you didn't cross the river for small talk. That never was your strong suit."

"No, it isn't, and you're right." Sam used a paper napkin to wipe her mouth after devouring the rest of the delicious muffin. "We're actually making some headway in solving Dad's case—the first real headway since it happened."

"Wow, that's amazing. You must be thrilled."

Sam shrugged. How to describe how the elation of getting much-needed answers was muted by the pervasive grief of his death? "I am, but part of me feels like it doesn't matter as much now that he's gone."

"It matters very much. The person who shot him robbed you and your sisters and your children and Celia of possible *decades* with him. And don't look at me like that. I loved that man for most of my adult life, and even after everything that came between us, I never stopped loving him. The day of his shooting…" Brenda shook her head and looked down. "I'll never forget that call from Tracy. My heart broke right along with all of yours."

Her mother's passionate words touched Sam deeply. In all the years she'd spent estranged from her mother, it hadn't occurred to her that her mother might still love her father. "Could I ask you—"

"Anything you want."

"If you loved him so much, why did you leave him for someone else?" It was a question that had tormented Sam for twenty years, and even though it wasn't the question she'd come here to ask, there'd never been a better opportunity to put it out there.

Brenda sighed and sat back in her chair. "Marriage is a complicated thing, as you certainly know. After Steven Coyne was killed, nothing was ever the same between your dad and me. I felt like I lost him almost as completely as Alice lost Steven. I tried for a long time to make things right between us, but after a while, when I didn't get anything back from him, I quit trying. By the time I met Bill, I didn't feel married anymore. It was wrong. I knew it then, and I know it now, but my only defense is that I was lonely and vulnerable, and I liked the way he made me feel important again. None of this is intended to excuse my behavior. I should've asked your father for a divorce, and I'll always regret how I handled that time in my life. I hurt you and your sisters and your father, the four people I loved the most. I'm very sorry for that. You have no idea how sorry I am."

Sam appreciated the apology, as she had the first time her mother offered it.

"I hope you believe me when I tell you it's my biggest regret, the one thing I'd do differently if I had to do it over."

"I believe you. But we can't go backward. Only forward, and I'm glad you're back, that we can see each other again."

"You have no idea how glad of that I am." Brenda blinked back tears as she placed her hand over Sam's. "No idea. I missed so much with you."

Sam gave her mother's hand a squeeze.

"Enough of that." Brenda wiped her eyes and smiled.

"You came here to talk about the case. What can I do to help? I'll do anything I can."

"Talk to me about Paul Conklin."

CHAPTER TWENTY-TWO

BRENDA'S BROWS FURROWED with surprise. "What about him?"

"Anything and everything. I'm looking for perspective from way back when."

Brenda gave that some thought. "He and your dad met at the academy, came up through the ranks together. Paul had some problems with alcohol, and your dad brought him home to stay with us for a while after his first marriage ended."

"Why don't I remember that?"

"You were really young. He stayed in your room while you slept with Angela."

Sam tried to remember but drew a blank. "Were you friends with him too?"

"I was friendly with him, but not *friends* the way I was with Joe, Jake and Steven."

"Were they competitive with each other?"

"Somewhat. Your dad and Joe were the rock stars of the group. They all said that. Jake never wanted to be chief or move beyond captain. He'd say he didn't want the headaches, but Joe and your dad… They wanted to go as far as they could on the job. Steven used to say he just wanted to go home to Alice every night. He didn't think much beyond that."

"What about Conklin?"

"I don't recall him being part of those conversations,

at least not while I was around. What has you asking about him?"

"I'm not supposed to talk about this, but we've learned that he knew more about Dad's shooting than he let on."

Brenda's mouth fell open. "What did he know?"

"We interviewed a man who rendered aid to Dad, and that man has contacted Conklin on every anniversary of the shooting. I heard his name for the first time two days ago. Conklin swears he wasn't on G Street that day, but we have a paramedic who can put him there."

"But *why*? Why would he withhold that info? Your dad was his *friend*."

"We don't know, but we're going to find out."

Slumping in her chair, Brenda shook her head. "This is just so hard to believe."

"For all of us."

"Joe must be reeling."

"He is."

"You should talk to Alice. She and Steven were closer to Paul and his first wife than we were. She might have some insight."

"I'll do that." Sam checked her watch. "I need to get going. Thank you for breakfast and the insight."

"Anytime."

Brenda got up to walk her to the door and gestured to the keypad lock. "The code is my birthday. Come by anytime and let yourself in. My home is your home."

Sam hugged her. "I'll do that."

"I'm here if I can help."

"Thank you."

When she was in the car, Sam put through a call to Malone.

"What's up?" He sounded rushed and stressed.

"I'm doing some background work. I'll be in shortly."

"Okay."

"I had a thought. I assume you and the chief spoke to Conklin the other night after I told you what Davis said?"

"We both did."

"Might be worth a shot to dump his phone to see who he talked to after you guys were there."

"Good thought, and if I wasn't so shocked, I probably would've already done it. I'll get a warrant and put Archie on it. People around here are buzzing about Conklin being arrested. We're going to need to put up or shut up soon."

"What's Forrester saying?"

"That we need more."

"Then let's get it for him."

"That's the plan."

"I'll let you get back to it. I'll be in shortly." Sam directed her car to the home of Alice Coyne Fitzgerald. Sam knew where she lived these days because her son had been involved in an investigation last year. Poor Alice had had more than her share of heartbreak. In addition to losing her first husband on the job, a son from her second marriage had been kidnapped and killed.

The case had been the only one of her father's career that had been left unsolved, and when Sam decided to dig into the cold case after taking command of the Homicide squad, her father had reacted badly. Later, she'd learned that Tyler Fitzgerald was Alice Coyne's youngest son from her second marriage, and her dad had been protecting Alice by not pursuing the case against her older son. The situation had caused an unusual rift between Sam and her father, who'd pleaded with her to leave it alone. Sam later learned that her dad had gone to great lengths to protect Alice's family, risking his own job, reputation and marriage.

Allowing someone to get away with murder wasn't her usual groove, but she'd deferred to her father's wishes and left the case officially unsolved, even as all the evidence had pointed to Alice's older son, Cameron.

Sam parked two blocks from the home Alice shared with her sons' father, Jimmy Fitzgerald. Sam had become acquainted with Alice after she reopened Tyler's case and had seen her most recently at Skip's funeral. Sam rang the doorbell and waited, hoping someone would be home. She didn't think Alice worked anymore, but she honestly didn't know what she did.

The inside door swung open, and Alice offered a warm, welcoming smile as she pushed open the storm door for Sam. "Hi there."

"Hi. It's nice to see you again."

She ushered Sam into the house. "How're you holding up? I was telling Jimmy that I was most worried about you. Skip talked about you all the time."

Even though she knew that, it still struck Sam in the heart every time someone told her. "I'm holding up okay. As you know all too well, it's a process."

"It is indeed." She led Sam to the back of the deep townhouse, into a sunny kitchen with white eyelet curtains on the window. "Can I get you anything?"

"A glass of water would be great." She'd had more than enough coffee. Any more and she'd be jumpy, which was the last thing she needed.

When they were seated at the table, Sam took a close look at a still-pretty face lined with years that hadn't been good to her. Sam took a sip of her water. "We're taking another look at my dad's case."

"I heard that on the news. It makes sense with everyone talking about it again."

"That's what we think too, and that's why I'm here."

"What can I do?"

"I'm looking for some background from the early days of my dad's career, the time he spent in the academy and with Steven as his partner."

"That was a very long time ago." Alice's wistful look indicated the lingering sadness over her first husband's sudden death. "A very long time ago." She stirred cream into her coffee, her gaze fixed on the swirl of the liquid.

"I'm sorry to resurrect old hurts, but I'm in bad need of some perspective."

"The old hurts are never far from the surface, even after all this time. I love Jimmy. I really do. But Steven, he was…" She shrugged helplessly. "You never really get over it. You just learn to live with it."

Sam ached for her.

"Your dad was so very good to me afterward. I wouldn't have survived it without him."

"He loved Steven like a brother."

"The feeling was mutual. They were quite a pair, those two." Alice chuckled and shook her head. "Always laughing and joking. I used to tell them I felt left out because they had a language all their own, and I didn't get their jokes half the time. Steven would tell me not to fret because the jokes weren't worth the bother of getting them."

"My partner and I are like that too. You spend so much time together, you develop a shorthand."

"Yes, that's it exactly."

"Who else were they close to at that time?"

"Well, Joe, of course, and Jake Malone, Paul Conklin, Roy Gallagher."

"The councilman?"

"Yes, he graduated from the academy with the guys, but he didn't last a year on the force. Said it wasn't for him after all. After he left the job, he didn't hang out with the guys as much as he had before, but he still came around from time to time."

"What did he do for work after he left the department?"

"I'm not really sure. We didn't see much of him after he quit, but he ran for council, and he's been there ever since, as you know."

Sam pulled out her notebook and made a note to check out Gallagher's life after his short stint in the department. "I had no idea he'd been a cop or that he was friends with my dad and the others."

"Roy wasn't like the rest of them. He had lofty ambitions that went far beyond the mundane life of a beat cop. Steven used to say Roy was too good for the job. It was clear early on that he wasn't going to last long on the force."

Sam took notes as Alice spoke. "What about Conklin? What're your recollections of him?"

"He was kind of a hot mess back in the day. He and his wife had one of those marriages that would be on reality TV nowadays. Always fighting and never caring who was listening, which made the rest of us so uncomfortable. They drank a lot, so much that we used to wonder how he managed to get up for work the next day. Then it all blew up—the marriage and the drinking. Your dad took him in for a time, helped him get sober and probably saved his career in the process."

Sam took notes of everything she said. "What was the first wife's name?"

"Jane."

"Do you know where she is now?"

"I have no idea. After they split, I never saw her again. She wasn't really close to the other wives. We kept our distance, because the two of them were no fun to be around. Truthfully, we wondered why she stayed with him. He thought nothing of going off on her in front of everyone, and she'd just sit there and take it, like she was so immune to his nonsense she barely heard him anymore. It was awful to witness."

"Sounds like it." Bad marriages, Sam had discovered, came in all shapes and sizes. Some were physically abusive, others emotionally abusive and still others were lacking in important elements that made it possible for two people to spend a lifetime together.

"What did you think of him specifically?"

"At the time, I thought he was kind of a bully. He'd get drunk and mouthy, and Jane was his favorite target. I understand that he changed a lot after he quit drinking. I wouldn't know. I never socialized with him again after Steven died."

"Conklin wasn't one of the officers who stepped up for you after he died?"

"No, he wasn't. Your dad was there the most, along with Joe and Jake and people like Norm Morganthau, who was the medical examiner and a friend of Steven's from childhood. But Paul never came around after the shooting. Of course, he was there for the funeral and everything, but not particularly for me."

"I'm trying to get my head around the timing of things. Maybe you can help me with that. The guys graduated from the academy, went to work for the department, got married, hung out together, et cetera. Steven was killed, Conklin's marriage broke up, he got sober... Do I have the order correct?"

"Paul and Jane broke up before Steven was killed. I remember that very distinctly. Steven expressed relief to me that their toxic soup of a marriage was over. He used those words—*toxic soup*. I remember thinking it was an apt description."

"Okay, the Conklins split, Steven was killed and then Conklin got sober?"

Alice thought about that. "Yes. Your mom was a saint to put up with all the time your dad spent with me during those first few years after I lost Steven. I know it caused a lot of problems between them, but I was so thankful for Skip's steady presence that I never stopped to question how hard it must've been for Brenda to share him with me." She paused and glanced at Sam. "Why does all of this matter now?"

"It's not public knowledge yet, but Conklin has been arrested for holding back info relevant to my dad's shooting." Sam told herself that the arrest would make the news at any time now, and everyone would know.

Shock registered in Alice's expression. "How could he do that? He and your dad were friends and colleagues for thirtysomething years."

"We'd all like to know."

"How did you find out?"

"A call to the tip line from someone who was on G Street that day and interacted with Conklin, who had claimed to not be there. We were able to track down a first responder who could also attest to Conklin's presence."

"That's just astonishing."

"Indeed, and it's imperative that you don't share that info with anyone. We're building a case that we hope will finally lead to answers in my dad's case."

"I won't say a word. I promise."

"You've been really helpful. I appreciate it."

"I'm happy to do anything I can to help you get answers for Skip. He was one of the best friends I ever had, and I'll never forget him. In many ways, he put me back together after I lost Steven."

"I know he thought the world of you both. He never got over losing Steven so suddenly. When we lost Detective Arnold earlier this year, his advice and counsel were so critical to me and the rest of my squad. He'd walked the walk, so he was such a huge help to us."

"I love that he was still participating at that level, even after such an awful injury."

"Because he was so sharp mentally, it made it easy to forget how precarious his physical condition really was."

"Which made his death that much more shocking."

"Right."

"I'm so, so sorry for your loss. I know how close you were to him and how hard it has to be to go on without him."

"It's hard, but I'm doing what he'd want me to do by getting back to work and staying focused on my family and my job."

"I can only imagine how proud of you he had to be."

"He was proud of all of us and never tried to hide it. We were very lucky to have him."

Alice stood to walk Sam out. "We all were, and I will hope and pray that you are able to finally get justice for him."

At the front door, Sam gave Alice a quick hug. "Thank you for all your help." She handed Alice a business card. "If you think of anything else that might be relevant, give me a call?"

"I will. For sure."

"Thanks again."

Thinking about everything she'd learned from her mother and Alice, Sam directed the car toward HQ. Halfway there, she took a call from Freddie. "What's up?"

"Hill is going to interview Conklin. Thought you might want to observe."

"You thought right. I'll be there in ten. Any word on the search of Conklin's house?"

"Only that it's ongoing."

"What about the dump of his phone?"

"Haven't heard anything on that."

"All right. I'll see you soon." She flipped the phone closed and focused on driving, darting between cars and changing lanes anytime she found an opening in the morning traffic jam. Her mind filtered through the details she'd been given by two women who'd had front-row views of the complex relationships between the various players who'd made up her father's inner circle—on the job and off duty.

The bonds formed between police officers could be deep and sometimes closer than family. They could also be acrimonious and competitive while appearing cordial on the surface. Sam had experienced every sort of dynamic with her colleagues during her years on the job. Some were closer than family. Others had become mortal enemies. And still others entered her orbit as needed and then exited without leaving much of an impact. Sifting through the information she'd gathered that morning, she tried to figure out which category Conklin and her father had fallen into.

Had Conklin been secretly jealous of Skip's promotion to deputy chief even while acting as his friend and supporter? It wouldn't be the first time someone had been two-faced when a friend moved ahead in the ranks. Jealousy could undercut even the most solid of friendships, but had Conklin been jealous enough to orchestrate what amounted to the attempted murder of his rival? Sam found that possibility hard to believe, but then again, she'd never understand how the deputy chief could've sat on information pertinent to her father's case for four years while pretending to be his close friend.

The jealousy motive seemed too simplistic, especially in light of their decades of personal friendship that had included Skip providing Conklin with a place to stay during a difficult time in the other man's life. A rational person would deduce that Conklin would be eternally grateful to Skip for what he'd done for him then, which by all accounts had helped to ensure that Conklin's promising career didn't get derailed.

No matter how she looked at it, she couldn't make sense of any scenario that would lead to Conklin either participating in or concealing evidence pertaining to her father's shooting.

Sam parked outside the morgue entrance at HQ and ducked inside, ignoring the larger-than-usual scrum of reporters gathered outside the main doors. On the way past, she'd noticed a couple of reporters who were usually assigned to the White House. Why were they slumming at HQ? Was there really that much interest in the death of the second lady's father? If so, it must be a slower-than-usual news week. Or maybe they were after more about Sam and Nick taking in the Armstrong children. Either way, they were going to leave disappointed. She had nothing to say about either of those things.

She navigated the hallways that led to the pit, which

was buzzing with activity when she arrived. "What's the latest, people?"

Cameron Green swiveled around in his chair to greet her. "We're still going through Conklin's files. Nothing new to report, but we're making headway."

Nothing new to report could have been the theme of her father's investigation until lately, when they'd finally gotten a few breaks, even if no one liked where they'd led.

Sam nodded in acknowledgment of Green's statement. "Can someone get me the files on the shooting of Officer Steven Coyne?"

McBride stood. "I'll do it."

"Thank you. What time is Hill talking to Conklin?"

"Thirty minutes," Freddie said.

"Got it." Sam unlocked her office, went inside and flipped on the lights, eyeing the huge stack of cards Malone had left for her. With some time to kill, she started opening the cards, most of them from people she'd never met but who'd had some sort of memorable encounter with Skip Holland during his time on the job.

I wanted you to know that your father once saved me on a night when my life exploded into violence at the hands of my ex-husband. Sergeant Holland's calm, cool, rational approach to a fraught situation not only saved my life, but my children's lives. He made a difference for my family that night, and I've never forgotten him. Wishing him eternal rest and Godspeed for you and your family.

As a faithful supporter of the city's Little League baseball program, Skip was a visible presence to the at-risk children who played the game for more than twenty years. He has our undying respect and admiration, and we extend our sympathy to the entire Holland family on the loss of a great man and dedicated public servant.

The District has lost a great man.

Our hearts are with you.

May he rest in peace.

Thank you for sharing your father with us. His enormous sacrifice will never be forgotten.

Sam read every message, her eyes filling more than once at the sweet words people had used to describe her dad. Though her heart broke all over again at the reminder of his death, she took comfort in knowing he'd been so loved and respected.

She kept opening the cards, reading each message and making a pile to take home to share with Celia, Tracy and Angela. Flipping open a card that expressed sympathy for the loss of her father, she read the message that seemed to have been hastily scrawled.

Look inside your own "house" and City Hall. The answers are closer than you think.

Sam read the message a second time and then dropped the card to her desktop. "Cruz!"

Freddie appeared in the doorway. "What's up?"

"Get me an evidence bag."

"What've you got?"

"Get the bag, and I'll show you."

When Freddie returned with the evidence bag, Sam used the tip of a pen to lift the card to open it, revealing the message written inside.

"Holy crap."

"The quotes around the word *house* lead me to think it's someone who speaks cop."

"For sure." Freddie slid it into a bag.

"Get it to the lab. Let them know my prints will be on it. Ask them to expedite."

"Will do."

As he left the room, her desk extension rang. "Holland."

"It's Archie. Can you come up here?"

"On my way." As she left her office, Jeannie McBride returned to the pit empty-handed.

"The Coyne files were checked out by your father one week before his shooting and never returned."

A charge of awareness went through Sam, leaving a tingle in the area of her backbone. She'd learned to trust those tingles as they usually meant she was onto something big. "Search my father's stuff again for the Coyne files. I want everyone on that. I'll be right back."

CHAPTER TWENTY-THREE

SHE TOOK THE stairs to the IT division two at a time, praying she wouldn't run into Ramsey up there, as his Special Victims division was located across the hall from IT. Thankfully, the hallway was deserted as she ducked into IT and walked toward Archie's office in the back, ignoring the curious stares of his team as she passed their cubicles.

People were so damned curious about her these days, which was ridiculous. So her husband was the vice president. His lofty job hadn't changed her daily existence all that much, except for the fact that she was recognized everywhere she went. Otherwise, she was still the same person and cop she'd been before his promotion.

She stepped into Archie's office. "Hey. What's up?"

"Come in. Shut the door."

Surprised by the unusual secrecy, she did as he asked.

"Come see this."

She walked around his desk to the computer terminal that boasted a massive monitor. As she took in the scene on his screen, she realized she was looking at G Street. "Is that…"

"It's from the day of your dad's shooting."

When she took a closer look, she could see her dad's black boots on the ground. That was the only part of him she could see as he was surrounded by paramedics and other personnel. Her stomach knotted, her heart began to beat faster. She recalled being told at the time that it took almost fifteen minutes after their arrival for the paramedics to stabilize her dad to the point where he could be transported.

"Watch." Archie played the video and Sam watched the chaos unfold in a stream of flashing lights, uniformed first responders, grim-faced cops and...Conklin.

Sam gasped. "Oh my God."

"Right smack in the middle of it."

Not just in the middle of it, but supervising, directing, barking orders. "Holy fuck."

"I've got to turn this over to Hill, but I wanted you to see it first."

"I...I appreciate the heads-up." Shock whipped through her like an extra heartbeat as she stared at the freeze-framed image of the man who'd taken her father's place as deputy chief after Skip was medically retired.

"Sam? Are you okay?"

"For so long I've craved answers for my dad, for all of us. But this..."

"It's inconceivable." Archie's blunt statement summed it up perfectly.

"Why haven't we seen this before now?"

"It had gotten archived somehow."

"What does that mean?"

"When we're working a case, we keep everything associated with the case as part of the active file, including the film. For whatever reason, this piece of film wasn't part of the case file. I found it in the archives."

Sam tried to process what he was saying. "How did you know to look there?"

"After scouring everything attached to the case file,

I went through all the other footage we have from that day in the archives, just to see if we'd missed anything."

"In other words, if you hadn't done that, this might never have been seen again?"

"Correct."

"Can you tell who archived it?"

"I'm going to dig into that and see what I can find out."

"But it had to have been someone inside this building?"

"That's also correct. It would be someone who had access to case files and had admin authority. Captain or above."

Sam's legs felt rubbery, so she took a seat, landing hard in his visitor's chair. "What the hell is this, Archie?"

"I don't know, but you can bet that our whole team is doing everything we can to get to the bottom of it."

"And when we do? What happens then?"

"Then we throw the book at the motherfuckers who did this." His eyes fairly burned with the same fury she'd felt for years.

She leaned forward and dropped her head into her hands.

Archie sat next to her and put a hand on her shoulder. "I can't begin to imagine how difficult this has to be for you."

"It's nothing compared to how difficult life was for him the last four years."

"Still, to have the trail leading in-house is a kick in the teeth for all of us, but no one more so than you."

Sam shrugged. "It's not going to change anything or bring him back."

"Maybe not, but at least the person or people who tried to kill him won't be walking around free anymore."

It would be, Sam realized, a smaller comfort to catch his shooter now that her dad was gone than it would've been when he was still alive.

"There is that, and at least he won't be here to find out that one of his friends might've been involved."

"True."

Marshaling her resources, she stood and took a deep breath. "Thank you for your hard work on this. It's much appreciated."

"I wish I could say it's my pleasure, but it's certainly a privilege to hopefully get justice for a great man and decorated police officer."

"Thank you, Archie. I appreciate the heads-up on this."

"No problem."

"Let me know if you find anything else."

"You'll be the first to know."

"You're the best." Sam left him with a small smile and headed downstairs, continuing to puzzle through the various things they'd learned in the last few days and trying to make sense of the new details in the larger context.

Freddie was waiting for her when she returned to the pit. "No sign of the Coyne case files in your dad's boxes."

Sam thought of the boxes they'd found in Celia's attic. "Do you recall seeing them in the stuff at the house?" They'd rifled through the boxes so fast, she barely remembered what she'd seen.

"They weren't there."

"Do you think it was a coincidence that Dad was shot

days after he checked out those files on a cold case involving his former partner?"

"My partner, a very wise woman, has taught me that there's no such thing as coincidences."

"She *is* a very wise woman to have taught you that."

"You won't hear me arguing. What did Archie want?"

"Come in."

He followed her into the office, closed the door and leaned back against it.

"He found archived footage from the day of the shooting that shows Conklin right in the middle of the emergency response."

"Wow."

"The thing is—only a captain or above can archive the footage."

"Was he able to determine who did it?"

"He's working on that."

"It's like one bombshell after another."

"After years of nothing."

"How're you doing?"

"I'm trying to make sense of things that make no sense, but otherwise, I'm fine."

A knock sounded on the office door. Freddie pushed himself off the door and opened it to Captain Malone.

"Could I have a minute, Lieutenant?"

Sam waved him in. "Of course." To Freddie, she said, "Let me know when Hill is ready to start."

"I will." Freddie left the office and pulled the door closed.

"What's up?" Sam asked the captain.

"After the chief and I were at Conklin's the other night, he made three calls right after we left—one to his wife, one to his sleazeball lawyer, Bagley, and the other to Roy Gallagher."

Tingles once again electrified her, feeding the buzz of being onto something big. "That's the second time today Gallagher's name has come up. I saw Alice Coyne Fitzgerald earlier, and she said something about him having been part of your posse out of the academy."

"He was. Lasted a year. Said it wasn't for him. He ran for council a year later, and that's where he's been ever since."

"Of course I knew he'd been on the council for years, but I'd never heard about him being a cop."

"He didn't leave much of a mark. Wasn't here long enough."

"Impressions?"

"Big opinion of himself. Wasn't one of my favorite people. I was glad when he left the department. He didn't have the stuff."

Sam knew exactly what he meant. People either had what it took to be a cop or they didn't. It was that simple.

"Can we get Hill to ask Conklin why he called Gallagher after your visit the other night?"

"Already passed it along to him."

Sam nodded. "Good. And the search of Conklin's place?"

"Ongoing."

"One other thing to note—I asked McBride to get me the files from the Coyne case, and when she went to Records, she was told my dad checked them out a week before his shooting and they were never returned. We've looked through the files from his office, but they're not there."

Malone pondered that for a full minute, his expression not revealing anything. "What the hell is this, Sam?"

"I don't know, but I'm starting to wonder if the two shootings were related in some way."

"Joe suggested the same thing last night. At first I thought, *They were decades apart. How could they be related?* But now… Who the fuck knows?"

"Roll with me here for a second… What if Coyne had stumbled onto something that got him killed? And then what if my dad stumbled upon the same thing that had him wondering if it had gotten Coyne killed? He starts to dig into it, the wrong people find that out and next thing you know, Dad is fighting for his life. The month before the shooting was a blank to him afterward, so he wouldn't have remembered what he'd been doing."

"It's as good of a theory as I've heard since Conklin was implicated."

"Do I have your permission to continue to explore the possible connection between the two shootings?"

Malone laughed—hard.

"What the hell is so funny?"

"I'm trying to remember the last time you asked for my permission to do anything."

Sam rolled her eyes at him. "I'm not *that* insubordinate."

"Ah, yeah, you really are, but since you do such a magnificent job of making me look good, I let it go most of the time."

"Whatever. Answer the question—can I pursue this without it coming back to bite us in the ass on the conflict of interest front?"

"Proceed with caution. Keep me informed of every development, no matter how small."

"Will do."

"And if you find something, I'll have to take the credit."

"I don't care about that if it leads to closing the case."

A knock on the door had Malone opening it to Freddie.

"Hill is ready."

"We're coming," Malone said.

Sam got up to follow them, anxious to hear what the deputy chief had to say for himself. Not that anything he could say would make up for the fact that he'd withheld pertinent information for nearly four years.

SAM, FREDDIE AND Malone stepped into the interrogation observation room, joining Chief Farnsworth and Tom Forrester. Sam couldn't remember the last time the U.S. Attorney himself had come to HQ to observe an interrogation. Assistant U.S. Attorney Faith Miller was also there and greeted Sam with a sympathetic smile.

Hill appeared in the doorway. "Is everyone here?"

Farnsworth nodded.

Sam made eye contact with Hill, hoping she was conveying everything she needed to tell him without saying a word that could compromise the case.

Hill gave a subtle lift of his chin to let her know he understood the magnitude of what he was about to do and how much it meant to her and so many others. Then he turned and headed into the room where Conklin sat with his attorney. Dressed in the orange jumpsuit that prisoners wore in the city jail and sporting stubble on his jaw, Conklin barely resembled the top-ranking cop they were used to seeing at HQ every day.

In his younger years, he'd been blond, but now his hair was thinning on top and was mostly gray. His face was pinched with strain, which Sam found enormously satisfying. *Good*, she thought. *You should be stressed, you evil son of a bitch.*

Avery's deputy, George Terrell, joined him in the interrogation room.

Terrell requested permission to record the interview.

Bagley gave permission, and Terrell turned on the recording device that sat in the middle of the table.

"Special Agent in Charge Avery Hill and Special Agent George Terrell in the interview of Paul Conklin, suspended deputy chief of the Metropolitan Police Department, represented by Charles Bagley." Hill also provided the date and time of the interview. "Mr. Conklin, you are charged with concealing evidence in the investigation into the shooting of Deputy Chief Skip Holland."

Sam absolutely loved that Hill referred to Conklin as *Mr.* Conklin and her dad as deputy chief. He had earned her eternal affection with that one sentence.

Conklin's eyes narrowed with disdain that also pleased her. "I didn't withhold anything."

"Did you speak to a man named Frank Davis on G Street on the date in question?"

"I wasn't on G Street that day."

"Special Agent Terrell, would you please play the footage from the scene of Skip Holland's shooting?"

At that, Conklin sat up a little straighter in his seat.

Bagley glanced at him, eyebrow raised.

Opening his laptop, Terrell called up the footage Archie had found and turned the computer to face Conklin and Bagley before pressing Play.

Sam held her breath, her gaze fixed on Conklin's face as he watched the clip.

His expression never changed, but his body language conveyed increased tension.

"As you can see from the video, you were present at the scene of Skip Holland's shooting, and according to Mr. Davis, you spoke with him. In addition, Lieutenant

Kevin Viera told investigators that he gave you Skip Holland's messenger bag. Can you tell us what you did with that bag?"

Conklin didn't blink. "I wasn't there. I don't know Frank Davis. And no one gave me anything of Skip's."

"The video puts you at the scene," Hill said. "Mr. Davis can attest to the fact that he spoke to you and called you annually on the anniversary of the shooting, looking for information about the investigation. We have his number on your call log on three straight anniversaries of the shooting. Viera, who had worked with you in the past, is certain he gave the messenger bag to you. That's a lot of evidence that indicates you *were* at the scene."

"I wasn't."

"Would you be willing to take a polygraph?"

"My client is a highly decorated police officer." To Sam, Bagley sounded like an arrogant ass. "That his reputation is being impugned this way is a crime, and your questions are opening the MPD and the FBI to a massive lawsuit."

"We'll take our chances," Hill said drolly. "Answer the question, Mr. Conklin. Would you be willing to undergo a polygraph examination?"

Conklin shifted in his seat.

"No polygraphs," Bagley said. "My client has answered your questions truthfully and should be released from custody immediately."

Hill's chuckle appeared to infuriate Conklin. "That's not going to happen. Your client will be arraigned in the morning on felony charges of withholding pertinent information in a manslaughter investigation that has been upgraded to a homicide. He will also be charged with lying to the FBI."

Conklin snarled at him. "I didn't withhold anything, and I'm not lying."

"Tell it to the jury. We have multiple witnesses who say otherwise, as well as video that puts you at the scene." Hill gathered his notes into a pile and stood.

"Wait." Conklin sounded nervous now. "Where're you going?"

"We're finished here."

Bagley stood to face off with Hill. "I trust that you'll be releasing my client?"

Hill leaned forward, getting right in the lawyer's face. "You trust incorrectly. Your client will be held until arraignment at which time he's apt to be ordered held without bail, which will be my recommendation to the U.S. Attorney."

Conklin stood, his face red and his eyes popping. "This is outrageous!"

"You know what's outrageous?" Hill spoke softly, but his words were laced with steel. "Withholding evidence involving the attempted murder of a fellow law enforcement officer who thought of you as a friend. That's truly outrageous, and you have only yourself to blame for whatever happens next. Let's go, Agent Terrell. We're finished here."

Sam wanted to stand and applaud the FBI agent who, at times, had been a thorn in her side. Today, he'd been an advocate for her father and the truth, and she'd never appreciated him more than she did right then.

"That was very well done, Agent Hill," Farnsworth said when Hill appeared at the door to the observation room.

"*Very* well done," Sam said. "Thank you."

"I wish I could say it was a pleasure." Disgust clung to his every word. Catching one of their own in a web of lies was one of the most difficult things any law enforcement officer confronted, but when those lies involved the shooting of another well-respected, decorated officer, it only compounded the disgust.

"Please keep us posted," Farnsworth said.

Hill nodded. "You do the same."

After Hill had left, Farnsworth turned to Sam. "Your team is still investigating Conklin?"

"They're on it. We'll let you know if we've got anything useful. In the meantime, I've got a few things I'm following up on."

"You're not working the Conklin case."

"Not directly. I'm digging into some background on my dad's case."

"Be careful, Sam. Be very, very careful. The last thing we need is to find the bastards who did this, only to get smacked with conflict of interest charges. This is no time to go rogue."

"I hear you, and I'm being careful." She looked around, saw they were alone but didn't trust that no one was around to overhear them. "Could I have a word in private?"

"Sure."

Sam led him into her office and waited until the door was closed before posing the question she'd asked Malone earlier. "What can you tell me about Roy Gallagher?"

The chief seemed momentarily stunned. "Where's that coming from?"

"His name has come up twice today."

"How so?"

"I spoke with Alice Coyne Fitzgerald, and she mentioned that he was in your group at the academy, which somehow I didn't know. And then I mentioned to Captain Malone that we might want to check to see if Conklin called anyone after you two went to talk to him the other night. He called three people—his wife, his skeevy lawyer and Gallagher."

Farnsworth's expression grew thunderous. "I thought you weren't working the Conklin case."

"I'm not. I merely suggested to the captain that the call info might be worth having. He's the one who followed up."

"I have to go."

"Where?"

"To see Roy Gallagher."

"Um, are you sure that's a good idea?"

"It's a very good idea, because if he's in any way wrapped up in this, I'm going to kill him with my own hands." He turned and headed out of the pit, toward the lobby.

"Chief, wait. Maybe you shouldn't…" Sam wasn't sure how to suggest to her boss that he not do what he was about to do.

Farnsworth whirled around to face her, and Sam nearly collided with him. "Go back to work, Lieutenant. That's an order."

The fierceness of his gaze surprised her as she rarely saw him so worked up about anything. Clearly the name Roy Gallagher had struck some sort of nerve in him. "I'm saying this as your friend, not your colleague." Sam spoke softly but had his attention. "Don't do anything foolish."

He gave a sharp nod to acknowledge her and walked away, his stride determined.

Watching him go, Sam had a sinking feeling that things were going to get worse before they got better.

CHAPTER TWENTY-FOUR

FURY. THAT WAS the only word to describe the feeling that had overtaken Joe when Sam mentioned Roy Gallagher's name. That arrogant, high-handed, self-serving son of a bitch. If he'd had anything to do with Skip's shooting, Joe would see him strung up. He walked by Helen, who held up a stack of messages.

Joe took them from her without comment and continued into his office, slamming the door behind him.

Roy Gallagher.

The name took him back to the earliest days of his career, beginning with the academy, where he'd met the men who became his closest friends and colleagues. Gallagher had been in their class, but he'd never been one of them. After a year on the force, he'd left to pursue loftier ambitions that had included a run for city council. To Joe's surprise, Gallagher had won that election and reelection every two years since, making him the longest-standing member of the city council.

Anytime he ran into Gallagher at City Hall, he made a point of reminding Joe that he'd supported his bid to be chief, almost as if Joe owed him something in return. The hell he did. He'd received a unanimous mandate from the council when he'd been hired as chief, and he didn't owe that swine Gallagher a damned thing.

Joe had never forgotten the night that Gallagher made a play for Marti when they were first dating. He'd actually told Marti she could "do better" than boring old Joe, and that she ought to go out with him instead. Marti had told Roy to go to hell, but Joe had never forgiven his former "friend" for the blatant disrespect. That'd been the end of their so-called friendship for Joe. Who needed friends like that? But Conklin had stayed close to Gallagher over the years, and as such, Joe and Marti had been forced to socialize with him on occasion. Neither of them ever gave him more than a passing hello to keep from being rude.

Running his fingers through his hair, Joe tried to get himself together. Sam was right. Going off on a rogue mission to give Gallagher a piece of his mind wasn't going to help anything, and it could actually make things worse. So he did what he always did when things got to be too much for him. He called Marti.

"Hi, hon. This is a nice surprise."

"I need you to talk some sense into me."

"How come?"

"You won't believe whose name has come up in the reenergized investigation into Skip's shooting."

"I'm almost afraid to ask."

"Gallagher."

Her gasp echoed through the phone. "You've *got* to be kidding me."

"Wish I was."

"What does he have to do with it?"

"Perhaps nothing, but he was one of three people Conklin called after Jake and I confronted him the other night. The other two were his wife and lawyer."

"Do you think he had something to do with Skip's shooting?"

"I don't know what to think. In light of this new

information, Sam is taking another look at Steven Coyne's shooting too."

"Oh, Joe. Oh my God."

"I should've retired when you wanted me to last year. If I had, none of this would be my problem."

"Even if you had retired, you'd still want to know who shot Skip—and Steven."

"Yes, you're right. I would've wanted to know." He sighed and took a seat behind his desk, mentally and physically exhausted. "Is it possible people we've known for decades could've been behind these unsolved shootings?"

"I suppose anything is possible, but I have full confidence in you and your team. If anyone can figure this out, you all can."

"I want to go over to City Hall and confront him."

"Don't do that, Joe. If he is involved, you'd be risking the case, not to mention the damage he could do to your career."

"Sam said essentially the same thing."

"She's right and so am I."

"I hate that son of a bitch." Hate wasn't a word he threw around lightly, but in this case and a few others it was the only word that fit.

"I know you do, and with good reason, but you have to keep your head about you. Your team will take their lead from you."

"Have I ever told you that marrying you was the best thing I ever did?"

Her laughter made him smile. "Only a few thousand times, and I'm always happy to remind you of it when you forget."

"I never forget."

"I know you don't, and I love you more than anything. I hate to see you struggling."

"I want justice for Skip so badly I can taste it."

"I want that too. Just as badly. But you can't sacrifice who you are as a man and a cop to get there. There's never been a time to be more 'by the book' than this."

"Thanks for talking me down. I was ready to go over to City Hall and have it out with him."

"If the trail leads to him, you'll know it soon enough."

"I guess so," he said, sighing. "I think I'm getting closer to having had enough of this place."

"Oh yay."

Joe laughed. "Tell me how you really feel."

"I'm ready to have you all to myself, but not until *you're* ready."

"I'm getting there."

"I'll be here waiting for you when the time is right. Keep me posted on what's happening?"

"I will. I'll try to be home for dinner."

"See you then. Love you."

"Love you too." He ended the call feeling calmer than he had before he talked to her. She was right—he had to play Skip's case completely by the book to ensure that no mistakes were made that prevented them from getting long-overdue justice for him and his family. But if the trail led to Roy Gallagher... God help that son of a bitch.

WITH THE REST of her team sequestered in the conference room digging through Conklin's digital and paper trail, Sam took the opportunity to reach out to Officer Matt O'Brien, asking him to come to her office when he got a chance.

He showed up a half hour after she called him. "You wanted to see me, Lieutenant?"

"Come in. Shut the door." She gestured for him to have a seat in her visitor's chair.

"What's up?" He had light brown hair, brown eyes and a rugged, muscular build that indicated many hours spent in the gym.

"As you know, we have an opening in the Homicide squad, and I wondered if you might be interested."

He smiled widely. "Hell, yes, I'm interested."

"Before you commit, I just want to make you aware that due to my higher-than-usual profile, which I hate in case you wondered, the squad is under the microscope far more often than we used to be. That can cause heartburn not only for me, but for the rest of you too."

"That's not a concern to me. It'd be an honor to work with and for you."

"You're sure about that?"

"Positive."

"We're still putting the pieces back together after losing Arnold. We have good days and bad days."

"I get it, and I totally understand. We were all affected by his death."

"I'll put in the paperwork and run it up the flagpole."

"I really appreciate the opportunity."

Sam stood to shake his hand. "I'll look forward to working with you."

"Likewise, Lieutenant."

"Keep it between us until the department makes it official."

"Will do."

After he left, Sam filled out the requisite forms to request that Patrolman Matthew O'Brien be promoted to detective to fill the vacancy left by Will Tyrone's departure earlier in the year and sent it to Malone for his approval.

With that task accomplished, she sat back in her chair to think, puzzling through the case and picking through each detail, letting her mind loose to ponder the various possibilities. She thought it through from every angle and sat up straight when an idea occurred to her that had her picking up the phone to call Malone.

"Need to see you. Your place or mine?"

"Mine."

"Be right there." Sam launched out of her chair and made a beeline for the captain's office, knocking on his door two minutes later. When he waved her in, she shut the door behind her.

"I got your email about O'Brien. Good choice. I'll send it through."

"Thank you."

"What's up?"

"Conklin's wife."

"What about her?"

Sam leaned against the wall and crossed her arms. "You said he made three calls after you and the chief were there the other night. One of the calls was to his wife. What if he was giving her instructions to get rid of things, such as the messenger bag?"

Malone sat back in his chair, balancing a pen between two fingers as he pondered that. "He was at the house. Why would he need to call her to make that happen?"

"Maybe what we're looking for wasn't at the house but somewhere else."

"I don't mean to be a buzzkill, but if Conklin had that bag or other evidence pertaining to Skip's shooting, don't you think he would've gotten rid of it a long time ago?"

"That's what you and I would've done, but who knows about him? Did either of us think he'd be capable of withholding information about my dad's case for four years?"

"No."

"So we can concede that anything is possible where he's concerned?"

"I suppose we have to." He picked up the phone and made a call to request a warrant to search Conklin's wife's car and office.

"Thank you," Sam said when he'd completed the call.

"I know you're sick of people asking if you're okay, but are you?"

"I'm frustrated because I can't be in the thick of this one."

"I know, but it's for the best. Keep doing what you're doing and working the edges."

"I'm heading to the library to do some research."

"Let me know if you find anything."

"You'll be the first to know." Sam left the captain's office and made her way to the department's library. She could count on one hand the number of times she'd made use of the resources contained in the library, but with the Coyne files missing, she needed context she could only get from news stories about the case. The library kept microfilm copies of old editions of the *Post* and the *Star* dating back to before the papers were digitized, and that was where she'd start to look for much-needed context on the Coyne shooting. Perhaps she was chasing her tail by bothering to take another look at that case, but she'd learned to trust the hunches that rarely disappointed her.

The librarian, a woman named June Mercer, perked up when Sam stepped into the third-floor library. Short and stout with gray hair cut into a bob and bright blue eyes, she'd been the department's librarian for more than thirty years.

"Good morning, Lieutenant."

"Good morning."

"How can I help you?"

"I'm looking for newspapers from decades ago."

"You've come to the right place. Do you have a date?"

Sam recited the date.

"That's the day Officer Coyne was killed."

"Yes."

June gave her a long look before seeming to realize she was staring. "Let me get that for you."

She set Sam up on a microfilm machine and showed her how to scroll through the coverage of the Coyne shooting.

"I took the liberty of getting you everything from the day after the shooting through the funeral. There were a number of stories in the months that followed until the case went cold and the coverage dried up."

"I'll take whatever you've got."

"I'll get you the rest."

"Thank you very much."

"I wanted you to know how sorry I was to hear about your father's passing. He was a lovely man and a great cop."

"I appreciate that, and I agree. He was the best."

"I'll leave you to your work."

Sam called up the first articles that detailed the

brazen shooting of a Metro police officer in broad daylight on a city street. The *Post* story mentioned how Coyne's partner, Officer Skip Holland, had been standing feet away from Coyne when he was struck down. Her father had never gotten over that happening when he was right there, just as Gonzo struggled with the similar circumstances of Arnold's shooting.

She took a good long look at the familiar face of Steven Coyne—he'd been handsome and intense with dark eyes. His dark hair had been buzzed per the department regulations at the time. Her father had always said Steven was one of the finest cops he'd ever worked with—a cop's cop, the kind who always had your back and never failed to do the right thing no matter the consequences. Skip had never forgotten his first partner or how he'd died.

There'd been few details about the make or model of the car from which the gunfire originated, with witnesses stating that it had happened so fast the car was gone before they realized the officer had been fatally shot.

For years after the shooting, Skip had agonized over the dearth of information in an investigation that had gone nowhere fast and quickly gone cold. *Just like his case*, Sam thought, *the similarities are remarkable in many ways*. The only difference being that Skip had survived—albeit just barely. He'd come out of the haze of the shooting with no memories of the weeks leading up to it, which had further hampered their efforts to find the shooter. Had he stumbled upon something that had led to the Coyne case or was his shooting entirely random? The not-knowing was maddening. She couldn't imagine how difficult that had to have been for Alice over the years. The Holland family had lived in a state of purgatory for four years. Her hell had spanned decades.

Sam continued to read the articles about the Coyne case, taking her time to read each word while hoping her dyslexia wouldn't kick in to scramble the text. By taking it slowly, she had a greater chance of getting through it without a problem. Tackling the reading earlier in the day also tended to help.

As Sam read, June continued to add articles to Sam's folder from her workstation behind the main desk. Sam opened a story from the *Star*, dated two months before Steven died, that showed a political rally for Roy Gallagher. In a photo that accompanied the article, Steven stood behind Gallagher on the dais, wearing a suit and an earpiece. He'd been named in the caption, which was why June's search for the name Coyne had yielded the photo.

Had he provided security for Gallagher? And why had Gallagher needed security?

"Hey, June? Would it be possible to get everything from Roy Gallagher's first run for city council?"

"Of course. I'll add that to your folder."

"Excellent. Thank you." Sam had a new respect for June the librarian, who was proving extremely useful.

She read for hours about Gallagher, his meteoric rise to political power on the District's city council. Gallagher was a Democrat raised by working-class parents in the city's Foxhall Village neighborhood, located blocks from Georgetown University. He'd been elected an at-large member of the council and was still there, making him the longest-serving member—and its most powerful member as the council chairman for the last sixteen years. Sam read how the council members each receive a salary of $132,990 with the council chair paid $190,000 annually.

"Damn. I'm in the wrong business."

"Did you say something, Lieutenant?"

"I'm marveling at how well paid the city councillors are compared to the rest of us."

"They do have a sweet deal."

What would someone like Gallagher do to protect that sweet deal? She read about his business interests—several five-star restaurants in the city, one of which had been a favorite of hers and Nick's back when they'd been able to move more freely. In addition, he owned several high-end apartment buildings and a boutique hotel.

Where in the hell did a guy with a working-class background who made $190,000 a year from his day job get the capital for all those businesses?

She rolled her chair to a computer workstation next to the microfilm machine and called up the search function on a browser and typed in Gallagher's name, looking for more information about his personal life and his businesses. The search returned a treasure trove of articles, most of them proclaiming him a genius when it came to business with just about everything he touched turning to gold.

A photo with one of the articles showed him with his gorgeous blonde wife, Crystal Sands Gallagher, the daughter of Maurice Sands, who'd done time in federal prison in the 1970s for gambling and racketeering. Before his death thirty years ago, he'd been rumored to have ties to organized crime, but that had never been proven.

Tingling sensations spiraled down her backbone, always a sign that she was onto something. But what?

Rubbing her tired eyes, she tried to put the pieces together, but they refused to yield anything that made sense. The first thing she wanted to know was more about Steven Coyne's connection to Gallagher and whether he'd done private security for Gallagher when he was a candidate for the council.

"Thanks again for your help," she said to June.

"Anytime."

Sam went back to her office, closed the door and picked up the phone to call Alice.

She answered on the third ring.

"Hi, it's Sam Holland. I had another question for you."

"Of course. Whatever I can do."

"Tell me about Steven's relationship with Roy Gallagher."

"They were good friends from the academy."

"Did Steven do private security for him during his first campaign for the council?"

"Not that I ever knew. He went to some of the rallies and fundraisers, but I wasn't aware of any formal role."

The earpiece Steven had been wearing in the picture was the only clue Sam had that he'd been providing security of some sort. "Would he have told you if he was working for Gallagher on the side?"

"I think he would have. We didn't keep secrets from each other." She let out a gasp. "Wait. The money."

"What money?" Sam held her breath, waiting to hear what Alice would say next.

"About two weeks before he died, he came home one night with a wad of cash that he said he'd found on the street."

Sam took frantic notes.

"I asked him why he hadn't reported it. He said he

did, and when no one claimed it they said he could keep it."

"*They* being?"

"I assumed it was MPD officials."

"How much was it?"

"Ten thousand dollars. That money paid my rent for six months after Steven died."

"And you never heard anything more from the department about the money?"

"No, nothing. Should I have?"

"I don't think so. I was just wondering."

"No one ever said anything to me, but about four months after Steven was killed, I came home one day to a package on my front porch that had another ten thousand dollars in cash. I...I didn't report it to anyone because I needed it so badly."

"Have you ever told anyone about the money?"

"I was afraid if I did, someone might ask me to give it back."

"This has been really helpful, Alice."

"Is there... I mean, if I had to pay back the money, I couldn't."

"You won't have to. Don't worry."

"Oh good." Her sigh of relief came through loud and clear.

"I know it's painful for you to think about, but is there anything about Steven's last few weeks that stands out in your memories? Anything different or unusual?"

Alice took a moment to think about that. "He was stressed out about something."

"He didn't say what?"

"Only that work was extra busy, but I sensed it was more than that. I never could get him to tell me what was wrong."

Sam wrote down every word she said. "If you think of anything else Steven ever said about Roy Gallagher or anything having to do with him, no matter how minor it might seem, please call me."

"I will. You don't think that Roy had something to do with Steven's death, do you? They were such good friends."

"I honestly have no idea."

"Wouldn't that be something? After all these years, to finally know what happened, to have answers."

"Yes, it would."

"Thank you for all you're doing. Even if it doesn't yield answers, it's nice to know that people still care about my Steven."

"Of course we do. He was one of us. He always will be."

"Means a lot."

"I'll be in touch."

For a long time after she ended the call, Sam sat perfectly still and tried to think it through from all angles. Someone had paid Steven ten grand before his death and then had made sure his widow was cared for afterward. Was it the same person? And if so, was that person the one who killed him?

Malone came to the door. "We found the messenger bag in the trunk of Conklin's wife's car."

CHAPTER TWENTY-FIVE

SAM SAT UP, feeling as if she'd once again been electrocuted. "Can I see it?"

"Not until we process it."

"Why did I know you were going to say that? Was there anything in it?"

"From what we could tell on first glance, it contained files and other personal items."

She took a series of deep breaths. "I feel like I'm going to be sick. That he had it for all this time and never told anyone…" Much to her dismay, tears flooded her eyes. Determined to keep it together, she blinked them back and forced herself to stay calm.

"If it's any consolation, you're not the only one who feels sick."

"It is. I know a lot of people around here loved my dad, and this will hit them hard. Tell me we're charging Conklin's wife too."

"You're damned right we are."

"Good."

Chief Farnsworth appeared next to Malone, and the two of them stepped into her office and closed the door, the chief's jaw pulsing with tension. "This might be the most unbelievable thing that's ever happened."

Sam wasn't sure that was true, but since it wasn't like the calm, cool, composed chief to make such pronouncements, she chose not to argue the point. After all, it was pretty fucking unbelievable. "What does he have to say about it?"

"Hill asked him that, and he said he doesn't know how that got into her car because he's never seen it before," Malone said.

"I hope we're dusting it for prints."

"As we speak."

"Does he realize yet that we've got him screwed, glued and tattooed?"

"I think it might be starting to register with him," Farnsworth said.

When someone knocked on the door, the chief opened it to Hill and Faith Miller. "Come in."

They stepped in and the chief closed the door.

Sam couldn't recall the last time she'd had that many people stuffed into her small office.

"Conklin's attorney is requesting a deal in exchange for his cooperation," Hill said.

"What kind of deal?" Sam asked, hesitant. The last thing she wanted was for him to get any leniency after what he'd done.

"A reduced sentence in exchange for information that'll help to hook a much bigger fish," Hill said. "Those are his words, not mine."

"I think," Sam said, "the bigger fish is going to be Roy Gallagher."

The others looked at her with stunned expressions.

"As in *Councilman* Roy Gallagher?" Faith asked.

"The one and only."

"I heard from City Hall this morning that he's championing legislation that would name HQ in honor of Skip," Farnsworth said.

The gesture, like so many things lately, hit Sam like a punch to the gut, leaving her momentarily breathless as tingles rained down her spine, making her more certain than she already was that they were onto something with Gallagher. Reading from her notes, Sam went through the things she'd discovered during her deep dive into the past relationships between her dad and Roy as well as Steven and Roy.

"Wait a minute," Hill said. "Are you suggesting the Coyne shooting might also be related?"

"I'm having one of my feelings about him, so I'm suggesting it might be possible."

Hill glared at her. "Explain."

Sam took them through the information she'd uncovered that morning, including the photo of Coyne providing security for Gallagher's first campaign—something Coyne's wife hadn't known he was doing. She told them about the money that had "appeared" twice—once before Steven died and again after. "Coyne's wife said he was stressed out about something in the weeks before he died. He told her work was getting to him. She sensed it was more than that but couldn't get him to tell her what was bothering her."

"I'm not seeing a solid connection to Gallagher," Hill said, "and if we're going to accuse a well-respected member of the District's government of being involved with possibly two police officers' murders, we'd better have it nailed down before it gets out that we're looking at him."

"He's right," Farnsworth said. "The last thing I need right now with my deputy chief implicated is a shaky connection to a powerful council member who'd have my job—and yours—so fast our heads would spin. Nothing you've uncovered would lead to motive for him to take out two police officers."

"Roll with me for a minute here." Sam felt the buzz

she often got from knowing she was onto something. "What if Coyne was working for Gallagher under the table to make ends meet? He didn't tell his wife because he doesn't want to concern her with their financial situation. What if, while working for Gallagher, he uncovers something that gets him killed. And then, what if, with retirement looming, Skip decides to take another look at the unsolved shooting of his first partner and close friend, wanting to wrap that up before he leaves the job? He checked out the Coyne files, which were never returned, and was nearly killed a week later. You going to tell me that's a coincidence?"

Malone shook his head. "We don't believe in coincidences around here."

"The alternative to investigating Gallagher," Faith said tentatively, "is to let Conklin make the case against whomever the big fish turns out to be, and then we'll know exactly who we should be looking at."

The group met the suggestion with total silence.

"It's going to be your call," Hill said to Farnsworth. "If you cut a deal with Conklin to get someone bigger, you're going to have to be able to live with Conklin doing less time than he deserves."

"I don't want to see him spend one day less than exactly what he deserves behind bars," Farnsworth said fiercely. "Let's see if we can make a case against Gallagher before we consider dealing with Conklin. I've learned to trust the lieutenant's feelings on these things. They're rarely wrong."

"Um, they're *never* wrong," Sam said, earning a glare from her chief.

Malone coughed, possibly to cover a laugh.

"I don't want anyone outside the people in this room knowing we're looking at Gallagher," Farnsworth said.

"Unless we have him locked and loaded, no one will ever know we investigated him. Am I clear on that?"

"Crystal," Sam said.

The others murmured their agreement.

"I'll need to inform Tom," Faith said of the U.S. Attorney.

"Only him," Farnsworth said. "No one else."

"Understood," Faith said.

"Everything you do is on deep background," Farnsworth said to Sam. "Malone's name is on anything that requires a paper trail."

Sam nodded.

"If this leads in the direction of Gallagher, it'll be nuclear for us," Farnsworth said. "There's absolutely no room for error."

"There won't be any errors," Sam said.

A knock on the door seemed to startle everyone in the room, as if they feared it might be Gallagher himself on the other side of the door.

Faith, who was standing closest to the door, opened it to Freddie, whose eyes bugged when he saw how many people were in the small office—and who they were.

Sam leaned around the others so he could see her. "What's up, Detective?"

"Frank Davis was just found murdered in his apartment."

SAM ACCOMPANIED CRUZ, Green and McBride to Davis's apartment, where they found the older man on the floor inside his front door, dead from a single gunshot wound to the forehead.

Cruz examined the door. "No sign of forced entry."

Green squatted for a closer look at the body. "Which means it was someone he knew or recognized."

"Who called it in?" Sam asked.

"His daughter," McBride said. "She's next door with his neighbor, who was also his friend."

Sam glanced at Freddie. "Let's go talk to them."

The door to the neighbor's apartment was propped open but Sam knocked anyway. While she waited, she took a look around for security cameras in the hallway but didn't see any. Many of the older buildings weren't wired for cameras the way the new ones were.

"Come in."

They found two women seated on a sofa. One had white hair and a sweet face lined with wrinkles and eyes filled with tears. She comforted a younger blonde woman, whose face was buried in her hands.

"Lorraine," the older woman said. "The police want to speak to you."

The younger woman raised her head, revealing a face ravaged with shock and grief.

Sam showed her badge as Freddie did the same. "I'm Lieutenant Holland, and this is my partner, Detective Cruz. We're very sorry for your loss."

"Th-thank you." Sobs muffled her words. "I don't know how this could've happened. My father didn't have an enemy in the world. Everyone loved him."

Sam and Freddie sat on a love seat across from the two women. "When was the last time you spoke to him?"

Lorraine wiped tears from her face. "Yesterday afternoon. He didn't answer the phone when I tried to call him this afternoon, so I came by after work to check on him. That's when I found him."

"When you talked to him yesterday, did he express any concerns or anything out of the ordinary?"

"Not at all. We talked about the Redskins, and he

mentioned that he'd met you. He said it was about your father's case?"

"That's right. We learned this week that your father had been a witness to the shooting."

"It's not a coincidence, is it, that this happened to him right after he gave a statement to you?"

Sam's stomach ached fiercely, the way it used to when she'd been hooked on diet cola. "I don't think it is."

Lorraine shook her head as more tears spilled down her cheeks. "I don't understand this."

"I don't either, but we're going to figure out what happened to him." To the older woman, Sam said, "Could I get your name, please?"

"Eleanor Lively."

"How long have you lived next door to Frank?"

"Oh, about fifteen years or so."

"And you were friends?"

"We were." Her voice caught. "He was a lovely man. He helped me with anything that needed fixing, and I cooked for him. It was nice for both of us to have the company, as we're both widowed. I don't know what I'll do without him." She took the tissue Lorraine handed her and dabbed at her eyes.

"Did you hear any sort of disturbance next door or the sound of the gunshot?"

Eleanor shook her head. "I didn't, but my television was on, so that might be why. I can't believe anyone would want to kill Frank."

"He was so sweet to everyone," Lorraine said softly.

They took down the addresses and phone numbers for both women and promised to be in touch when they knew more about what happened.

In the hallway, Sam leaned against the wall and took

a series of deep breaths, but that did nothing to quell the nausea swirling in her gut. "I think I'm going to be sick." She headed down the stairs and burst into the cool autumn air, bent at the waist and took more greedy deep breaths, hoping she wouldn't vomit.

That was where Captain Malone found her when he arrived at the scene. "Lieutenant."

Sam straightened. "Our investigation got Davis killed."

The captain grimaced. "You know that for sure?"

"How could it *not* be related?"

As the medical examiner's truck arrived, Malone took Sam by the arm. "Let's take a walk."

Sam didn't want to walk, but she let him lead her around the corner, away from the prying eyes of the other first responders and the neighbors who'd gathered, as they always did, hoping for a look at someone else's disaster.

After a short walk, Sam stopped and turned to face the captain. "What *is* this?"

"I don't know." He ran his fingers through wiry gray hair, frustration rolling off him in waves.

"It's like we've stirred a hornet's nest, and now the hornets are coming at us and everyone we've talked to in the process of stirring the nest."

"Or the hornets are running scared and attacking anyone who's threatening them."

"Which means we need to protect everyone else involved, including Kevin Viera, the paramedic who gave us a statement."

Sam had reached for her phone to call Viera when Cameron Green came running around the corner. "Lieutenant!"

Sam's stomach dropped with dread.

"We just got a call from Dispatch. Viera, the paramedic, was run off the road a short time ago as he was leaving the gym."

Sam swallowed hard, the nausea swirling. "Is he alive?"

"Yeah, but they had to cut him out of his truck. They're taking him to GW. It was called in as level-one trauma."

She glanced at the captain. "Let's go." To Green, she said, "Stay until Crime Scene gets here and talk to all the neighbors. See if anyone heard anything from Davis's place."

"Yes, ma'am. We're on it."

Sam handed her keys to Cameron. "Tell Cruz to take my car back to the house when you're done here."

"Will do."

She followed the captain to his SUV and got into the passenger seat. As he drove them to GW, she focused on breathing and not vomiting in his car.

Malone put through a call to Hill, keeping the phone on speaker, which Sam appreciated.

"What's up?" Hill asked.

"We've got witnesses turning up dead or injured." He filled Hill in on what'd happened to Davis and Viera.

"Jesus. We got the lab back from the card that Lieutenant Holland submitted. The only prints on it were hers, so that's a dead end. And Lieutenant Archelotta was unable to determine who archived the footage from G Street."

Sam boiled with frustration as two leads failed to turn up anything that could help.

"It's time to put some serious pressure on Conklin," Malone said. "He's the key to this whole thing."

"Agreed. I'll get him back into interrogation within the hour."

"Lieutenant Holland and I are going by the GW ER to check on Viera, and then we'll be back to the house."

"I'll wait for you."

The line went dead.

Sam realized her hands were shaking so she tucked them under her legs.

When they were stopped at a red light, Malone glanced over at her. "Talk to me."

"What do you want me to say?"

"Tell me what you're thinking."

"I'm thinking someone is going to an awful lot of trouble to make sure we don't solve this case—and they've been doing that for four years now with my dad, perhaps as long as decades with Steven Coyne. Knowing it was all intentional... The roadblocks, the dead ends... That makes it so much worse."

"I know." He tightened his grip on the wheel. "Makes me want to kill someone. I can only imagine how you must feel."

"I want to see the messenger bag and what was in it."

"Let's see what's up with Viera, and then we'll check it out."

She appreciated that he understood her need to see that bag. "We need people on Viera to make sure whoever put him in the hospital doesn't try to finish the job while he's there."

Malone put through a call to the Patrol officer in charge and requested coverage at GW.

"Yes, sir. The officers who took the initial call are accompanying him to the ER. We'll instruct them to stay with him."

"Very good. Thank you."

Sam breathed a small sigh of relief at knowing Viera would be protected. "What about Alice?"

"Alice Coyne?"

"Yes. She's been talking to me, giving me context. I was there earlier today. If I was being followed, they know she's cooperating."

Malone redialed the Patrol officer in charge. "Get me two people at the home of Alice Coyne Fitzgerald as well." He recited the address. "Immediately."

"Yes, sir."

Malone ended the call. "You should call her and tell her what's going on, so she knows why there're cops posted outside her house."

Sam's hands were still trembling when she placed the call to Alice.

"Hi, honey. Did you think of something else you needed to know?"

"Not yet." Sam closed her eyes and said the words that Alice needed to hear, hating that she had to bring a new horror to a woman who'd already seen more than her share.

Alice gasped. "What would they want with me?"

"I don't think they'd want anything, but I'm not taking any chances with your safety."

"Sam…"

"We're closing in on whoever shot my dad and possibly Steven too. They're getting desperate. You have to let us keep you safe."

"Of course, but I'm afraid."

"Don't be. Our officers will be there until this is over, and I'll check on you myself later. I promise."

"Okay." She sounded shaky but resolved.

"I'll be in touch."

"It's the right thing to do," Malone said after Sam ended the call.

"Even if it scares the hell out a woman who's already had more than her share?"

"Even if. Better safe than sorry."

They arrived at GW and entered through the emergency doors to find the waiting room full of uniformed paramedics.

Sam recognized Branson among them and made her way to him. "How is he?"

"We don't know anything yet." The same man who'd been so friendly to her only a few days ago could barely look at her now, which meant he blamed her for the fact that his friend and colleague had been hurt. "But the first responders said it was bad. They had to cut him out."

"Were there witnesses?"

"Not that I know of."

"We'll pull the film from the area."

"You do that."

"I get that you're pissed—"

"I'm glad you get it. He's a good guy who did the right thing, and where did that get him? Did you know his girlfriend is expecting their first child? That's her over there. She's had a difficult pregnancy and is supposed to be on bed rest. They're going to admit her because they're afraid she'll lose the baby."

"I'm sorry this has happened to them both. To all of you."

"So am I. If he dies…" Branson shook his head.

"Let's pray that he doesn't."

Someone called to Branson, and he walked away, leaving her feeling completely alone in a room full of people.

Malone pushed his way through the crowd to her. "Come on."

Sam didn't ask where they were going as she followed him through the double doors to the treatment area. They stopped outside a cubicle where several Patrol officers stood with Dr. Anderson, whose grim expression only added to Sam's tension.

"What've you got?" Malone asked.

The Patrol officer consulted her notes. "Viera was headed south on 21st Street Northwest, between Virginia and Constitution Avenues, when he was forced off the road by a white vehicle."

"How do you know it was white?" Sam asked.

"The streaks of paint on the side of Viera's navy blue pickup truck were white. Viera's truck was found upside down. The other car had fled the scene by the time we arrived. We've put out an APB for a white vehicle with damage to the passenger side."

"Who called it in?"

"An Uber driver who happened upon the wreck after it had happened."

"Contact Lieutenant Archelotta to find out what we've got for cameras in the area."

"I've already done that," the Patrol officer said.

"Good work, Officer Densley." Sam took note of the young woman's name after being impressed by her thorough report.

"How's he doing?" Malone asked Anderson.

"He's in rough shape with broken ribs, clavicle, femur and a head injury that's our biggest concern."

"Will he survive?" Sam asked.

"I hope so. We'll know more in a few hours."

"We need him, Doc," Malone said.

"His girlfriend and unborn child need him too," Sam added.

"We're doing everything we can. Let me get back to him." Anderson returned to Viera's room.

"Don't leave this hallway for any reason," Malone said to the Patrol officers. "If anyone tries to get to him, do whatever is needed to keep him safe."

"Yes, sir."

The two young officers seemed nervous but determined to follow orders.

As she followed Malone back to the waiting room, Sam wished she felt better about leaving them to protect Viera's life.

Malone walked through the crowded waiting room, which went silent as they passed through.

Sam wondered if they were all blaming her for the fact that their friend was in critical condition and fighting for his life. She'd gone looking for him and dragged him into the investigation, and now...

"Don't go there," Malone said gruffly as they walked to his vehicle. "It's not your fault or our fault that this happened."

"Try telling that to his pregnant girlfriend or the people who work with him every day."

"It's not your fault. You were doing your job, and it led to him."

"Who else knew that it led to him besides his colleagues and ours?"

"What're you getting at?"

"Am I being followed?"

"Have you felt like you were?"

"Nope, but my head hasn't been a hundred percent in the game the way it usually is. I probably wouldn't have noticed if I was being trailed."

"Conklin knew we'd talked to him. Don't forget that."

"True."

They were in his SUV and seat-belted in, but he made no move to start the engine.

Sam stared out the passenger window as the silence stretched into minutes. "Let's deal with Conklin before someone else ends up dead."

"Sam—"

"At this point, what does it matter if he does ten years or twenty? I just want answers. I want it to be over, Cap, for my dad, for my family, for everyone who loved him. I want justice any way I can get it—for him and for Steven, if his case is related."

"All right, then. Let's go see what the son of a bitch has to say for himself."

CHAPTER TWENTY-SIX

UPON THEIR ARRIVAL back at HQ, Malone asked that Skip's messenger bag and the contents be brought to his office immediately.

Filled with a strange mix of anticipation, dread and excitement, Sam paced the small room while they waited. She had no idea what she'd find in that messenger bag or what it would mean to the case, but she knew for certain that having that piece of her dad back in her custody would mean the world.

Memories of early-morning coffee dates and happy-hour gatherings at O'Leary's siphoned through her thoughts, along with the many times she'd had to implore him not to intervene on her behalf when she was struggling with Stahl at work. The reminders of the life they'd led before someone tried to kill him were bittersweet. On the one hand, she loved to think about the way things used to be. On the other hand, it was almost too painful to remember him before the devastating injury, especially in light of how he'd been forced to live afterward.

And to know, all that time, someone close to them had held the answers they'd craved and had chosen to protect himself rather than do the right thing… It would take her years to get her head around that.

Malone eyed her warily. "You look like you're about to spontaneously combust."

"I feel like I might."

"We're close, Sam. Closer than we've ever been."

"I know."

"But?"

"I'm still trying to wrap my head around Conklin's involvement."

"You're not the only one."

"How many do you think there are? Out of four thousand, how many are crooked?"

"Maybe one percent."

"That'd be forty. That's too many."

"We've gotten rid of two of the worst with Conklin and Stahl."

"Or so we think. Who knows how deep the cancer has permeated the department."

"I have to believe that most of the people we work with are on the side of right. The day I no longer believe that is the day I'll turn in my badge." He placed his hands on her upper arms, forcing her to stop pacing and meet his intense gaze. "Don't let a few bad apples ruin your love for the job. Don't give them that satisfaction. Your dad would hate that."

"Yes, he would. I'm glad he didn't live long enough to find out that Conklin was involved."

"Me too. That would've broken him."

A uniformed officer appeared at the door, bearing a large plastic evidence bag. "Per your request, Captain. It's been fully processed, so no need to glove up."

Malone took it from the officer. "Thank you." He closed the door and handed the bag and a printed report to Sam.

She took it from him, hugging it to her chest while reading the report that indicated Deputy Chief Conklin's prints had been found on the bag, along with those of Deputy Chief Holland and Conklin's wife.

"Take as long as you need. I'll tell Hill to wait for you." The door clicked shut behind him as he left the room.

Sam went around to sit at his immaculate desk. She would never understand how neat-freak people like him and Nick got anything done in such sterile work spaces. As she broke the seal on the plastic bag containing the messenger bag, tears filled her eyes. She refused to give in to them. Not now. Not yet. Soon... But not yet.

Handling the worn leather gingerly, she removed it from the plastic bag and placed it on Malone's desktop. For the longest time she only stared at it as if it somehow had the power to bring back the man who'd once carried it. The bag couldn't bring him back to her, but perhaps it could yield some of his secrets. Touching the Kiss Me I'm Irish key chain, she let it slip through her fingers, recalling his over-the-top pride in his Irish heritage and mourning the fact that he'd never made it to Ireland. That'd been on his retirement bucket list and was another thing that'd been taken from him by the shooter.

She flipped open the outer flap, unzipped the largest pocket and withdrew a stack of file folders that included those pertaining to the Coyne shooting. Sam set them aside to go through later. In addition to the Coyne files, she found a stack of newspaper articles about Roy Gallagher, sending a new zing of tingles down her backbone.

"I knew it. I fucking *knew* it."

She found a piece of paper with the names Santoro and Ryan circled in red ink.

Sam knew she ought to find Malone and update him

on what she'd found, but she took one more minute to go through each of the other pockets, finding his business cards, a pack of the mint gum he'd loved, pictures of her sisters and their children, a photo of him with Celia, and Sam's official police portrait. In yet another pocket, she found a spare set of keys to his house as well as the department SUV that had been transferred to Conklin after her father was medically retired.

She put everything back exactly where she'd found it, knowing she would never again unzip the pockets or remove the items from where he'd kept them. The bag would remain in evidence through the trials of those involved, but it would one day return to Sam's custody and she would find a place to keep it where it could never be lost again.

Taking the files and the copies of the Gallagher newspaper stories with her, she went to find Malone in the lobby, conferring with the chief.

"Find anything?" Malone asked.

She handed him the stack of photocopies of news stories pertaining to Gallagher. "Told you so."

With the chief looking on, Malone flipped through the articles about Gallagher opening yet another restaurant, buying yet another apartment building and running again for reelection.

"What I want to know," Sam said, "is where a working-class kid from Foxhall Village got the money to build such a massive business conglomerate and how he manages it all while also serving as a full-time member of the city council. We also need to find out who Santoro and Ryan are." She showed the piece of paper on which Skip had written their names and circled them with red ink.

"The answer to those questions may very well break this entire thing," Farnsworth said. "Let's go."

Sam followed them to the interrogation room, where Hill waited with Terrell, as well as Faith Miller, outside the door. Malone updated them on the items they had found in Skip's bag.

"Ready?" Hill asked, his gaze landing on Sam.

She nodded and stepped into the observation room.

The others followed, but she paid them no mind as she set her sight on Conklin's unshaved face, bracing herself for whatever he might say and how it would change everything. He looked like he hadn't slept in days. *Good.* She hoped his guilty conscience was causing havoc.

"You requested this meeting," Hill said. "We're listening."

"Deputy Chief Conklin is willing to make a statement that will provide information that should help to resolve two outstanding homicide cases, in exchange for leniency and isolation from the general prison population."

There. Confirmation that Coyne and Holland were related. She'd known it, but hearing it confirmed left a hollow pit in her belly.

You dirty fucking rat, still looking out for yourself when two good men are in the ground. It was all she could do to remain in observation when she wanted to burst into the interrogation room and claw Conklin's beady eyes from his face. She wanted to pummel him with her fists until he hurt a fraction as much as her father had hurt in the last years of his life. She wished she could beat him to a bloody pulp for all the years Skip had been denied and his family cheated.

But she didn't do any of those things. Rather, she

stood stoically and silently and let the process play out the way it needed to. There'd be time for howling later.

"In exchange for what?" Hill asked in response to Bagley's offer.

"He'll tell you everything he knows about the shootings of Steven Coyne and Skip Holland."

Conklin had the good sense to look down at the table as his lawyer all but acknowledged that his client had information relevant to both cases. He also verbally confirmed that the two shootings were related.

Under normal circumstances, Sam would be euphoric to have a break in either of the cold cases. Under these circumstances, her hands rolled into tight fists, and her entire body ached from the tension that had every muscle on full alert while her stomach burned with bile that threatened to come up at any second. If anyone so much as breathed on her, she'd shatter.

Hill got up and left the room. As far as Conklin was concerned, Hill was conferring with the Assistant U.S. Attorney. But they'd worked out their plan in advance, so Hill merely took a few minutes in the hallway while Conklin twisted in the wind, coexisting in uncomfortable silence with his lawyer and Terrell.

The door opened, and Hill stepped back into the room, closing the door.

"Well?" Bagley asked. "Do we have a deal?"

"That depends on what Mr. Conklin has to say."

Sam loved that Hill continued to refuse to refer to Conklin as deputy chief. For that alone, she would forever count Avery Hill as a close personal friend.

Conklin sputtered with outrage that Bagley quelled with a hand to his client's arm and a tight squeeze.

"Deputy Chief Conklin is under no obligation to share any information with you. He has offered to do so out of respect for Officer Coyne and Deputy Chief Holland."

That finally broke her. Sam slammed both hands against the two-way glass that separated the observation from interrogation. They couldn't hear her, but she screamed anyway, filled with rage that he would pretend to have *respect* for either of the deceased officers.

Malone calmed her with his hands on her shoulders. "Take a breath, Lieutenant."

The chief moved closer to her, the two of them protecting her from whatever outrage would come next.

"Respect," Hill said, "is an interesting choice of words in light of the fact that Mr. Conklin sat on information relevant to the shootings of two of his fellow officers, for years in one case and decades in the other."

"I didn't know about Coyne for decades," Conklin shouted, the words bursting from him in an urgent tone.

"*Shut up*, Paul," Bagley said in a low growl. "Not another word." Glaring at Hill, Bagley said, "Either you offer us something tangible or this conversation is over."

"I guess it's over, then." Hill was the picture of calm coolness as he stood. Taking his lead from Hill, Terrell did the same.

They were to the door when Conklin cleared his throat. "Wait."

"Paul…"

"Be quiet, Charles. This is my life on the line here, and I want to talk."

Bagley scowled at him. "You're a fool to do that without a deal on the table."

"What kind of deal do you think they're going to give me? The chief was Skip's best friend. They're going to throw the book at me."

Sam growled. "You got that right, you worthless son of a bitch." She held her breath waiting to hear what he would say.

Conklin sighed, seeming resigned to his fate. "I have one condition."

"What's that?" Hill asked.

"Drop the charges against my wife. She had no idea what I was asking her to do and shouldn't be caught up in this. If you leave her out of it, I'll tell you what you want to know, and I'll hope that in exchange, the USA will do what he can for me. If you refuse to drop the charges against her, I'm not saying another word."

"I'll make that recommendation to the U.S. Attorney, but as you know, that's his call."

"She's a victim in this. I'll swear on a stack of bibles that she knew nothing about that bag or what was in it."

"So noted."

Sam wanted to laugh at Conklin offering to swear on a stack of bibles. Didn't he know his word—with or without the bibles—was shit at this point?

"You aren't going to confer with the U.S. Attorney?"

"Not now, but I'll make your wishes known."

Conklin didn't seem too pleased with that response but apparently realized it was the best he was going to get.

Sam had to give Hill credit. He never lost his cool when he probably wanted to reach across the table and shake the truth out of Conklin. That was what she'd want to do, which was another reason it was probably better that Hill was handling this interrogation rather than her.

Hill projected a casual, disinterested attitude, but after having worked with him for some time, Sam knew that was only a facade. He was one of the sharpest law enforcement officers she'd ever encountered, and if she couldn't do this interrogation herself, she was thankful it was in the hands of someone she respected and trusted to get the answers she needed so badly.

"If you have information pertaining to the shootings of Officer Coyne and Deputy Chief Holland, I'm listening."

After a long pause, Conklin sighed, his shoulders slumping into the position of a man accepting that life as he'd known it was over. "The person you've been looking for all this time is Roy Gallagher." Conklin glanced at Hill, apparently expecting a big reaction to the name, and seeming disappointed when he didn't get one. "The councilman."

"I'm aware of who he is."

"I'm telling you he's behind the shootings of Coyne and Holland."

"We already suspected that."

Conklin's expression registered his shock. "How?"

"Never mind how. Keep talking."

Conklin sighed again and propped his elbows on the table.

Sam watched him so intently her breathing began to sync with his.

"You know Gallagher graduated from the academy with us—me, Skip, Steven, Joe, Jake and Wallack, among others, but that group was tight. Steven and me, we were the closest to Roy. When he was leaving the department, he came to both of us with a business opportunity. He'd been approached by some 'backers,' as he called them, who were encouraging him to run for the council. They were interested in taking back some of the power, as they put it, that'd gone to what they considered outsiders—people who'd lived here a short

time before running for the council. They wanted to get
the natives back in charge. Because Roy asked us to, we
met with them, heard what they had to say. Steven, he
was interested. He and Alice wanted to have kids right
away, and she wanted to stay home with them. There
was no way he could swing that on a patrolman's salary, so he signed on to help Roy get elected and earn
some extra money."

"And you didn't?"

Conklin shook his head. "I was already having trouble with my drinking. My first marriage was falling
apart, and all my time was spent either working or
drinking. I had no interest in politics, and frankly, I
didn't think Roy would make for a very good councilman. He'd been a terrible cop."

"Why do you say that?"

"He didn't care, took shortcuts, looked the other way
so he wouldn't have to do the paperwork. I was actually relieved when he said he was quitting. I liked the
guy as a friend but not as a coworker."

Sam wanted to know how Conklin went from being
offended by a lazy coworker to breaking the law. Was
it something that'd happened gradually, or had it been
all of a sudden?

Even though the interview was being recorded, Hill
took notes. "So he ran for council, he won and while
he served the city he has presided over a very successful business empire."

Conklin nodded. "You should look at how he came
to have the money for that business empire. His father
was a bus driver, his mother a cook at the Georgetown
cafeteria. His grandparents were all immigrants with
blue-collar jobs."

"Sounds to me like you know where he came by the

money, so how about you save us all some time and fill in the blanks."

Excellent, Sam thought. That was exactly what she would've said. Quit beating around the bush and spill it.

"Gambling."

"What kind of gambling?"

"The illegal kind that happens off the grid where federal regulators and the IRS can't get to it. The kind his father-in-law was into before the Feds caught him doing other stuff, but the gambling… That continued after Maurice Sands died. Gallagher picked up the reins and has kept it going all these years."

Now we're getting somewhere, Sam thought, her skin tingling as her heart beat so fast she could hear the echo.

"Gallagher and his business partners, Mick Santoro and Dermott Ryan, were running the gambling entity since before Gallagher left the force. It's an all-cash business that yields a billion dollars a year."

Sam stood up straighter at the words *billion dollars*. *And Dermott Ryan. How do I know that name?*

Conklin continued, "It's my belief that while working for the campaign, Coyne figured out what they were up to. He was by the book, and my theory is that when he confronted Gallagher about it, Coyne got himself killed."

"By Gallagher?"

Conklin shook his head. "No, it would've been Santoro or Ryan."

"Why do you say that?"

"They've kept Gallagher clean to protect his council seat. Having him there has been good for business."

"And how do you know all this?"

"I've been friends with Gallagher a long time. I've

known about the gambling from the beginning." Conklin paused, looked down at the table. "A couple of weeks before Skip was shot, I was at a party at Gallagher's house when I overheard them talking about Skip digging into Coyne's killing and how he was determined to solve that case before he retired. Gallagher told the others that if Skip picked up their scent in the Coyne case, something would have to be done." Conklin glanced at Hill. "Two days before he was shot, Skip went to see Ryan, asked him a bunch of questions about Gallagher."

"That's not in any of his files or notes," Sam said.

"He might not have had a chance to document it yet," Malone said, "but clearly he was onto the same thing Coyne had uncovered."

"He was meticulous about the paperwork."

"Something this nuclear, he might've kept out of the files until he had it sewn up."

"Why do I know Dermott Ryan's name?"

"He owns O'Leary's, among other things, but he's not there very much, so you may not know him personally."

Stunned, Sam stared at the captain. The owner of the bar that had been like a home away from home to her dad was involved in his shooting? She staggered under the weight of that information.

Malone braced her with his hands on her shoulders. "Breathe."

Sam couldn't move or think or do anything other than reel.

"Sam! *Breathe, damn it.*"

She forced a shaky breath into lungs that felt like they belonged to someone else. Time seemed to stop and the roaring in her ears became so loud it was all she could hear. People close to her father at work and away from work had hidden information that could've solved his case years ago. Right under her nose, under their own roof at HQ.

"I…I think I'm going to be sick."

Malone hustled her toward the garbage can in the corner.

Sam heaved up the meager contents of her stomach, and that she didn't care her captain was holding her hair back as she puked would've concerned her under normal circumstances. However, there was nothing normal about these circumstances. When her stomach stopped heaving, she tied off the trash bag, her fingers fumbling through the basic steps of tying a basic knot.

Sam felt hot and cold at the same time, as her brain whirled and her heart pounded. Adrenaline raced through her system, as if she'd downed six large cups of coffee all at once.

And then she heard Conklin sobbing in the interrogation room and was doubly glad she wasn't in there because there was no way she'd be able to hold back the burning need to punch him in the face. She'd like to think she'd learned her lesson about punching her fellow officers after the Ramsey incident, but in this case, it would surely be justified.

Straightening, she took the tissues Malone handed her and wiped her mouth with shaking hands. He looked as undone as she felt, which brought her comfort. At least she wasn't the only one who found this excruciating.

"You should go home. We can take it from here and get it done."

Sam looked up at him. "No fucking way am I going home."

He gave her a long, piercing look before he nodded.

They turned their attention back to the interrogation room, where Conklin had his head down on his folded arms, his entire body shaking with sobs.

"I loved Skip. I truly did."

Sam wanted to claw his eyes out. "Fuck you, you son of a bitch. You motherfucking rat bastard—"

"Sam."

The chief's stern tone ended her vocal diatribe, but the diatribe inside her would never end. She wanted to stab that cowardly bastard straight through the heart with the rustiest steak knife ever.

"When did you figure out that they were behind the killing of Steven Coyne?"

"About a year before Skip was shot. When he said he was going to take another look at the case, I tried to tell him to leave it alone." Conklin sniveled as snot leaked from his nose. "But he wouldn't listen to me."

"You warned him off the investigation?"

Conklin nodded as he wiped his face on his sleeve. "I tried to. I told him that messing with Gallagher wasn't a good idea."

"I feel like my head is going to explode," Sam said.

"Mine too," Malone replied, his teeth gritted.

"What did he say when you tried to warn him off?" Hill asked.

"He was determined to get justice for Steven, even if it led to people who'd rather forget what'd happened to him. He said he would never forget."

"Did you tell Gallagher that Skip was onto them?"

Conklin dropped his head into his hands and muttered something.

"What was that? I didn't hear you."

"Yes, I told him!"

"And you did that knowing it could get your friend killed?"

"Yes."

"Why?"

"Gallagher had shit on me that could ruin my life."

"What kind of shit?"

"I…I was involved with the gambling. I made a small fortune. My wife… She had no idea where the money came from, and she would've left me if he told her because her father bankrupted their family gambling when she was a kid. I…I really love her. She saved my life in so many ways. I couldn't lose her. And if it got out, it would've ruined my career along with my marriage. If he found out I knew about Skip digging into the Coyne case and didn't tip him off, he would've come at me hard. He might've even tried to kill me."

"So in order to save your career, marriage and your own skin, you were willing to sacrifice Skip's life?"

Conklin's sobs echoed loudly through the speaker connected to the interrogation room.

"Tell me how Skip's shooting went down."

Conklin took a minute to pull himself together. "Santoro was waiting for him. When he was leaving that day, Santoro pulled out ahead of him and then started darting in and out of traffic and generally causing chaos. Skip did exactly what they expected him to, by turning on his lights and giving chase."

"Why that part of G Street?"

"It's mostly deserted after GAO lets out for the day."

"What else is there? What else have you been hiding while pretending to serve as a decorated police officer?"

"Nothing! There's nothing else."

"That's good, because I've heard more than enough."

Hill pushed a yellow pad across the table. "Write it all down and sign it."

Bagley cleared his throat. "I assume my client will be treated with leniency due to his cooperation."

Sam wanted to punch him too.

"Your client will get exactly what he deserves." Hill stood and left the room, slamming the door behind him.

After a minute, when Hill didn't enter the observation room, Sam went looking for him and found him in the hallway, leaning against a wall, his head down. Everything about his posture expressed his dismay at having to extract that information from a fellow law enforcement officer.

"You did a great job," Sam said.

"I'm sorry you had to hear all that. I can't imagine how painful it had to be for you."

"At least now I know."

"I imagine that's a small comfort."

"It's better than not knowing. What happens now?"

Hill straightened out of his slouch. "Now we arrest Gallagher, Ryan and Santoro, blow the lid off their entire operation and throw their asses in jail for the rest of their miserable lives."

CHAPTER TWENTY-SEVEN

ALL THREE MEN were arrested by the FBI at the exact same time, so they couldn't tip each other off. The operation went off with surgical precision, overseen by Hill. Gallagher was hauled out of a meeting at City Hall, his arrest chronicled for all to see by the media that stalked the building. Ryan was found at one of the restaurants the three men owned, and Santoro was pulled naked from his bed in a penthouse apartment in Georgetown. A woman who'd been in bed with him raised such a fuss that she was arrested too.

Charged only with the murder of Metro PD Deputy Chief Skip Holland initially, each of the men proclaimed their innocence. However, as she watched the news coverage of the bombshell arrests on the conference room TV, Sam saw the fear in their eyes. They knew what they'd done and that they were screwed, glued and tattooed every which way to next Tuesday.

Her phone rang nonstop with calls from Darren Tabor and other reporters, but she didn't take any of the calls.

A hollow feeling gnawed at her. For the longest time, she'd imagined what this moment would be like, to have the answers that had eluded her and the others who'd loved Skip and Steven for so many years. But the reality was just…empty.

Her dad was still dead. Steven was still dead.

Yes, she was glad to see the people responsible dragged out of their comfy lives, fully aware that they were going to do hard time for what they'd done to two honest, hardworking, dedicated police officers—and their families.

Normally, Sam would hate being relegated to the sidelines, but in this case, it was for the best. She would've been tempted to shoot them in their necks, so they'd have to live the same way her father had, trapped in a useless body while their minds remained as sharp as ever. That would be the least of what they deserved.

She ought to call Celia and her sisters but couldn't bring herself to do it. She hadn't been allowed to call them or anyone before the operation went down. They would hear the news soon enough, if they hadn't already.

Sam had no idea how long she'd stood there staring at the TV when she heard the door to the conference room open and close. She was about to turn to see who it was when arms slid around her waist and the fragrance of home filled her senses. He'd come. Of course he'd come.

She sagged into Nick's embrace. "How did you hear?"

"Freddie called me. He thought I'd want to be here for you."

Thank God for the two of them. What would she ever do without them? She hoped she'd never have to find out.

"I don't know whether to say congratulations or I'm sorry or I love you."

"All of that works."

"I can't begin to imagine what you must be feeling."

"I'm numb."

"The whole thing is simply unbelievable for me, but for you it has to be such a massive betrayal."

She nodded because she didn't trust herself to speak.

"Samantha." He tightened his arms around her and kissed her neck.

Safe in the arms of her love, Sam finally broke down.

Nick turned her to face him and gathered her into him, his fingers in her hair, his arms tight around her as she shook with sobs that she'd held off until now, until she finally knew why her father had been taken from them far too soon.

"Let it all out, sweetheart." He rubbed her back and kissed her forehead. "You've been so strong for everyone when your own heart was breaking."

She cried until there were no tears left, until his shirt was damp under her face, until her body ached like it'd been run over.

"Let me take you home."

She knew she ought to stay, to see this through to the end, but there was nothing left for her to do. "Okay but give me a minute." She didn't want her colleagues to see her red-faced and unhinged.

He handed her a monogrammed handkerchief. "Take all the time you need."

Sam breathed in the familiar scent of starch and citrus-scented cologne as she wiped the dampness from her face. She took the bottle of water he handed her and drank half of it while wondering how he always seemed to have exactly what she needed when she needed it.

"Thank you."

He tucked a strand of hair behind her ear. "No need to thank me."

"Yes, there is. The only reason why I'm holding it together at all right now is because of you."

"I always want to be where you are, especially at a time like this."

"Didn't you have a thing at the White House tonight?"

He shrugged. "I called in sick."

"Can you do that?"

"Well, I did it. I guess we'll find out if I'm allowed to."

She smiled up at him, surprised that she could smile, but leave it to him. "You're the best."

"I love you, and I ache for you over this."

"I love you too. I'll get through this knowing that the people who killed him and Steven, and those who let them get away with it, are going to pay."

"That's what really matters."

She released her hair from the clip that held it up while she was working and ran her fingers through it, attempting to bring order to it. "I need to call Celia and my sisters."

"Go ahead. I'm sure they're anxious to hear from you."

She called all three of them, went through the facts of what had been uncovered and talked them through their tears of outrage and despair.

"It's so unreal," Celia said. "It's just unreal."

"I know. It'll take me years to wrap my head around this, but at least now we know."

"Yes, for all the good it does."

"I'm going to start a grief group for people like us who're the victims of violent crime. I want you to be part of it. It might help."

"I'll think about that. Come see me when you get home?"

"I will. For sure."

Angela and Tracy had expressed similar disbelief and had cried when Sam told them about the connection to the owner of O'Leary's. That detail had been difficult for all of them to hear, knowing how much their father had loved that place. After she ended the call with Tracy, she turned to Nick. "I need to see Alice."

"Alice Fitzgerald?"

Sam nodded. "She's waited far longer than we have for this news."

"I'll ask Brant to get us there. Give me one minute."

After he left the room to confer with Brant, Sam tuned back into the TV. The local news was on fire over the long-awaited arrest in the shooting of Deputy Chief Holland. They hadn't yet made the connection to the Coyne case, so Alice still didn't know.

"Babe." Nick stuck his gorgeous face through the door. "Let's go."

She took his outstretched hand, made a quick stop in her office to get her keys and walked with him through the winding halls that led to the morgue exit, where his motorcade was parked. Along the way, she ignored the curious stares of her coworkers, who had to be reeling right along with her. And if they weren't, they ought to be. He helped her into the backseat of one of the black SUVs and then followed her in. When he was settled, he reached for her and Sam curled up to him.

"It's amazing."

"What is?"

"That I was as agitated as I've ever been, and then you show up and make everything better."

"That's my job."

"You do it exceptionally well."

"Why, thank you. I try."

She tipped her head so she could see his face. "Now we know."

"Now we know."

"I want it to change everything, but it doesn't."

"No, because it can't bring him back or undo the nightmare of the last four years."

"And it can't bring back Steven. In all this time, never once did it ever occur to me that their shootings were related."

"Why would it? They happened decades apart. There was never any reason to suspect they were related, was there?"

Sam shook her head. "Still… It's so hard to know that the answers were right under our noses all this time."

"You can't blame yourself for that, babe. You were betrayed by someone you thought you could trust."

"True. And get this—one of Gallagher's cohorts owns O'Leary's."

"Wow."

"It makes me sick. My dad put that place on the map by making it a favored bar for MPD officers, and this is the thanks he gets?"

"It's so disgusting. Every bit of it."

"I wish I had a dollar for every time greed was the motive in one of my cases. I could retire early."

"You could retire early even without those dollars. Your husband would be more than happy to support you while you attend tea parties and have facials. Just tossing that out there in case you're tempted."

Sam laughed. "Can you see me working the tea party and facial circuit?"

"I can totally picture it. You'd be awesome at it."

"You're just saying that because you want me to quit being a cop."

"I'd only want that so people would stop shooting at you and running you off the road and hitting you with their cars and—"

Sam hooked her hand around his neck and drew him into a kiss. "Thanks for offering to keep me, but I'd go mad without the job."

He leaned his forehead against hers. "I know."

A short time later, the car came to a stop outside Alice's modest home.

Sam glanced at the house. "She's not going to know what's going on with the motorcade stopping here."

"You want me to come with you?"

"Do you mind?" She didn't want to leave him, even for the fifteen minutes she would need to explain the unexplainable to Alice.

"Not at all. Happy to be wherever my beautiful wife is."

"You're the best."

They walked hand in hand up the sidewalk to the door, where Alice stood waiting for them, her eyes wide at the sight of Nick and the motorcade. She opened the storm door for them. "What is all this?"

Sam dropped Nick's hand and put her arm around Alice. "I have news. Let's go sit so we can talk."

"Okay…"

The two women sat together on a sofa while Nick took one of the chairs.

"I know what happened to Steven—and my dad. Their two shootings were related after all."

Alice gasped. "How do you know that?"

Sam took her through the whole thing, connecting

Gallagher, Ryan, Santoro and Conklin to the shootings of Steven and Skip.

"Paul Conklin knew this and never said anything?"

"Yes." Sam sighed. She understood how Alice felt. "He claims he only found out that Steven's shooting was connected to Gallagher and the others a year before my dad was shot, but he knew all along that they were behind my dad's shooting. He's the one who tipped Gallagher off that my dad was looking into Steven's shooting, hoping to finally solve that case before he retired."

Alice wrapped her arms around herself, her body trembling violently. "Brings it all back," she whispered. "Like it just happened."

"I know, and I'm so sorry to do that to you."

Alice's eyes flashed with anger. "Don't you apologize to me. You're as much a victim of their evil as I am, as Steven and Skip were." She began to cry. "Two of the best men I ever knew."

Sam wrapped her arms around Alice and held her as she sobbed. Her own emotions were all over the place, pinging from rage to sadness to despair and then, when she noticed Nick watching her intently, to hope. As long as she had him and Scotty, the twins and the rest of her family and friends, she would survive this. She could survive anything with them on her side.

"How could Paul have done this?" Alice asked.

"I don't know, but without him coming clean, we might never have gotten Gallagher and the others."

"Roy was Steven's friend." She hiccuped on a sob. "Steven trusted him, looked up to him, even."

"We may never understand this, Alice, but they're going to pay for what they did to Steven, my dad, Frank Davis, Kevin Viera and who knows who else. As we speak, the FBI is raiding their offices, their homes, their businesses. The Feds will build an airtight case against them. They'll never see the light of day again."

"Doesn't bring Steven or Skip back, though, does it?"

"No, but at least we'll get justice for them. Finally."

The back door slammed shut, startling Alice. She sat up straighter, wiped her face and made a visible effort to pull herself together. "That'll be Jimmy, home from work."

"Alice?"

"In here."

"What're all those cars in the street for?" Jimmy came into the room, stopping short at the sight of Sam and Nick. "What the..."

"Jimmy, this is Sam Holland, Skip's daughter, and her husband—"

"I know who they are. What's going on?"

"They've arrested the men behind Steven's murder. And Skip's."

"Oh. Well. That's good news, isn't it?"

Alice nodded and dabbed at the tears that continued to spill down her cheeks.

"I, um, I'm sorry about your dad," Jimmy said. "Alice... She said he was a good man."

"Thank you. He was."

"I'll, ah, I'll give you a minute. I'll be in the kitchen if you need me, Alice."

After he walked away, Alice wiped her face and seemed to shake off the despair. "It's hard for him to see me upset about Steven. He's always felt second best, like the runner-up or something. I tell him that's not true, but Steven... He was..." Alice grimaced.

"I know."

"I so appreciate you coming to tell me this yourself. It means the world to me. It's what your father would've done."

Sam took Alice's hand and gave it a squeeze. "Hearing that means the world to *me*."

They stood, and Alice hugged her for a long time. "People have used the word *closure* over the years. That's what you brought me today, and I'm thankful to you and everyone else who worked on Steven's case. Will you pass along my thanks to them?"

"I will. And I'll keep you posted of any developments." Sam was struck with an idea that was too powerful to resist. "I met a woman this week, someone just like you—newly married, madly in love with her husband, a DEA agent who was shot and killed."

"I read about that."

"I'm starting a support group for victims of violent crime. If you are willing, perhaps I could introduce you to Roni. As someone who has taken the same journey, you might be able to help her."

"I'm not sure if I could do anything for her, but I'd be happy to try."

"I'll call you about it."

Alice walked them to the door and held out a hand to Nick. "I'm honored to have had you visit my home."

"The honor was all mine. I'm sorry for your loss."

"Thank you."

"I'll wait for you outside, Sam."

When they were alone, Alice smiled at Sam. "Got yourself a handsome one there."

"He is that."

"Hold on tight to what you have with him and enjoy every minute."

"I will." Sam hugged her again, feeling closer to her

dad in Alice's presence, knowing how important she and her late husband had been to Skip.

"You stay safe, you hear me? Nothing is more important than your life, and if you're in the area, come by and see me."

"I'll do that." Sam left her with a smile and went out to the front porch, where Nick waited for her. "And I'll be in touch about the group."

"I'll look forward to hearing from you."

Sam took hold of the hand Nick held out to her. "Let's go home." Her dad wouldn't be there, but her house was full of people who loved her, and she would carry Skip in her heart everywhere she went for the rest of her life. His voice would be in her head every day, his hand on her shoulder, guiding her the way he always had. He wouldn't want her to get sucked into the rabbit hole of despair and grief. He'd tell her to quit her moping and get back to doing the best job ever.

So that was what she'd do even if she'd miss him every step of the way.

EPILOGUE

SAM RAISED HER right hand and swore to tell the whole truth and nothing but the truth while making a studious effort not to look at the repulsive face of the man who'd tried to kill her—twice. He would be tried for both attacks at this trial, and Sam focused on remaining calm.

Nick sat in the front row of the gallery, his steady gaze fixed on her as she talked about events they'd both sooner forget.

"Can you identify Leonard Stahl in the courtroom today?"

Sam pointed to the defendant. He'd lost a significant amount of weight since he'd been in jail, but he stared back at her with the hateful, beady eyes that brought back horrific memories she hoped she'd never again have to think about after today.

They went through the events that had led to him attacking her on her front porch.

"Did you feel that Mr. Stahl intended to kill you that day?"

"Absolutely. If my son's Secret Service detail hadn't been there, he probably would've succeeded."

"Objection."

"Overruled."

Faith gave Sam a smug look that only she could see. "Why would Mr. Stahl want to kill you?"

"I don't know exactly. He hated me from the time I

first joined the force and went out of his way to make my life miserable when I worked for him. I always suspected his animosity stemmed from his dislike of my father."

"Objection."

"Overruled."

"Do you know why he disliked your father?"

"No, neither of us knew. We suspected he might be jealous because my father, who was a year senior to him, had been more successful in his career. But beyond that, we never knew why. And then when Stahl was reassigned to Internal Affairs and I was put in charge of the Homicide squad, his ire toward me seemed to intensify." If she were to glance in Stahl's direction, she suspected his face might be that hideous shade of purple that it took on when he became enraged. She'd seen a lot of that colorful face over the years.

But she didn't look. She didn't care enough to be bothered looking.

"Prior to the incident on your front porch, had anything happened between yourself and Mr. Stahl?"

"So many things. We constantly butted heads, most of the time over manufactured offenses that he used to try to discredit me."

"Had he ever threatened you before the day on your front porch?"

"Numerous times. He brought me up before the Internal Affairs Board on charges of misconduct on two occasions, the first over my involvement with Nick Cappuano during the O'Connor investigation. When I only received a suspension for that, he said, 'You may think you've won this round, Holland, but you mark my words—I'll get rid of you if it's the last thing I ever do.'" Sam had memorized the details of the various incidents in anticipation of testifying.

"Did you feel personally threatened by that statement?"

"Not in a physical sense, but I definitely felt he was threatening my career."

"And did he have the power to hurt your career?"

"Absolutely. He was the lieutenant in charge of Internal Affairs at that time, so he could definitely make trouble for me. And he outranked me as a more senior lieutenant."

"Did anyone else hear him threaten you?"

"Yes, my partner, Detective Cruz, heard it." As she spoke, Sam felt the heat of Stahl's gaze on her, but she continued to look at Nick while ignoring the hatred coming from Stahl.

"What was the second reason you were brought up on IAB charges?"

"Stahl overheard one of my officers joking about having to work while the rest of my squad attended my wedding. He decided to make something of that."

"Did it go anywhere?"

"No."

"And what was his reaction?"

"He was pissed and seemed to increase his efforts to try to get me in trouble, always inferring that my father's friendship with the chief was the only reason I hadn't been fired."

"Did you argue with him?"

"All the time. I will admit that I often enjoyed needling him. I enjoyed watching his face turn purple with rage every time he was anywhere near me, but I never imagined he'd take it as far as he did."

"Objection, Your Honor. Could you ask the witness to stick to the questions and quit the editorializing?"

"Sustained. Lieutenant, please answer the questions and leave it at that."

Was she allowed to tell the defense attorney to fuck off? Probably not… "Yes, Your Honor."

"Lieutenant Stahl was arrested for tipping a reporter off to a detail you had withheld from the public during an investigation. Can you tell us about that?"

"Yes, when we investigated the murder of DC Feds player Willie Vazquez, we didn't disclose that his body had been found in a dumpster. I heard from Darren Tabor, a reporter with the *Washington Star*, that he'd received that information in an anonymous tip. Working with IT Lieutenant Archelotta, we determined the tip was made by Stahl in a call from the Lieutenant's Lounge at MPD Headquarters. Lieutenant Archelotta produced video that showed Stahl making the call. Upon seeing the video, the chief ordered that Stahl be relieved of his weapon and shield and that he be arrested."

"How did Stahl react?"

"He blamed me, even though the video plainly showed him disclosing information we had deliberately withheld from the public reports."

"Did he threaten you?"

"Yes." Sam had memorized this part too. "His exact words were 'You're going to pay for this, Holland! You'd better watch your back, little girl! That stupid bitch set me up! This is all her fault!' After he said that in front of myself, Chief Farnsworth, Deputy Chief Conklin and Captain Malone, Stahl was charged with a felony count of threatening a public official."

"Did he make good on that threat?"

"He did. After he was released on bail, he showed up at my house and attacked me on my front porch."

"Can you please describe the attack?"

"He arrived in uniform and wrapped an arm around my neck, squeezing so tightly I couldn't breathe. Luckily, I was able to knee him in the groin and then kick him in the knee before my son's Secret Service detail intervened." The two agents who'd been there were scheduled to testify to what they'd seen.

"Were you injured?"

Sam nodded. "My neck was black-and-blue and very painful for some time afterward."

"Was it your feeling that he intended to kill you?"

"Yes, I believe he would've killed me if I hadn't been able to defend myself or had help from the agents."

"Objection."

"Overruled."

"When was the next time you saw Stahl after the attack on your doorstep?"

"I next saw him at the home of Marissa Springer during an investigation."

"What was he doing there?"

"I learned he was in cahoots with Marissa, who blamed me for the death of her son Billy. Our investigation into the murder of Marissa's youngest son, Hugo, implicated Billy. He was later killed by police after he took hostages."

Faith led her through the details of that day—arriving at Marissa's house to ask her a few more questions pertaining to the investigation, realizing she'd made a critical mistake going there alone, watching Marissa kill her maid with a shot to the forehead, being marched to the basement that had been a crime scene and made to sit in a chair to await her fate.

"What happened once you were in the basement?"

"Marissa made a call, said she'd gotten me to come back and to get over there."

"Did you know who she was talking to?"

"Not until he showed up."

"You're referring to the defendant?"

"Yes." Sam would never be able to properly articulate the shock she'd felt when Stahl had arrived, and she'd put two plus two together to figure out that Marissa had paid his bail on the assault charges and entered into some sort of unholy alliance with him.

"What happened then?"

"He said some stuff to me, which I ignored, and then he slapped me in the face and pulled my hair, hard, trying to get a reaction from me."

"Did he get one?"

"I spit at him."

"How did he react?"

"He punched me in the face. Then he tied me to the chair as tightly as he could. I also learned they'd set up my partner, Detective Cruz, by having someone mess with his girlfriend, so he'd be out of the picture when they took me hostage."

Faith asked her a series of questions that revealed the next few hours of hell to the jury—Stahl's unpacking of an arsenal of weapons, his argument with Marissa about who was in charge before he shot her in the gut, how he told Sam he hated her because she thought she was better than everyone else. He insulted her father and his relationship with the chief and generally ranted his hatred toward her as he wrapped her in razor wire.

The jurors, who'd withheld reactions up until then, gasped at that detail.

"What did you say to him as this was happening?"

"Nothing." Faith had told her she wanted to get that detail into the record—that Sam hadn't said a word to him during the prolonged attack.

"At all?"

"I didn't say a single word to him the entire time."

"Why?"

"Because it was bothering him that I refused to speak to him, so I stuck to my plan to stay quiet and let it unfold however it was going to."

"What were you thinking about?"

Sam kept her gaze locked on Nick, who barely blinked the entire time she was testifying. "My husband, my son, the rest of my family. I focused on thoughts of them and that kept me focused."

"Did you think you were going to die?"

"I was fairly certain I was going to, especially when he doused the area around my chair with gasoline. His intention was for me to burn alive, knowing that I'd be sliced by the razor wire if I so much as moved."

More gasps from the jurors.

This was going well. Very, very well indeed. Nick's small smile indicated that he thought so too. Even though it was hard for her to relive and harder for him to hear, they were in this together, like always. She just needed to get through this, and then she would be taking a few days to spend alone—or as alone as they ever were with the Secret Service underfoot—with him and the kids. She'd let Lilia know she wasn't up for socializing after the week she'd had, and Lilia had promised to hold another dinner party with the same guests as soon as Sam felt up to attending.

"Did you find out more about Stahl's actions while you were his hostage?"

"Yes, I learned from what Marissa said that Stahl

had tipped the Springer family off that we were closing in on their son Billy as the perpetrator of the murders that had occurred in their basement, which had included their younger son, Hugo." Sam's niece Brooke had also been gang-raped that night. "After Stahl shot Marissa, when she asked him why he would do this to her when she'd been his friend, he said she'd outlived her usefulness."

"Did he say anything else that indicated why he was attacking you?"

Sam nodded. "When Marissa continued to criticize him, he dumped gas on her too, and made sure to get it in her wound. He said, 'I'm so fucking sick of women who think they should have an *opinion*. Shut your fucking mouths and do what you were put on this earth to do—spread your legs and breed.' He also indicated that he'd given Lori Phillips, a known drug addict, cocaine in exchange for sex. He said, 'Worst thing they ever did was let bitches into the police department. Ruined everything.'"

"Objection."

"Your Honor," Faith said, "Lieutenant Holland is quoting the official police report from the incident in which the defendant's words were documented."

"I'll allow it."

The defense attorney sat but was clearly pissed with the judge.

"How did the incident end?" Faith asked.

"He began lighting matches and teasing me that he was going to drop them on the gas he'd spread all over the place. He went through an entire box that way and was down to the last one when SWAT burst in through the windows and took him down."

"Can you detail your injuries?"

"I was told my face was unrecognizable, and I had cuts all over my body, several that required stitches."

"One final question, Lieutenant. Did you determine a motive for the defendant's actions?"

"Other than satisfying his vendetta against me, we believe he was out to discredit the department and the people who ordered him arrested for leaking sensitive information during an investigation, among other things he held against them, such as their success while his career had stalled—no pun intended."

"Thank you, Lieutenant. Nothing further."

Now came the fun part, the cross-examination from Stahl's attorney.

The man stood and gave her a steely look that had her stomach pinging with nerves.

"The defense has no questions for Lieutenant Holland."

Shock zinged through her, quickly followed by relief so profound it made her light-headed. It was over.

She could walk out of there and never have to see that revolting bastard's face again.

The judge turned to her. "Lieutenant Holland, you're dismissed."

She stood, gave herself a second to get her legs under her and then stepped down from the witness box, walking directly into the arms of her husband. He kept one arm around her as they exited the courtroom, which had gone completely silent.

Neither said a word as the Secret Service whisked them out of the courthouse and into one of the waiting SUVs.

"You were fucking brilliant," Nick said as the car pulled away from the curb. "I've never been so proud of you. If your testimony doesn't put that bastard away for life, I don't know what will."

"It's out of my hands now."

"The jury was outraged by what he did to you."

"It seemed that way." She relaxed into his embrace and took a couple of deep breaths as adrenaline continued to zip through her. For so long, she'd dreaded having to face off with Stahl in court, but now it was done, and she could finally put it behind her. "This has been a rather monumental week. We solved my dad's case and Steven's, and hopefully disposed of Stahl once and for all. We got rid of a whole bunch of scumbags."

"A good week indeed, but a tough one for my love." He kissed the top of her head and ran his hand up and down her arm. "What can I do for you?"

"I want two days with you and the kids and nothing to do."

"Let's go to the cabin and take them to the farm to ride horses."

"That sounds like perfection."

AS USUAL THESE DAYS, it took some doing to organize an impromptu getaway to the cabin in Leesburg that John O'Connor had left to Nick. The cabin was located a short distance from the home of John's parents, Graham and Laine O'Connor.

The press had been relentless in their attacks against the department, shining the light on the "cancer" that had been permitted to fester under the watch of Chief Joe Farnsworth, who had been equally criticized and lauded for pursuing the truth that had led to arrests in cold-case killings of two respected cops. No one knew for sure whether Farnsworth would be able to hold on to his job or if he even wanted to after the sickening discoveries about his deputy chief. Having Stahl's trial happening at the same time hadn't helped to take the heat off the department. Faith had told her it would be at least another week before the trial went to the jury.

Sam had avoided all requests for comment about the arrests in her father's case and didn't plan to speak publicly about it until after the trials had been completed. In the meantime, she hoped and prayed that her beloved chief and uncle Joe would weather the storm, even if she wouldn't blame him if he decided to retire. In the good news department, she'd heard that Kevin Viera was expected to make a full recovery, and his girlfriend had delivered a healthy seven-pound baby girl. Sam had personally called Lorraine Davis and told her why her father had been killed, making a point to thank her again for what her father had done to save Skip's life that day on G Street.

Sam had received the green light from both the department and the White House to pursue her grief group for victims of violent crime and had mentioned the group to Lorraine Davis. With Trulo's help, she hoped to have it up and running in the next couple of months.

On the second night they were at the cabin, Graham and Laine invited Scotty and the twins to spend the night, so they could ride the horses some more and make the homemade ice cream Laine was known for. At first, Aubrey and Alden had been hesitant to go, but Scotty had convinced them, telling them Sam and Nick would be right down the road and could come get them if they missed them too much.

Aubrey had taken a liking to one of the horses, so she'd been easier to convince. As usual, Alden seemed wiser than his years as he carefully considered the invitation before agreeing to go, but only because Scotty was there.

"Alone at last," Nick said when they returned to the cabin after having dinner with Graham, Laine, their longtime housekeeper, Carrie, and the kids.

"How long do you think Alden and Aubrey will hold out before they want us?"

"With Scotty there, we might get the full night. But since it's possible they could call us at any minute, what do you say we make very good use of the time we have alone together?"

Sam gave him a blank look. "To do what?"

His wolfish grin was the sexiest thing ever.

She whipped her top over her head and unbuttoned her jeans.

Nick followed suit, kicking off his shoes, removing his sweater and stripping down to boxers in record time. He wrapped an arm around her waist, taking her by surprise when he lifted her.

"If you throw your back out, you'll put a damper on things."

"Oh please. You're light as a feather."

Sam snorted with laughter. "Sure I am. Where're we going?"

"Right here." He lowered her to the soft carpet they'd bought to put in front of the fireplace.

"This carpet was the best idea I ever had."

"Mmm," he said, kissing her. "Definitely one of your best."

"You know what my very best idea ever was?"

"What's that?" He released the front clasp of her bra, his eyes going dark with lust when her breasts sprang free.

"Marrying you. Single best thing I ever did in my entire life."

"That was a pretty damned good idea you had."

Cupping her breast in his hand, he took her nipple into his mouth and sucked hard, just the way she liked it.

Sam squirmed under him, pushing at his boxers until she could wrap her hand around his erection. "Now. I want you right now."

"Whatever my baby wants." He withdrew from her only long enough to remove her panties and his boxers before coming down on top of her again, making her gasp from the pleasure of his skin rubbing against hers.

If there was anything better than this, she'd yet to find it and had no desire whatsoever to look for it.

He slid into her in one deep thrust that nearly made her come. "Scream." His lips brushed against her ear, setting off goose bumps. "I want to hear you. There's no one around."

"The agents…"

"Are next door." They'd rented the houses on either side of the cabin, so they could provide security when the second family was in residence. "I told them to give us some space tonight."

"God, you think of everything."

"Not everything. Only the important stuff."

She raised her hips to meet his deep stroke. "And this is *very* important."

"The most important thing."

Sam clung to him as their lovemaking took on an intense, almost desperate tone that came from being entirely alone.

He held her so close she could barely breathe, but she wouldn't have it any other way. She loved him like this, when there was no one around and they could give in to the ravenous desire that raged between them.

Sam reached down to where they were joined, which drew a deep groan from him.

"Do it, babe," he said, his breathing choppy. "Touch yourself."

She pressed her fingers to her clit and felt him get even harder inside her, as he always did when she coaxed herself. It didn't take long for her to bring herself to a screaming orgasm.

He pounded into her, coming right after her with a shout of pleasure before sagging into her arms. For a long time, they were quiet as their bodies cooled and their breathing slowed.

Sam broke the long, contented silence. "I want to tell you something."

"What's that?"

"I tell you all the time how much I love you, but…"

"That's never a good word to add after you tell me you love me."

Sam laughed and poked him in the ribs, drawing a laugh from him too.

"It's a good 'but.'" She took a second to gather her thoughts, which were scattered after he'd made her see stars. "I never could've gotten through the immediate aftermath of losing my dad, of working his case, of finding out the truth, of testifying against Stahl, without you there beside me. Just knowing you are there, even when you're not physically there, it makes all the difference." She looked up at him looking down at her, his eyes always so gorgeous but even more so in the firelight. "What I'm trying to say is that I love you even more than I did two weeks ago, and that was an awful lot."

"I feel the same way—that anything is possible, that I can get through anything, as long as I have you. You're the one who makes it all happen for me."

Sam drew him into a sweet kiss and felt herself settle somewhat into her new reality. Her life would never be the same without her dad, but she was somehow surviving the loss because she had Nick by her side to take the journey with her. She pictured Skip as he'd been before the shooting. It was an image she would carry with her always as she continued on without her dad.

She would strive every day to make him proud—at home and on the job.

* * * * *

ACKNOWLEDGMENTS

THANK YOU FOR reading *Fatal Reckoning*, a very special installment in the Fatal Series. Many of you know that I lost my own dad during the writing of this book. He was perfectly fine when I began it on May 1 and gone on July 12. I had to come back from burying him to finish Skip's story, which was one of the bigger challenges I've faced in my career. Sam's relationship with Skip is very similar to the groove I shared with my dad, and I want to thank him for giving me such a great basis for Skip and many of the other dads who appear in my books. I joke that he was my "best girlfriend," but it's really true, and I will always miss him. I referred to him as the Chairman of the Board of my company, with one distinct job—to call me every morning to make sure I was up and writing. No one— and I do mean no one—enjoyed the wild ride my career has been more than he did. This book is dedicated to the chairman, my best girlfriend, with gratitude for a lifetime of laughs and good times.

Many thanks to the team at HQN, especially my editors, Allison Carroll and Alissa Davis, and to my HTJB team: Julie Cupp, Lisa Cafferty, Holly Sullivan, Isabel Sullivan and Nikki Colquhoun. As always, thank you to my friend Captain Russell Hayes, Newport, RI, Police Department (retired) for his input into this and every Fatal Series book—and for playing the bagpipes so beautifully at my dad's funeral.

As always, I send my love and appreciation to the readers who wait patiently for every new Fatal book and who continue to love Sam and Nick as much as I do.

xoxo
Marie

Get 4 FREE REWARDS!

We'll send you 2 FREE Books plus 2 FREE Mystery Gifts.

FREE
Value Over
$20

Both the **Romance** and **Suspense** collections feature compelling novels written by many of today's best-selling authors.

YES! Please send me 2 FREE novels from the Essential Romance or Essential Suspense Collection and my 2 FREE gifts (gifts are worth about $10 retail). After receiving them, if I don't wish to receive any more books, I can return the shipping statement marked "cancel." If I don't cancel, I will receive 4 brand-new novels every month and be billed just $6.74 each in the U.S. or $7.24 each in Canada. That's a savings of at least 16% off the cover price. It's quite a bargain! Shipping and handling is just 50¢ per book in the U.S. and 75¢ per book in Canada.* I understand that accepting the 2 free books and gifts places me under no obligation to buy anything. I can always return a shipment and cancel at any time. The free books and gifts are mine to keep no matter what I decide.

Choose one: ☐ **Essential Romance**   ☐ **Essential Suspense**
                        (194/394 MDN GMY7)   (191/391 MDN GMY7)

Name (please print)

Address   Apt. #

City   State/Province   Zip/Postal Code

Mail to the **Reader Service:**
IN U.S.A.: P.O. Box 1341, Buffalo, NY 14240-8531
IN CANADA: P.O. Box 603, Fort Erie, Ontario L2A 5X3

Want to try 2 free books from another series? Call 1-800-873-8635 or visit www.ReaderService.com.

*Terms and prices subject to change without notice. Prices do not include sales taxes, which will be charged (if applicable) based on your state or country of residence. Canadian residents will be charged applicable taxes. Offer not valid in Quebec. This offer is limited to one order per household. Books received may not be as shown. Not valid for current subscribers to the Essential Romance or Essential Suspense Collection. All orders subject to approval. Credit or debit balances in a customer's account(s) may be offset by any other outstanding balance owed by or to the customer. Please allow 4 to 6 weeks for delivery. Offer available while quantities last.

Your Privacy—The Reader Service is committed to protecting your privacy. Our Privacy Policy is available online at www.ReaderService.com or upon request from the Reader Service. We make a portion of our mailing list available to reputable third parties that offer products we believe may interest you. If you prefer that we not exchange your name with third parties, or if you wish to clarify or modify your communication preferences, please visit us at www.ReaderService.com/consumerschoice or write to us at Reader Service Preference Service, P.O. Box 9062, Buffalo, NY 14240-9062. Include your complete name and address.

STRS19R